THE BONES BENEATH MY SKIN

THE BONES BENEATH MY SKIN

TJ KLUNE

TOR

TOR PUBLISHING GROUP • NEW YORK

THE BONES BENEATH MY SKIN

Copyright © 2018 by Travis Klune

A Tor Book
Published by Tom Doherty Associates / Tor Publishing Group
120 Broadway
New York, NY 10271

www.torpublishinggroup.com

Tor® is a registered trademark of Macmillan Publishing Group, LLC.

The Library of Congress Cataloging-in-Publication Data is available upon request.

ISBN 978-1-250-89043-6 (hardcover)
ISBN 978-1-250-40655-2 (international,
sold outside the U.S., subject to rights availability)
ISBN 978-1-250-89044-3 (ebook)

Our books may be purchased in bulk for promotional, educational, or business use. Please contact your local bookseller or the Macmillan Corporate and Premium Sales Department at 1-800-221-7945, extension 5442, or by email at MacmillanSpecialMarkets@macmillan.com.

First U.S. Tor Hardcover Edition: 2025
First International Edition: 2025

Printed in the United States of America

0 9 8 7 6 5 4 3 2 1

For those who dream of stars

Who are we? We find that we live on an insignificant planet of a humdrum star lost in a galaxy tucked away in some forgotten corner of a universe in which there are far more galaxies than people.

—Carl Sagan, *Cosmos*

THE BONES BENEATH MY SKIN

You won't understand. At least not right away. And that's okay. You may even think I'm a liar, and that's okay too. All I ask is that you listen until the very end before passing judgment. I have a story to tell you. Of a place under a mountain. Of the minds of men. Of what it means to be human, to make a home out of a place where one should not exist. And of what the future holds. For you. For me. For all of us.

CHAPTER ONE

He sang along with the radio.

Something about taking a sad song and making it better.

After, he laughed until he could barely breathe.

✦

He crossed into Douglas County just before another song ended. There was a news break at the top of the hour, every hour.

A singer named Selena had been shot at a hotel in Texas. He'd never heard of her before.

TAROM Flight 371, leaving Bucharest and heading for Brussels, crashed shortly after takeoff. All sixty people on board died. An investigation was underway. Terrorism was not suspected at the moment.

The comet discovered last year, Markham-Tripp, was getting closer. Already it could be seen if you knew where to look, but no worries, folks. It's going to swing right by us before heading back out into the great beyond.

And there was still no official word on the helicopter that went down outside of the Marine Corps Mountain Warfare Training Center in Northern California last week. The cause was still under investigation, though it was implied it was related to that big storm that blew through the area. Officials weren't saying if there were any fatalities.

And now for the weather. It's gonna be a beautiful day, would you look at all that sunshine, can you just *believe* it?

It was March 31, 1995.

He continued south.

✦

The air outside grew cooler the farther he went into the mountains. The sun warmed the hand he hung out the window. The blue sky stretched on and on. There were clouds, but only a few.

Nice day, he thought. *Of course it is. That's the way things go.*

He hit the town in late afternoon. There was a sign, old and faded. It'd been there since he was a kid and his parents had taken him up to the cabin for a few weeks during the summer. It said:

Roseland, Oregon
Pop. 827 Established 1851
Elevation 2345 ft.
Gateway to the Cascades!

He passed by a diner. A church. Shops on either side. Some of them were open. The town wouldn't hit tourist season for another month or two, but they'd be ready. People driving up from the bigger cities looking for an escape from the heat and grind would spend their money, take their photos, and then disappear back from where they came.

The air was filled with the scents of pine needles and earth. It was like he was ten years old again and his mom and dad were still in love, love, love. They would laugh and sing along with the radio. They would play road games. I Spy. Twenty questions. The license plate game where you'd try and get all fifty states. He'd learned early on that *that* was impossible. The most he'd ever gotten was seven. That had been a good day. One had been Maine, an impossibly faraway place.

He saw the sign for the gas station before the gas station itself. It spun lazily, but not before he caught the words BIG EDDIE'S GAS AND CONVENIENCE. He breathed a sigh of relief. It was good to see that some things remained the same. Even after everything.

He pulled in, the tires of the truck hitting the thin black cord. A bell dinged somewhere inside the station as he stopped next to the pump. He turned off the truck, listening as the engine ticked.

He ran a hand over his face before opening the door, setting his feet on the ground. He stretched his back, hearing it pop. He was only twenty-seven years old, but gone were the days when he could sit in a car for hours without a problem. His muscles pulled. It felt good.

The glass door to the gas station swung open and a large man walked out, wiping his hands on a rag. If it wasn't for the smile on his face, the man would have been alarming. He'd never seen anyone that size anywhere else. Must have been the mountain air.

"Well, look who the cat dragged in," Big Eddie Green said, his voice a deep timbre. "Nate Cartwright, as I live and breathe."

Nate forced a smile onto his face. "Big Eddie. Good to see you're still running this dump."

"You watch your mouth," Big Eddie said, but he was still smiling, his teeth a little crooked but endearingly so. He held out a large hand streaked with a bit of oil. Nate didn't mind. He held out his own. Big Eddie's grip was firm, but he wasn't trying to be an asshole about it. He wasn't like that, at least not that Nate knew. He hadn't seen Big Eddie since he'd turned twenty-one, the last time he'd been up to the cabin. And it wasn't like they were *friends*, though Big Eddie could make friends with just about anybody he set his mind to. There was something about the way he smiled that put Nate at ease. It was familiar, this. Heartbreakingly so.

"Heading up the mountain?" Big Eddie was already moving to the pump. "Unleaded okay?"

"Yeah, it's fine," Nate said, leaning against the truck. He glanced inside the gas station window. There was a kid inside bent over the counter, scribbling furiously on something, his tongue stuck out between his teeth like he was concentrating really hard. "Jesus, is that Benji?"

Big Eddie laughed. "Yeah," he said, and Nate could hear the fondness in his voice, rough and sweet. "Sprouting up like a weed. His ma and me can barely keep up with him. More than a handful. Crazy, right?"

"It is," Nate said because he was supposed to agree with it. That was how conversation worked. That was how people talked to each other. He wasn't so good at that. And now that he was running away to the middle of nowhere, he didn't think he'd get much more practice at it than this.

The gas pump hummed.

Big Eddie whistled as he looked in the bed of the truck. "Quite a few supplies you got back here. Planning a long stay?"

Nate shrugged. "A while, anyway."

The smile softened. "Real sorry to hear about your folks. That . . . well. I don't know much else to say beyond that. Must have been tough. I can't imagine what that's like, so I won't insult you by pretending to."

Nate wasn't sure what to say to that. Tough, sure. Oh yeah, it'd been tough. Murder-suicides usually were. His father had come to his mother's house, feeling hurt and ornery like he usually did when he drank. There'd been a fight. Neighbors said they heard shouting but thought it was the TV or just a regular old domestic that they couldn't find the wherewithal to get involved in. Nate didn't blame them, especially when his father had gone out to the very truck Big Eddie and Nate were leaning against, grabbed his shotgun, hoofed it back inside, and blown his ex-wife away before turning it on himself.

It's hard to do, the detective had told him, sounding soft and worn. Committing suicide by shotgun. But Nate's father had found a way. Sat in a chair, propped it between his legs. The barrel had gone under his chin, and he'd used his big toe, of all things, to pull the trigger. It'd been a mess.

At least Nate assumed it had been. He hadn't been inside his mother's house after. His brother had taken care of all that. There are services, his brother told him over the phone. It was the first time he'd spoken to his brother in years. They come in and clean up crime scenes. They charge you out the ass, but they take care of what they can. They can't get it all, of course, but that's what contractors are for. They'd fix up the house before it got put up for sale.

And later, they'd spoken one more time. Dad left you the truck, his brother said. Mom left you the cabin.

Oh was all he could say. Oh.

What he'd *wanted* to say was how could this have happened? How did it get this far? Sure they'd had their problems—they were divorced, for fuck's sake. But his father had never raised a fist. Not to *anyone*. He hadn't been the nicest guy, but he'd never hit them. Or her. Not once. That wasn't who he was.

"Yeah," Nate said to Big Eddie. "Tough."

Big Eddie nodded. "You get the water turned on?"

"Called a couple of days ago. They're supposed to come tomorrow. Generator will take care of the rest. Shouldn't be too cold. Not for long."

"Oh yeah. Snow's gone. Mild winter this year. Christmas was sixty degrees, if you can believe that. I take it you'll want me to fill the gas canisters you got back here."

"If you could."

"Will do, Nate. You been up there since—"

"No."

Big Eddie nodded slowly as he lifted the empty canisters out of the truck. "Your ma was out here. Last September, I think. Brought one of her girlfriends. Josie? Is that right? Josie?"

"Joy."

"That's right. Joy. They were cackling like a pair of old hens. Stayed up there for a couple of weeks. Didn't see them when they came back down. Your ma was happy, Nate. In case you needed to know."

"Thanks," Nate managed to say because wasn't *that* the consolation he was looking for. She'd been *happy*. She'd been *laughing*. He hadn't heard from her in years, but hey, she'd been having the time of her life. Fucking good for her. "That's . . . nice. Thanks."

"She talked about you, you know," Big Eddie said like it was nothing, like they were shooting the shit. "Said you were big-time. Living in Washington, D.C. Reporter or something."

"Journalist," Nate corrected by force of habit.

Big Eddie took the pump from the truck and put it down into one of the canisters. "Journalist. That's right. A *journalist*. Working for the *Post*. She seemed awfully proud of that."

Nate wanted to laugh. He wanted to scream. He wanted to smash his hands against the truck and *demand* Big Eddie shut the fuck up about things he didn't know about. Sure, maybe his mother had been *proud*, maybe she'd been talking out her ass, but what gave her the right? She'd done *nothing* when his father had told him to get the fuck out, that he wouldn't have a fucking *faggot* for a son. She hadn't spoken a goddamn *word* in his defense while his father had shouted that he'd get fucking faggot *cancer* like all those other queers. She'd done nothing when he'd looked at her, begging for her to say something, anything. Her eyes had been wide and shocked, her bottom lip quivering. But she'd stayed silent, so she'd stayed complicit.

They'd been standing in the doorway to the cabin, hadn't they? They weren't even supposed to be up there. They'd already told him they were getting a divorce months before, so the fact that they were together at all was confounding. He'd been frantically trying to cover himself and his boyfriend at the time, their skin slick with sweat, his heart racing. He'd felt *ashamed* for reasons he couldn't quite understand. He wasn't doing anything wrong. He was an adult. He was allowed to be in the cabin with whomever he wished, but he'd felt *bad* at the look of disgust on his father's face, at the way his mother's eyes were wet. He'd felt *awful*.

He and the guy left after that. Hastily, overnight bags stuffed but not zipped up. His parents hadn't even looked up at him from where they sat at the kitchen table. He'd forgotten one of his hiking boots. It'd been sent to him in the mail two months later. No note, no return address, but he'd known it'd come from his mother.

He'd thrown it away.

The boyfriend hadn't lasted long after that day. Another couple of weeks. It didn't matter. It wasn't serious. A distraction, that's all it'd been.

He'd gotten the cabin.

He'd gotten the truck.

That was fine. They were dead, and he'd gotten two things that were essentially useless to him.

Maybe he'd burn them both. He had time now that he didn't have a job.

How wonderful for her that she'd been proud. How fucking *grand*.

"Great," he said, voice even. "I'm glad to hear that."

Big Eddie hummed under his breath. The first canister filled up, and he moved to the second one. "You got a phone hooked up there?"

Nate shook his head.

"Got a cell phone?"

He did. "Why?"

"Give you my number. In case you need something. You being up there all by yourself, things could happen, Nate. Just being cautious is all."

"Doubt it'd work up there." His service was already spotty as it was, being this far into the mountains. It probably wouldn't work at all by the time he got to the cabin.

"Still. Better to be safe than sorry."

Right. Nate went back around to the driver's-side door. The phone was sitting on the bench seat, a red Nokia, the screen cracked down the middle from where he'd dropped it on a sidewalk while trying to juggle a couple of coffees. Big Eddie spouted off his number, and Nate dutifully typed it in, saving it under EDDIE.

Big Eddie hoisted the gas cans back into the bed of the truck before he wiped his hands on the rag he stashed in his pocket. He glanced at the pump, then said, "That'll be $36.50, unless you need anything else from inside. Last stop before all that nothing."

Nate shook his head, pulling his wallet out and finding his debit card, something he'd only gotten a few months ago. They were new, and it boggled his mind a little how much easier it was than cash or a check.

Big Eddie grinned at him again. "Be right back."

Nate watched him go.

The sun was low in the west. It'd be dark in another couple of hours, and he was itching to get back on the road. He had another hour to go, the last half of which was on bumpy dirt roads that weren't great to navigate in the dark. He should have gotten an earlier start, but his hangover had been harsh this morning, his tongue thick in a mouth that felt stuffed with cotton. Even now he had remnants of a headache, the last little gasps of something that had dug deep into his brain for most of the morning.

Big Eddie was inside the gas station, saying something to his son. Nate watched as he ran a hand over Benji's head. Benji knocked it away, and Big Eddie chuckled. He said something else, and Benji glanced out the window. Nate gave a little wave. The kid waved back, his arm thin, his whole body shaking. Big Eddie laughed over his shoulder as he came back out and didn't see his son scowling at his back.

"Math," Big Eddie said as he approached. "It's not going so well."

"Sucks," Nate said. "Never understood that much myself."

Big Eddie handed him his card and receipt. "He doesn't get why he needs it if he's going to be running the station. I told him he needs to set his sights a bit higher than Roseland. He wasn't too happy about that."

"Sometimes you need to let them do what they think is right." Nate instantly regretted the words.

"Yeah." Big Eddie rubbed his chin thoughtfully. "I suppose. I just—it's being a parent, I guess. You want the best for your kids, to see them spread their wings and fly. He's going to do great things, I think. One day. I just don't know if he can do them here." He shrugged. "You'll know one day. When you got kids of your own."

That wasn't going to happen. Nate didn't have the patience for kids. He didn't like them, and they didn't like him. It wasn't in the cards. But he said "Sure" because that's what he was supposed to say.

"I better let you get on, then," Big Eddie said. "I know you've still got a ways to go. I could stand out here jawing all day. That's what the wife says. And her sisters. And Benji. And most of the town."

Nate bet he could. Big Eddie was just the type—friendly and open. Nate wasn't like that. Not at all. He put his wallet back in his pocket. "Thanks. I appreciate it."

Big Eddie shook his hand again. It was a little tighter this time, like he was trying to tell Nate something without actually saying the words. "You need anything, you give me a holler, you hear? Those supplies won't last you forever. You need something, let me know, and we can meet halfway. Save you a bit of a trip."

"You don't have to—"

"Nate, just take it for what it is. Kindness. Sometimes people need it, even if they don't know how to ask for it."

Looking away, Nate cleared his throat. "Thanks. I will." He turned for his truck.

Before he pulled out, he glanced back into the gas station. Big Eddie was bent over the counter next to his son, frowning down at the paper. Benji was doing the same. It was strange how obvious it was they were related. Like father, like son.

Nate pulled out and left Roseland behind.

✦

There was a sign, barely visible behind a gnarl of greenery, trees and bushes growing wild. If you didn't know it was there, you wouldn't even see it, or the turnoff. Nate almost passed it by accident, distracted by a deer moving off in the trees to the left. He hit the brakes a little sharper than he meant to, the seat belt digging into his hips. The tires squealed against the pavement, and he looked in the rearview mirror to make sure he hadn't just pulled that asshole move in front of another car.

There wasn't one. He hadn't seen another vehicle since he'd left Roseland.

HERSCHEL LAKE, the sign said. 15 MILES.

An arrow pointed toward a dirt road.

He sat there on the road, in the middle of the forest in the mountains, for far longer than he should have.

And then he hit the blinker and turned the truck onto the dirt road.

✦

It was smoother than he expected, which meant Big Eddie had been right about the mild winter. If it'd been normal, there would have still been snow on the ground. It wasn't surprising to see spring snowstorms come ripping through, the air different than the winter squalls. It always felt more electric in the spring, the snow falling on blooming flowers, the reds and violets almost shocking against the white.

But it was easier this way. He hadn't thought to put chains on the truck's tires when he'd set out from Eugene after meeting with the estate attorney. He'd flown in from D.C. The attorney had picked him up from the airport, given that his brother had been busy. Or so he'd said. Nate knew better, and he could tell the attorney wanted to ask questions (*whywhywhy*), but somehow, he'd minded his own business. He'd been balding and talkative, saying how sorry he was about Nate's parents in one breath, and then talking about the Trailblazers in the next.

"Didn't see you at the funeral," he'd said at one point.

"Don't expect you did," Nate had replied, staring out the window.

"No money," the attorney said later. "People always want to know how much money they're getting. Just be up front with you about that now. Everything went to your brother's family. His kids. College ain't cheap."

He didn't want their money.

He didn't even want the cabin or the truck.

But he'd taken them anyway because there was nothing else left for him.

"Sign here," the attorney had said. "Sign here, initial here, and here, and here, and would you look at that, you're the proud owner of a 1974 Ford F100 and a cabin on four acres in the middle of nowhere. Congrats. Shelly, would you make copies for Mr. Cart-wright."

His secretary had popped her gum loudly and done exactly that.

He'd been given keys. Front door. Back door. Shed. Two for the truck.

He'd been given copies of all the paperwork.

He'd been shown the door.

"Let me know if you need anything," the attorney had said, both of them knowing this would be the last time they'd ever speak to each other.

The truck had been sitting in the parking lot, dropped off by his brother a couple of days before.

It was white with green trim. The tires looked a little bald. There was a gun rack against the rear window, the same one that had held the shotgun his father had used on his mother and then on himself. Nate had stood in that strip mall parking lot, staring at the gun rack for a long time.

He'd stayed in Eugene for a few days, making phone calls from the room he'd rented at the Motel 6. Calling for the water to be turned on. Paying for a few more months at the storage locker back in D.C. His mail was forwarded to a PO box that he could check monthly.

And just like that, Nate Cartwright's life was all wrapped up in a neat little bow.

He'd stayed one more night in the Motel 6, staring up at the ceiling, listening to the trucks out on the highway passing by at three in the morning.

The next morning, he'd been at Walmart as soon as it'd opened, buying everything he needed to stay away for a long while. He hadn't even winced at the amount he'd spent when it was read to him. It didn't matter.

He hit a pothole.

The truck's frame shuddered.

He slowed. He didn't want to get a flat tire this far up in the mountains. He didn't have a spare.

Herschel Lake had once been a popular tourist destination in the fifties and sixties. Where there'd once only been a handful of cabins, there suddenly were dozens. Vacation rentals, second homes, all set far enough away from each other to feel *just* out of sight from the rest of the world, Herschel Lake and the forest around it would echo with people on picnics or kids in the lake, jumping off docks or rope swings.

It'd fallen off in the late seventies, the company that owned most of the cabins going under. Things had fallen apart. The Bureau of Land Management had come in and purchased most of the land, but nothing had been done with the rental cabins. They'd been left to rot.

Nate's parents had come up in 1980. They'd fallen in love with the area and found a cabin for sale, farther away from all the others. An elderly man was being moved into a retirement home by his kids, and they wanted the cabin sold. A couple of months later, the Cartwrights had a cabin in the woods.

He'd been thirteen the first time he'd come to Herschel Lake.

The quiet had scared him.

He'd gotten used to it after the first week.

Going home after had always seemed so loud.

It's what he wanted now. Quiet. Room to think. To figure shit out. He needed to decide what was going to happen next.

His first glimpse of the lake came twenty minutes later, a flash of sun on the water. He blinked away the afterimages that burned in his eyes.

He thought about stopping. About taking off his old pair of Chucks and putting his feet in the water. It'd be cold. The lake was fed from streams that came from farther up the mountains. The air was already considerably cooler than it'd been even in Roseland. Maybe it would shock him. Cause his brain to reboot.

But the sun was getting lower, and the sky was starting to streak. He wanted to make it to the cabin by dark. He still needed to get to the other side of the lake.

He drove on.

✦

The first stars had appeared overhead by the time he reached the long driveway to the cabin. He'd turned on the truck's headlights ten minutes before, the thick trees blocking out much of the dying sun. He'd rolled up the window too, telling himself the chill on his skin had only to do with the mountain air.

He used the signal again as he turned onto the road to the cabin. Force of habit. There was no one else out here.

The driveway was a little rougher than the main road. The truck rattled and groaned. The beam cast by his headlights jumped, bouncing through the trees. He kept the speed low, listening to his meager belongings bounce around the bed of the truck, the gas canisters scraping loudly.

And there, as it had been fourteen years ago when he'd first laid eyes on it, was the cabin.

It wasn't anything grand. Single story. A small porch. Two bedrooms, one slightly larger than the other. Two bathrooms, both of which had showers where the water was either scalding or ice. A perfunctory kitchen with a stove and an ancient refrigerator. A living room with a couch his mother had insisted upon, saying they weren't going to live like *savages* out in the middle of the woods, could you *imagine*? And *that* had been an ordeal, having that thing tied down to the back of the truck with bungee cords, bringing it up the mountain only to find it didn't fit through the front door. There'd been a moment of panic, his parents getting those looks on their faces, the ones that said *someone* was going to start yelling, but then Nate's brother had pointed out the rear doorway was larger, and they'd made it work. A cushion had torn and the paneling around the doorway chipped, but they'd finally made it in, all of them laughing, sweat dripping down their faces.

Nate's favorite part of the cabin, however, had been the books.

The cabin had been sold as is. The elderly man's children had taken everything of sentimental value but had left other things that Nate couldn't believe. The head of a deer—an eight-point buck—mounted on the wall in the living room, its eyes shiny and black. ("Take it down," his mother demanded almost immediately.) Dozens of cans of Spam. ("I don't think it ever expires," his father muttered, squinting at the pantry.) Two packs of cigarettes, both opened and missing a few. ("Don't tell Mom," his older brother warned. "I'm going to smoke the shit out of these.")

And the books. So many books.

They lined the old set of shelves on the far wall in the living room. Hundreds of them, most of them Westerns by Louis L'Amour (*The Burning Hills* and *High Lonesome* and *Hanging Woman Creek* and *Under the Sweetwater Rim*). There were a few books he'd barely gotten to look at before his mother had snatched them away from him (*Teacher's Pet* and *Perversity* and *Anything Goes*), the women on the covers half-dressed and posed salaciously, the covers promising to tell the story of how Judy stayed after class and earned her diploma through special tutoring or how a love-starved temptress gave in to her insatiable desires. Those books were gone quickly.

But the rest were fair game. And his summers became Westerns, frontier stories of cowboys and Indians and red plateaus under the scorching sun. He'd take a book or two and disappear into the trees for the day, eating blackberries for lunch, his fingers and lips a tacky purple, the pages stained by the time he headed back toward the cabin.

He'd been happy here. He'd been free.

And maybe that's why he was here again. Maybe that's why he'd come back. Nate Cartwright hadn't been happy in a long time. Things had been simpler when he'd been thirteen or fourteen or fifteen years old, his body changing, zits on his forehead, voice cracking, hair sprouting in places where it hadn't before. He'd been an awkward kid, all gangly arms and legs, perpetually pushing his glasses back up his nose. His brother had bitched and moaned about being away from his friends and girlfriend *again*, his parents were already checked out mentally, but Nate had just grabbed the books and gone away for hours, sitting at the base of a tree, sometimes reading, sometimes pretending he was a settler on the frontier, that he was in the wilds, the cabin he'd built somewhere behind him, and he was alone, truly alone, just the way he liked it.

Maybe that's why he'd come back here. To be alone.

It wasn't because he was trying to find some last connection with the two people who had cut him out of their lives. Of course not. He'd gotten over that a while ago. The fact that they'd left him the cabin and the truck hadn't meant a damn thing. Maybe their guilt had gotten the better of them. It didn't matter. Not now. Not anymore.

The cabin was dark.

He was exhausted.

If his mother had been here in September, it wouldn't be too bad inside. He'd open a couple of windows to air it out, maybe wipe down the thin layer of dust that had settled. But it wouldn't be much. For that, he was thankful.

He turned off the truck. The headlights went dark.

The stars blinked above as he opened the door.

The sky was red and pink and orange.

The surface of the lake looked as if it were on fire.

He heard birds in the trees, the lap of waves against the shore.

He stepped out of the truck.

Gravel crunched under his feet.

The door creaked as he closed it behind him, the sound echoing slightly.

He went to the back of the truck and grabbed his duffel bag. In the side pocket was a flashlight that he'd put there earlier after his shopping spree. He clicked the button on the side, and the beam flashed on. He shined it in the bed of the truck until he found one of the canisters Big Eddie had filled for him. He reached in and grabbed it too, shirt lifting slightly, a line of thin skin pressing against the cold metal of the truck. He shivered as he pulled the canister out of the truck.

He walked toward the cabin, trying hard not to think about the last time he'd been here. The guy had been sucking on his neck as they stumbled toward the porch, one hand in Nate's back pocket, the other under his shirt and rubbing against the hair on his chest. He'd always been on the lean side, but at twenty-one, he'd been making daily trips to the gym. He'd been harder then, more defined. His dark hair had been newly cut, tight against his skull. He'd been groaning at the teeth sinking into his neck, the tongue dragging along his skin. They'd lost most of their clothes as soon as they got inside, the guy on his knees, Nate's pants around his ankles, his cock being swallowed down into wet heat as he leaned against the door, head back and eyes closed.

His parents had shown up unexpectedly two days later.

"Give me the key," his father had snapped, eyes blazing. "Give me the key, and don't let me catch you here again."

He was a shadow now. Thinner, his hair shaggy. His shoulders were a little bony, sharp. He was softer, too. He hadn't had time for the gym like he'd had before. It'd all been cups of coffee and sitting in front of a computer, working the phones or shouting questions at some senator who tried to walk as fast as he could, a thin smile fixed on his face as if thinking that affair he'd had or the money he'd embezzled would just fade away if he ignored the kid demanding to know why, an electronic recorder held toward his face, cameras flashing again and again.

Nate had caught his reflection in a store window not that long ago and wondered who the man staring back at him was. The man with the sharp cheekbones, slightly sunken cheeks. The man whose blue eyes looked faded and cold. The man sporting three-day-old stubble on his face that made him look dirty and tired. The man with the wrinkled shirt and purple lines under his eyes and no job because he'd fucked up big-time and done something he never thought he was capable of, and here he was, a useless degree and six years on the street beat, chasing down stories that didn't matter while daydreaming of breaking something wide open, a scandal that would rock the city to its very core. He had Pulitzer dreams on a lower-middle-class salary that barely kept him afloat in a city that bled red, white, and blue, oozing in time with the beat of a diseased heart.

It had been killing him.

So yeah. His brother had called him again. He'd been spinning his wheels. He'd heard *cabin* and *truck* and thought why the fuck not. He had some savings, enough to get by for a little while. He broke his lease on his tiny apartment, packed up his shit and sent most of it to storage, and headed west.

Best damn idea he'd had in a long time.

He'd figure things out. He'd take a few days, clear his head, and then he'd sit down and figure things out. He always did. He was good at it when he allowed himself to be.

He walked to the side of the cabin, heading toward the back where the generator sat inside a small storage shed. He fumbled with the keys, the flashlight slipping slightly, the beam pointing at his feet. The gas canister sloshed against his leg. His footsteps were soft in the grass.

He found the key he needed for the shed, thankfully marked *S* in the tape that wrapped around the top. There was *FD* for front door, *BD* for the back. There was one marked *BH* for boathouse, the wooden structure next to the dock on the lake. They'd never had a boat and had ended up only using it for storage. He'd have to take time to clean it out later. To see what had been left behind.

The shed was—

He stopped.

The metal of the gas canister's handle dug into the skin of his folded fingers.

The padlock hung open on the shed door.

The door was open slightly. Just a sliver, really.

That wasn't—

He shook his head.

It was fine. His mother had forgotten to latch it all the way when she'd been here last. An honest mistake. Hopefully nothing had happened to the generator in the interim. The winter had been mild, but there *had* been snow. And rain.

He went to the shed door, setting the canister in the grass.

He reached, and just to be sure, he closed the padlock. It clicked. Locked. He slid the key into the keyhole and turned it. The padlock popped open.

Honest mistake. She probably had been distracted. Maybe Joy had been calling for her and she just hadn't slid it closed before turning back toward the cabin.

Except when he opened the shed door, he was hit with a wave of warm air. As if the generator had been running. Recently.

He frowned.

He stepped inside the shed. Reached out and touched the generator. The metal was hot to the touch. Not a fluke.

Had she left it on this whole time?

But that couldn't be right. Even if she had, it would have run out of gas months ago. Even with all the lights off in the cabin. It wouldn't have—

There was the unmistakable click of a gun being cocked.

Something hard pressed against the back of his head, digging into his scalp.

A voice said, "You're going to set the flashlight on the ground. And then you're going to bring your hands up slowly. Lace your fingers on the back of your neck. If you try anything, if you reach for something I cannot see, or if you don't do *exactly* as I've said, I will put a bullet in your head. Without question."

Everything felt sharp around Nate. His vision narrowed. His heart thumped wildly in his chest. There was blood rushing in his ears. His mind was utterly blank, bathed in a sheet of white.

He'd been mugged once. In Bethesda, down in the Metro. There'd been a small knife and a look of desperation on the man's face, eyes darting back and forth. He'd demanded Nate's wallet. "Now," he'd chanted. "Now, now, *now*, man, I swear, you need to move, give it to me *now*."

It'd felt the same. There was fear, sure, and it was causing his muscles to freeze, his brain shorting out with what felt like an audible *pop*. The knife hadn't been anything to sneeze at, a pigsticker with a sharp blade, and somehow—*somehow*—Nate had managed to hand over his wallet. The man had snatched it from his hand and taken off.

People had kept walking around him as if nothing had happened.

He'd stood there for a long time.

Eventually he'd moved. He'd found a Metro cop and filed a report.

"Probably won't ever see it again," the cop had told him. "It's a pain in the ass, but just cancel your cards and get a new license. It won't ever turn up."

He'd done exactly that.

His wallet had never been found.

It'd been leather, a gift. Nothing extravagant. And he'd had twenty bucks in it. But that was all.

But for months after, every time he'd gone down into the Metro, he'd kept an eye out. He didn't know what he'd do if he found the guy again, if he saw him on the train. Confront him? Say, hey, remember when you held a knife to my stomach and took away my sense of security?

Of course he'd never seen the guy again. It's not how those things happened.

But it was that *same* fear. Like he was outside of himself. He felt separate. Mechanical. He knew it was cold, but he didn't feel it anymore. He knew the inside of the shed was warm, but that was a thing of the past.

Now it was only the gun against his head.

The deep, hoarse voice at his back.

He bent slowly, the press of the gun barrel never leaving his head. He dropped his flashlight. It bounced on the floor of the shed with a wooden *thunk*.

He stood again, moving as though he were underwater. He brought his hands back up behind his head as he'd been told, the keys pressing against his neck.

They were taken from him before he could lock his fingers.

They jangled somewhere behind him.

The gun barrel never wavered.

He gripped the back of his neck tightly.

He said, "I don't have much money. My wallet is in my back right pocket. You can have whatever's in it."

"You have anything else on you?" the voice asked again.

"No."

"Who do you work for?"

And that—that was not a question he was expecting. He couldn't process it. He didn't understand. He said, "I don't work for anyone."

"Bullshit," the man growled, sounding angrier. "Are you alone? Who else is with you?"

"No one."

"Who knows you're here?"

He blinked rapidly. "Uh—Big Eddie. From the gas station in Roseland. My brother probably." He swallowed thickly. "The attorney who gave me the keys. That's it."

"What the fuck are you talking about?"

"You asked who—"

"You came from the mountain?"

"I drove up the mountain, yes. It's how I got here."

"You're lying. How did you find us?"

"I didn't find *anyone*." He was starting to sound a little hysterical. He couldn't help it. His throat was starting to close, and panic was clawing at his chest. "My parents died and left me the cabin, and I drove up here to get away, okay? That's all. That's it. I had nothing else, and this is it. This fucking cabin. That goddamn truck. It's all I have left and—"

Another voice. This time female and younger. "I think he's telling the truth."

The barrel pulled away slightly. "I told you to stay inside the house."

Nate closed his eyes.

"I know," the girl said, and Christ, she sounded so *young*. "But here I am anyway."

"He's lying." The barrel was back. "What did I tell you about this?"

The girl sighed. "That there's no such thing as coincidence. Everything happens for a reason."

The man coughed. It sounded painful. "And now he's here."

"Maybe he's meant to be. Maybe he's—"

"Don't."

"You're still hurt. You should be resting."

"I told you, I'm *fine*. We need to figure out who he's working for. They could be—"

"Is he going to piss himself?" The girl sounded far too curious. "Isn't that what happens when you get really scared? I read in a book that you can lose control of your bowels and—"

"Art. Get. Inside. *Now.*"

"No. I won't leave you. You promised."

The man made a noise that sounded pained. "God. I know. Okay? I know I promised, but we can't take chances. There's no such thing as coincidence. If he's here, then it's for a reason. And we need to—"

"She's right," Nate heard himself say. "I'm not lying. I swear, I'm not—"

The gun barrel was back. "Don't you talk to her," the man snarled. "Don't you *ever* talk to her. Tell me how you found us. Tell me who else is coming."

"No one," Nate croaked. "There's no one. This is my parents' cabin. They're dead. This is my only home now. I can't—"

The gun barrel fell away.

Nate heard the man step back away from him.

He gulped in a deep breath. It hurt his throat.

"Keep your hands where they are," the man said. "And turn around slowly. I will shoot you if you don't do what I say."

Nate almost laughed hysterically.

Instead, he turned.

There in the dark was a man with a very large gun pointed in his direction. The man himself had short black hair that was almost a buzz cut and dark eyes that watched every move Nate made. He was older, lines around his narrowed eyes and mouth. He had stubble across his cheeks and jaw. His skin was pale, and his hand was shaking slightly. He had an arm wrapped around his waist, a big hand holding on to his side. He wore jeans and an open flannel shirt. Nate could see the skin and hair on his chest and stomach, and what looked to be a thick bandage on his side.

And next to him was a little girl.

She wasn't scared. Not like the man whose leg she stood next to, a hand wrapped in the hem of his shirt. She wasn't angry like he was either. Instead she looked merely curious. Her hair was blond and pulled back into a loose ponytail, with escaped tendrils hanging around her ears. She had big eyes and a little upturned nose. She wore a shirt that had a Care Bear on it. It swallowed her small frame.

The man was large. He had a few inches on Nate. He seemed

almost as wide as he was tall. He dwarfed the little girl, the top of her head barely coming past his waist.

"Howdy, partner," the girl said. "My name is Artemis Darth Vader. It's nice to meet you, I reckon."

"Art," the man growled down at her.

"You said I have to act normal, Alex," the girl said, staring up at the man. "Normal people introduce themselves. I read that in a book."

"What the fuck," Nate said faintly.

"I also told you that you need to not talk to *strangers*," the man—Alex?—snapped at her. The aim of the gun went off to the left. He looked as if he was swaying.

"He's not a stranger," the girl said, suddenly looking down. "His name is Nathaniel Cartwright. He lives in Washington, D.C."

"How the hell did you—is that my *wallet?*"

She glanced back up at him. "Yes. This is your wallet. Very astute."

"How did you—" He hadn't even *felt* her take it.

"You said we could have it. Oh boy. You were right. There's not much money in here. That's too bad. I like money. It smells weird."

"Art!" the man barked again. "Get inside the house. *Now.*"

And then, just because Nate's night couldn't get any stranger, the man's eyes rolled back up in his head and he collapsed to the ground.

The gun fell from his hand.

"I told him not to push it," the girl who'd introduced herself as Artemis Darth Vader said. "He needs to listen to me more." She looked up at Nate. "Nathaniel Cartwright of Washington, D.C. I'd sure appreciate it, hoss, if you could mosey on over here and help a fellow cowpoke out. Need to get this guy into the cabin over yonder."

Nate did the only thing he could.

He passed out too.

CHAPTER TWO

". . . you should have secured him. We can't take any chances."

"I'm not going to tie him up. One does not tie up *guests*, Alex."

"He's not a guest. He's—"

"He's in the photos."

"What?"

"The photos. In the bedroom. In the hallway. Above the fire-place. He's in the photos. He's telling—no. Don't *move*. I can show you if you need to see. If you would just trust me, I could—"

"It's not about trust. I told you that. It's about survival. We're not—"

Nate groaned.

"Oh look," the girl said. "He's waking up."

"Get away from him. Art, just—"

Something poked his cheek.

He opened his eyes.

The little girl was staring down at him. Her eyes were the brightest green he'd ever seen before in his life. They were enchanting.

He made a little strangled noise in the back of his throat, jerking up.

"Howdy, partner," she said, stepping back. "Welcome back to being awake. You were unconscious for twenty minutes, seventeen seconds. That's a long time for someone like you."

Nate was on the couch. His Chucks had been removed. A blanket was laid over him, which fell to his lap as he sat up. His head felt stuffed, his muscles stiff.

The man sat across from him in a wooden chair Nate recognized as being from the kitchen. His shirt was buttoned a little, enough to cover the bandage. The gun sat on his thick thigh, his hand around the grip. He was breathing shallowly, his eyes never leaving Nate.

"You can't kill me," Nate said, the first thing that came to his mind.

"I can," the man said, a sneer on his face. "Very easily. You'd be surprised at just how easy it would be."

"He's not lying," the little girl said solemnly. "He's a gunslinger. A lonely man, a six-shooter on his hip, the iron hot as he fixes the brim of his hat and rides off into the sunset on the mesa—"

"I told you not to read those damn books," the man said.

"Well, I found those other books, but you wouldn't let me read them. The ones you said were inappropriate for someone my age, even if I'm—"

"Art."

She rolled her eyes. Then, "Did I do that right? Did I look exasperated because you wouldn't let me find out why Judy needed to stay after class to meet with the teacher in order to raise her grade? I mean, why couldn't she just get extra work to take—oh. Oh." She frowned. "That can't be ethical."

"Who are you?" the man asked.

"Nathaniel," he said. He coughed and shook his head. "Nathaniel Cartwright."

"Wow," the girl said. "Just like I told you earlier. How about that."

"And why are you here?"

"This is my cabin," Nate said, wondering where the anger was coming from. Because yes, he'd had a gun pointed at him. Yes, he'd been threatened. Yes, these people were here, and he didn't know who the fuck they were. And maybe he was a little embarrassed too. He'd passed out for no goddamn reason, for fuck's sake. That added to it, sure. His blood was boiling. He stood, the blanket falling to the ground. It was an afghan his mother had knitted. He hated the sight of it.

The man immediately raised the gun.

The girl took a step back.

"This is *my* cabin," Nate said again, the words stronger. "You don't have the right to ask me what I'm doing here when I *live* here. Who the fuck are you? You know what? I don't care. I'm calling the cops."

The man cocked the gun. "You're not going to do shit."

"You would have shot me already if you were going to," Nate said, looking around for his cell phone before remembering it was still sitting on the bench seat in the truck.

"Oh boy, hoss," the girl said. "You should *not* have said that."

The man fired the gun. The blast was flat and sharp in the small space of the living room. Nate swore he felt the buzz of the bullet right by his cheek. He turned slowly to see a ragged hole in the wall behind him. His skin felt like it was vibrating.

"Don't think I won't do it," the man said coldly. "Because I will do whatever it takes to keep her—" He grimaced then, leaning forward and groaning.

The girl was at his side in an instant, hands running over his stomach and chest.

"What's wrong with him?" Nate asked, feeling like he was floating above himself, secured by a thin tether.

"Nothing," the man said through gritted teeth. "It's just—"

"He was shot," the girl said. "By a jerk who wouldn't get out of the way."

"Shot," Nate repeated dully. "Like he almost just shot me."

"He missed," the girl said.

"I didn't *miss*," the man said, a thin sheen of sweat on his forehead.

Nate didn't know what to do with that. "Why don't you take him to a hospital?"

She glanced over her shoulder. "Because that's not how being on the run works. Don't you know that?"

"Art, I swear to god, you're going to—"

"He doesn't know how it works," Art said, turning back toward the man. "I'm just telling him so he knows. You need to stop talking. The more you talk, the more you hurt, and I don't like it when you hurt. I need you to be okay again so we can be together. I cried, Alex. You made me *cry*. That's not very nice of you."

And wonder of all wonders, the man's scowl softened. "You don't need to cry. Especially not over me."

She fussed over him, tugging on his shirt. "You don't need to get shot. Or be rude. I don't like it when either of those things happens."

"You've never seen me get shot before."

"Yes, but I've seen you be rude all the time, so."

The man slumped back in the chair, tilting his head back. His grip was loose on the gun. It would be so easy to just—

"Here," Art said, taking the gun from the man's lap, holding it toward Nate.

The man's eyes flashed open. "What are you doing?"

"He was thinking about going for the gun," Art said. The gun looked huge in her small hand. "I figured if I gave it to him, he would know he could trust us." She frowned. "Or at least trust me, seeing as how you almost shot him in the head trying to show how manly you are." She looked back at Nate. "Wasn't he manly? Say yes so he feels better."

"Yes," Nate said immediately.

Art turned back toward the man. "Do you feel better?"

He tried to sit forward. "Give me the gun."

"No. Nathaniel, come get the gun."

"Nathaniel, do *not* touch that gun, I swear to—"

Nate stepped forward and took the gun. He didn't know the first thing about how to use it, but he pointed it directly at them.

"Nathaniel," the girl said. "Don't be rude."

The man stood with a groan and forced the girl behind him. She squawked but stayed where he'd put her, peeking around his hip to look at Nate. "If you point that thing at me, you better be ready to use it."

The barrel shook.

He put pressure on the trigger.

"He looks unsure," the girl whispered. "That's not a good look to have when you're pointing a gun."

Nate blinked. She didn't even sound scared. He felt bad, yeah, of course he did. Whatever was happening, she was just a little girl, and this wasn't her fault.

He said, "I'm going to get my phone. I'm going to call the cops."

"You're still pointing that gun at me," the man said, pushing the girl farther behind him, much to her visible irritation. "I told you—"

It was a distraction, of course. Even while he was still talking, the man moved. One moment they were facing off, the gun in

Nate's hand, the man several feet away. The next, the man had moved, and the gun was now in *his* hand. It took Nate's brain a few seconds to catch up, to understand what had just happened. His arm was still raised.

He lowered it slowly.

The man wasn't pointing the gun at him anymore. He sat back down in the seat with a groan.

The girl glanced between the two of them. "Now that *that's* out of the way, y'all reckon we could patch this up here, buckaroo?"

No bars.

The fucking Nokia had no bars.

He sat in the truck, staring down at the green screen in the dark.

They hadn't tried to stop him when he'd gone outside. Well, that wasn't entirely true. The man *had* made some kind of noise, trying to push himself up, but the girl put her hand on his shoulder, forcing him back down. Which for such a little thing was rather remarkable.

"He'll be back," the girl said as Nate fled out the door.

Fuck that.

He raised the phone above his head, hitting the top of the cab of the truck.

No bars.

"Come on," he muttered.

He got out of the truck.

The air was cold. The sun was gone.

He turned in circles.

No bars.

He got into the bed of the truck.

No bars.

He jumped into the air as high as he could.

Still no bars.

He eyed the roof of the cabin.

Probably not the best idea.

He should just leave. Get back in the truck and head back down the mountain.

If he took it slowly, he'd be back in Roseland in a couple of hours. His phone would work.

He could find a cop. Hell, he could call Big Eddie. He might not even have to get all the way back to Roseland before it worked.

Yes. That sounded like a plan.

"All right," he muttered to himself. "I'm going to do that. That's what I'm going to do. It's smart. It's safe. Good plan."

He got back into the truck and reached down to turn the key.

Except there was nothing there.

Because he didn't have his keys.

"Mother*fucker*," he growled, slamming his hand against the steering wheel.

When had he last had his keys? It would have been at the shed before he—yeah, fine, before he *fainted*. He'd felt them cool against his neck, buried under all that terror of having a fucking *gun* pointed at his head. Either they were still sitting on the ground by the shed, or they were inside after they'd carried him in—

And that—something buzzed a little at that, didn't it? Like an electrical pulse in the back of his brain. It was disbelief mixed with ??????? because *how* had that happened exactly? The man had passed out. The girl couldn't have carried him in herself. The man must have woken up and carried Nate inside, but . . . he was *injured*. He'd been *shot*. Nate had never been shot, but he could imagine what kind of pain he'd be in. Nate may have been thin, but he was a hair over six feet. He wasn't *small*. Yes, the man was much larger— probably had a good sixty pounds on Nate—but if he was hurt, and if Nate could take him by surprise . . .

Unless they were just *pretending* the man had been shot.

Or if there was another person in the cabin. Someone he hadn't seen yet. Maybe the girl's mother.

He had a feeling the keys weren't by the shed.

He got out of the truck.

He turned toward the road.

He started walking.

He made it three steps before he stopped.

He turned back around.

They were in *his* cabin.

He wasn't the one that needed to go.

He took a step forward, determined.

They had a gun that had already been fired in his direction.

His next step was less determined.

As were the ones after that.

By the time he reached the porch steps, he was sweating despite the cold mountain air. His hands were shaking, and his head was pounding.

He managed to make it up the steps, the wood creaking underneath him.

The door was still open partway. He couldn't see much.

He steeled himself, took a breath, and pushed the door open.

The man was still sitting on the chair, head tilted back, eyes closed.

The girl was next to him, her hand on his side.

The gun was sitting on the coffee table.

"Told you he'd come back," she said without turning around.

The man cracked an eye open. "Huh."

"Who else is in this house?" Nate asked, going for firm but landing somewhere around shrill.

The man closed his eye. "What?"

"The house," Nate repeated. "Who else is here?"

The girl cocked her head, waited a beat, then said, "No one. Just us three."

Nate nodded, head jerking up and down. "Fine, then you're not really shot."

The man snorted.

"He is." The girl patted the man on the knee. "He shouldn't have been, but he's an idiot. Do you like sunglasses?"

"Art," the man said, a warning in his voice.

"What?" the girl asked. "It was just a question."

Nate wasn't sure what was going on. "I don't *care* about sunglasses—"

"Oh," the girl said. "That's too bad." She brightened. "Are these your books, partner? Going down the dusty trail on your horse named Benny with your clichéd and borderline racist caricature of a Native American sidekick that—"

"Yes," Nate said. "Those are mine. The books are mine. That chair you're sitting on is mine. *Everything you see here is mine.*"

"Okay. Jeez. You don't need to brag."

Nate sputtered. "Jesus, I'm not *bragging*. What the fuck is wrong with you?"

The girl squinted at him. "Nothing. What's wrong with you?"

"Listen, little girl—"

"My name is Artemis Darth Vader. I told you that already."

"That's not a real name!"

"It is," she insisted, and for the first time since this craziness had begun, the girl looked almost . . . upset. "It's mine. It's my name. No one else can have it. It belongs to me. You can't take that from—"

The man winced, but he lifted a hand and dropped it on her shoulder, squeezing gently.

The little girl's chest heaved once, twice, three times before she sighed.

"Her name is Artemis," the man said quietly. "Art, for short. She's . . . very partial to it."

Nate didn't know what to say to that.

"He's my Alex," Art said. "And he's been shot. There's no one else in the house. We didn't know who lived here. We didn't hurt anything. I read some of your books. We ate some of the food, canned stuff that didn't look like it'd be missed. We slept in the beds. He needs to feel better. Okay? That's all I want. I need him to feel better."

"Where are my keys?" Nate asked quietly.

"I dropped them," Art said, looking back at Alex. "By the shed. I couldn't get them and you and Alex at the same—"

Alex coughed. "*We* couldn't lift you and grab the keys at the same time. Not with how weak I am."

"Right," Art said. "Because you've been shot. In your skin."

Nate moved across the living room, giving the two strangers a wide berth.

Neither of them went for the gun.

He was out the door before they could speak again.

✦

There they were. Just . . . sitting in the grass next to the shed.

He bent over and picked them up.

The generator hummed.

He looked down at the keys in his hand.

All he'd need to do was get back in the truck. That's it. He had what he needed. His phone was in his pocket, his keys in his hand. He hadn't even unpacked anything. He hadn't had time. If the man *had* been shot, he didn't need to know how. He didn't need to know what they were running from. Who was after them. He didn't need to be involved. Hell, he didn't even have to tell anyone about them. He could go back inside, tell them they had a day to clear out before he called the cops, and he could sleep somewhere down the road in the truck. He'd come back tomorrow and they'd be gone, and he could pretend none of this had happened. He would go about living his strange, isolated existence where he was going to figure out what he'd do next. He'd grieve over that *lack* of grief he felt at his parents' loss and then move on. He wouldn't have to worry about a dangerous man and his weirdly named daughter.

Yes. That sounded good.

He turned back around.

The girl was standing there.

He jumped and made a rather embarrassing sound.

"Howdy," she said, staring up at him.

"Don't *do* that," he snapped at her.

"You're really jumpy."

"You snuck up on me!"

"Yes. I'm really quiet. It's one of my strengths. What are you doing? Are you contemplating? I do like contemplating. It's so . . . normal."

He stared back at her.

She smiled up at him. If he hadn't felt the air splitting around a bullet near his ear only a little while before, he might have thought her beautiful.

But as it stood now, she was obviously a fugitive on the run and had somehow involved him with her crazy father.

"Yes, well," he said stiffly. "If you don't mind, I think I'll be leaving—"

"Do you have more food?"

"Yes. No! I don't—"

"Which is it?" she asked, cocking her head.

"What?"

"I asked if you had more food. You said yes and no. It can't be both. It's paradoxical."

"How old are you?"

"How old are *you*?"

"Don't you—I'm twenty-seven."

"Oh. Alex is forty. He's older than you. Do you have more food? There wasn't much in the pantry. And he needs to eat to get his strength back. I was going to go to another cabin to see if there was more food, but then you came, and now we're standing here with you saying both yes and no to a question that was either-or." She paused, staring up at him, barely blinking. Then, "I like sunglasses. Alex got me some. They are inside. I'm not wearing them now because it's nighttime, and Alex says you can't wear sunglasses at night because it makes you look stupid."

"Yes, I have more food," Nate said, desperate to get this strange girl to stop talking. "I can—"

"Oh good." She reached out and took his hand. He barely flinched. "Let's mosey on over, then, to that thar horse and buggy you pulled up in, partner. I like your books. They make me happy. Do they make you happy?"

They were walking toward the truck. Nate hadn't even known they were moving. "I don't . . . know?"

"Oh. That's okay. Sometimes not knowing something makes it wonderful. That's what Alex said. But he only says that when I ask him a question I don't think he knows the answer to. He's clever like that."

They were at the truck. She watched with interest as he lowered the tailgate, like she'd never seen such a thing in person before. "Do you have soup?" she asked politely. "I read that soup makes you feel better when you are sick." She grunted lightly as she pulled herself up into the back of the truck and started rooting through his stuff.

"He's not sick," Nate said. "He's been shot. Don't touch that."

"Yes. Do you have soup?"

He did. It was cheap and easy. Most of what he'd brought were nonperishables or stuff that could sit in the freezer for months on end and still be edible after being nuked in the microwave. "He needs a hospital."

"No. I'm on it."

"The wound could get infected."

She stared at him. "That's what the soup is for."

"Look, I could take you both down the mountain to—"

"We're fine here."

"This is *my* cabin."

"Yes, but there's only you, and there's so much room. We can share. Oh look. I found the soup. Wow, there is a *lot* of it." She looked back over her shoulder. "Are you sick too?"

It would explain all of this if he were trapped in a fever dream of some sort. Maybe he'd wake up soon in his apartment in D.C. and none of this would be real. "No. I'm not sick."

"Not like Alex. But I think you're sick somehow."

"Would you stop going through my—why do you call him that?"

She had stacked four or five cans of soup in her arms. "Call who what?"

"Alex."

"That's his name."

"Why don't you call him—let me carry that. You're going to drop it."

She looked at him defiantly, her chin propped against the cans of soup stacked in her arms. "I can carry it."

"Fine, but how are you going to get down?"

She looked at the tailgate. Then back at him. Then she walked toward the edge of the truck. She crouched down and let the cans fall. They clanged against the truck. She turned them all upright at the end of the tailgate. She jumped down. She turned back toward the truck, then reached up and grabbed the cans before stacking them once again in her arms. "Like that," she said simply before turning toward the house. She stopped at the porch steps. "Hey," she said, looking back at him. "Do you also have bread? Because I read that soup goes with toast and bread becomes toast when you put it in the toaster."

"I have bread," Nate said.

"I know. I saw it. I was just seeing if you would tell the truth. Can you bring it, please?"

Then she was up the steps and through the door.

Nate stared after her.

The keys were still in his hand.

He pushed the tailgate up and locked it in place.

He could leave now. He had everything he needed. He'd helped them as much as he could. There was nothing else he could do. All he needed now was to get in the truck and drive away.

He walked around to the driver's door.

He reached for the handle.

Or at least he tried to.

Instead, he reached into the back of the truck into one of the paper bags. He found the loaf of whole-grain bread he'd bought at the market in Eugene.

"Leave," he told himself quietly. "Just leave."

He walked toward the house.

CHAPTER THREE

Alex had moved (been moved?) to the couch. He was covered with the same afghan Nate had been under when he'd awoken. His eyes were closed, his breaths shallow. Nate didn't think he was asleep.

The gun was sitting on the chair Alex had been on before.

Art was in the kitchen, carefully putting the cans on the counter, her tongue poking between her teeth as she concentrated.

Nate gave a wide berth to the couch, wondering if he should go for the gun. But he'd already had it in his hand once, and that hadn't ended well for him the first time. There were knives in the kitchen. Maybe he would get one of those.

"None of these are chicken soup," Art told him as he entered the kitchen.

"I know."

"This one says it's *hearty chili*. That's not even soup. The word *soup* isn't listed anywhere on it."

"That's because it's not soup."

"That's what I just said." She looked up at him. "Chicken soup makes you healthy. None of these have chickens. How is Alex supposed to feel better if he doesn't get chickens?"

Nate didn't know how to answer that. So he said, "This one," and tapped the top of a can.

She eyed it dubiously. "Vegetable beef."

"Yes."

"That will make him better."

"Yes."

"This is scientifically proven. Like the chicken."

"It's not *science*—yes. Yes, it is scientifically proven. Like chicken."

She nodded. "Okay. I reckon this will suffice, partner."

He watched as she moved away from the cans and went to a

drawer near the sink. She pulled a can opener from it like she knew exactly where it was. Like she'd done this already. Which, if she was to be believed, she had.

She set the can opener down next to the vegetable beef and went to the dining table. She pulled one of the chairs toward the counter. Once it was pressed flush with the bottom cabinets, she climbed on top of it and then onto the counter.

"I can help you—"

"I know how to do it," she said. She opened the cabinet and found what she was looking for. Bowls, old things that had been there since he was a kid. She pulled down three of them, setting them on the counter before she shut the cabinet and slid back down to the chair. She picked up the bowls and brought them next to the can opener and the soup. Then she went *back* to the chair and moved it in front of the stove. And then it was back to the cabinets again, this time to a lower one. She pulled out a pot and closed the cabinet. She went back to the stove and climbed onto the chair before setting the pot on one of the heating coils. She climbed back down the chair, crossed the kitchen to the soup, grabbed the can opener and three cans of vegetable beef, and went to the stove again.

Nate hadn't moved through the entire process.

"Can you turn the bread into toast?" she asked without looking at him. "I've never done that before and don't want to ruin it."

"What is happening?" Nate whispered.

"We're making soup and toast, Nathaniel," Art said, grunting as she squeezed the can opener. "Obviously."

Obviously.

The toaster was sitting where it always had been, next to the bread box. It felt like he was moving in a dream as he crossed the kitchen, an unopened loaf of bread in his hand. He set it on the counter as Art poured the first can of soup into the pot. She leaned over the stove and twisted the dial. He thought about telling her that children shouldn't play with the stove. He didn't, though. He didn't want to be rebuked by what had to be a ten-year-old little girl. He'd already had enough of that for one evening.

"We didn't have bread to make toast," she said as she poured the second can. "I looked, but there wasn't any. I found crackers, but they were hard, and Alex doesn't like hard crackers because he said they were stale. I didn't think they were bad, but I didn't want to make him sicker, so I threw them away. I'm sorry if you liked them."

"It's fine," Nate muttered, wondering what he'd done in his life to get to this point. "They were old."

"Not all old things need to be thrown away."

Nate didn't know where to begin with that. So he said, "I guess."

"And I also threw away rice. Because a mouse had chewed on the bag and it spilled."

"I don't care."

"I cleaned up the rice too."

"I don't care."

"I put it in the garbage."

"Why are you telling me this?"

She looked at him from where she'd started stirring the soup. He didn't know where she'd gotten the ladle from. "Because these were things that were not mine that had to be dealt with. I wanted you to know in case you worried about them. Alex said that this wasn't our house, and we had to be respectful. I am showing you respect."

"I don't—just—" He shrugged helplessly. "Thanks."

"You're welcome. Is that how you make toast? You hold the bread in your hands?"

"What?" He looked down. He was holding a couple of pieces of bread. "No. You put it in the toaster."

"Oh. Because you're just standing there holding the bread in your hands."

He glared at the bread as he shoved it in the toaster, slamming down the switch.

"Hey, partner?"

"My name is Nate."

"I thought it was Nathaniel."

"It is. It's short for—your name is Artemis, right?"

She nodded. "Artemis Darth Vader."

He wasn't even going to touch that. Because that would mean her father was Alex Darth Vader and his fever must *really* be bad. "Art is short for Artemis."

"That's what Alex says."

"Nate is short for Nathaniel."

She frowned. "Oh." Then, "Why is Dick short for Richard?"

The air smelled of toast and soup. "What?"

"If Art is short for Artemis, and Nate is short for Nathaniel, why is Dick short for Richard? It's not even the same!"

"I don't . . . know?"

"Oh. That's okay. You know how to make toast. That's good enough for me."

Nate didn't think he'd ever received such simple validation in his life.

The toast popped up.

"Whoa," Art said, squinting over at him. "So that's how that works, huh? Okay. I'm impressed. Can you do it again, or do you have to wait twenty-four hours for it to recharge?"

"I can do it again."

"Nice. Good job. Please do it again. Two for Alex. Two for you. And six for me."

"You can't eat six pieces of toast."

"Why not?"

"No one eats six pieces of toast."

"Says who?"

"The same people who say vegetable beef can be used instead of chicken."

"Oh. So, scientists."

"Yes."

She narrowed her eyes at him. "Sometimes scientists can be wrong."

"I know. But not this time. Two pieces of toast."

"Four."

"Two."

"Three."

"Two."

"You're really good at that. Two it is."

He made more toast.

She switched off the stove before ladling the soup into the bowls carefully, steam wafting up toward her face. She brushed a lock of hair behind her ear. The chair wobbled slightly. And before he could stop her, she brought a hand down onto the stove to steady herself, right next to the heating coil.

She hissed, dropping the ladle into the pot, bringing her hand up quickly.

He was moving before he could think. He'd burned his hand on this very stove once, the first summer they'd come here. It'd been an accident, but the blister had been swift. His mother had told him to put his hand under cold water. It'd helped. A little.

She squawked as he grabbed her and carried her to the sink. He intended on putting her hand under a stream of water, but nothing came out when he flipped the handle.

"Shit," he muttered. "The water's not turned on yet. It won't be until—"

"Let her go."

He paused.

She stopped moving.

He looked slowly over his shoulder.

The gun was pointed at him for the third time in less than two hours. Alex's face was pale, but he was stock-still, finger on the trigger.

"She burned herself on the stove," Nate said, trying to keep his voice from wavering. "All I wanted to do was put her hand under the water."

"Art."

"It was hot," Art said with a sigh. "A mistake."

"Put her down."

Nate did.

"Art, come over here."

She grumbled under her breath, words Nate couldn't make out, but did as Alex asked. Alex didn't lower the gun as she held her hand up for inspection.

"All right?" he asked, glancing down at her hand.

"I'm *fine*. Look, see? There's nothing there."

Nate frowned. "What do you mean there's nothing there? I saw you—"

"It must have been fast," Alex said, dropping the gun back to his side. "Barely had a chance. Just a little red."

"Can I finish now?" she asked, sounding irritated. "You shouldn't be up. I'm making soup. Nate had some. There were no chickens, but he said vegetable beef is the same and that toast will help too and will help you heal."

And he saw it again there, briefly. Alex's expression softened *just* a little, the sharp lines in his face relaxing to the point he looked almost normal. If he didn't have an oversized gun in his hand, Nate would have thought he wasn't brutish at all. Alex grunted at her and leaned against the counter. Art looked as if she was going to say something but decided against it.

Nate understood. He wasn't going to be left alone with Art again. Not when he could grab her so easily.

He wondered if he could do that. If it came down to it. He wouldn't hurt her, just . . .

His stomach twisted at the thought.

Art came back to the stove and climbed onto the chair again.

More toast popped up.

She ladled soup into the last bowl.

Nate wondered what the fuck was going on.

There was whiskey in the cabinet above the fridge.

He wanted it desperately.

Instead, he stayed in the corner in the kitchen, struggling against the urge to run screaming with his hands over his head.

Art looked rather proud of herself, setting the bowl of soup on the table in front of Alex. She ran back into the kitchen and grabbed a spoon and put two pieces of toast on a paper towel before coming back to him.

She left her own bowl on the counter next to Nate's, instead choosing to drag her chair from the stove back until it was right next to Alex's. She climbed onto it, set her elbows on the table, chin in her hands, and watched Alex.

Nate wanted to ask. Somehow, he kept his mouth shut.

Alex picked up the spoon and dipped it into the soup.

"You have to blow on it," she said. "That's how you eat soup. You blow on it before you put it in your mouth."

He did just that.

She never looked away.

Alex chewed.

Art was enraptured, leaning forward.

Alex swallowed.

"Well?" Art demanded.

"'Sgood," Alex said.

Art sighed, slumping down in the chair. "That's just swell." She turned to look back at Nate, still standing in the kitchen. "You were right. Vegetable beef *is* just like chicken."

Nate nodded, unsure of what to do next.

She turned back around. "Are you feeling better?"

"Yes. I'll be fine."

"If you don't try and be stupid again. You're very lucky you have me."

Alex ate another bite of soup.

Nate looked at the bowls still sitting on the counter next to toast that was growing cold.

Then back at the table.

Art watched every bite Alex took.

He shouldn't be doing this. He should be leaving. He should be getting the fuck out of there before whatever they were running from caught up with them. He should be demanding answers. He should be shouting at them, telling them again to get the fuck out of his house. His parents were on the walls, frozen smiles from years long past, and he wondered if this was what it felt like to slowly lose your mind.

He had so many things he should be doing. To save himself. To ensure his safety. There was a crazy injured man with a gun and a girl who sometimes spoke like she was trapped in a bad spaghetti Western and loved sunglasses and didn't get burns when she put her hands on a hot stove.

He picked up a bowl of soup.

Two slices of bread.

He carried it over to the table.

Set it down in front of her.

Alex watched his every move, spoon stopped halfway to his mouth, broth dripping down to his bowl.

Art tilted her head back at him.

Her teeth were little, trapped in a wide upside-down smile.

"Thanks, Cook," she said, that long, slow drawl coming out again. "I reckon it's time to dig in myself."

He nodded and retreated back to the kitchen.

He watched them eat.

Art spoke every now and then, saying strange things like, "This doesn't taste like the vegetable paste on the mountain" and "I tried to have six pieces of toast, but Nate said two, and I think I like bread better when it's toast."

Alex slowed partway through his meal. His eyelids looked a little heavier.

She made him eat every last bite.

He did so without complaint.

He finished just before she did.

She peered into his bowl to make sure it was all gone.

It was.

She looked pleased at that. "Maybe vegetable beef is better than chicken after all."

She took both their bowls to the sink. Nate flinched at the clatter. She looked at him, then at the full bowl of soup and toast still sitting on the counter. "Were you not hungry?" she asked.

"No."

"Oh." She frowned. "Why didn't you say so? Isn't that a waste? You can make bread toast, but you can't make toast bread. Sometimes things can be made into one thing, but it's impossible to turn them back, no matter how hard you try."

He said, "Why are you named Artemis Darth Vader?"

"Because I like it," she said. "Why are you named Nathaniel Cartwright?"

"Because that's what my parents named me."

"Are your parents those people on the walls?"

He nodded.

"Do you like your name?"

"It's the only one I have."

"You're not toast."

He felt off-kilter. "What?"

"You're not toast," she said. "You can be Nathaniel Cartwright. Then you can be someone else. And then if you don't like it, you can be Nathaniel Cartwright again. You're not toast. Bread doesn't have a choice. You do."

"Jesus Christ," he muttered.

"Exactly," she said, sounding pleased. "I'm sure your parents wouldn't mind if you became someone you liked instead of the person you are. It's better to be happy a little bit than to not be happy at all."

"Who are you people?" he asked, voice hoarse.

"I am Artemis Darth Vader," she said, enunciating each word slowly. "And that is my Alex Delgado."

Artemis Darth Vader Delgado. Nate didn't know what to do with that. He didn't know what to do with any of this.

"Art," Alex said, voice deep. "That's enough."

"I'm just trying to—"

"No more."

She sighed. "You heard the boss," she said to Nate. "Back on the trail, partner."

Maybe she was mentally . . . ill. Deficient? Nate didn't know the proper terminology. Maybe she was sick somehow. In the head. And her father had stolen her from a hospital or wherever, and someone had shot him, and now they were here. They were fugitives on the run from a mental hospital, and they just ate his soup. He made them toast. That made him complicit in . . . whatever this was. He was harboring fugitives and making them toast. He would go to jail.

"I don't want to go to jail," he said.

Alex looked at him sharply. "Why would you go to jail?"

"Because you stole your daughter from the mental hospital and they shot you and I made you toast."

Alex and Art both stared at him.

Nate didn't know what else to say. It was out there now.

"You're so bread," Art finally said. "I can't wait to see you toasted."

Nate swallowed thickly. "Was that . . . was that a threat?"

She shook her head. "Did that sound like a threat?" She looked back at Alex. "Is that one of those things that sounds like one thing, but also could mean another?"

"I think he's overreacting," Alex told her. He pushed up from the table, grimacing as he moved. The muscles in his arms strained against the flannel he wore, something Nate *really* should not have been noticing. He had other things to worry about. Like a little girl threatening him with . . . maybe being murdered. Somehow.

She was at Alex's side in an instant, hovering as he stepped away from the table. He took a step. And then another. And then another before he stumbled a little. He caught himself before he fell, but she was there too, tiny arms around his waist, as if that would help a man five times her size if he was going down.

Nate didn't move at all.

Alex stopped, breathing deeply. He let it out through his teeth and then made his way to the couch. He sat without further incident before lying down on his back, one foot hanging off the side, the other on the cushion. Nate stared at the hole in the sock near the big toe. It wasn't big, but it was there.

"I need to see it," he heard Art say.

"Not now."

"Alex."

"Art."

She glanced back at Nate. He didn't know if she was asking him for help. He didn't know how he *could* help.

She turned back toward Alex. She leaned forward and whispered something to him. Nate couldn't hear what was said.

Alex sighed. "A little."

The gun was on the table. Just sitting there.

Art unbuttoned his shirt, fumbling a bit.

It fell open.

The bandage was white, taped against skin. There wasn't even a hint of blood. Alex breathed shallowly, the muscles in his stomach flexing under a mat of dark hair. Art tugged at the tape gently. "Careful," he said, wincing as it pulled against hair.

"Maybe if you weren't a hairy monster, this would be easier."

Alex huffed out a sharp breath, almost like he was laughing.

The tape pulled back.

Nate could go for the gun. Right now. He could get the gun and maintain enough distance between himself and Alex so he wouldn't be surprised again. So Alex couldn't do his quick ninja moves again. He was built like a linebacker, but Nate had never seen someone move like that before. He wondered just how close he'd come to a bullet to the head when he'd grabbed Art to try to put her hand in water.

He took a step toward the table.

Art pulled back the gauze.

He passed the table, leaving the gun where it was.

Once when he'd been covering a protest in Columbia Heights, there'd been anger over the death of a Black homeless man at the hands of a police officer. Los Angeles was still burning after Rodney King, and Nate was in the middle of it on the other side of the country, wide-eyed and breathless. He'd been taking the scene in, people shouting, looks of pure fury on their faces, when there'd been a loud *crack* that echoed around them. People ducked and began to scream, shoving each other as they tried to get away. Nate had stood there, getting knocked from side to side. In the crowd, he saw a hand rise, a black pistol held high, firing into the air. People screamed again. There came a third shot. The gunman (later found to be a white guy named Keith Blair who *needed* to put himself in the middle of it all, *needed* to cause as much pain as he could) was tackled a moment later.

But there was another man on the ground, a man writhing, shoes scraping along pavement as he gasped for air. His hands were on his stomach, and the blood that had been welling between his fingers was so dark it was almost shocking.

Nate hadn't moved. It was a story. He couldn't get involved with a story.

He hated himself, after.

For a very long time.

Others stepped in. They came and shoved the man's hands away. Before they could cover the wound with a shirt that had been handed over, Nate had seen the *wound,* the ragged hole in the man's stomach, the skin torn, blood gushing.

The man had died at the hospital two days later.

One of his colleagues had written the story on it.

He knew what bullet wounds looked like.

The bandage was lifted almost all the way off, and there was—

The smallest amount of blood on the underside. Just the barest amount, a splash of red against white.

But there was no open wound.

No stitches.

Oh, the skin was red and inflamed, yes. And there was bruising. There was even a circular indentation that could have been an entry wound. But it looked as if it'd had time to *heal*. As if Alex hadn't been shot recently, as had been implied. Maybe Nate had heard it wrong. Maybe he'd misunderstood.

But then why was Alex moving as if it was a recent thing? Yes, there'd been those shocking ninja moments, but . . .

"Looks better," Art said quietly. She glanced back at Nate. "Thank you."

He stood at the edge of the couch, staring down at Alex's bare skin. "For?"

"Vegetable beef. You were right. It helped. And for the toast."

"When did you say you were shot again?"

Alex stared at him coldly. "I didn't."

"When were you shot?"

Alex said nothing.

Art sighed.

"Uh-huh. Right. Okay." Nate took a step back. "I'm . . . going to just—"

He turned and moved down the hall to the bedroom.

The cabin shuddered as he slammed the door behind him.

CHAPTER FOUR

He didn't sleep.

Not much, anyway.

When he wasn't pacing the length of the bedroom that had once belonged to his parents, he was lying on top of the musty comforter, dozing fitfully.

His phone had no bars no matter where he stood in the room or what furniture he climbed on top of. He wasn't surprised.

For almost a full hour, he stood at the door, ear pressed against it, listening. He heard the brief, low mumble of sporadic conversation, but nothing more.

His duffel bag was still in the truck.

He didn't undress. He had to be ready. For whatever. Just in case. It wouldn't do to be caught unawares without pants on.

There was toothpaste in the en suite bathroom, halfway rolled up. His mother must have forgotten it the last time she'd been here. There was no toothbrush. He squeezed some directly into his mouth and swished back and forth. It burned his tongue and caused his throat to close. He hacked it up into the sink. The water guy wasn't coming until tomorrow, so he cleaned it up with an old hand towel. His mom had always hated when he or his brother left bits of toothpaste in the sink.

He lifted his head and stared at himself in the mirror.

His eyes were wide.

He had toothpaste on his chin.

He wiped it off.

Stepped out of the bathroom.

And began to pace.

It went on for hours.

Nate wasn't stupid. He had a keen mind able to make the connections that most people couldn't see. It was why he'd been good at his job. He could find the story that others couldn't. He was charming when he needed to be. Cunning when the situation called for it. He could be ruthless, too, when he had to. You couldn't survive in D.C. and not be. He would have been chewed up and spit out a long time ago.

It hadn't hurt (helped?) that he'd been so young. A beat reporter covering fluff pieces bordering on puffery (Agnes Richards is eighty-seven years young and completed her first marathon! Moxie may be blind, but she is still man's best friend, and oh! Would you look at that! She's been *adopted!*) that had somehow managed to work his way up the ladder, stepping on whoever he needed to, slashing throats of those who'd considered him a friend. He didn't *have* friends. He couldn't and do what he did.

Not that that mattered anymore.

That was gone now.

Back and forth he went in that little room.

Eventually birds began to sing in the trees outside the cabin.

The sky began to lighten.

He wondered if he should just escape through the window.

Or maybe yesterday had been a weird dream.

He'd open the door and he'd be alone. There would be no one there named Alex Delgado with bushy eyebrows and a weird little girl called Artemis Darth Vader. He wouldn't have to worry about guns or becoming toast or how a padlock to a shed housing a generator could be unlocked without the aid of a key.

He would make himself breakfast. Maybe some eggs. No toast. An omelet. Yes, he would make himself an omelet and coffee, and he would take his meal to the back deck, bundled up in a coat and breathing in cold, cold air.

After, he'd unload the truck, putting everything in its place exactly where it should be. It would be fine. Everything would be *fine*.

Yes, there would be some questions later, like how he could have imagined such a thing as Alex Delgado and Artemis Darth Vader and bullet wounds that weren't gaping wide open. But he could potentially chalk it up to his grief. He was here, after all, in this cabin, for the first time since his parents had died violently. This place held terrible memories of his father's bigotry and—maybe even worse—his mother's complicit silence, and he was *dealing* with it. Why, *anyone* would go a little bit crazy, right? It was a wonder he'd held himself together for *this* long.

Of course none of this was real.

Of course he'd made it all up in his head.

He felt better.

He wanted to change his clothes. He'd been wearing these same jeans for damn near twenty-four hours. The same *underwear*, even.

He'd get his duffel and take a shower, and *then* there would be breakfast on the deck with as much coffee as he could possibly stand.

He tilted his head side to side, feeling his neck pop.

It felt good. That, and having a plan.

He moved to the door.

He opened it.

And was met with . . . silence.

Because of course he was. There was no one there. He was alone in the cabin in the middle of the woods in the Cascade Mountains, just as he had expected to be when he'd made the decision to come here in the first place. There was no gun being pointed at him. His imagination had always been overactive. All his teachers had said so come report card time. He'd even toyed with writing a novel— most journos did at one point or another. But every time he sat in front of that open Word doc, cursor blinking, he would *freeze*. He could deal in facts. He didn't understand fiction.

He'd been tired the day before. The events of the past few months had finally caught up with him. He'd made it to the cabin, stumbled inside, and dreamed the whole thing.

Yes. Yes, that sounded just fine.

There was a bedroom door across from him.

It was shut.

He tried to remember if it'd been closed the night before.

He couldn't think clearly.

He was tired.

It was still too early. Which was why he'd thought about taking a shower. He couldn't. The water was still off.

He needed coffee. And his toothbrush.

THE BONES BENEATH MY SKIN • 51

And underwear.

He thought about opening that door.

He put his hand on the doorknob, but then a little voice in the back of his mind whispered *what if?*

What *if* he opened the door to the second bedroom with the two twin beds that he and his brother had shared to see a little girl in one and a large man in the other? Granted, the bed would almost be too small for a figment of his imagination that size, but what if?

He stepped away from the door.

He needed coffee and a toothbrush and underwear.

He'd feel better after that.

He moved down the hall quietly.

It felt like he was sneaking, which was *ridiculous* since he was alone.

The wooden floor creaked in that one spot it always did. He'd forgotten about it.

Nate winced and stopped. Listening.

The house was quiet.

Of course it was.

He could see the couch.

The afghan was folded neatly and laid across the back.

There were no dishes on the dining room table.

It didn't even smell like soup or toast.

Outside, the generator hummed.

Sunlight filtered in through the east windows.

He looked around the living room.

He was alone.

He breathed a sigh of relief.

"What are you doing?" a gruff voice asked.

He didn't scream.

He *didn't*.

It was more of a gasp that he choked on as he twisted around, almost losing his footing. He stuck his hand out and held himself up against the wall, heart pounding as he struggled to take another breath.

There, standing in the kitchen, leaning against the counter with a cup of coffee in his hand, was the man the girl had called Alex

Delgado. He wore the same pair of pants from the day before. The flannel shirt was gone. Instead, he wore a white undershirt. Nate couldn't tell if the bandage had been removed.

"Why did you sneak up on me like that?" Nate demanded, sounding more breathless than he would have liked.

Alex scoffed derisively. "Haven't moved."

Nate didn't know what to feel. Embarrassed, probably. Angry, sure. There was the urge to find the biggest knife in the kitchen and stab the man right in his face. Nate wasn't violent by nature, but he figured everyone was allowed to be at some point in their lives.

It was just finally his turn.

"What are you doing?" he asked instead.

Alex looked down at his steaming mug, then back up at Nate. "What's it look like?"

It was too early for Nate to be dealing with breaking-and-entering strangers who also turned out to be assholes. "I'm going to my truck," he announced grandly.

Alex didn't say anything.

Nate waited.

Alex sipped his coffee.

"Right," Nate said. "You just . . . you stay right where you are. And don't touch anything else. This is my house, and I don't want your dirty hands on my things."

Alex snorted.

Nate backed away slowly, keeping his eyes on Alex.

Alex stared back.

Nate bumped into the dining room table. It scraped along the floor.

Nate flushed.

Alex was stoic. With coffee.

Nate was out of the kitchen, and he turned around, ready to rush the front door when—

He stopped.

There in the living room was everything he'd brought with him.

Well. Not *everything*. All the foodstuffs were gone. The water. The cooler.

But there was his duffel bag.

His boxes of books.

His PowerBook.

His Nokia, sitting on the old coffee table.

Someone had unloaded the truck for him.

He turned slowly.

Alex sipped his coffee again.

"Where's all the food?" he asked, even though that wasn't the question he'd intended.

Alex didn't answer him. Instead, he jerked his head toward the pantry.

Nate didn't believe him.

He went to the pantry.

All of it was there. The cans. The flour. The baking soda. Hamburger Helper. Boxes and boxes of Hamburger Helper, because he was a single man in his twenties. Stacks of bottled water. An empty cooler.

He went to the fridge. Eggs sat on the shelf next to packs of bacon. Lunch meat. Mustard. Mayo.

The freezer held hamburger meat. Chicken. A bag of peas, because he'd felt guilty about not having any vegetables. He never planned on eating them. He thought peas were disgusting.

"You unloaded my truck," he said, staring into the freezer.

Shockingly, Alex didn't say a word.

Nate closed the freezer door. He took a breath. He said, "Where is the little girl, and are you on the run because you murdered someone?"

Alex choked on his coffee.

Nate felt great satisfaction at that. He hoped it burned.

Alex set down the mug on the counter, black liquid sloshing out. He was muttering something under his breath, flipping on the faucet.

Nothing came out.

"No water," Nate said mildly. "Hasn't been turned on yet. Used to be from a well, but it went on the county in the late eighties."

Alex grabbed a paper towel instead, wiping it over his face. He had thick stubble on his cheeks and neck that was thicker than it'd been the day before.

Alex threw the crumpled paper towel on the counter.

Nate waited.

Alex glared.

Nate waited some more.

Then, "I know there's no water. I had to use the bottled stuff you brought for the coffee. It's the first time I've made any since we got here."

"Uh-huh. Right. Okay. Why are you—"

"I didn't—I'm not. *We're* not on the run because of murder."

Nate squinted at him. "But you are on the run."

Alex didn't say anything.

"You don't speak much, do you?"

Alex proved his point and didn't say a word. He picked up his mug instead.

That's when Nate noticed it for the first time. Ink, on Alex's right arm.

His shirtsleeve covered most of it, but there looked to be the tip of a knife. Talons of some kind of bird. The bottom curves of what looked like letters. As he lifted the coffee again, the sleeve stretched *just* a little against his biceps, pulling back slightly. Two of the letters were clearer.

MC.

It only took him a second.

The talons probably belonged to an eagle.

The knife would be a Ka-Bar.

MC belonged to USMC.

United States Marine Corps.

A grunt. The haircut made sense now. But he was older, right? The girl had said he was . . . what. Forty? Career, then. He was built for it, sure. Big arms. Big chest. Thick thighs that probably looked—

Nate coughed. "Eggs," he managed to say. "I need to make eggs."

Alex didn't say a word.

Nate got out the eggs. He'd only brought a dozen, figuring they'd last until he made a supply run down in Roseland. He hadn't expected to have guests. Granted, they weren't guests as much as they were squatters, and he didn't owe them a *damn* thing. He had plans—*omelet* plans—for breakfast on the deck. He rarely ate breakfast, usually having no time for such indulgences. Instead, he'd be gulping down coffee on the Metro. Sometimes he'd even have a banana. Or an apple.

So he didn't have time for such things. He was a busy, busy man. Or rather, he used to be.

Now he was a jobless man standing in a kitchen with a large Marine who might or might not have murdered someone and stolen a child.

He made all the eggs.

He didn't mean to.

He started with three, planning on his omelet.

They turned scrambled instead.

And he just kept going.

The whole dozen.

He took down plates.

He made more toast.

He wished he'd thought to bring cheese.

There was bacon. Yes. The bacon would do.

He made that too.

"What is that?"

He startled slightly.

Standing next to him, yawning quietly, was Artemis Darth Vader. She had pajamas on. They were pink and a little small, the sleeves not quite reaching her wrists. Her hair was a mess.

She was also wearing a pair of oversized neon-green sunglasses that slid down her nose.

She looked ridiculous.

"What?" he asked, unsure of what else to say.

"That," she said, pointing to the bacon sizzling in the pan.

"That's . . . bacon."

"Bacon," she repeated slowly. She looked over at Alex. "Will I like that?"

Alex shrugged.

"Where does it come from?"

"The store," Nate said.

She grunted, and the noise sounded so much like Alex that Nate wondered if he'd stolen her or if she was actually his daughter. "No, *where* did it come from?"

"I don't—"

"A pig," Alex growled.

Art cocked her head and stared at the bacon. "I thought sausage came from pigs. I've never had it, but I read about it."

Nate wasn't sure what was going on. "It does."

"And pork chops."

He nodded. "Those too."

"And hot dogs."

"Well, I wouldn't go *that* far—"

"And now *bacon* comes from pigs too?" She shook her head. "What magnificent creatures. I wonder who looked at them for the first time and thought to themselves how many meals they could make out of them."

Alex made a noise that coming from anyone else would have possibly been approaching a laugh. But coming from *him* it sounded like a monotonous release of air.

Suddenly and quite viciously, Nate felt the need to find a way to break him in two. To crack him right down the middle and see what spilled out. Curiosity had always been his downfall. He'd always stuck his nose where it didn't belong. And the fact that there was this—this *mystery* before him was causing his skin to itch. He was pragmatic, yes. The world had an order to it. If something didn't make sense, if something was unknown, he would poke and prod until he found the thread that led to the truth.

He was confused. He didn't like being confused.

"Did you sleep well?" Art asked him, pushing the sunglasses back up her nose.

"I don't . . . know?"

"Oh. Why don't you know?"

"Art."

She glanced back at Alex. "What?"

"Leave him alone. Come here."

She went.

He put a hand on the top of her head as she leaned against him. It might have been endearing if Nate hadn't thought it was meant to be protective. Alex was protecting her from *him*. As if he thought

Nate would take a scalding pan of bacon and smash it upside her head.

Which—okay. He hadn't exactly thought of that, but . . .

And besides. He wouldn't do that to the girl.

To Alex, yes. Hell yes. If he thought Alex was going to hurt him, he'd burn his fucking skin off and beat his face in with a pan of bacon, no question.

She leaned against Alex, yawning.

The sunglasses slid down her nose again.

He turned back to the bacon.

He put some on each plate next to the eggs.

He switched off the stove.

Alex and Art didn't move as he put the pan in the sink. They both watched him instead.

He went back to the plates. Maybe he was showing off a little as he held one in each hand and the third on his forearm. He'd worked his way through school slinging hash and waiting tables in Tucson, where most of the staff and patrons didn't speak English. He'd picked up serviceable Spanish quickly. The pay had been shit, but he could put in the hours he needed for a little pocket money. His parents had paid for the tuition and the dorm and the books just like they'd done for his brother, but anything more, he'd needed to earn himself.

Alex didn't look impressed.

Art stared avidly.

You win some, you lose some.

He set the plates on the table. He went back for forks. Napkins. Those went on the table too.

There was a half-full pot of coffee.

He poured himself a cup. There was sugar in a tin above the pot. It was a little crusty, but he broke off a chunk and dropped it in.

He went back to the table, sat down in front of a plate, and sighed.

It wasn't an omelet on the deck by himself.

But it could work.

Maybe.

He looked back toward the kitchen.

Alex's eyes were slightly narrowed. Art was fidgeting.

"Well?" Nate asked.

Alex hesitated. And just when Nate thought he'd have three full plates all to himself, Alex gave a little push to the back of Art's head.

She ran to the table and climbed on the chair, nostrils flaring as she gnawed on her bottom lip. The eggs on her plate were reflected back in the lenses of her sunglasses.

Alex came too, though he didn't run with enthusiasm as Art had.

He moved much slower.

Art didn't touch the silverware until he sat next to her, the chair groaning under his weight.

He said, "You don't need to use your fork for the bacon."

She looked at him, then down at the plate, then back at him. "Fingers?"

He nodded.

"But not for the eggs."

"No. Use the fork for those."

"I've had eggs before."

"I know."

"I had to use my fingers."

Alex's jaw ticced as his mouth thinned. "I know."

"Okay. Just making sure." She looked down at the bacon. Then in a move Nate thought was *dainty*, she reached down and pinched a piece of bacon between two fingers and brought it up to her face. She studied it carefully, turning it from side to side. She sniffed it. Eventually, she stuck her tongue out and licked it, a little flash of pink.

Her eyebrows shot up behind the sunglasses.

She stuck the whole thing in her mouth at once and chewed loudly.

"This is *pig*?" she said through a mouthful of meat. "Holy *wow*, what the heck!"

She reached for another piece, but Alex put his hand on top of hers. "Chew that first. Carefully. Swallow. Then you can have more."

She nodded, cheeks bulging.

Nate gaped at her.

"She's never had bacon before," Alex said quietly.

Nate nodded, unsure of what to say.

He had barely forked a bit of egg into his own mouth before Art gasped around a fresh piece of bacon, groaning as she shoved the whole piece into her mouth again.

Alex ate too, but not quite in the same fashion. He was neat and quick, chewing perfunctorily before eating another measured bite.

It was the weirdest meal Nate had ever been involved in. Even more than vegetable beef soup and toast.

Art wasn't as enamored with the eggs as she was with the bacon, almost looking forlorn when it was gone. She looked at Nate's plate enviously, the bacon sitting next to his barely touched eggs. Nate thought about handing it over to her, but he wondered if this was part of their plan. If they were trying to endear themselves to him (well, endear *her*, because Alex was a fucking asshole) so that they could get on his good side before they . . . did whatever they planned on doing with him. He wasn't sure if he was being held hostage. Or being robbed. Or was becoming the third person in their cult.

The gun had yet to make an appearance.

He was thankful for that.

He ate his own bacon defiantly. He wasn't going to fall for their tricks.

She didn't look very happy about that.

He felt savagely pleased. And oddly guilty.

Then he changed the subject in the worst way possible.

He said, "Thank you for your service."

Alex's fork froze halfway to his mouth with the last of the egg on it. It didn't even shake.

Art was staring at him.

Nate cleared his throat, wondering how he'd made it this far in his life without being murdered.

Alex set down the fork on the plate.

He could probably use it as a weapon if he wanted to.

"What was that?" Alex asked, voice hard.

"Your tattoo," Nate said as evenly as he could. "Marines, right? Semper Fi and all that?"

Alex's grip tightened on the fork.

Nate didn't want to die. He wished he'd kept his mouth shut.

"How did you know that?" Alex asked.

"Uh. I lived in D.C. You end up knowing what grunts look like. And I mean, come on. Your tattoo says USMC. You don't see those on someone who hasn't served." Right? That had to be right.

Alex nodded slowly, though his grip didn't loosen on the fork.

Breakfast had been going so well too.

Mostly.

"Oh boy," Art whispered, glancing back and forth between the two of them.

Nate wasn't sure of what else to say.

Surprisingly, Alex said, "Yes."

Nate blinked. "Yes?"

"Yes."

"Okay. That's . . . thank you. For that. Clarification."

Alex nodded. He lifted the fork and ate the last of his eggs.

It was as if Art had been waiting for him to finish. She took his plate and fork from him and stacked it on top of hers. She looked at Nate, down at his plate, then back up at him.

He looked down.

He still had eggs.

He finished them.

She didn't look away.

Neither did Alex.

It wasn't so bad.

Once his plate was clean, Art cleared her throat. "May I clear your plate, sir?" she asked politely.

Nate nodded, wondering where the *sir* had come from.

She looked back at Alex. "Did I do that right?"

"Yes."

"Cool." She turned and grabbed Nate's plate. "I hope the meal was to your satisfaction."

"It . . . was?" Nate said, because what.

She stacked his plate on the others, the forks on top. She got down from the chair first before reaching back up for the plates. She took them to the counter and set them next to the sink.

Nate stared after her.

"She met a waitress for the first time a couple days ago," Alex said, and Nate looked at him, disbelieving that Alex had volunteered information. "She liked her."

Nate didn't know what to say to that.

Because how had she never met a waitress in her entire life? She had to be ten years old if she was a day.

He said nothing, because *now* he was thinking that this man, this crazy fucking man, *had* kidnapped this girl when she was a *baby* and kept her prisoner her entire life, and only *now* was letting her out in the world and—

She came back to the table and climbed into the chair. "Thank you," she told him. "For the bacon and the eggs. But mostly the bacon."

"You're. Welcome?"

She grinned at him.

She looked at Alex.

He sipped his coffee.

She coughed.

He ignored her.

She coughed louder.

He side-eyed her.

She poked his cheek.

Strangely enough, she didn't lose her finger.

"What?" he asked.

"You know what."

"You said it already."

"Be polite, Alex," she said. "You told me that you have to be nice when you can because you don't know when it could mean everything to someone."

Alex sighed. He mumbled something under his breath.

Art frowned. "None of us heard that. Do better."

"Thank you for the eggs," he muttered.

"And?" Art asked.

He scowled. "And the bacon."

"*Especially* the bacon."

"I'm not going to say that."

"We'll work on it," she said, patting his hairy forearm. She looked back at Nate expectantly.

"You're . . . welcome."

She beamed.

There was a knock at the door.

The gun was out even before Nate could blink. He didn't know where it'd come from. One second there was no gun, and the next there was *all* the gun, that massive thing that looked straight out of a Dirty Harry movie that he and his brother had snuck into without their mother knowing.

Alex was standing and scooping up Art in his arms. She went quietly, hands going around his neck, face buried in his throat.

"Who is it?" Alex whispered furiously. "Who else knows you're here?"

The gun wasn't pointed at him, but at the door.

"No one," Nate managed to say. "No one knows I'm—okay. That's not true."

Now the gun was pointed at him.

Nate felt his eyes bulge. "No, no, not like *that*. Not . . . *whatever* you're thinking. My brother knows. Or at least I think he does. Big Eddie from the gas station. The lawyer who gave me the keys. I told you that last night. But I swear, that's it. That's *all*."

"Then who the *fuck* is at the door?" Alex hissed. He was backing away from the table slowly, arm wrapped protectively around Art's back, holding her close to him. The gun was again pointed toward the door.

"I don't *know*," Nate snapped back. "Why the hell do you think it's something *I* did? For fuck's sake, maybe they're here for *you*."

And he felt instantly guilty when Art whimpered against Alex.

He rose from the table. He raised his hands, placating. "Just . . . stay there. I'll see who it is. Okay? It's fine. I swear it's fine."

It was absolutely *not* fine if the thunderstorm on Alex's face meant anything. Minutes ago, he'd been begrudgingly thanking Nate for eggs and bacon, looking rather put out at even having to say the words.

Now he looked terrifyingly like a killer.

Nate thought back to the question he'd asked almost first thing this morning.

Are you on the run because you murdered someone?

He moved toward the door. He heard Alex following him closely. He didn't look back.

The knock came again.

"Coming," Nate managed to say.

He reached the door.

He breathed in.

He breathed out.

He put his hand on the doorknob.

A grunt came from behind him.

He looked over his shoulder.

Alex shook his head, holding up the hand with the gun, raising one finger.

Nate waited.

Alex looked through the window next to the door. The blinds were drawn, and he lifted a wooden slat the barest amount. It lasted only a second.

"A truck," he muttered. "White. Yours is blocking it. I can't see who it is."

"What should we do?" Nate asked.

Alex looked at him.

"What?"

He shook his head. "Just . . . open the door. If I think there's even the *slightest* chance something is wrong, I'll put a bullet in the head of whoever's out there. Remember that before you speak."

Nate felt his hands shaking.

Alex pressed his back against the wall, Art still in his arms. He raised the gun and nodded at Nate.

The knock came again.

Nate opened the door.

CHAPTER FIVE

There was a man on the porch.

Nate blinked against the bright sunlight. The cool air caused his skin to break out in gooseflesh.

The man was wearing jeans and boots and a polo shirt under a light jacket. His dark hair was thinning away from his forehead, and he had wire-framed glasses that sat perched on the tip of his nose.

There was a badge hanging from his jacket.

"Nathaniel Cartwright?" he asked, his voice a little reedy.

"Yes?" He hoped this man didn't die in front of him.

"Douglas County Public Works." He held out his hand. "Name's Randy. Had an appointment this morning to get your water hooked up, right?"

Nate had no idea what he was talking about. Then he did. "Right," he said quickly. "I wasn't—I thought . . . You're early. You weren't supposed to be here until this afternoon."

Randy shrugged. "You're the farthest out on my route today. Decided to start way out here and work back in. Don't have a lot of people up here. At least, not this early. Don't see some of these cabins start to fill up until June or so. Usually still snow on the ground. Mild winter, don't you know."

"I heard," Nate said, skin buzzing just a little.

"Shouldn't take much time, no it won't. Valve's supposed to be near the meter. Know where that's at?"

He nodded. "I can show you."

He started to step out. "Whoa," Randy said, holding up a hand. Nate stopped.

"Little cold out here. Got a jacket? Don't want you to freeze." He smiled.

"Give me just a second."

"Oh sure," Randy said. "Gotta get a couple of things from the truck. Take your time."

He stepped off the porch, whistling as the gravel crunched under his shoes.

Nate closed the door.

"Did you call for him to come here?" Alex growled.

Nate nodded. "Yeah. It's—made the appointment days ago. It's—he's supposed to be here."

Art peeked at him over her sunglasses, secure in her place in Alex's arms. "I don't like him."

Alex looked down at her. "Why?"

Art glanced at Nate, then back to Alex, and said a strange thing. Well. *Another* strange thing. "Is he the Macho Man?"

Even Alex looked confused, eyebrows rising. It took only a moment for him to sigh. "No. That's not him."

"Who?" Nate asked.

"The Macho Man," Art said. "Randy Savage."

"I don't—are you talking about the *wrestler*?"

She nodded solemnly. "He hates Hulk Hogan. And I like Hulk Hogan."

"Who the hell *are* you people?" Nate asked fervently.

"I'm Artemis D—"

"Darth Vader, yeah, I *know*. And he's Alex Delgado." Nate threw his hands up. "That doesn't explain—you know what? It doesn't matter. I'm going outside with the water guy, and he's going to turn on the water. And then I'm going to come back in and take a *shower* because I am still wearing the same goddamn underwear—"

"We used your dish soap in the lake," Art said, patting Alex on the cheeks. "Alex said it was the same, but the water was cold. You could have borrowed some of his underwear."

Nate made a wounded noise. "I'm not—that's not the *point*. Jesus Christ, I don't—I'm going outside!"

He put his hand on the doorknob and was about to jerk it open dramatically.

"Don't forget your jacket," Art said.

Nate almost screamed.

Instead, he turned and stomped to his duffel bag. He pulled it open and found a sweater with a zipper down the middle. It would do. He pulled it on, left arm and then the right, all the while glaring at the two people he'd known for less than a *day* who had already upended his life.

He stomped back to the door.

"If he says *ooh yeah*," Art told him as he threw open the door, "you need to watch out for his signature move. It's called the Savage Elbow, and it will take you *down*."

He slammed the door behind him, the wood rattling in its frame.

A head poked up near the white truck. "All right?"

Nate forced a smile on his face. It came more easily than he expected. "Yeah. Fine."

"Good, good. We'll get you all set up, and everything will be right as rain."

Nate sighed. He doubted that very much.

✦

"There she is," Randy said, pointing at the meter on the side of the house. The sky was already a deep, wonderful blue, with only traces of clouds. It was cold, and Nate could see his breath with every exhalation. The lake was flat and almost still.

Randy put his toolbox on the ground near a small metal grate. He sank to his knees, then opened the toolbox, staring at the meter. "So what brings you up here?"

Nate saw movement out of the corner of his eye. He looked up. A window, with the drapes drawn. It was in the second bedroom. At first nothing happened. And then the drapes moved again slightly, a finger pulling them back.

Nate glared.

The drapes closed again.

Randy turned back to look at him.

Nate said, "Sorry. Um. What was the question?"

Randy chuckled. "A little early for ya, is it?"

"Yeah. Something like that."

"Early riser, I am. Always have been. Early to bed, early to rise, as my ma used to say. More things to see in the daytime, I suppose."

"Uh. Yeah. Sure." He looked up again in time to see the drapes shaking furiously. He didn't know what the hell was going on until Art poked her head through the curtains, sunglasses askew, mouthing at him and pointing at her elbow, then down at the man. *Savage Elbow*, she overenunciated.

Nate choked.

Randy looked at him again.

Nate scratched the back of his head to cover it up.

It wasn't very convincing.

"You all right?"

Nate nodded. "Yeah. I'm—it's early. Like you said."

Randy moved the grate. He pulled a long, thin wrench from his toolbox. "Hold that for me, will ya?" he said, handing Nate a flashlight. "Keep it pointed down, if ya don't mind."

He did exactly that.

The beam was shaking.

He steadied it with his other hand.

Randy leaned down toward the opening. "Like I was saying, what brings you up here?"

"Oh. Uh—just—it's my cabin. I guess."

"You guess? It either is or it isn't."

"Right. Yeah. It is. I . . . inherited it. Recently. From my parents."

"They pass on?" Randy asked, grunting as he leaned lower to the ground.

"Yeah."

"Real sorry to hear that. They're with the Lord now, having earned their just reward."

Nate didn't do religion. He never had. He didn't even know what he believed in. The idea of a supreme god and heaven and hell and judgment seemed almost like a fairy tale. But he learned early on you didn't say such things out loud to the religious sort, so he said, "Sure." It was easier that way.

He looked up again.

Art's face was pressed against the glass. When she saw him watching, she blew as hard as she could, lips spreading wide, eyes bulging.

Nate coughed explosively.

She looked furious as a big hand pulled her back, the drapes closing against the window.

He looked back down.

Randy was staring at him.

"Swallowed a bug," Nate managed to say. "Big fucker."

Randy nodded, rubbing his jaw. "Oh sure. They get huge round the lake. Usually in the summer, though. You'll want to get some bug spray if you're gonna be around that long."

It felt like a question that he didn't know the answer to. "Maybe."

Randy was back in the ground. "What do you do that you can stay out here, if you don't mind me asking? You write books? You look like the type."

Nate didn't know if that was an insult or not. "No. Not a writer. Well. Not books, anyway."

"There's other kinds?"

"Yeah. I was—I *am* a journalist."

"A reporter?"

Nate bristled a little at that. Old pride coming through. "A *journalist.*"

"For the news? You on camera? That sounds fancy."

"Print."

"Oh! Good on ya. I don't read the paper. Don't read much at all, if I'm being honest. Never had the patience for it. That's what the TV's for. Besides, too much bad in the world, ya know? I want to hear the good stories. Last summer, they had a squirrel up here that could water-ski, if you could believe that! Those are the types of stories I like to hear. Darnedest thing, too. Little son of a bitch behind a remote-controlled boat. The strangest thing. Too many bad things in the world already. Just watch squirrels on skis."

"I wouldn't—I don't know anything about that."

"Don't do water-skiing squirrels?"

"No. I was . . . in D.C. More . . . political. There were squirrels, but they didn't ski."

Randy pulled a face. "Don't know how you can stand that. All those bigwigs in Washington. What the hell do *they* know about the working man? I don't trust a word out of ol' Slick Willie's mouth. Now Reagan. You want to talk about a good man? You talk about Ronald Reagan. He knew how to take care of business, yes, *sir.*"

There was a man with a gun above him holding the weirdest

child Nate had ever seen while another man grunted into a hole in the ground at Nate's feet discussing politics and belief in God.

He should have stayed in Washington.

At least he was used to that kind of crazy.

"And . . . there it is," Randy said. He sat back up, eyeing the meter, watching it start to tick slowly. "Looks like we're up and running. I checked out the plans filed with the county. Looks like pipes were replaced here in '87, so you should be good to go. Any issues, I got a friend that can help you out cheap. You just let me know. Sometimes these houses settle. Pipes shift. They can break, especially with the winter having passed. Pipes could have frozen."

Nate frowned. "I thought the winter was mild up here this year?"

Randy laughed. "Oh yeah. You nailed that one on the head. Don't know where my mind is sometimes." He pushed himself to his feet and went to a spigot on the side of the house. Nate's mom had had it installed for her flower beds. He turned it on. It spat and gurgled for a moment before clear water came out.

Randy turned it off and grinned at him. "There ya—"

A loud thump came from the house, followed by a crash.

Randy turned to look back at the window. "Someone with you in there?"

"Uh. No. Just—probably the pipes."

Randy nodded slowly. "The pipes. Right. Don't know that I ever heard pipes like that before. But there's a first time for everything."

"Or it could be my dog," Nate said quickly. "He's—big. And mean. And always getting into things. Probably just found what was left over from breakfast."

Randy grinned at him. "I love dogs. What's his name?"

"Fido," he blurted before wincing. "Uh. Yeah. Fido."

"What kind is he?"

"Oh, you know. He's just a mangy mutt. All kinds, I guess."

"Mean, you say?"

"The meanest. Doesn't like strangers. Tends to bark at them for no reason at all, even when he's the one in the wrong."

Randy began to put his tools away. "Funny. Didn't hear him bark when I knocked on the door."

"He was . . . hiding."

Randy arched an eyebrow. "Mean dog that hides? How strange."

"You have no idea," Nate said truthfully.

✦

Randy had him sign an invoice before shaking his hand and telling him to enjoy his day. "You let me know about those pipes!" he called as he started to climb into his truck. "Remember, I got a guy. Will help you out real cheap. He owes me a favor or two."

Nate waved in acknowledgment. He figured the pipes were the least of his problems.

Randy tipped his head and then started his truck. He backed out slowly before heading down the dirt road.

Nate breathed a sigh of relief.

He turned to head back into the house, only to see Alex standing on the porch, glowering down at him. Art stood in front of him, sunglasses sitting on the top of her head.

"You called Alex a mean dog," she said. "Even though you said Fido, you meant Alex. I know what subtlety is, even if Alex says I don't."

Nate looked toward the sky, begging silently for strength. It was hypocritical, but he knew no other way. "It was the first thing I could think of, since apparently neither of you understand how to be quiet."

"I knocked over a lamp by accident," Art said. "It broke. I am supposed to feel bad because it didn't belong to me, but I thought it was ugly and was going to break it yesterday but I forgot. So I accidentally did it today."

Nate just went with it. He had to. "Of course you did."

Alex stepped around her and down the stairs. His large feet were bare, little wisps of black hair on his big toes. Nate didn't know why he noticed that. It shouldn't have mattered.

He also carried his gun.

He didn't come for Nate.

Instead, he went around the side of the house.

"He's gotta check," Art said.

"For what?"

"In case Macho Man Randy Savage was a spy."

He opened his mouth to say *something,* but for the life of him, he didn't know how to parse that sentence, so instead he shook his head and followed Alex.

He was on his knees in front of the water meter, gun on the grass at his side. He reached up and felt along the meter, hands going over the plastic covering and reaching around the back like he was looking for something.

When he didn't find anything, he moved the grate covering the valve and bent down, reaching in all the way to his shoulder, eyes narrowed.

"You know," Nate said. "For someone who just yesterday was having a hard time moving because he'd been shot, you seem to be doing okay."

Alex didn't respond.

"Granted, the wound looked old, but still. Old man yesterday, bright and spry today. Was it the coffee? Which, by the way, you're welcome for. Thanks for unloading the truck and then helping yourself."

Not a word.

"It was probably the bacon," Art said, suddenly appearing beside him as if out of nowhere. He hadn't heard her coming. "Bacon makes everything better."

"Right," Nate said slowly. "Because you've never had bacon before. Or met a waitress."

"She was so nice," Art said. "She brought me juice when I asked. And ice cream. And meat loaf. And carrots. And mashed potatoes."

"That's—"

"And butter for my bread that wasn't toast."

He waited.

She smiled up at him.

"You're a reporter," Alex grunted as he sat back up, as if conversational whiplash was a thing they did.

"Excuse you. I'm a *journalist*—"

"You should have said something."

"Oh. *Riiiight.* Because you've shared so much with me already. How could I be so goddamn rude and not tell you about my career path, man who broke into my house? You have my most sincere apologies. Please consider forgiving me."

"He will," Art said. "He's starting to like you, even though he normally doesn't like anyone besides me. You can tell by the way he hasn't pointed the gun at you in over ten minutes."

Nate felt himself flushing. He didn't know why. He didn't give a *fuck* if this man liked him in the slightest. He still wasn't convinced that some crime wasn't happening here, and if it involved the girl, he would do everything he could to get her away from Alex. What Alex thought about him shouldn't matter.

It shouldn't.

"No wonder you ask so many questions," Alex muttered, wiping his hand off on his leg. "Reporters don't know when to mind their own goddamn business. Always sticking their noses where they don't—"

"I came up here to do exactly that," Nate snapped. Normally he didn't give two shits what others thought about what he did. Or rather, had done. The work was important, and he wasn't in it for the popularity. But even he could admit to himself that Alex's dismissal stung the tiniest bit. "Mind my own goddamn business. But in case you couldn't tell, *someone* had broken into my cabin and made themselves at home. Which is *illegal*."

Alex pulled himself to his full height.

Nate wasn't intimidated. Well, he *was*, but he'd faced assholes before. This was just another one.

He was a little relieved the gun stayed on the ground.

"Fine," Alex said, a scowl on his face. "There's plenty of other cabins around here. We'll find another one."

"But those don't have water," Art said. They both looked down at her. "This one does. And the lake is cold and I like my bed and I've only read fifteen of the books, which means there are three hundred and sixty-two left to go." She nodded, the sunglasses sliding off the top of her head and down on her face. "Besides, Nate will be sad if we leave. He likes us."

"I don't like either of you at all," Nate said.

"You made us bacon."

"That doesn't mean I like you."

"It certainly seemed that way," she said. "If you give someone something that good, it has to mean *something*. You can't just give a gift without having feelings behind it."

"It was just *breakfast*."

Alex crouched down before her. "It'll be okay," he said, not looking at Nate. "We'll find another place. And I know the water is cold, but if we move fast, it'll be over soon and we can get warm again. And there might even be more books. Different kinds. It'll be okay. I promise."

It was the most Nate had heard him speak.

He wondered if he was being manipulated.

He felt like he was being manipulated.

Art looked up at him, pulling her glasses off slowly. Her eyes were wide, like she was a goddamn anime princess.

Definitely manipulated. But he thought it was just by her. Alex didn't seem like the type. He was fists and guns and violence. He didn't understand subtlety.

But Artemis Darth Vader?

She was *all* about manipulation.

And it was *working*.

"Tomorrow," Nate said through gritted teeth. "You guys can leave tomorrow. At least let her have a hot shower. You too. But goddammit, I get to go first because this is still *my* fucking cabin. You hear me? I get the first shower, and I am going to stay in it as long as I want, so you don't get to bitch at me for that."

Art looked smug.

Alex scowled.

Nate almost smashed his face in.

Instead, he turned and headed back around the house.

He thought he heard a little girl laughing.

CHAPTER SIX

Nate stuck to his guns.

He took the first shower.

The water was either ice or scalding. No in-between.

It didn't matter.

It was wonderful.

He leaned against the seafoam-green tiled wall, feeling his skin start to redden.

The shower was where he did some of his best thinking.

Back home in the suburbs of D.C., he would spend thirty minutes every morning in the shower, the sounds of water falling around him soothing. He'd lived in an overpriced apartment (it was D.C.— unless he chose to live an hour away, *everything* was overpriced) in Chevy Chase, an eighth-floor one-bedroom, sparsely furnished. He didn't have *time* to own things, didn't have the sort of people he'd call friends who'd come over and sit on the couch and shoot the shit and watch bad TV. He worked too much. He liked it that way. It was easier to depend on himself than it was to depend on others.

Did it get lonely?

Sure.

But he never let himself dwell on it too much. There wasn't time.

His alarm would go off at four thirty, and he'd trudge to the first-floor gym, where he'd run on a treadmill, Discman attached to his hip, headphones in his ears, blasting *Dangerous* by Michael Jackson. He'd dutifully put in his three miles, and then he'd be back up to his apartment.

One time, he thought about getting a cat. But then he remembered he hated cats.

He wasn't home enough for a dog.

By five, he'd be standing in the shower.

And there he'd stay for thirty minutes.

Thinking.

It helped him focus.

Toward the end of his illustrious career with the *Post*, he'd taken to having a shower at night too.

It hadn't helped.

So yes, here he was now, standing in a too-hot shower, steam rising thick and heavy, as he'd forgotten to turn on the overhead fan. The tile was chilled against his back, the water burning against his front.

He could only take shallow breaths.

He needed them to leave.

He did.

They needed to go. As Alex said, there were other cabins. Many, in fact. He wasn't advocating for them breaking and entering, but . . . they shouldn't be here. They were complicated. Both of them. Nate didn't need complicated. The reason he'd come to Oregon at all was to make things *un*complicated.

Did he have questions?

Of course he did.

They *ravaged* his mind. He'd always been curious. Always. Ever since he was a kid. He wanted to know everything, even those things he shouldn't. His mother had called him nosy. She'd caught him once trying to listen in on a conversation between her and his father, and she'd told him that he needed to mind his own business. That one day, it was going to get him into trouble.

She'd been right, of course.

He was here now because of that.

He'd pushed when he shouldn't have.

There were ethics guidelines when it came to journalism. Especially at a paper with a storied history like the *Post*.

They had to go.

So what if a little girl had to bathe in a cold lake.

There were people in the world that didn't even *have* water to bathe in.

And the less he knew, the less of a chance there'd be that he'd be called to testify against . . . whatever was happening.

But *fuck*, did they both intrigue him.

He groaned.

No.

Absolutely not.

He wouldn't ask a single question.

And that was final.

✦

Alex was in the shower when Nate asked, "Why are you called Artemis Darth Vader?"

Art was sitting on the couch in an awkward position, slumped almost as low as she could go, her socked feet dangling toward the floor but not quite reaching. She had another Louis L'Amour in her hands. *The Tall Stranger.* Ned Bannon versus his brother over control of Bishop's Valley. Bad guy dies, and ol' Ned gets the girl.

"What's that now, partner?" Art drawled without looking up. She was wearing her sunglasses. He wondered where she'd gotten them from. If they'd been stolen.

"Artemis Darth Vader."

She lowered the paperback slightly. "That's my name, don't wear it out." She chuckled quietly. "Now I get why that's funny. Interesting. I like that."

"Why are you—"

"Haven't we already done this?"

He glanced down the hall, listening to the shower running. After he'd come out, Art had taken her turn. It'd been quick, much quicker than he'd expected for someone like her. She'd come out only ten minutes later, a towel wrapped around her head expertly, wearing jeans that looked a little big on her, purple socks, and a Chicago Bulls T-shirt that hung off one shoulder.

Alex, for his part, looked conflicted at the idea of leaving her alone with Nate. Art had told him to stop being silly. He'd growled wordlessly at her before he glared at Nate for at least a minute.

The threat there was evident. No words were necessary.

Nate wasn't going to ask a goddamn thing. He *wasn't*.

He wasn't very surprised when, as soon as the shower turned on again, he'd opened his mouth.

"You never answered," he said.

"I did," Art said, flipping a page in the book. "I told you that I like it. And you said you're Nathaniel Cartwright because it's what your parents named you. But you don't like your parents very much."

He blinked. "What the hell are you talking about?"

"They're dead, right?"

"How did you—"

"That's what you told Macho Man. But you didn't seem very sad when you said it. You were angry, I think. Or something like it."

Shit. She was right. And they'd been listening in. "That's not the point. It doesn't matter."

"Oh. Okay. It's just, if you don't like them very much, and they named you, why didn't you pick something else?"

Nate felt helpless. This wasn't going like it was supposed to. "That's not how it works."

She pushed the sunglasses up until they rested on the towel on her head. "Says who?"

He didn't know how to answer that. "Says *everyone*."

"Not Alex."

"What?"

"Alex said I could be whoever I wanted to be. That no one could ever tell me what to do if I didn't want them to. I could pick my own name. So I did."

"But what about your mom?"

"What do you mean?"

"What name did she give you?"

She rolled her eyes. "One that you wouldn't be able to pronounce, you can trust me on that."

That . . . didn't sit right. "But why—"

She grinned. "Do you know *Star Wars*?"

"Everyone knows *Star Wars*."

"Okay, good. So you know there's this guy Darth Vader."

"I know."

"He's, like, part machine and part man and carries a red—"

"I know who he is!"

"Well, I like him."

"You like him," Nate said slowly. "Why?"

She shrugged. "Because he was bad, but he really wasn't. And also, he could raise his hand and choke people. Granted, the entire Star Wars universe is a little unrealistic, because that's not how—" She cut herself off. She cocked her head at him. The towel drooped. "Anyway. Darth Vader."

"And Artemis."

"She was the goddess of the hunt. Of wilderness. She protected girls."

"And you liked that."

She nodded. "More than any of the others. Do you think they were real?"

"I don't . . . are you asking me if I think ancient Greek deities are real?"

"Yes."

"No. No, I don't think ancient Greek deities are real."

"That's too bad." She sat back against the couch and opened her book again.

Nate wasn't sure how they'd gotten to this point.

The shower was still running.

Could he do this?

"Art, listen."

"Listening."

"I need you to be honest with me."

"I can do that, Nate."

"Good. That's good. Could you look at me, please?"

"I can multitask. I'm actually quite good at it. And Ned Bannon is about to—"

"For me. Please."

She sighed the great sigh of the put-upon, but she closed the book and looked at him.

"Thank you. Now. I need you to think about your answer. Okay? *Really think.* Can you do that for me?"

"Sure."

"Did Alex kidnap you? Is he hurting you? Do you need me to help you get away from him?"

She didn't answer.

"Art?"

She stared at him.

He leaned forward. "Are you okay?"

She nodded. "I'm showing you that I'm really thinking like you asked me to. When you really think on something, you don't answer right away."

"That's—"

"Okay, done thinking. No. Alex is not hurting me. I don't need to get away from him. He's my Alex. There's no one else in this world I want to be with."

Nate didn't know if she was telling the truth or if this was some form of Stockholm syndrome. He needed to push. "Has he ever hurt you?"

She squinted at him. "Not intentionally. One time he grabbed my wrist too hard, but it was only because we were running really fast and he didn't know he was squeezing too tightly. My legs aren't as long as his."

Nate felt a chill run down his spine. "What were you running from?"

"Men."

"What men?"

"The men with guns."

"Like . . . the police?"

"No."

A terrible thought struck him. "Are you on the run from the Mafia?"

She laughed brightly. "Oh, Nate. I like you. I'm so glad we chose to break into your cabin. You are so strange."

"What's going on?"

Nate jumped.

Alex was standing in the hallway, water dripping over his naked chest, holding a towel that barely seemed to wrap around his waist. The tattoo was clear now. The Ka-Bar. The eagle. USMC. A ribbon with the words DEATH BEFORE DISHONOR wrapped around the bird and blade. The dark hair on his chest and stomach was matted down and wet. The bruising on his stomach, which just yesterday had been blue and purple and vivid, was now mottled green and *fading*.

"Nate was just asking me if we were running from the Mafia," Art answered cheerfully. "Isn't he funny?"

"Hysterical," Alex said, staring at Nate.

But Nate wasn't going to be cowed. Not by a little girl. Not by a wet, barely covered man. "So," he said. "Not the Mafia, then. But she did say it was men with guns."

"Did she?"

"Sure did," Art said, flipping through the next page of the book. "Oh, Ned Bannon. She's too good for you. You've got your heart set on revenge. Hey, Alex. Did you know that Nate's seen *Star Wars?*"

"Has he," Alex said in such a way that Nate was sure it almost meant *I am death, destroyer of worlds.*

"Yes. He also asked me if you kidnapped me."

"Traitor," Nate muttered.

"And you said?"

She looked at him. "You're dripping on the floor. Why aren't you wearing clothes? Are you trying to show off?" She glanced at Nate, then back at Alex. "I think it's working."

Nate looked away, face heating.

"Art, keep your mouth shut," Alex warned. "And *you.*"

Nate swallowed thickly.

"You just . . ." He made an aggravated noise before spinning on his heel and stomping back down the hall. A door slammed shut a moment later.

Art looked at him with wide eyes. "You're in so much trouble," she whispered.

He didn't like the smile on her face.

Nate Cartwright wasn't a stupid man.

He wasn't.

He had a strong sense of self-preservation.

Which is why he immediately grabbed his keys and phone and took off down the side of the mountain as fast as he dared to go.

He watched in the rearview mirror, sure that he'd see Alex charging after him, half-dressed (and why did he even have to add in *that* little detail?), gun pointed forward, ready to blow Nate's head off.

But there was nothing but dust being kicked up behind the truck as the cabin grew smaller behind him.

He waited until he'd gotten to the main highway before he looked down at his phone.

He had bars. They flickered, but they were there.

He pulled over to the side of the road.

He left the truck running.

He started to dial 911.

He stared down at it, thumb hovering over the Send button.

His heart was jackrabbiting in his chest.

Instead, he deleted the 1 and the 1 and the 9.

He pulled up his contacts. Highlighted who he was looking for. Hit Send.

It rang three times before—"Hello?"

"Big Eddie?"

"Nate!" Big Eddie said in that deep voice of his. "Didn't expect to hear from you this quickly. Everything all right?"

"Yes. No. I don't know."

"You okay?"

"I'm fine. It's just—" What? It was just . . . *what*? "Have you . . . is there anything? On the news?"

"There's a lot of things on the news," Big Eddie said slowly. "No TV up in the cabin, right?"

"Yeah. Mom, she—it was too expensive. And she didn't want us watching TV during the summer anyway."

"Makes sense. You sound . . . I don't know how you sound. What's going on?"

"A girl. A man."

"What girl? What man?"

"Anything on the news? About people . . . missing? Or something?"

"No," Big Eddie said. "Not that I've seen. I haven't—hold on a second. Abe. Hey, Abe!"

A muffled reply.

"You hear anything about a missing girl? Just—I don't know. A missing girl. Little, Nate?"

"Yes."

"Yeah, like—okay. Right. Right. I'll be right there, you old fart."
Big Eddie sighed. "Nothing doing, Nate. Why do you ask? You see
something?"

He thought fast. "No, just—a man and a girl up near the lake.
Just a weird feeling, you know?"

Big Eddie hummed. "Oh sure. You can't ignore your gut, right?
Especially you. You'd probably know better than anyone. You sure
it's not someone staying in one of the other cabins? Just because it's
the off-season doesn't mean some don't still get rented out."

"I know. I—"

Big Eddie lowered his voice. "You see something, maybe? I can
call the sheriff if you want. I think Griggs is on shift if you need
me to—"

"No," Nate said hastily. "No. No sheriff. I'm probably just overreacting. Tired, you know?"

"Sure," Big Eddie said. "And being up there for the first time is
probably bringing back all kinds of memories. It's tough. I know."

"It's nothing," Nate said, closing his eyes.

"If you're sure."

"Yeah."

"Get your water turned on okay?"

Nate sighed. "Yeah. Guy came up bright and early this morning."

Big Eddie laughed. "Jimmy doesn't do anything bright and early."

"No. Not Jimmy. A guy named Randy."

"Well, there you go. Just when you think you know everyone.
That's good. Nate, you get settled in, all right? And if anything else
happens, you call me, okay? It might be nothing, but . . ."

"Yeah. I will. Thanks, Big Eddie. Sorry to bother you."

"No bother, friend. Be safe."

"Bye."

The phone beeped in his ear.

He tapped it against his forehead.

Roseland was a small town. Everyone knew everyone's business
there. It was a fact of rural life. But that didn't mean they'd come
from Roseland. They could be from anywhere. He should have given
Big Eddie a name. Not Artemis Darth Vader. No. That couldn't be
real. But Alex Delgado? That could be—

An idea hit.

Hard.

He scrolled through his phone again.

He checked his watch.

It was only ten in the morning.

Which meant it would be one on the East Coast.

He found the name he was looking for.

He hit Send.

It rang once.

A voice said, "This is Davis."

"Ruth. It's me."

There was a pause. Then, incredulously, *"Nate?"*

"Yeah."

"Holy fucking *shit*. Do you know how many messages I've left for you? You goddamn asshole, you—hold on a second. I swear to god, if you hang up, I will *end* you." Ruth Davis muffled the phone on her end. He heard the faintest of sounds coming through, her low, smoky rasp the loudest of all. He closed his eyes, imagining her sitting in the newsroom, people rushing around her, desks lining the floor cluttered with papers and files and fat computer monitors. He felt a sharp twinge in his chest at the thought of it. He'd been so wide-eyed the first moment he'd stepped inside, on his way to interview for an internship that didn't pay him a dime but that he wanted more than anything.

Ruth had been there, even then.

She'd been there for decades. She was a tough old broad who still used a typewriter and lamented about the days gone by when she could chain-smoke right at her desk rather than having to take the damn elevator down to the courtyard. If asked, no one could say *exactly* what Ruth's job title was, but she did a little bit of everything and was more than willing to help out if asked—if only she liked you. And *liked* might have been too strong a word. If Ruth Davis tolerated your existence, chances were you were going to make something of yourself. If she hated you, you'd most likely be working somewhere else within six months. No one fucked with Ruth. One guy had tried to complain about her to the higher-ups. He'd been fired three days later.

For some reason, she'd liked Nate. Not just tolerated but *liked*. Of course, she'd chewed him up and spit him out on numerous occasions, but that was the only reason he'd become better at what he did. She was harsh, but only because she cared. Or so she said.

She was a tiny thing, Black with a frizzy white Afro and rings on each finger that wouldn't be repeated within a month's time. Nate had often wondered just how much jewelry she had, but he didn't want to take a chance in asking her and facing her wrath.

He adored her.

He also hadn't said goodbye to her when he'd been marched out by security, his meager belongings in a box, his skin vibrating, the panic still simmering at a low level because this couldn't be real, this couldn't *be real*—

So. He was expecting what was about to come. He hadn't spoken to her in the weeks since.

"Nate," she said, coming back to the phone. Her voice was a growl, not unlike Alex, if he were honest. He'd never tell either of them he'd thought that, of course. One had a gun. The other carried a Taser. "Where the hell are you?"

He thought about lying. Instead, he said, "Oregon."

"Oregon," she spat at him. "*Oregon.* As in the *state?*"

"I didn't know there was any other Ore—"

"Are you sassing me, kiddo?"

"No, ma'am."

"Let me tell you how this is going to go," she said, and he could hear the furious *clack* of her typewriter in the background. "I am going to ask you questions. You are going to answer these questions. If at any point I feel you're not being truthful with answers to said questions, I will find a way to tear your intestines out through your asshole. Do we have an understanding?"

He missed her quite a bit. "Yes."

"Good. Now. First question. Why Oregon?"

"My parents had a cabin here. They left it to me."

"And when did you find this out?"

"A couple of weeks ago."

"Where in Oregon?"

"Outside Roseland. Near Herschel Lake."

"Sounds scenic and absolutely terrible. I'm writing this all down. Mind ain't what it used to be. I don't want to forget in case I need to get my fat ass on a plane to hunt you down."

He wisely said nothing.

"Herschel . . . Lake. Now, since I know fuck all about Oregon, I assume this is in the middle of nowhere and you're surrounded by trees and nature and birds and shit."

"That's . . . apt." Because yes, he was in the middle of nowhere surrounded by trees right at that very moment.

"Are you turning into a hippie? Communing with nature? Working on some secret pot farm and trying to find yourself again because you're lost?"

He smiled despite himself. "No, Ruth."

"You know how I feel about pot-growing hippies."

"I do."

"Goddamn draft dodgers."

"So you've said." Many times. Even without provocation.

"Are you safe?"

And what an *odd* question for her to ask in the grand scheme of things. And even then, he hesitated. "Yes."

Of course she picked up on it. "Are you sure about that?"

"I . . . think so. It's—complicated."

"Make it uncomplicated."

"I need you to look up a name for me."

"Do you."

"Yes."

"Go."

"Alex Delgado. He's . . . forty. Marines. Maybe former. But you know what they say, once a Marine—"

"Always a Marine," she agreed. "Please tell me I'm not doing a search on someone you're wanting to fuck."

"Oh my god."

Ruth ignored him. "Because if I *am*, I have to say that's pretty damn smart, using your resources like that. Maybe it's slightly reprehensible, but you can't be too safe."

"For fuck's *sake*, Ruth!"

"I had to ask. So you don't want to fuck him?"

"No!"

"Hmm. I'll let that go. For now. Why am I looking up this man?"

"Just—he's up here. In the cabins. And he's—different. There's something off. And I can't figure it out. He has a girl with him. I think she's his daughter, but . . ."

"But . . ."

"I don't know!" he said, exasperated. "Nothing about *either* of them makes any sense. And it's pissing me off."

"So instead of asking, you're going behind their backs and coming to me to do the searching for you."

"Yes. Exactly. This."

"I approve," she said. "But if you think that little girl is in any danger, you need to call the cops. Better to be wrong about doing the right thing. You can always apologize after. You don't take chances, not when kids are involved."

He's my Alex. There's no one else in this world I want to be with.

"I don't think it's like that," Nate admitted. "But if that changes, I will do what I can. I promise."

"Good. This will take a few days. Can't just drop everything because you finally decided to call me back."

"I know. I'm sorry. It's just . . . I had to get out. I had to leave."

"Is . . ." She sighed. "Rumors, you know?"

"I know."

"They true?"

"Depends on what they're saying, I guess."

"Bathhouse," she said, dry as dust. "Married junior senator. You using him as a source while still getting your dick wet."

"Well. Then the rumors would be true."

She whistled. "You sly dog."

"It's not something I'm proud of."

"No, I suppose you wouldn't be. Wife's got photos, huh?"

"PI. Didn't know we were being followed."

"How long did this go on?"

Of course she would ask that. "Three months."

"Jesus, Nate."

"I know."

"I would have fired your sorry ass too."

"After you beat the shit out of me."

"Damn right. You're lucky I didn't find out before you left D.C. What are you going to do now?"

He shrugged, even though she couldn't see him. "I don't know. That's what Oregon is for. To clear my head."

"And now you're calling me about big, bad Marines named Alex Delgado."

"It's not like that."

"Sure, kiddo. If you say so."

"It's *not.*"

"I don't give a shit whether you lie to yourself. But don't you lie to me. That's your only warning. I won't push, but I don't deserve that, Nathaniel."

He huffed out a breath. "Fine."

"I'll get back to you when I can."

"If I don't pick up, it's because I have bad service up here in the mountains. Just leave me a message, and I'll call you back."

"Because you called me back the last eight messages I left, right?"

"You know you're my only girl, Ruth."

She snorted. "Don't you try and pull that charmer bullshit with me, Nate. You leave that for your married senators." She paused, considering. "Or your Marines."

"He's *not my*—"

"I'll call you back when I got something. But remember, that little girl needs help, you help her. Don't let anything stop you. Children are the most precious thing in this world. They need someone to fight for them when they can't fight for themselves. You get me?"

The forest was alive around him. "Yes, ma'am."

"Good." Her voice softened. "Take care of yourself, okay?"

His eyes burned a little. He missed her greatly. "Thanks, Ruth. You too."

The phone beeped in his ear.

He sat on the side of the road in his truck for another twenty minutes before he made a decision. He turned the truck around and headed back up the mountain.

CHAPTER SEVEN

He regretted it almost immediately.

Alex was waiting on the porch, watching for the truck.

He had dressed. Jeans and flannel again, which—thank god. Nate didn't need distractions. Yes, Alex was . . . attractive. But Nate didn't *want* to think that. Especially since so much was unknown. Everything, really. Add in the fact that Alex was more likely to murder him than look at him in any way other than as a nuisance. Times, oh they were a-changing, but Nate had been the subject of smear-the-queer a handful of times by guys that looked just like Alex. They'd stand outside the gay bars in D.C. and shout shit at the queens, who blew air kisses at them defiantly. They were aggressive, and everyone knew you couldn't leave alone. You had a buddy. A system. You carried Mace. You wanted to live your life the way those that had come before had fought for, but you had to be careful. There were people out there who wanted to hurt what they didn't understand.

He'd never been *hit*, per se, never been attacked. Not physically. But he'd been in the Pride Parade last year along with thousands of others. He'd been in Freedom Plaza for the street festival. He'd seen the men and women with their Bibles, their faces red, screaming about Sodom and Gomorrah, about how the faggots and the dykes were bringing about the End Times, that God him*self* found them to be a sin, a *blasphemy* against nature. He'd seen the cops in their uniforms turning an indifferent eye. He'd seen men in military uniforms looking upon them with disdain, even as some of their brothers and sisters marched, knowing that with the newly passed Don't Ask, Don't Tell, they could be discharged, even though it was technically supposed to *protect* them to an extent.

He didn't know Alex. But he knew the type.

Or maybe he'd be the type that'd fuck to get his rocks off and then still spit on you as you passed him by on the street. Nate knew those types too. They were worse. They were angrier.

It didn't matter.

Nate wasn't thinking about this. None of it.

He turned off the truck. He opened the door.

He wouldn't be intimidated. This was his home.

Alex didn't speak as Nate made his way toward the cabin. Art was nowhere to be seen. She was probably still inside. Nate didn't think Alex would let her wander off on her own.

He reached the porch, and before he put his foot on the first step, Alex said, "Where did you go?"

"Away."

That was apparently the wrong answer. "Where?"

"For a drive, man," Nate said, keeping his tone even. "You don't own me. I'm allowed to do what I want." He wasn't sure where the bravado was coming from, but he sure as hell wasn't going to question it.

"You took your phone."

"Yeah. I did. Because it's mine."

"Who did you call?"

He wasn't dumb. Nate had to keep reminding himself that. "If I even called anyone, I don't see how it's your business."

"You call the cops?"

"No." That wasn't a lie.

"Do we need to run?"

That startled Nate. It was so . . . blunt. "Why would you need to run?"

Alex remained as stoic as ever. He was good. "In case you have someone coming after us."

Nate laughed a little wildly. "Who the hell would I send after you?"

"You're a reporter. You probably have contacts."

"I'm a *journalist*," Nate snapped at him, unnerved by just how close Alex was. "And I worked for a paper on the other side of the country. That I was *fired* from. Do you really think *anyone* there would be willing to help me?"

"Why were you fired?"

Nate scowled. "I don't owe you shit. I didn't call the cops. No one is coming after you. At least not from *me*. I obviously can't say the same for *you*—"

Alex nodded stiffly. "We need to talk."

That . . . was surprising. "Are you breaking up with me?" Nate asked before he could stop himself. He winced. "Uh. Pretend I didn't say that."

"I don't know if I can now."

Nate gaped. "Did you just . . . make a joke?"

"I don't joke," Alex said. "If we're staying here, you need to know a few things."

"What do you mean, if you're staying here—don't walk away from me when I'm talking to—goddammit."

He sighed before climbing the steps and following Alex into the cabin.

✦

Art wasn't sitting on the couch. Instead she'd pulled a chair from the kitchen out to the living room. She swung her legs as she sat on it. The sunglasses were gone, as was the towel. Her hair was dry and looked a little fluffy. She grinned when she saw Nate. "Hey."

"Hey," Nate said. "Hi."

"I told you he'd come back," she said, looking up at Alex as he passed her by.

He grunted at her on his way down the hall.

She rolled her eyes fondly.

Nate wasn't sure if he was supposed to follow. Alex said he wanted to talk, but Nate didn't feel comfortable being in a bedroom with him. He wanted to be able to run if Alex pulled the gun again.

"He'll be right back," Art said. "He's going to get the scrunchies."

"The . . . scrunchies?"

"Yep."

Once again, Nate didn't know what to do with that. "He said we had to talk?"

She sighed. "What is he doing, trying to break up with you?"

"That's what *I* said!"

"I know. I heard you talking. The door was open."

"Jesus."

"You say his name a lot. Did you know he hung out with beggars and whores?" She frowned. "Though, 'whore' isn't a very nice thing to call someone. Anyway. It's weird, right? He had all these friends who weren't what someone like him was supposed to have, but he did anyway. But most people don't talk about that when they pray to him. They're all so focused on his death. That's just morbid."

He felt like everything was upside down. "I have no idea what you're talking about."

She waved a hand at him. "It doesn't matter. I just think it's important sometimes to be remembered for what you lived for rather than what you died for."

The floor creaked as Alex appeared in the hallway again. Nate realized he had to duck his head just a little to keep from hitting the lintel. Even his shoulders seemed in danger of brushing the walls on either side of him.

Nate groaned inwardly. Not the time. Not the time. Not the—

"Did you bring the scrunchies?" Art demanded.

"Yes," Alex said. And he *had*. In his hand was a baggie filled with brightly colored bands. Some were thin—like rubber bands—and others were larger and covered in polka dots. She made grabby hands at the baggie, and Alex handed them over.

She hummed a little song under her breath as she dug through the baggie before eventually setting aside a couple of the small bands. They were teal.

"One or two?" Alex asked her, standing behind the chair.

"Two please." Then, "Ha! Pigtails. Because bacon makes everything better. I get that now."

Nate wondered yet again if he was caught in a dream.

Alex nodded and then did the most remarkable thing.

He reached those big hands down, the skin callused, the fingers thick, and began brushing them through her hair with purpose, separating it right down the middle. Art continued to sing quietly as he did so.

Nate watched, helpless to do anything else. He couldn't look away.

Alex, massively intimidating and scary Alex, began to braid the little girl's hair.

"I'm keeping her safe," he said, not looking up at Nate.

Nate struggled to find his voice, entranced by the sight in front of him. "I—that's what she said."

"I can't tell you everything," he continued, fingers moving deftly. "Not because I don't trust you, but—"

"You don't. Trust me, that is."

He didn't even hesitate. "I can't. I don't know you. She's—if there's a chance, even the smallest one, that something will slip, that you'll say something to someone without meaning to, it could end . . . badly."

"For who?"

He shrugged. "Us. You. You could be brutally murdered or—"

Art coughed pointedly.

He jerked her hair a little harder than necessary.

She tilted her head back slowly, glaring up at him.

Alex sighed before pushing her head forward again. "You've been . . . nice."

"Wow," Nate said. "That sounded like it hurt for you to say. Congratulations for being able to get that all out on your own."

"It did," Art said. "Showing feelings hurts him all the time."

"I'm not *showing feelings*," Alex said. "You told me I had to say this."

"Well, *yeah*. But I didn't say to tell him he's been *nice*." She looked at Nate. "I told you to say you've been hospitable. There's a difference. You haven't been nice. Not really."

"Thank . . . you?"

She beamed at him. "You're welcome." She tried to look back at Alex again. "See how easy that was?"

He pushed her head forward. "It's a synonym."

"Well, that's just a lazy excuse. Do better."

His mouth thinned. "You have been hospitable. And you didn't have to be."

"You pointed a gun at me," Nate reminded him. "Multiple times. I don't think I had a choice. Forced hospitality isn't hospitality. It's a hostage situation."

THE BONES BENEATH MY SKIN • 93

"You left," Art said. "You could have stayed gone. But you came back."

Which—yes. That was true. He had no idea why. "I did."

She started humming again.

"She's my responsibility," Alex said, halfway done with the left braid. "And I take that very seriously."

"You're not her father. Are you?"

He looked up, eyes boring into Nate. He kept still, waiting for Alex to find whatever he was looking for. Finally, he gave a small shake of his head. "I'm her bodyguard."

"My protector," she said, snapping a scrunchie against her fingers. "My big, brave Alex."

"What are you guarding her from?"

Alex finished one braid and snapped his fingers near her ear. She handed him a teal rubber band over her shoulder. He snapped it around the bottom of the braid with a practiced twist of his fingers. "She's important."

It was like pulling teeth. "To?"

"Me. Others."

"Appropriately vague. How expected."

Alex wasn't amused. "I told you that I couldn't tell you everything."

"You're not telling me *anything* I couldn't figure out on my own—"

"You said Mafia earlier," Art said. "That wasn't right at all."

"It was a *guess.*"

"A terrible guess. Maybe I'm a space princess."

Nate groaned. "*Star Wars.*"

Her smile was luminous. "I do love those movies."

"Then why are you Artemis Darth Vader and not Princess Leia?"

"Eh. That's a little on the nose—*ow.* You didn't have to pull so hard!"

Alex was scowling down at her. "Maybe you should stop talking."

"Maybe you should—*oh.* Right. Copy that. Let's get on down this old dusty trail, then, partner. You're starting to mosey a bit."

"Look," Alex said. "All you need to know is that I am doing all I can to protect her from people who want to hurt her, and that's final. I haven't kidnapped her, I'm not abusing her—"

"I never said—"

Alex looked up sharply. "You thought it. I know you did."

Nate couldn't deny that.

"And I don't blame you for that," Alex continued. "I know how this looks. I know what . . . you must be thinking. A guy like me. Her . . . the way she is. But you have to understand. You have to believe me when I say I would rather die than see anything happen to her. I'm doing everything I can to help her. Everything."

"You're not going to die," Art said, a frown on her face. "I don't like it when you talk like that. Don't say it again."

"How long?" Nate asked him.

"How long what?"

"How long have you known her?"

"A long time," Alex said, the second braid almost finished. "Longer than it seems."

"And her parents?"

The skin under his eye twitched. "That's . . . who we're trying to find. Who we're trying to get her back to."

A thought struck Nate. A terrible thought. "You didn't kidnap her. She was already taken."

"Yes." Alex looked relieved. "That. Exactly that."

Nate's mind was already moving, connecting bits and pieces. "Was it—" Oh shit, that was an awful thing. "A . . . ring? Like . . . slavery?"

Alex looked confused for a split second before it hit him. His eyes went wide. "No, no. Not like . . . that. Nothing like that. It was—"

Art rolled her eyes. "I know what you're talking about. No, Nate. I wasn't being trafficked."

He stared at her. "How old *are* you?"

"Ten," she said. "Thereabouts."

"And you're on the run. Hiding out. Here. In my cabin."

"It was the farthest one away," Alex mumbled. "It didn't look like it'd been used in a long time." He snapped again, and she handed him the other scrunchie.

"It's almost like fate," Art said seriously. "Do you believe in fate,

Nate?" Her nose wrinkled. "That rhymed. I don't like rhymes very much."

"I don't—no. I don't. Believe in fate."

"Kismet? Destiny? Nothing?"

"No."

"Huh." She squinted at him. "Then what *do* you believe in?"

"I don't know."

"Ghosts?" She clapped her hands. "I like ghosts. Have you ever seen one?"

"No."

"I haven't either," she said, sounding strangely disappointed.

"Done," Alex said. He tugged on the ends of each braid. "It's a little off-center."

Art reached up and ran her fingers over the top of her head and down the braids. "Still. You're getting better at it. Remember the first time you tried? You growled at me the whole time, and it ended up looking like I'd been attacked by an owl."

Nate laughed. It came out sounding slightly hysterical, but he couldn't stop it. Both Art and Alex looked surprised. "You're just— how am I supposed to believe any of this? You're asking me to take you at your word. To trust you. How can I do that when you don't trust me?"

"We'll get there," Art said, putting the remaining scrunchies back in the baggie. "I know it. It'll take time, but most things do."

Alex was staring down at her, an undecipherable look on his face.

"How long are you going to stay here?" Nate asked quietly.

Alex scratched the back of his neck. "I don't know. It's . . . complicated."

"It's not time to leave yet," Art said, hopping down from the chair. Her pigtails bounced behind her head. Nate didn't know the first thing about how to do such things, but they still looked good. She was achingly pretty. "I'll know when it's time."

"How—"

She walked over to him, stopping with the tips of her sock-covered toes against the tips of his Chucks. She motioned for him to lean down. He looked at Alex. Alex was watching Art, that same odd look on his face.

Nate did the only thing he could.

He crouched down until he was eye level.

She tilted her head at him as she studied him. Her eyes were bright and knowing. He didn't flinch as she reached up and cupped his face. Her hands were warm. "Sometimes you need to take things on faith," she said quietly. "Even if you think you have no faith left, I promise you, you do. All of you do. It's easier, I think, to stay lost. But when you're found, when you open your eyes, you can finally see the truth for what it is."

He didn't understand. She made no sense. But there was a lump in his throat he couldn't seem to swallow past.

She leaned forward and kissed his nose with a loud smack.

He was stunned.

"I'm glad you found us," she whispered, her breath on his face. "I think we needed you to."

And then she *smiled*.

He was speechless as she let him go. She stepped away, already demanding that Alex get her a mirror so she could see how pretty her braids were. Alex looked at Nate, and there was almost a *crack* in that stoic mask he wore, something that looked strangely vulnerable, but it was gone only moments later.

Art took him by the hand and led him down the hall to the second bathroom.

He could hear her squeals of delight, telling Alex how much better he was getting at this, that give it another week and he'd be *perfect*, and did he like how she looked? Was she the prettiest Artemis Darth Vader in all the world?

He didn't hear what Alex said, but he had a good idea.

He was still crouched, blinking slowly, when they came back out. "Time for lunch, huh?" she said. "I think we should probably have more bacon, just to make sure this morning wasn't a fluke."

✦

She was standing off the back deck, staring up at the sky. Alex and Nate were watching her. Nate had spent the last couple of hours trying to gather his thoughts, trying to put everything in order so it made some sort of sense. He was missing large pieces, pieces that he'd likely never know. At least not with things how they were now. He didn't regret making the phone call to Ruth. But he wasn't going to tell Alex about it either.

If Alex was telling the truth, *if* what Art was saying was possible, then there would be a trail. Somehow. Whoever her parents were. Whoever Alex was. Whoever *she* was.

"Your last name isn't Delgado, is it," he muttered, not looking at the man standing only a few feet away.

"No."

"Is your name even Alex?"

There was a brief hesitation. Then, "Yes." And, "Her name isn't really Artemis Darth Vader. In case you were wondering."

Nate turned slowly to gape at him. "Did you just make another joke?"

"Of course not."

"That . . . sounded almost like a joke."

"I told you, I don't make jokes."

"He's funny only sometimes!" Art called up to them. "And usually he doesn't even mean to be."

"See? Now *that* I believe."

Alex scowled. It was starting to get familiar.

And it shouldn't be. Nothing about this should feel familiar. That way lay danger. This was temporary. All of this was temporary.

This time yesterday, he was just outside of Roseland, wondering if Big Eddie's Gas and Convenience was still there. He was driving toward the mountains, getting ready to hunker down and lick his wounds, to deal with all that he'd done to get to this point. He was going to drink himself into a stupor for a few days, feel a little sorry for himself. And when he was done, he was going to pick himself up and gather up all the pieces that had broken off, try to see if there was any way to fit them back together.

These people, this man and this girl, didn't fit into any of that.

And how that *burned*. There was a maddening itch just below his skin that begged to be scratched, to demand the truth. Oh, he'd believed what Alex had said while braiding Art's hair. For the most part. He was good at picking through bullshit, setting aside truth from untruths. But the *vagueness* of it all was driving him up the wall. He was sure the scenarios running through his head were far more outlandish than reality. Mysteries, when solved, usually ended up disappointing. When the spotlight shines down, when all the shadows melt away, all that's left isn't going to be as impressive as the secret made it seem. He'd been here before time and time again. He'd always forced himself to remain pragmatic, even when he was a kid.

Still. What if . . .

"How long?"

"How long what?"

He didn't look at Alex, trying to sound nonchalant. "How long have you been on the run?"

"Why?"

"I'm trying to get to know you, man."

"Why?" And that sounded infinitely more suspicious.

"You're staying in my cabin," Nate said, irritated. "I think I'm allowed to ask questions."

"Do you ever not ask questions?"

"No. Never."

Art bent over, picking up a rock and staring down at it as she bounced it in her palm.

"A week," Alex finally said.

That . . . didn't sit right with Nate. "And how long have you been here?"

"Here."

"Yes. *Here.* On the lake. In my cabin."

"Fucking reporters," Alex muttered.

"I heard that."

"You were *meant* to."

"Be nice!" Art said without looking. She bent down and picked up another rock. The waves lapped at the shore. The sun was shining. There were barely any clouds in the sky. It was a perfectly normal day.

"Five days," Alex said.

Nate finally gave in and glanced at him.

He was watching Art. His arms were crossed over his chest, the sleeves of his shirt straining against his biceps. He was scowling, of course, because that was most likely the default expression on his face. The scruff on his cheeks and neck was a little thicker than it'd been the day before. He didn't seem the type to grow a beard. Nate thought he would have shaved every day as part of a strict, regimented routine. He'd get up even earlier than Nate was used to. He'd do sixteen thousand push-ups. He'd eat thirty hard-boiled eggs. He'd drink coffee as black as his soul. He'd glower at everything while he watched the sunrise, contemplating whatever it was men of his caliber did. After, he would shower, using shampoo that probably smelled like medicine. And once finished, he would floss and brush his teeth. Finally, he would shave. Any hint of facial hair would be gone by 6:00 A.M.

But here he was, stubble on its way to becoming something more. Nate had never been able to grow a beard. It'd always come in patchy and wiry. He'd had a goatee in college, something he'd been proud of at the time. In retrospect, it was a wonder he ever got laid with that thing.

It didn't matter, though. He didn't know this man. He didn't know this girl. And they didn't trust him. Alex had said as much. Not that Nate had given them any reason to, but still. Art wasn't . . . normal. At least not like any other ten-year-old he'd ever seen before. Maybe she was older than she claimed to be. Maybe she was Alex's young teenage bride, and they were on the run from irate parents that—

"How did you get shot?" he blurted.

The scowl deepened. "It was a mistake."

"How does one mistakenly get shot? Did you shoot yourself?"

Alex turned slowly to look at him.

"Right," Nate said hastily. "Stupid question. Of course you didn't shoot yourself. What was I thinking? I've seen you handle a gun."

Alex looked back to where Art was continuing to pick up rocks.

"So, I guess we're not going to answer that question, huh?" Nate asked.

"I told you. It was a mistake."

"Yes. You did say that. Which . . . doesn't really say anything at all. Must have happened a while ago, though."

"Why?"

"Because it's healed."

"Rubber bullet."

Nate blinked. "Oh. Right. I guess that—huh. So you got shot mistakenly while rescuing Art from people who want to get her back, and they carried guns with rubber bullets instead of real bullets because . . ."

Alex didn't take the bait.

"That must have hurt."

Alex grunted.

"Has anyone ever told you that you're aggravating?"

"No," Alex said. "No one. Ever." Then he walked down the steps off the deck.

Nate stared after him. "Was that another joke? Because if it was, you have a terrible sense of humor."

Alex didn't acknowledge him. Nate thought that was rude. He watched as Alex approached Art. She didn't look up at him, but Nate thought she knew he was coming. When he stood beside her, she showed him the rocks she had in her hands. "Which ones?" she asked. "Because some of them are better than others, but I like this one because it's pretty."

He reached down. "This one. And this one."

"But not the pretty one?"

"No. It wouldn't bounce right."

"Oh. Because it's not flat enough?"

"Yes."

"So that means I can keep it."

Alex sighed. "How many rocks have you kept so far?"

"Today? Or since we've been here?"

"Art."

Her face scrunched up. "Seventeen."

"You can't take them all."

"Seventeen isn't all the rocks, Alex."

"You know what I mean. If we have to go, we can't take it all. There will be some things we'll have to leave behind."

Art glanced back at Nate. The hairs on the back of his neck stood up. "Maybe. But not now. Not yet."

"Not yet," Alex said quietly.

"Okay. Now show me. You promised."

"Did I?"

"Alex! Don't be mean."

"Never," he said, and for some reason, Nate believed him.

They walked closer to the water. The beach was rocky, tufts of grass growing through the stones. Alex hovered right behind her as she carefully stepped on the rocks, hands ready in case she slipped. She didn't. He stopped her before she could get any closer, telling her he didn't want her to get her shoes wet.

"Because the world would end if that happened, right?" she asked him.

"Do you want me to show you this or not?"

"Yes."

He picked a rock from her hand. "See how I'm holding it? You need to let it rest against your thumb and pointer finger."

"Like this?"

"Almost." He reached down and fixed her grip. "There. That's better."

"Feels a little weird."

"Does it?"

"Yeah. Rocks are strange."

"You don't have—it's fine. You have a good hold on it?"

"I do."

"Okay. Watch me. Watch my arm."

She did.

He brought his arm back, then swung it out in a flat arc. He let go of the rock. It skipped along the surface of the lake. Nate counted. Of course he counted. It was what you were supposed to do when skipping rocks. One. Two. Three. Four five *sixseveneight*—

It splashed and sank below the surface.

"Wow," Art said, sounding suitably impressed. "That was a good one."

And it was. Nate remembered standing in almost that exact same spot, doing that exact same thing with his brother. They'd do

it until their arms were sore, making a game of it, trying to outdo
the other for hours. His brother always won. Always. Oh sure, Nate
would get a few good skips in, but Ricky had been better at it. He'd
never been mean about it, not really, but he'd gloat, sure. They were
kids. That's what kids did.

After—when they'd found him, when his parents had walked
into the cabin and found Nate and his boyfriend in flagrante, Nate
had returned home to D.C., tail between his legs, the sting of his
father's words and his mother's silence still piercing his skin again
and again. He'd heard the anger in his father's vitriol. He'd seen the
look of shock and horror on his mother's face.

He'd thought about telling them before. He had. He really had.
But he'd been living on the other side of the country, and it'd
just . . . gotten away from him. But when he *had* thought about it,
it'd made him feel itchy. A little queasy. He didn't know how they'd
take it. They weren't religious. Oh god no. They'd only been to
church once, some midnight mass at Christmas that they'd never
done again because it was late and boring. Even his father had
said so.

And, if he *really* thought about it, had he ever heard his parents
say anything about gay people? He didn't know if he had. Of course,
that hadn't meant a damn thing. Not in the long run.

They'd caught him, though, and at the worst possible time.
He'd felt that nauseous slick twist in his stomach when they'd first
walked in the door, and they had just *stared* at each other for a long
minute. He'd found his voice first, telling them it wasn't what they
were thinking (it was), and if they would just let him explain (they
didn't), everything would be fine.

His father had started yelling.

His mother hadn't said a word.

He'd fled.

Three days after he'd flown back to D.C., his brother had called.

"Is it true?" he'd asked.

"Yes," Nate had said, because there was no way around it. And
he was tired. He was so goddamn tired, and he just couldn't find a
reason to lie.

"Why?"

"Why didn't I tell you?"

"No," his brother had spat. "Why are you *like* this?"

Nate had closed his eyes.

He'd hung up on his brother a few minutes later, cutting him off mid-shout.

Nate had spoken to him twice more. The first was for his brother to tell him their parents were dead and that there were *services* that could come in and clean crime scenes, all while Nate struggled to not hyperventilate. The second time, of course, had been a couple of months later.

"The cabin," he'd said, the same brother who had laughed when he'd skipped a rock six times once, telling him he was getting better at it. "The truck. That's yours. Nothing else."

"Oh," he'd said. "Oh."

"You're not getting anything else. Don't try and fight me on it."

"I won't."

Rick had given Nate the attorney's information and then hung up without saying goodbye. He didn't scold Nate for not coming to the funeral. Nate hadn't expected that. He'd been *waiting* for it, for some sign that things could be different now that they were gone, that maybe Rick could think for himself, could—

But there'd only been the dial tone in his ear.

He watched as Alex repositioned Art's arm, pushing her elbow down just a little bit. She nodded, eyes narrowed slightly in concentration. She listened to every word he said. Nate couldn't take his eyes off them.

"Okay," Alex said. "You're good to go."

He stepped back.

And she hurled the rock.

One. Two. *Threefourfive*—

"Whoa," she breathed as the rock disappeared into the lake. "That. Was. *Awesome.*" She threw her hands up in the air, pigtails bouncing as she jumped around. "Did you *see* that? Alex! Did you— Nate! Nate, did you see what I just did?" She looked up at him still standing on the deck. She was smiling.

Alex looked at him too. He wasn't smiling, but he wasn't scowling either. It was . . . different. For just a moment.

"Yeah," Nate said, voice hoarse. "Yeah. I saw it. You did . . . It was good."

She immediately demanded they do it again.

And they did. For two more hours.

Nate watched them the entire time.

CHAPTER EIGHT

Three days later, nothing had changed.

Well.

Maybe that wasn't entirely true.

They existed here in his cabin, the three of them.

Nate would wake early, not able to sleep in no matter how hard he tried. His body had been trained to be up by five at the latest. He had no real reason to be up before the sun, but there he'd be, blinking slowly in the dark, the only light from the clock radio on the nightstand beside him, the numbers burning a dim green, switching from 5:01 to 5:02 even as he watched.

And he'd lie there, staring up at the ceiling, listening to the cabin settle quietly around him. He'd think the muddled thoughts of those still waking up: *What do I have to do today* and *Where am I?* and *Oh, that's right, that's right, everything is weird and different. I'm in Oregon. I'm in a cabin in the woods with people I don't know who are running from something they aren't explaining—*

Everything would be startlingly clear then.

✦

Alex was always up and in the kitchen before he was.

The second morning after Nate had arrived at the cabin, Alex hadn't said anything as Nate had come into the kitchen. He'd been drinking coffee at the window, staring out at the sky as it began to lighten. Nate made his own cup of coffee, pulling the mug down from the cabinet, mixing in two spoonfuls of sugar. They stood there, not speaking until Art came out an hour later, blinking blearily.

The third morning, Alex had grunted something that could have been *hello*, but Nate was mid-yawn when it'd happened, so he missed what was said. He had muttered something in return and gone to the coffeepot.

His mug was already sitting on the counter next to the sugar bowl.

He paused. Then he shook his head and went about making his coffee.

The fourth morning, the mug had been ready and waiting for him, still steaming, sugar mixed in.

"Thanks," he said.

Alex grunted in return.

Art went through the books quicker than Nate would have expected. She didn't seem picky, not necessarily perusing until something caught her eye. Instead, she'd finish one, put it back on the shelf, humming to herself under her breath before picking the next book. There was no order to the books; his mother had said she was going to organize them one day, maybe by author or subject or *something* to give some sense of order. She'd never done it. The L'Amour books were always together, though. They'd been Nate's, his mother not quite understanding his fascination with them. He was surprised she hadn't gotten rid of them after they'd found him in the cabin.

It was just another thing he would never know the answer to.

Art and Alex were outside again, skipping rocks on the lake, when Nate made a decision.

He could hear them through the open window. Art was laughing, and Alex was being Alex and saying as little as possible.

He went to their room.

His room, he reminded himself, because this was *his* cabin.

He ignored the tiny twinge of guilt.

The door was shut. For a moment, Nate wondered if it would be locked, which would be ridiculous, of course, because the bedroom doors didn't *have* locks. His dad had said they didn't need them, that nothing good ever happened behind a locked door.

And Nate, curious bastard that he was, tended to agree with that, much to his chagrin.

He stopped in front of the door, cocking his head. Listening.

He could hear Art.

They were still down by the lake.

He pushed the door open.

The room was sparsely furnished. There were the two twin beds separated by a small wooden chest. The beds were made immaculately, the matching green comforters pulled tight and folded underneath the mattress. Nate and Rick had shared this room when they'd come here for the summers, Nate always taking the bed closest to the window. Art would fit just fine. For Alex, on the other hand, the beds would be too small.

Nate didn't let himself think about that much. That way lay danger.

There was an old dresser against the far wall near the small closet. It was the same one that'd been there when Nate was a kid. The large photograph on the wall was new, a framed picture of a lighthouse shot in black-and-white. The lamp on the chest between the beds was new too.

Other than that, there wasn't anything else in the room.

Aside from two green duffel bags, one at the foot of each bed.

They were the same, a deep forest green with a silver zipper that ran down the middle. They looked military issued, something Nate had expected.

He went to the closest one first, at the foot of the bed nearest the door.

He unzipped it.

It was Alex's.

Three pairs of jeans rolled up tightly. A few shirts. Undershirts. Socks. Boxers.

Nothing else.

Nate felt almost guilty.

Almost.

He zipped the bag back up.

The contents of the second bag were more . . . colorful.

It was all clothes belonging to a little girl.

A bag of scrunchies.

There was a side pocket filled with rocks of different shapes and sizes.

And nothing else.

It almost hurt to see. He didn't know what he'd expected to find. Something, maybe. Something that could have given him any further clue as to what he was dealing with. Where they had come from. Who or what they were running from. *Something.*

Instead it was the barest of possessions.

✦

In the hall bathroom, there were two toothbrushes lying side by side next to a half-empty tube of generic toothpaste.

In the shower was a bottle of bright pink shampoo with flowers on the label. A bar of green soap sat in the soap dish.

It was like they barely existed at all.

✦

"What about school?" he asked.

Alex stared at him. "School?"

"Was she—should she be in school?" He was floundering. But he had to push. He had to. The pink shampoo made him. It meant that Alex had gotten it for her. It was the type of shampoo a dad buys for his daughter when she visits after a divorce. Like he didn't know what else to get and only got it because it looked girly.

But there was no other shampoo in the shower, and that meant he used it too.

He had to ask.

When Alex didn't answer, he said, "You're taking her back to her parents."

Alex said nothing.

"Where are they?"

"I told you," Alex said tightly. "I can't—you need to stop. You're not going to get the answers you want."

Nate backed off.

For now.

✛

They ate all their meals together.

Art insisted on it.

"People need to eat together," she told Nate the second night when he'd tried to take his meal to his room. "You don't have to be alone when others are near."

He'd thought about arguing against it.

But she had big, big eyes and she knew how to use them.

It was unfair, really.

But he'd set his plate back on the table and pulled out the chair.

Alex said nothing.

But Nate noticed he didn't take a bite of his own food until Nate did so first.

✛

Ruth didn't call back.

Nate checked.

He thought about driving down the mountain. Just to be sure.

He didn't.

✛

The weather held. The stretches of days were bright and sunny, though still cool. Sometimes Art would take her book out onto the dock and lie on her back, holding the book above her face, her oversized sunglasses blocking out the sun. She would flip through page after page.

Alex always followed her out.

He would stand at the edge of the dock, eyes scanning the tree line.

Nate could see the outline of the gun tucked into the back of his jeans.

✛

"Let me see," Nate heard Art say as he came out of his room on the afternoon of the fifth day he'd been at the cabin. He'd just woken up from a nap he hadn't meant to take, feeling particularly self-indulgent. He reminded himself he was on a vacation of sorts, though it wasn't turning out like he'd expected.

"It's fine," Alex said.

Alex was sitting at the kitchen table. Art was standing next to his chair, her hands on her hips, glaring up at him. His beard was fuller now, almost looking a little wild. He'd need to trim it soon or it'd be out of control.

"I *know* it's fine," Art said. "But it's still good to check and make sure."

"I already checked."

"I don't believe you."

He arched an eyebrow at her.

She smiled sweetly at him. Then, "Nate, would you please tell Alex to take off his shirt?"

Nate stumbled.

They both turned to look at him.

He ignored them, sure his face was bright red.

"See?" Art said. "Even Nate thinks you should."

"Leave me out of this," Nate managed to say. "Whatever you're doing, I don't want to know."

"I need to make sure his side is doing better," Art said. "And he won't let me check."

"If he says he's fine, then he's fine."

"Wow," Art said, the glare turning to Nate. "I didn't know it'd be *you* who betrayed me. Now I know what Old Man Brannagan felt when his nephew turned him over to the sheriff. Real bad, hoss. I feel real bad."

"You need to stop reading those books."

She shrugged. "I like them. Things make sense in them. Good guys are good guys. Villains are villains. The good guys always win."

"They do," Alex said quietly, and it was one of those things that meant more than he understood.

Art softened just a little. "I know. But that still won't get you out of being checked out. Come on, partner. Off with your shirt."

"Why did you wait until right this moment to ask this?" Alex asked her, glancing at Nate for some reason.

"I have no idea what you're talking about," Art said sweetly. "Are you going to do it? Or are we going to have to do this the hard way?"

Nate didn't want to know what that meant.

Alex sighed. "Fine. But this is the last time."

And he lifted his white undershirt over his head.

Nate should have looked away. He should have. It was the right thing to do.

He knew this.

But.

He looked. For strictly professional reasons. That was it. He only wanted to see how Alex was healing. It had absolutely nothing to do with the miles of skin and muscle and hair on his chest and stomach. At all. It wasn't like that for him.

It wasn't.

The bruising was almost gone. There was the barest hint of color against his skin, but that was it.

Even the scar had disappeared. Or the indent. Whatever it'd been.

Art looked pleased. "Looks just fine. Nate? What do you think?"

"Yeah," Nate said. "Yeah."

Alex grumbled at the both of them and pulled his shirt back on.

"You're getting scruffy," she said, reaching up, the tips of her fingers disappearing into the hair on his chin. "I can barely see your face anymore. Which is too bad. It's a good face."

Alex almost looked embarrassed. "I don't—it's not." He sighed. "I don't have a razor."

That hit Nate square in the chest for reasons he couldn't explain. "Why didn't you say anything?"

Alex didn't look at him. He stared down at the table. "It doesn't matter."

"He doesn't like having a beard," Art said to Nate. "He likes to be clean-shaven."

Nate said the only thing he could. "I have . . . a razor. A spare blade. Shaving foam. You can—you can use it. If you want."

Alex put his hands on the tabletop. He flexed his fingers against the wood. His brow was furrowed. He looked put out.

He was fucking aggravating.

Art cleared her throat pointedly.

"Fine," Alex said.

Art coughed loudly.

Alex's hands curled into fists. "Thank you."

After the door to the second bedroom was shut for the night, Nate went to the hall bathroom and left the razor and foam next to the sink.

Alex was in the kitchen like he always was first thing in the morning, coffee in hand.

A second mug sat filled next to the coffee maker.

He had shaved.

His face had an almost square shape to it, blunt and firm. His jawline was sharp, his neck thick. He had a small dimple in his chin.

Nate stared.

Alex snorted.

"Feel better?" Nate finally asked.

Alex shrugged. He tilted his head toward the coffee he'd made for Nate.

They drank in silence.

Art squealed when she saw him, demanding he come down to her level.

He did.

She ran her fingers over his face.

"There you are," she said. "I see you."

One of the first things he'd learned when he'd begun his internship at the *Post* was that a good journalist knew which questions to ask, but they also knew when to keep their mouths shut and observe. "You can see things you might not have if you'd wasted your time talking," Ruth had told him gruffly. "You don't always have to talk. Let others do what they do and adapt from there."

Artemis Darth Vader did not go anywhere without Alex Delgado following.

He was her protector, she'd said.

A bodyguard, he'd said.

She wanted to go outside?

That was fine.

Alex was right there behind her.

She wanted to read on the couch?

That was okay too. Alex was standing in the living room, near the window.

She was in the bathroom?

Alex was in the kitchen.

Sleeping in the bedroom?

Alex would open the door quietly, sticking his head in as if to check to make sure she hadn't disappeared in the last fifteen minutes.

He made sure she ate. Sometimes Nate made their meals. Other times, Alex did. When it was Alex, it was always from a can. He would set the bowl in front of her and made sure she took at least the first bite before he'd go back to the kitchen.

He always served himself last.

She had his attention. Always.

✦

"You can ask him," Art was whispering. "He likes us. He's not going to say no."

Alex muttered something in response, but Nate couldn't make out what it was.

"Fine." Art sighed. "I'll do it. You're so weird. Nate. Hey, Nate!"

He looked up from his laptop, where he'd been going through notes of stories that would never be written. He couldn't bring himself to trash them, though it was close.

"Yeah?"

"Can we use your washer and dryer? We don't have many clothes. We need to wash them."

Alex wouldn't look at him.

"Yeah," Nate said. "Shit, sorry. I didn't even think. Of course you can. The laundry room is down—"

"I know where it is," Art said. "When we first came here, I went through every room in the house. Alex said I was being nosy, but I was just trying to make sure no bears had gotten inside. They hadn't. Which was good. I've never seen a bear in person before, but I imagine they are quite large."

Nate just nodded, which was beginning to be his default reaction when Art said something that didn't quite land right.

She beamed at him. "Thank you! Alex. *Alex.* He said we could. Come on. Get *up.* You are so *heavy,* jeez, get up, get *up!* You promised you'd show me how to do laundry!"

Alex got up.

Art raced down the hall toward their bedroom.

Alex followed, albeit at a much slower pace.

He stopped near the table.

Nate looked up at him.

"Thank you," he said.

"Wow," Nate said. "You're getting better at that. I'm proud of you."

Alex scowled at him before going after Art.

＋

It rained.

The surface of the lake was dark.

Art stared out the window and sighed, her book forgotten on the couch.

Alex asked, "Do you have a deck of cards?"

It was the first time anyone had spoken in almost an hour. Nate looked up from his own book at Alex, who stood near the kitchen table. "What?"

"A deck of cards," he repeated. "Do you have one?"

"Uh. Yeah. There should be one in the—hold on a second."

"You don't have to—"

Nate ignored him, pushing himself off the couch. He felt Alex watching him as he walked down the hall to the closet across from the bathroom. He opened the door and pulled the metal string for the light overhead.

There were four shelves inside. The bottom held old towels.

The next shelf had spare sheets for the beds.

The third shelf had light bulbs and batteries and a couple of flashlights.

The top shelf was stacks of board games.

Sorry! Monopoly. Trivial Pursuit. Guess Who?, which had been his favorite, though no one else had liked that one much. He'd hated Trivial Pursuit since it'd been an edition from the seventies. His dad had always won whenever they'd played.

When he could convince Rick to play Guess Who?, it usually only lasted a few minutes before Rick would get bored and start to cheat.

Next to the board games were a couple of packs of playing cards.

He grabbed the one from the top and closed the closet door.

Alex was still standing in the same spot.

Art was staring out the window. The rain sluiced down the glass.

"Here," Nate said.

Alex glanced down at Nate's outstretched hand. "Thanks," he said. "It's . . . I know it's—"

Nate shrugged. "It's fine. You're welcome."

Alex nodded. Then, "Artemis."

She looked over at him.

He held the deck of cards up, shaking it slightly.

Her eyes lit up. "Where did you get those?"

"Nate had them."

"We have to play!"

He jerked his head toward the kitchen table.

Thunder rumbled overhead as she pulled out a chair and climbed onto it. He sat across from her. "You going to play?" she asked, looking up at Nate.

He shook his head, unsure of what was happening.

Alex pulled the cards from the box.

He didn't set the Joker aside.

He shuffled the deck expertly. The cards sounded like the rain on the roof.

He dealt two hands until the deck was gone.

He waited as Art picked up her cards. She frowned in concentration, the number of cards too big for the size of her hands. "Cover your eyes," she told Alex.

And wonder of all wonders, he did. He reached up with one hand and put it across his eyes.

Art pushed herself up on her knees in the chair, reaching across the table and waving her hand in front of his face.

Nate swore Alex's lips twitched.

Once she appeared satisfied that Alex couldn't see, she spread her cards on the table. She picked up any pairs and discarded them to the side.

Nate knew this game. He couldn't remember the name of it, but he knew it.

She had the Joker.

She looked up at Nate. "No helping him," she ordered.

Nate could do nothing but nod.

She picked up the remaining cards and held them in front of her face, peeking over the tops. "Okay," she said. "You can look now."

Alex dropped his hand. He picked up his own cards and moved his matches back to the table.

"You can pick first," Art said. "Because I did last time."

"How generous of you," Alex said, dry as dust. He reached out and took a card from her, the one that stuck out above all the others that Art obviously wanted him to take.

It was the Joker.

She cackled.

Old Maid. These two people whom Nathaniel Cartwright had been living with for a week now, who were on the run from something unknown, were sitting in his kitchen in a cabin in the middle of nowhere playing Old Maid.

Art won the first game.

And the second.

And the third.

By the time they finished, the rain had stopped, and she said they needed to go outside because there was nothing like the smell in the air after the rain.

It was when she was standing by the door, Alex's hand in hers, that she turned back toward Nate. "Are you coming?"

Alex was looking at him too, waiting for his answer.

Eventually, Nate nodded.

They went outside.

Art was right. There was nothing like the smell in the air after the rain.

✝

His skin was chilled by the time they came back in. He told them he was going to take a shower to warm up.

He stood under the spray for a long time.

He wondered how much longer they were going to stay.

The water felt good on his skin.

Art had changed into a pair of sweats that looked to be a size too big for her. The bottoms had been rolled up several times. She wore a sweatshirt that said DIVA on it. She looked ridiculous.

She was standing in the hall, looking up at the photographs on the walls. He could hear Alex moving off in the kitchen.

Nate hesitated.

She knew he was there. "What are their names?" she asked.

"Art," Alex said, a warning in his voice.

"I'm just *asking*."

"It's okay," Nate said, surprised when he meant it.

Alex grunted, as he was wont to do.

"Linda," Nate said, coming to stand next to Art. "My mother. And my father was Mitchell."

She reached up and fixed a frame that was slightly off-kilter. The photograph was of a fourteen-year-old Nate standing with his parents on the dock near the cabin. Rick had taken it. Nate had a fishing pole in his hands, the tip of which was bent, the line taut in the water. His father was next to him, a net in his hand, ready for the bluegill that was on the hook. His mother was laughing, her head rocked back, her smile wide, teeth bright, eyes closed.

"And they're dead."

"Yes," Nate said.

She looked up at him, head tilted. "You still don't sound sad. Just angry. I thought when someone died, you were supposed to be sad."

"It's not like that. Not always."

"Oh. Why?"

He shouldn't be talking about this. Not with a little girl. Not with *anyone*, really. He didn't ask for this. He'd come up here wanting to be alone, wanting to deal with his grief that was more rage than anything else. He should have told her to stop asking questions. Told her to mind her own business, which, honestly, was just a fucking *hoot*, given all the questions he had for *them*.

Instead he said, "Because sometimes people don't deserve for me to feel sad over them."

"But you feel something."

"Yes."

She nodded as if she understood. He didn't know if she did. "And him?" She pointed to another photo. The first summer at the cabin. Rick had his arm slung around Nate's shoulders. They both wore shorts and tank tops. They were barefoot on the porch. There was a little troll statue his mom had bought in Roseland sitting at the bottom of the steps. It'd be broken a few years later when a great storm rolled through the mountains in the fall. His mother had been weirdly sad over it when they'd come up on the weekend to inspect the damage. The cabin was fine—just a couple of shutters off their hinges. But that damn troll had been knocked over and broken into several pieces, and she'd been *upset*.

"Rick," Nate said. "My brother."

"He doesn't look like you. Not very much."

And yeah, he'd heard *that* before, hadn't he? Rick had been the handsome one, the *cool* one, the brother who played football in the fall and basketball in the spring. He'd been popular, always with a girl on his arm and a devilish twinkle in his eye. Nate had been in the marching band. He'd played the trombone. He hadn't been very good at it.

He'd also worked for the *Shout*, the biweekly newsletter that went out at Northwest High. He'd been the intrepid reporter, chasing down leads for such riveting stories as new sod being laid down on the football field and Mr. Harrison's retirement after teaching his-

THE BONES BENEATH MY SKIN • 119

tory for thirty-nine years ("I'm old, kid, I don't know what the hell else you need for me to tell you"). He had *loved* it, had run it almost single-handedly. And yeah, it'd looked *great* on college applications, but he wasn't Rick. Oh god no. Sure, Rick had washed out playing college ball at Arizona State. Had torn his ACL his sophomore year. He was a real estate agent now. A wife. A picket fence. Three kids. Nate had only met one of them. The others he'd seen in a Christmas card he thought had been sent to him by mistake.

"He took after my father," Nate said, keeping his voice even.

"Oh," Art said. "I guess I can see that. Did he die too?"

"No."

He knew the question that was coming next. Could see it working its way through her mind and down to her lips. "How did—"

"Art. That's enough."

She had an irritated look on her face when she glanced over her shoulder at Alex. "I'm just asking questions."

"I know that. But it's not polite. Not always."

"How can we ever learn anything if we don't ask questions?"

"You have to respect boundaries."

She looked back at Nate. "Am I not respecting your boundaries?"

Nate . . . didn't know what to say to that. "It's not—I don't. I haven't seen any of them for a long time. It's . . . I don't like talking about it."

She nodded, reaching out and grabbing on to a couple of his fingers, squeezing them gently. For a moment, he thought he felt a warm pulse of *something* roll through his skin, but then it was gone. "I'm sorry."

"For?"

She shrugged. "This."

He didn't know what *this* was. "It's okay."

"Do you want to take them down?"

Yes. He did. He said, "It's not—it's fine."

"Okay. But if you change your mind, let me know. I can help. You'll have to get the ones I can't reach, but it won't take long." She frowned. "It's like a Band-Aid, right? Just gotta pull that sucker off."

"You're very strange."

Her smile was blinding. "You have no idea."

✦

It surprised him when it was Alex who asked instead.

Later that night, Nate was on the couch, a book in his lap and a little girl curled up against him, snoring loudly. Her legs were folded up underneath her. Her head was on his shoulder, her mouth hanging open. They'd been reading *The Ferguson Rifle*. Ronan Chantry's wife and son had died in a fire that he'd been blamed for, and he was heading west to try and start a new life. Art had been enthralled. She'd lasted all of ten minutes before her eyes had closed and a loud sound that no little girl should have been capable of making began falling from her mouth.

She was wearing her sunglasses too, because of course she was. They sat at an odd angle on her face. He thought about taking them off.

"What happened?" Alex asked. He was sitting at the kitchen table, a half-empty glass of water near his hand. Nate thought he had the gun, but it was out of sight. Alex never went anywhere without it.

"What?"

Alex's brow furrowed. He looked pissed off and wary and confused, all at the same time. He jerked his head toward the photographs on the wall.

"What happened to boundaries?"

Alex looked down at the table. "You're right. It's not my place."

Nate sighed. "It's fine. It's . . . complicated."

"They're dead."

"Yes."

"How complicated can that be?"

He felt irrationally angry. "My mother was murdered."

Alex didn't flinch. "That's rough."

Nate snorted. "That's one way to look at it."

"When did that happen?"

"Just after Christmas."

"Sorry."

"Thanks. I think."

Alex looked frustrated. "I—it's. I have a hard time. Sometimes. Saying . . . things."

"Wow. That was as succinct as usual."

"Nate."

"Right. Right. Sorry. That was unnecessary."

"I'm trying."

"Are you?" Nate asked. "Why?"

"Art told me I needed to." He looked faintly embarrassed.

"That was . . . blunt. Do you often do things she tells you to do?"

"Only the things that won't get her hurt."

She huffed out a little breath, smacking her lips. Nate and Alex waited, but she resumed snoring only moments later, a child-size chainsaw rumbling against Nate's shoulder. "Still."

"She wasn't wrong."

"About?"

"Trying harder. I'm not . . . good at these things."

"What things?"

Alex scowled. "You're being difficult."

"Maybe a little," Nate admitted. "But this is weird. Everything about this is weird."

"I know."

"Do you? Because I don't know if you do."

"You have no idea."

He stared at Alex for a beat too long. Alex didn't look away. Nate wanted to get a reaction out of him. Something. Anything. He said, "My parents walked in on me with someone they didn't expect when I was twenty-one. It didn't go well. That was the last time I saw them."

Alex's shoulders stiffened slightly, but that was it. "And your brother?"

"Wants nothing to do with me."

Alex shifted awkwardly in his seat. "Because of . . ."

"Yes. Because of."

"Okay."

"Okay?"

Alex shrugged. "Okay."

"That's not . . . God. You're so . . ."

"What?"

"Frustrating."

"You're not the first person that's said that."

"I don't get you."

"There's nothing to get."

Nate rolled his eyes. "You're on the run with a little girl you're protecting from people you won't tell me about. I'm pretty sure there's something."

"Don't."

"I'm not."

"You *are*," Alex snapped. "You're . . . pushing."

"Or maybe I'm trying. Just like Art told you that you needed to."

"It's not the same."

"Whatever."

Alex made a low sound in his throat like he was growling. "You're aggravating."

"Pot, kettle."

"You don't know when to keep your mouth shut."

"Not the first person who's said that about me. Won't be the last."

"I don't understand you."

"There's nothing to understand," Nate said, flip and a little cruel. He couldn't help it. He was feeling cornered, and he didn't know how they'd gotten there.

"Why are you here?" Alex asked.

"I don't know," Nate said honestly. "I don't know much about anything anymore. I thought . . ." He shook his head. "I thought I could use a change. That something would happen if I came here. I lost my job, and I . . . I don't know. I thought I'd use this place to clear my head."

"And then we were here."

"Yeah. There is that."

"I offered to leave," Alex reminded him.

"I know."

"We still could."

"Can you?" Nate asked. "Where would you go? Do you have a plan? Money? Any other place to stay?"

Alex looked uncomfortable. "I'd figure it out."

"Because of her."

"Yes."

"Because it's your job to protect her."

"Yes."

"To get her back home."

"*Yes.*"

It was close. This *thing* that was happening around him, that was happening *to* him, was almost within reach. There were things he wasn't being told. He knew that. Obviously. But everything he *had* been told had sounded plausible, regardless of how ludicrous it was. Still, it felt slightly off. He didn't have the full picture. He didn't even think he was close.

He said, "You can trust me. You know that, right?"

Alex shook his head slowly. It shouldn't have stung as much as it did. "It's not . . . it's not *you.* It's just . . . she's. She's special. More than you could ever know. And I—can't take chances. Not with her. It's not you."

Nate chuckled. "It sounds like you're breaking up with me again."

He swore he saw the smallest of smiles on Alex's face, there and then gone again. "I would, you know."

"Would what?"

"Trust you. If I could."

They didn't say much after that.

✦

She's special.

Nate would remember that. For a long time to come. That moment. Those words.

He didn't understand. Not then. Not how far it went. How far it could go. There was this girl, and there was her giant shadow. She wore oversized sunglasses and pink socks and said things like, "Hey, partner, how 'bout we mosey on outside and see what we could see on that thar dusty trail?" with a ridiculous drawl that would have been grating coming from anyone else. But from her, it was oddly charming in ways Nate couldn't quite put his finger on.

He didn't understand, no, but he followed them as they did what she'd asked. They moseyed on outside to see what they could see on that thar dusty trail. Nate wondered if he could find a cowboy hat in Roseland for her. He thought she would love it.

He didn't understand her. Or her shadow. He didn't know where they'd come from, where they were going, what was going to happen next.

But he followed them all the same.

She's special, Alex had said.

She skipped sometimes as they walked along the barely there trail that led away from the lake. She hummed to herself too, songs that almost sounded familiar. Every now and then, she'd bend over and pick up a rock, inspecting it up close before discarding it or handing it over to Alex, who would put it into his pocket without question.

Nate could see the bulge of the gun tucked into the back of his pants.

He followed them still.

He thought of his phone, turned off for a couple of days.

He'd get to it. Eventually.

There was a clearing half a mile away from the cabin. A field, really, where in late spring and early summer, wildflowers bloomed in bright colors, stretching as far as the eye could see. In warmer months, people would bring blankets and picnic baskets and eat ham sandwiches and potato salad and drink pop and lemonade.

The field was partially in bloom now as they walked into it. Tulips, mostly, red and yellow and white and a purple so dark it almost looked black.

"Wow," Art breathed. "Would you look at that."

Nate frowned. "Usually there are more by now. I know it's been drier than normal, but. Or maybe it's already past peak bloom and this is all that's left."

But that didn't seem right. Getting closer, it looked as if many of the flowers had yet to open. Maybe if they had time, they could come back here in a week or two to see if anything had changed. He wanted her—them—to see what it looked like when they were all open. When the entire field was filled with almost every color imaginable.

He'd come here with his mother. She'd been told about it by someone in Roseland. It was summer, so it wasn't like it'd been in the spring. But she'd wanted to see it anyway. Rick hadn't wanted to go, saying he didn't want to see *flowers*. His father was on the dock, fishing pole in hand, beer in a cooler buried in melting ice.

So he'd gone with her.

He would always remember the look on her face when she'd seen the field. Like someone seeing color for the very first time and unsure of how to process it. Her eyes had widened, her hand coming to her throat. She hadn't spoken for a long time, and Nate had stood by her side, wondering what it was that had taken her breath away.

He hadn't understood then.

He didn't know if he did now.

But he wanted to. He wanted Art to see it. To see if *she* would see it as his mother had. And then maybe she could explain it to him.

He walked through the field.

Alex stayed at the edge.

He heard Art following behind him, humming her quiet little song.

He didn't hear it when it happened. He was too focused on each step he took, careful to avoid crushing any flowers beneath his feet. He said, "It's different. Later, when it's all here. All the colors. When the wind blows through them. It rustles. Like bones. But bright bones, if that makes sense."

"Art," he heard Alex say. "This isn't—"

"It is," Art said. "It is."

Nate didn't turn. "It's something to see. They don't have things like this back in D.C. Not really. It's all steel and stone and potted plants that you forget to water that sit out on tiny balconies. It's a half life. A sleight of hand. An illusion."

"But it's real here," Art said.

He nodded, closing his eyes and inhaling. His allergies would probably give him hell for it later, but right now he didn't care. "It's real here."

"Is that why you came back here?" Art asked him. "To feel real?"

"I don't know."

"It's okay not to know."

"Is it?"

"I don't know."

He laughed, the tangle of knots in his chest loosening for the first time since he could remember. He turned. "It's—"

And that's all he got out.

That's all he could say.

Alex stood on the other side of the field, watching them both.

Art was only a few feet away, smiling quietly at Nate.

Behind him, the flowers had bloomed.

Every single one of them.

The entire goddamn field.

In a matter of *minutes*.

Gooseflesh prickled along his arms. His chest. His neck. He felt hot and cold at the same time. He said, "What."

"They must have been listening," Art said, shrugging slightly. "The sun is shining, and maybe they just needed some encouragement. The earth is like that, you know. It needs to hear that someone is waiting for it. People are like that too, I think."

She's special, Alex had told him.

He didn't understand it. Not then.

He allowed himself to believe she was right. That that's all it was. The sun. The fact that it was spring. It was rational. Logical . . . mostly. That was how his mind worked. He dealt in facts. Discernable truths. There was no room for flights of fancy. For esoteric bullshit about the earth *listening*. They just happened to pick the exact day, the exact hour, the exact *minute* to walk through this field on a bright, sunny morning when the flowers opened.

That was it.

Alex was watching him with an indecipherable expression.

Art pushed her sunglasses up on her nose. "You're right," she said. "It really is something."

And not for the first time, in a field of flowers, Nate wondered if any of this was real.

CHAPTER NINE

They were out of bacon.

The world was ending.

"You don't understand," Art lamented, throwing herself on the couch. "What will we do? Are we going to *starve?*"

"There's plenty of other food," Alex reminded her.

Nate didn't say anything. He hadn't said much at all since the flowers the day before.

"I *know* that, Alex," Art said. "But nothing is as good as bacon. Why can't you understand that? It's like you're being difficult on purpose."

"I'm not difficult."

"A little."

"Art."

"Alex."

"If you're hungry, there are plenty of other things to have."

"But I don't *want* other things. I want *bacon.*"

Nate said, "I can go to town. Pick up some supplies."

They turned to look at him slowly. It was probably the first time he'd spoken today, and it was already approaching noon.

"She doesn't need anything," Alex said quietly.

"Says *you.*" Art pushed herself up off the couch. "If Nate needs to run away—I mean, if he's *volunteering,* then we should let him."

He wasn't running away. Flowers bloomed all the time. That was a fact. It was how they worked. "Yes," he said. "I'm volunteering."

Alex stared at him suspiciously. "Are you—"

"You need things too," Nate reminded him. "You have to shave daily, because of the whole *grr* mountain-man thing you have going on."

"I don't have *anything* going on—"

"You shaved this morning, and you already have a five-o'clock shadow," Nate said. "You're going to dull my razors."

Alex scowled. But that was okay, Nate was used to that. He could *deal* with that. "Besides, it'll give me a chance to get some air. I didn't expect to have roommates, after all."

"Right," Art said. "Didn't expect that. We're probably getting on your nerves."

"Exactly," Nate agreed. Then, "Wait. No. Not like that."

"She doesn't need bacon," Alex said.

"Get as much as you can," Art said cheerfully. "I don't have any money, but I'm sure I can pay you back somehow."

Nate didn't want to know what that meant.

Alex got up from the kitchen table, chair scraping against the floor.

He still carried the gun.

He disappeared down the hall.

Nate wondered if he'd done something wrong. He looked at Art, who just shrugged.

Alex came back a moment later, still scowling of course. He thrust his hand out toward Nate.

In it were two twenty-dollar bills.

Nate stared at them.

"Just take it," Alex said, huffing out a breath.

Art coughed.

"It would be *nice* if you would take it," Alex said.

"Annnnnd?"

He shot a glare at Art. "And if you could get us a couple of things. A razor would be helpful."

"Do you want shampoo?" Nate blurted. "Because I know you use the pink shampoo."

Alex took a step back. "What?"

"The shampoo. In the bathroom. It's pink."

"Very girly," Art agreed.

"Fine," Alex said through gritted teeth. "Shampoo. Bacon. A razor."

"And grapes," Art said. "I would like some grapes. I've never had them before, and I read in a book a long time ago that the green kind are better than the red kind."

"You've never had grapes," Nate said faintly.

She shook her head. "I've always wanted to try them."

If he took the money and fled the house, well.

That was nobody's business but his own.

✦

There was a small grocery in Roseland. Nothing spectacular. But they had razors and bacon and shampoo and grapes.

He stood in front of the grapes for the longest time.

"Hard decision?"

Nate blinked.

A man stood next to him, looking familiar. He carried a plastic basket on his arm. It was empty. "Pardon?"

The man nodded his head toward the fruit. "You've been staring for a couple of minutes."

"Oh. Right. Sorry. Just . . . a lot on my mind."

The man smiled. "Oh, I get that. Those pipes holding up okay?"

Nate blinked. "The pipes . . . ? Oh. I'm sorry, I'm completely spacing on your name. It's been . . . a long week."

The man laughed. "No problem." He held out his hand. Nate took it, pumping up and down a couple of times. "Randy. Douglas County Public Works."

"Right," Nate said. "Sorry. Nate. Nate Cartwright."

"I remember," Randy said. "How's that dog of yours?"

"Dog?"

"The one you have at the cabin."

"I don't—" He coughed. "Right. The dog. He's, uh. He's fine. Just fine."

"What'd you say his name was again?"

"Fido."

"That's right. Fido. Funny name for a dog."

"Is it? I thought it was normal."

Randy shrugged. "Never heard of a dog actually named Fido before."

"I guess."

"Just as long as—"

"Nate! You're down here quicker than I expected."

He turned. Big Eddie Green was walking toward him, an easy grin on his face. He clapped his hand on Nate's shoulder, squeezing gently. "Yeah," Nate said. "I, uh, needed. A few things."

"Everything good up at the cabin?"

Well, no. There was a man with a gun and a girl who might have caused flowers to bloom. But that wasn't something he could say out loud, because that was *crazy*, right? He hadn't even allowed himself to *think* about it, much less say it aloud. Oh sure, he'd come to terms with the gun thing. That was just Alex. That was fine. He didn't care about that anymore. It hadn't been pointed at him in days, after all.

The flower thing, though.

That was just something else, wasn't it?

So he said, "Fine. Fine. Everything is fine."

"Good," Big Eddie said. He glanced over at Randy. "Oh, sorry. Didn't mean to interrupt. Howdy. I'm Eddie Green, but everyone calls me Big Eddie."

"Randy," he said, though he looked slightly angry.

They shook hands.

"You a friend of Nate's?" Big Eddie asked.

"No," Nate said. "He's the water guy."

"The water guy," Big Eddie repeated. "That so? Don't believe I've had the pleasure. You work for the county? Thought I knew everyone in public works. I know Jimmy's been complaining about needing someone else helping out around here. County's pretty big for just one person. They able to fit you into the budget, I guess?"

"Sure," Randy said, though his mouth was in a thin line. "Haven't been here long."

"How's Jimmy doing? Come to think of it, I haven't seen that old coot in a couple of weeks."

"He's on vacation," Randy said. "Out of town."

Big Eddie frowned. "Really? Normally he asks me to water his plants when he leaves. I didn't hear from him."

"He probably already has someone doing it for him."

"Probably," Big Eddie said. "I'll stop by, just to make sure. He gave me a key years ago. Better to be safe than sorry."

"You do that," Randy said coolly. "I'm sure he'll be grateful."

Big Eddie nodded slowly. "I'm sure he will. Nate, all right?"

Nate was sure Big Eddie was asking more than just *all right*, but he couldn't quite get where he was going with it. He couldn't know about the two waiting for him up at the cabin, right? Unless they'd come through Roseland. Alex had said a couple of days before that they'd ditched the car they'd been in but wouldn't say where. Or how. If it'd been found, couldn't it be traced back to Alex somehow?

"Yeah," Nate said. "All right." It wasn't *true*. Not exactly. But he didn't know what else to say. Not to Big Eddie. And not in front of Randy, who he didn't know from Adam. He was the water guy. That was it. He smiled weakly at Randy. "Sorry about that. What were you saying?"

"You were talking about your dog," Randy said.

"Dog?" Big Eddie asked. "I didn't see—"

Nate bumped him with his plastic basket filled with four packs of bacon, a razor, and the manliest shampoo he could find. He didn't know how he'd gotten to this point.

Big Eddie seemed to understand. "Yeah. The dog. Big fella, right?"

"Yep," Nate said, shrugging awkwardly. "You know how he is."

"Very true," Big Eddie said. He shook his head. "Well, enough talking for me. Wife's at the gas station, but she's got things to do. If I'm going to check on Jimmy, I should get to it before the missus sends a search party after me. Nate, you keep in touch, y'hear? Let me know if you need anything. Anything at all."

Nate nodded.

"Randy, it's sure nice to meet you. I hope you love this place as much as we do. There's just something about Roseland you can't find anywhere else."

"Oh, I'm sure there is," Randy said. He didn't sound too impressed.

Big Eddie squeezed Nate's shoulder again before walking away.

"Nice guy," Randy said once Big Eddie was out of earshot.

"The best, really," Nate said, and it was *awkward* now, and he didn't know why. His first thought had been that Randy was trying to hit on him maybe, however absurd that sounded. If so, he was flattered but not interested in the slightest. He had bigger things to worry about at the moment. "Well, it was nice seeing you again—"

"I get it," Randy said, taking a step closer. "It's gotta be rough, being all the way up there all by yourself."

That . . . he didn't know what to do with that. "It's all right. I'm doing okay."

"Are you?"

"Yes." Nate cocked his head. "Why?"

"Just thinking out loud, is all. That far out. Cell phones don't work. Cut off from pretty much everyone, ya know?"

"I . . . guess so?"

"You see anyone else up there?"

"No."

"You sure about that?"

"Why?"

Randy grinned. It didn't quite reach his eyes. "Just shooting the shit. Be careful up there, Mr. Cartwright. There are probably things in those woods you wouldn't expect."

He pushed by Nate, leaving him standing in the middle of the store.

✦

He was halfway back when he remembered his phone.

He fished it out of his pocket and powered it on. He'd turned it off since it'd been essentially useless up on the mountain. He'd meant to call Ruth back on the drive down, but he'd been distracted. It was stupid of him. It should have been his first priority.

The Nokia lit up.

And a moment later, the voicemail icon appeared on the screen. He called it first.

"You have . . . six . . . new messages."

He frowned.

The first message was from three days before. "Nate, it's Ruth. I need you to call me back when you get this. It's . . . Just call me back. I've got information for you."

The second message was from two days before. Ruth again.

"Nate. Your phone is going straight to voicemail. You know I hate it when you turn your phone off. You better call me back. Now."

The third message was a couple hours later. "Nate, I swear to god, if you don't call me back, your ass is grass. What the hell have you got yourself mixed up in? I found some things, okay? Old sources who told me things they shouldn't have and—call me. You need to hear this."

The fourth message was from yesterday morning. "Nate. You— Jesus Christ. Boy, if you make me get on a plane, I am going to kick your fucking *dick,* do you hear me? And I'll make you pay me back for a first-class ticket because there is no way my ass is sitting in coach."

The fifth message came yesterday afternoon. "I think they know I've been asking questions. Nate, this isn't normal. I need to hear from you. Please. Hurry."

The final message was from earlier that morning. It would have come as Nate was arguing with Alex over going to the grocery store. Ruth spoke in a furious whisper. "Nate. I don't know what's happened. There are men here. Government. They think they're slick in their expensive suits and ridiculous sunglasses. They're asking questions. I don't think they know it's me. I don't—*shit.*"

End of messages.

Nate pulled the phone slowly from his ear.

His head was pounding.

His skin was slick with sweat.

He breathed in and out.

He highlighted Ruth's name. Pressed Send.

It rang once. Twice. Three times. Four and five and—

"You've reached Ruth Davis with the *Post.* If you have this number, you know who I am. If it's important, leave a message. I'll decide if it's *truly* important enough to call you back."

He didn't leave a message.

He called again. One ring. Two. Three—

"Davis."

"Ruth."

"*Nate,* why the hell—hold on a minute. Don't you go anywhere, you hear me?"

"Yeah, I—"

He was put on hold. Muzak crackled through the phone. It felt like it stretched on for hours and hours. Then, just before he thought he'd go out of his mind, a beep sounded above the Muzak. It was a number he didn't recognize. He clicked over. "Hello?"

"It's me."

"Ruth? Why are you calling me from a different number?"

"Went to an empty office. Different phone line. Couldn't take any chances. Don't think they know about this one."

"What are you *talking* about?"

She grunted. "Boy, you are in a world of hurt. Do you know what the hell you've stepped in?"

"I don't—what's going on? What happened? Who were the men that—"

"NSA," she snapped. "Or so they claimed. Bullshit, if you ask me. I've been around here long enough to know a smokescreen when I see one. You called me here, talking about some random *man* in your house, a Marine with a little girl. And then I start looking around, putting out some feelers on an Alex Delgado, and here they are."

"Do they know it was you?"

She snorted. "Boy, I cover my ass better than that. They were looking for a man named Hank Williams."

Nate couldn't stop the grin on his face. "Mom always liked him."

"I bet she did. They wanted to see computers and such. They came to my desk, and I pointed toward my typewriter. They weren't happy."

"So much for freedom of the press."

"Oh, you and I both know that's an illusion if you go far enough. And I went *far*. Nate, there is no Alex Delgado."

He closed his eyes. "Yeah. I figured as much."

"His name is Alex Weir. And he went AWOL two weeks ago from a base in Northern California. The Marine Corps Mountain Warfare Training Center."

Nate frowned as he opened his eyes. "Why does that sound familiar?"

"You listen to the news?"

"No. Not since I've been at the cabin."

"A helicopter went down there a couple weeks back. Right around the time your Alex Weir disappeared."

"That's—I heard that on the radio. Right before I pulled into Roseland. They said it was a training exercise."

"That's what they *said*. Just like they *said* the whole base is nothing but what's in the name. A training center."

"Ruth," Nate said slowly. "What are you trying to tell me?"

She sighed. "I couldn't get deep, Nate. I tried. Lord knows I did. But the more I dug, the more doors closed. I have—*had*—some people I trusted. Old friends. But even they couldn't get very far. I haven't heard back from them, even though I've called repeatedly."

"What did you find out?"

"It's not a training center. Something big happens there, Nate. Something that no one outside is supposed to know about. Alex Weir was career. By all rights, he was exceptional. Some high-profile missions. Decorated. Until he disappeared completely ten years ago. And we're not talking like he went AWOL back then. No. He was just *gone*. Everything just *stopped* for him. He wasn't a person anymore. It wasn't until two weeks ago that he resurfaced. And *that's* when he was listed AWOL, but not by the usual channels. This is all completely in the dark. And they're looking for him."

"I don't understand," Nate said hoarsely.

"That little girl. Nate, is she . . . ?"

"Is she what?"

"I couldn't get much. They called it the Mountain. That's what the place is called. The training center is just a cover."

"But it's—"

The first day.

Alex, with his gun.

You came from the Mountain?

Nate had thought he was—off. He'd come *up* the mountain, yes. But . . . that wasn't what Alex meant, was it?

Mountain. Capitalized.

And then after.

Art.

Artemis Darth Vader.

This doesn't taste like the vegetable paste on the Mountain.

He hadn't asked what that'd meant. He hadn't *asked*.

"What about her?" Nate asked roughly. "What about the girl?"

"There wasn't any mention of a girl," Ruth said. "It was always called the Seventh Sea. S-E-A, like the ocean. Whatever it is, it's the Seventh Sea. And they're *looking*, Nate, okay? They're looking. Whatever it is, they want it back."

"I don't understand."

She laughed wildly. "You and me both, kiddo. Look at you. You get fired for getting your fucking *dick* wet, and here you are, smack dab in the middle of a story that people are probably getting killed over. Don't you see? Nate, they're *coming*. You need to get your ass in gear and *run*."

There was a storm in his head. Everything felt surreal. "I have to go."

"Goddamn you, Nate. You need to stay safe. Get as far away from that Marine and the girl as possible. I don't know what's happening, but you can't get mixed up in it—"

"More than I already am?"

"Nate. Please. I'm asking you to do this. For me. Please. Just . . . drive. As fast as you can. Head east. Hole up somewhere until this blows over. Use cash. No cards. This doesn't have to involve you. This doesn't have anything to do with you. Leave, Nate. Do it now."

He remembered the way Alex had braided Art's hair, gentle and soft, snapping near her ear for the scrunchie.

How big the sunglasses were on her face.

How Alex had been embarrassed to ask for a razor.

He's my protector.

You have to believe me when I say I would rather die than see anything happen to her. I'm doing everything I can to help her. Everything.

The way they'd both looked back at him after playing a game of Old Maid, asking if he was going to come outside with them, because nothing smelled as good as the air after it rained.

The way the flowers had bloomed.

God, the field looked like it'd been so fucking *alive*.

"I can't," he whispered.

"Oh. Nate. No. No. Please. Please don't do this."

"I have to tell them. I have to—"

"You *don't*. You don't owe them a *damn* thing!"

Ruth couldn't understand. She hadn't seen the way Alex had shown Art how to skip rocks. She hadn't had a cup of coffee waiting for her made just right by a man who didn't know how to smile. "I think I do."

"If anything happens to you, I'm going to *murder* you, do you get me?"

He laughed. It cracked right down the middle. "Yeah. God, yeah. I understand. You be safe, okay? Don't let the Man get you."

"Kiddo, I've been around these types longer than you've been alive. They don't know who they're fucking with. You call me if you can, you understand? Don't you be someone who disappears. Okay?"

"Yeah, Ruth. Thank you. I—thank you."

"Yeah, yeah, yeah. Get the fuck out of here."

But he could hear her smile.

The phone beeped in his ear.

He tossed it on the bench seat.

He headed toward the cabin, pushing the truck as fast as it could go.

+

He was almost to the turnoff when his phone rang again.

He thought about ignoring it.

He glanced down.

EDDIE across the display.

He picked it up.

The line crackled.

"Hello?"

"—ate, you—hear me?"

"Big Eddie? Yeah, I'm here. We've got a bad connection. I'm almost up—"

"—immy. He's—need the guy. They—who he is."

"What? Eddie, you're breaking up. I can't hear—"

A clear burst. "Jimmy. Nate, Jimmy is *dead*."

"Who the fuck is—the *water* guy?"

"Yes. He's been shot. It's been *days*. I called—and they don't—"

"I can't hear you! What did you say?"

"*Randy.* There is *no one named Randy employed by public works.*"

Nate's stomach twisted. "How do you know?" he asked dully.

"I called. Spoke with the big boss. Nate, who is he? Where did he come from? Did he give you a last name? They're going to want to know. The police. It's—"

"No," Nate said, his own voice sounding far away. "No. He never . . . said . . . Eddie, I've got to go. I've got to—"

"Nate, don't do this, okay? Just—stay—we'll find him—don't *move*—"

Nate threw down the phone and gunned the engine.

A minute later, he saw the sign for Herschel Lake.

✦

He went as quickly as he could up the mountain, dust kicking up in great clouds behind him. The old truck rattled and groaned as the tires bounced in potholes. He hit his head on the ceiling of the cab. His phone was knocked off the seat. The groceries rattled on the passenger-side floor.

He gritted his teeth together, pressing harder on the gas pedal. The needle crept toward forty.

He exhaled sharply when his cabin finally came into view. He started honking the horn frantically, the sound low and weak.

Alex must have heard, because the front door opened and he stepped out onto the porch, gun drawn. Art peered out from behind him, eyes wide.

Nate slammed on the brakes, the end of the truck fishtailing slightly as he came to a stop. He threw it into park before shoving the door open.

"What's wrong?" Alex asked, voice flat.

"Seventh Sea," Nate said, gasping for air. "It's about Seventh Sea."

Alex's expression hardened almost immediately. The gun was pointed in Nate's direction yet again.

"Whoa!" Nate cried, raising his hands and taking a step back. "Goddammit, Alex, I'm not—"

"How do you know that name?" Alex asked, voice cold.

"I have a contact, okay? Back in Washington. The first day I left here. When you asked if I'd made any phone calls. I lied, okay? I called my contact. Asked questions. Asked her to look up Alex Delgado."

"Uh-oh," Art breathed.

The gun didn't waver.

Nate took a step toward the porch, hands still raised. "I'm not here to hurt you. I swear. I would never do that. To you. To her. You both are my—"

"Don't," Alex snapped. "Don't you fucking say a goddamn word."

"You're my *friends*," Nate said, ignoring the warning. "The water guy."

Alex's eyes narrowed. "The guy that came up here? What about him."

"I don't think he's who he says he is. He was in town, and there was—it doesn't matter. A man is dead, and I don't know what's going on."

"Who did you call?" Alex demanded. "What the hell did you do?"

"I asked questions. I'm sorry. I didn't—I had to. It's not—"

"Alex," Art said, pulling on his pant leg.

"I *told* you," Alex growled. "I *told* you that you couldn't ask questions. That you had to take it for what it was. That you could get hurt. That you could get *her* hurt."

"I know," Nate said weakly, taking another step. "I wasn't—I didn't think. It wasn't supposed to be like that. I didn't know."

"Alex," Art said again.

"I'm doing what I'm doing for a *reason*," Alex said. "Why did you think I was—"

"*Alex*."

"*What*, Art? I'm trying to—"

"We need to go."

The barrel of the gun shook. "Are you sure?"

She nodded. "We have to hurry."

"Get to your room. Pack what you can. Now."

She glanced at Nate before disappearing into the cabin.

Alex glared at Nate once more before following her inside.

Nate froze for a moment. His heart was thundering in his chest. His throat felt tight. He could barely take a breath.

He was up the steps into the cabin before he even realized he was moving.

Alex was in the kitchen, taking cans of food from the pantry, lining them up on the counter. He ignored Nate, leaning down and grabbing the block of water bottles.

Art was in the bedroom, her duffel bag and Alex's opened on the bed. She was shoving clothes inside in big handfuls.

Nate went to his own bedroom. He didn't know what to do. Should he be packing too? Should he be trying to talk to Alex? Should he just crawl into bed and pull the comforter up over his head until all the noise around him fell away and he could pretend these past days hadn't happened?

Instead, he grabbed his own bag and began to pack.

There was no order to it. He grabbed everything. Jeans and underwear and boots. His toothbrush. His hands were shaking, and the band wrapping around his chest made it harder to breathe. His movements were jerky, almost mechanical. He could only hear Ruth's warning in his head, telling him to run, that he needed to *run*.

He heard Art grunting out in the hall. He zipped up his bag, slung it over his shoulder, and went out the bedroom door.

She was trying to drag both bags. Nate knocked her hand away on one of them and lifted it for her. Her smile was a little wobbly, but she was able to pull the remaining bag much more easily.

The kitchen was empty.

The front door was still wide open.

For a brief moment, Nate wondered if Alex had left them both behind.

He came back in through the door, a dark look on his face. The gun had been tucked away again. He saw Art. "You get everything?"

"Yeah," she said. "I think so."

"It'll have to do. Keys."

Nate blinked, unsure of what was happening.

"Nate," Alex snapped, holding out his hand. "Give me the goddamn keys."

Nate reached into his pocket. The keys pressed painfully into his skin, but he managed to pull them out. Alex snatched them out of his hand before he grabbed his duffel from Nate. He bent over to pick up Art's too. "We need to go," he told her. "You stay behind me. Hold on to the back of my shirt. You don't let go. This is just like on the Mountain, okay? We move quick. We move quiet. And we don't look back."

"Okay," she said in a small voice.

"Good. Let's go."

"Come on, Nate," she said, glancing back at him.

And Alex stopped. "What?"

"Nate's coming too."

"No," Alex said. "He's not. This is—"

"We're not leaving him," Art insisted. "We need him, Alex. He's part of this."

"You can't know that—"

"Do you trust me?"

"That's not fair," he snapped at her, and for the first time since Nate had known him, there was a heartbreaking look of *fear* on his face. Of desperation. It was naked and fierce, and Nate almost couldn't take it. "You know I trust you more than anything in this world."

"And you made me a promise."

"I know."

"Then you need to trust me now," she said. "We need him. *You* need him."

Nate thought Alex was going to argue. He looked up at Nate, scowl ever-present, but he was *panicking*. Nate hadn't thought it was possible for Alex to be anything but stoic, but here he was, eyes wide, searching Nate's face for *something*. It was a dissonance Nate hadn't prepared himself for. He'd seen Alex threaten. He'd seen him braid hair like it was the easiest thing in the world.

He wasn't supposed to be scared.

Neither of them were.

"Fine," Alex said, shaking his head. "Nate, you will do what I say when I say it. If I think there is even a *second* that you're not, I will shoot you in the head and leave your body where it lands. Do you get me?"

"Yeah." Nate could barely breathe.

"He won't shoot you." Art patted Nate on the hand. "He likes you too much for—"

"Art," Alex barked.

She rolled her eyes. "Yeah, yeah. Not the time. I got it. It's *never* the time."

"Art, behind me. Nate, behind her. We move quick. We don't stop. We're in the truck. I'm driving."

"He's really good at driving," Art said, looking up at Nate. "Especially when people are shooting at us."

"That's not as comforting as you think it is," Nate said faintly.

"I know. But it needed to be said."

Alex was at the door, slowly scanning the tree line. His stance was stiff, a duffel bag over each shoulder. Art went behind him and grabbed the tail of his flannel shirt. She looked back at Nate. "Stay close," she said. "It'll happen fast."

"What will happen fa—"

"Now," Alex said. "Move. Now."

Nate did the only thing he could.

He followed.

They were on the porch, the wood creaking beneath them. Alex stopped at the top step for a moment, looking around again. And then he was moving down the steps and onto the gravel, rocks crunching under his feet. Art was his shadow, holding tightly to his shirt. Nate felt like he was moving underwater.

Alex tossed the duffels into the back of the truck. He motioned for Nate to do the same. There were white garbage bags already sitting on the bed. It looked as if they were filled with the cans Alex had been taking from the pantry. The water was there too. Some blankets. Nate dropped his duffel next to theirs. He turned in time to see Alex lifting Art into the truck. He turned to round the back to the passenger side when—

He stopped.

A little farther down the dirt road stood a man.

"Uh," Nate said. "Alex?"

"What?"

"I think the water guy is here again."

"What the hell are you—"

Nate was shoved back behind Alex, the gun already drawn and pointing at Randy.

Art whimpered inside the truck.

"Staff Sergeant Weir," Randy said merrily. "What a pleasure it is to finally meet you."

"Who the fuck are you?" Alex asked, voice low and dangerous. He had one hand behind him, holding on to Nate's arm, keeping him in place. It took Nate a second to realize Alex was *protecting* him. He peered over Alex's shoulder to see that Randy hadn't moved. He was about twenty yards away. He looked unarmed.

"Who I am doesn't matter," Randy said. "You have something that doesn't belong to you. I'd like you to return it now. This little test has gone on long enough, I think."

"What test?"

Randy smiled. "You really think we didn't know where you were? We could have come in at any time, Weir. In fact, that was the plan to begin with. But the powers that be decided that a field test was in order. To see how the Seventh Sea would react to . . . outside stimulus. There were those of us that disagreed, but. You know how it goes. Rank and file. Rank and file. We do what we're told." His smiled widened. "Well, most of us do, anyway. You certainly caused a bit of a hullabaloo, didn't you? They weren't expecting that. Though I must commend you, as it definitely pointed out the faults in our security system. I'm sure those in charge will take that into consideration when deciding your fate. You helped us, after all."

"You can't have her."

Randy laughed. "Her? *Her?* Weir, there never has been a *her.* You know that as well as I do. And you don't get to decide what happens to *it.* It doesn't belong to you, no matter what your misplaced paternal instinct is telling you. It's tragic, don't you think?"

Alex stiffened.

Randy picked up on it almost immediately. "Oh, yes. I know all about you, Alex Weir. Your history. Where you came from. Your file is rather . . . detailed. Did you ever wonder why they picked you? Out of everyone? You were a *grunt.* A machine. Brute force without a brain. You were a weapon, and you went where you were pointed.

But you never stopped to ask *why*. Why they chose you. Why they gave you the access to it they did."

"Don't," Alex said in a thunderous voice.

Randy's eyes narrowed. "They picked you because you were broken. They picked you because they wanted to see if it would latch on to you. Like a host. Symbiotic. They wanted to see what it was capable of in the face of human grief. I think even they were surprised just how far it went. You thought you were a glorified babysitter. You didn't know that you were part of the test."

"I don't care. You can't have her. She doesn't belong to you."

"And you think it belongs to *you?*" Randy asked, sounding incredulous. "Alex. *Alex*. It's not real. None of what you're feeling is real. It is using you. It has *manipulated* you. That is not a little girl. That is a monster. It doesn't give two shits about you. It never has. In your sorrow, you just couldn't tell the difference. And for that, I am sorry."

"Who do you work for?" Alex asked.

Randy shrugged. "Does it matter? Probably not a division you've ever heard of. Let's just say I'm the one they call when something has been taken and needs to be returned."

"You're an Enforcer."

Randy arched an eyebrow. "Okay, so you *have* heard of us before. Interesting. And here I was thinking you were just a sorry grunt with dumb luck. I won't make that mistake again. I would have taken it from you sooner, but—well. The last few days have been enlightening, and I had my orders." He glanced over Alex's shoulder. "Mr. Cartwright. The Mafia. Really. That's what you thought. That's where your imagination took you."

"How did you—"

"You wired us when you came here," Alex growled.

"I did. Just not near the water meter. Nice of you to check, though, after I left. Can't be too careful, I'm sure. Not in this day and age when paranoia can keep you alive. But the time for all of this has come to an end, I'm afraid. I didn't expect that local to get involved. Small towns, right, Mr. Cartwright?"

"Big Eddie," Nate breathed. "You leave him alone. He's got a *family*—"

Randy waved a hand in dismissal. "I don't care about him. We'll all be long gone by the time he even thinks of you again. Mr. Cartwright, it's time for you to listen to me. You stand behind a man wanted by the United States of America for treason. He has defected and, in the process, has taken something that did not belong to him. If you don't surrender immediately, you'll be considered an accomplice. You will not like what happens then. However, if you yield, I will see to it myself that you are treated fairly. You have thirty seconds to decide. Starting now."

Nate didn't know what to do. He didn't know what they were talking about. This had nothing to do with him. He'd come here to grieve for a life lost. For the mistakes he'd made. To lick his wounds and figure out what to do next. He didn't ask for this. He didn't ask for any of this.

"If you do this," Alex said quietly, still staring straight ahead. "If you . . . I won't blame you. But you can't stop me. They can't have her. Not again. I need to get her home. Please, Nate."

"Tick tock, Mr. Cartwright," Randy called. "Twenty seconds."

Nate pressed his forehead against Alex's back. "Will they hurt her?"

"Yes."

"And they'll kill us anyway."

"Maybe. Either we die here, or we never see daylight again."

"He's not alone, is he."

Alex snorted. "You're smarter than you look."

"Asshole. Can you get us out of here?"

"I don't know. But I'm going to do everything I can."

"Five seconds, Mr. Cartwright."

He glanced into the truck. Art was watching him, head resting on her hands against the bench seat. He didn't know what was happening. He didn't know who she was or what she was supposed to be. But he couldn't stand the way the man down the road had said she wasn't a person. That she was an *it*.

So he said the only thing he could. "I'm with you. Both of you."

She smiled.

"Mr. Cartwright. You're out of time. Do you have an answer?"

"Yeah," Nate said, raising his voice. "In fact I do. Here it is. Fuck off."

The smile faded on Randy's face. "That's not a good decision, Mr. Cartwright."

"Real heartbroken over it. I don't know how I'll go on."

"That's enough," Alex hissed at him even as Art giggled, covering her mouth.

"Remember," Randy said, voice cold, "that I gave you a chance." He spun on his heel, dust kicking up around him, and began walking into the trees.

"Where the hell is he going?" Nate asked.

"Get in the truck," Alex said. "Now. We have to—"

In the distance came a faint *thumpthumpthump*.

"Shit," Alex breathed. "Now. We have to move *now*."

"Not again," Art muttered. "Didn't they learn after what happened last time?"

"What is that?" Nate asked as Alex turned and shoved him toward the truck. "What's that noise? It sounds like—" He grunted as he went sprawling inside the cab of the truck. He felt Alex shoving his flailing legs farther. Art scrambled up and over his back as Nate pulled himself in. He sat upright against the passenger door, turning to glare at Alex. "I can get in my*self*, thank you very—"

The *thumpthumpthump* grew louder. He turned slowly and looked out the back window. Art was on her knees, chin resting on the back of the bench seat.

In the distance, above the trees, were two black smudges against the bright blue sky.

"Are those . . ."

"Helicopters," Art said ominously as Alex climbed into the truck and slammed the door behind him. "Black Hawks."

"Oh," Nate managed to say. "That's . . . not good."

"Nope. They're really big. And fast."

"You're not making me feel any better."

"Hold on to something," Alex growled.

The truck roared to life and lurched almost immediately as Alex threw it into reverse. Gravel kicked up around the truck as the wheels spun briefly before catching solid ground. The truck groaned as it shot back. Alex expertly twisted the wheel, the truck spinning around until it faced the dirt road leading down to the highway. He shifted it into drive, and as soon as they'd stopped reversing, they were moving forward.

"Careful," Nate snapped as Art squawked, falling against him. He turned her around, holding her tightly at his side. "This thing doesn't exactly have a roll bar."

"I know what I'm doing," Alex said, hands tight on the steering wheel.

"He says that even when he doesn't mean it," Art said. "It's supposed to make us feel better about our chances of survival. Do you feel better? You don't look like you feel better. Your face is a little green."

"This has been a very weird day," Nate muttered, the trees flying by them out the window.

"There's going to be a roadblock," Alex said.

Art looked up at him. "I know."

"No matter what direction we go."

"I *know*, Alex."

"Which way?"

She hesitated.

"Art." Alex sounded frustrated. "I made you study those maps for a reason. We planned for this. I need you to tell me *which way*."

"East. I think . . . I think we're supposed to go east."

"Are you sure?"

"No."

"Fuck," he groaned.

"I don't like it when you curse."

"Now's not the time, Artemis."

"He says a lot of bad words when he's anxious," Art told Nate.

Nate's hands were shaking. "I don't blame him in the slightest."

They hit the tree line, the canopy thick above them. Even from inside the cab, he could still hear the thumping sound of blades spinning from somewhere overhead. Alex leaned forward, face almost against the steering wheel, peering upward. "This cover won't last long."

"Do you have a plan?" Nate asked.

Alex glanced at him. "Sort of."

"*Sort* of? What the hell is *that* supposed to—holy shit, look *out*!"

Ahead of them on the dirt road stood a row of men in full fatigues, rifles pointed in their direction.

Alex didn't slow. If anything, he pressed the gas pedal down farther.

The cab rattled around them.

"What are you doing!" Nate shouted at him. "They've got guns, Jesus Christ, they've got—"

He saw the exact moment the soldiers in front of them realized they weren't going to stop. Everything slowed down around them as a large man on the end raised his arm in the air and then brought it down in a slashing motion. There were bursts of fire from the tips of the rifles.

They weren't going to make it.

From the corner of his eye, he saw Art move forward, hand raised toward the windshield, fingers extended.

The air was sucked from the cab.

He thought his eyes were playing tricks on him. He saw the licks of fire from the ends of the automatic rifles. The windshield should have shattered. The truck should have been riddled with bullets. They should be dead.

Instead, there were sharp sounds from the front of the truck, and he saw *sparks* right outside the windshield, as if the bullets were *ricocheting* off some invisible wall. He cringed at the sounds, sure that what he was seeing wasn't real, that any moment the windshield would shatter around them, the bullets entering their heads, splattering the back window with bits of skull and brain.

It didn't happen.

The men in front of them began to shout, lowering their rifles.

Alex pressed the gas pedal down harder.

The soldiers began to move, shoving one another to the side.

The last few managed to jump out of the way right before the truck plowed into them.

Alex kept a tight grip on the steering wheel as they took a soft curve at speeds that could have caused the truck to flip.

Art sighed and sat back down in the seat, lowering her hand.

Nate said, "What—I don't—What is—I can't."

"You okay?" Alex asked.

"I don't know," Nate said, voice high-pitched and frantic.

"I wasn't talking to you. Art?"

"I'm fine," she said, shaking her head. "That won't be all of them."

"Oh," Alex said, "I'm counting on it."

Nate stared at both of them.

Art patted his knee. "So later, after we escape the bad men with the guns and the helicopters, we probably should tell you that I'm pretty much not from around here. And by around here, I mean this planet." She paused, considering. "Or even this galaxy, if we're being specific."

"*Art*," Alex snarled.

She winced. "Oops. That didn't come out like I meant it to. My bad. I really need to work on my timing."

"Space princess," Nate breathed.

She grinned at him. "You remembered! How fun."

He managed to roll down the window before vomiting.

✦

They didn't talk much until they neared the highway. The sounds of the helicopters never left, though it seemed as if they were keeping their distance.

"Turning left will take us into town," Art said, glancing at Nate warily as if she thought he was going to throw up again. She hadn't seemed too fond of that if the look on her face had meant anything. "We could probably avoid it and go around."

"And right?" Alex asked.

"Will take us farther into the mountains. North. But we'll eventually be able to go east. There's not much that way."

"Fewer people."

She hummed. "Fewer bystanders."

"They're going to be waiting for us."

"I know."

"Can you handle it?"

"I've been resting. I'll be okay."

"The flowers."

She sighed. "I didn't mean to. I just wanted to see Nate smile."

They both glanced at him.

He was as far away from them as he could be and still be inside the truck. He was plastered against the passenger door, eyes wide. His mouth tasted disgusting, and he was pretty sure there was a drying string of bile on his chin. But that was the least of his worries. Everything else had faded into the background. His sole focus was on the two people in the truck with him.

"You okay?" Art asked him.

He nodded once.

"You don't look okay."

That was probably an understatement.

"I think I broke him," she said with a frown.

"You did that on purpose," Alex said through gritted teeth.

"I just stopped the car from filling up with bullets. I had to tell him *something*."

"Jesus Christ," Alex muttered. "Look, we're—"

The trees fell away beside them.

They were almost to the highway.

"Right?" Alex asked.

"Right," Art said.

They hit the road at the same speed they'd been traveling. Nate tried to make a sound—*anything* to remind them that the highway wasn't *that* wide and the other side had a metal barrier thing before it dropped into *nothing*—but the only thing that came out was a thin rush of air. Alex spun the steering wheel hand over hand, and the truck felt like it was *leaning* to the left. Nate was sure that for a moment, they weren't on all four tires. Somehow Alex managed to maintain control of the truck and straighten it out, the back end fishtailing slightly before he crossed the yellow line back to the right side of the road.

Nate knew there wasn't much farther up into the mountains. A few towns, though they had to be an hour or so away. He thought one of them was called Green Creek, really nothing more than a village. He'd been there once when his mother and father had gotten the itch to explore farther into the mountains. The road leading up was winding, with pullouts every few miles for tourists.

And currently, it was empty.

No blockades. At least none that he could see.

As if she could read his mind, Art said, "Oh they'll be there. You can count on that, partner. We're the frontier settlers trying to save our land from the big, bad gang of bandits trying to take it over, I reckon."

He gaped at her.

She winked at him.

"Not helping," Alex said.

"I'm trying to keep him *calm*—"

A loud roar rattled the cab as two Black Hawk helicopters flew overhead, so low that Nate thought they could have scraped the top of the truck. He shouted at the sight of them, head hitting the window as he jerked away. A bright flash of pain shot through his skull, eyes narrowed as he watched the helicopters fly ahead of them.

He thought Alex would slow. Would stop. Would turn the fucking truck around and drive in the opposite direction of the helicopters that rounded the corner ahead.

He didn't.

If anything, he went faster.

"You're both fucking insane," he managed to say.

"It's a good thing you're not a doctor, because insanity isn't a medical diagnosis," Art said. "You should stick with what you know."

They rounded the corner.

Down the road, maybe a quarter of a mile, was the blockade.

The highway wasn't anything big. One lane in either direction. Most of the time in the winter, the roads were closed to everyone but residents. They were plowed when the county could get to it. Sometimes the towns in the higher elevations were cut off for a couple of weeks at a time before the roads became passable again. But the people were used to it. They knew the risks of living so far into the Cascades.

Both sides of the road were blocked off. Four Humvees—two on each side of the road—faced them, headlights on. More soldiers stood in front of them, rifles raised. The left side gave way to nothing, a drop-off of at least five hundred feet to the forest below. The right was a sharp rock face. There was no way they'd be able to get up and through.

The helicopters had made a wide arc, circling back and hovering a dozen yards above the Humvees. Stunted bushes on the rock whipped back and forth from the force of the spinning rotor blades.

There was no way through.

"We're going to die," Nate said. "We're definitely going to die."

"We're not going to die," Alex snapped at him.

He didn't slow.

He sped up.

Nate glanced over in shock to see the speedometer climbing above forty.

"Art," Alex said. "We only get one shot at this."

"I know," she said, voice dreamy and soft. She climbed to her knees, leaning forward, hands flat against the dashboard.

"Hold on." Alex glanced at Nate, a thin sheen of sweat on his forehead.

"To *what?*" Nate demanded. "What are you—"

The truck began to vibrate.

Nate could feel it down to his bones. It felt like his skin was crawling.

There was a pulse of *something* that emanated from the little girl sitting next to him. He thought he saw the air ripple in front of the truck, hurtling toward the blockade. They were so close that he could see the whites of the soldiers' eyes, and he tried to look away, tried to steel himself for the impact and—

The rippling air struck the soldiers in front of the Humvees. They were knocked off their feet, spinning into the air, rifles falling from their hands. It looked as if they were *floating* when the rippling *something* struck two of the Humvees behind them. The hoods crumpled in a shriek of metal they could hear from inside the cab of the truck. The windshields cracked, then shattered, chunks of glass spiraling off, glittering in the sunlight.

They were so fucking *close and—*

The two Humvees shot up into the air, striking the bottoms of the helicopters, causing them to list alarmingly close to each other. The rotor blades began to brush together, sparks shooting out and raining down.

They hit the blockade a split second later.

Nate looked out his window.

It was a storm of steel and fire. The passenger-side mirror snapped off when it struck one of the remaining Humvees. There was the screech of metal against metal. Nate jerked his head away from the door, sure the passenger window would break.

It didn't.

One moment they were in the middle of the blockade, surrounded by fire and men spinning off through the air, and the next they were through.

He turned to look out the back window in time to see the Humvees that had crashed into the helicopters fall back onto the ground and explode with a dull *fwump*, shrapnel flying, black smoke curling. The helicopters were spinning out of control, looking as if they were about to collide at any moment.

And then the truck rounded another corner and the destruction behind them disappeared.

Nate turned back around slowly.

Art rolled her shoulders slightly as she pushed back from the dashboard.

Alex said something to her, and she responded, but for the life of him, Nate couldn't make out a single word they said.

His focus was on the two small, perfect handprints embedded into the dashboard.

They drove on.

CHAPTER TEN

It was dusk before he found his voice again.

They'd been driving for hours, mostly in silence. They'd passed by Green Creek without stopping. There was a turnoff for another town called Abby, but it was thirty miles off to the east. They hadn't seen another car in a long while.

At one point—and Nate couldn't be sure when because time had lost all meaning for him—Alex had demanded Nate hand over his cell phone. He didn't argue. He didn't even *think* to argue. Once Alex had it, he rolled down his window and tossed the phone outside.

Nate thought about arguing with him, demanding to know why the hell he'd done that. Because Nate *needed* his phone, right? How else would Ruth know he was alive? How else would Big Eddie call him after hearing of the mess up on the mountain?

But he couldn't even find the strength to do that, because it hit him then that those were the only two people in the world that would even know he was gone. No one else would care. That . . . didn't hurt as much as it should have. He figured it was because he was numb.

It probably didn't help that Art sat between them, staring at him and barely blinking.

Sometimes he stared right back, trying to see something, *anything* that would show him how full of shit she was. How full of shit *both* of them were. But he couldn't find a thing. Not that he knew what he was looking for, anyway.

Other times he ignored her outright, knuckles white as he held on to his own knees, knowing there'd probably be bruises later but not caring in the slightest. He had to hold on to something to keep from flying apart.

He tried to form thoughts. Some sense of order. But everything came in fragments, shards of a whole he couldn't quite put together. He knew the way the world worked. He'd seen its teeth, its sharp edges, but there was an *order* to it. There was a *reason*. Maybe he wouldn't always know said reason, but he was at least comfortable in the knowledge that it was there. All he had to do was dig for it. Ask the questions that needed to be asked. Push the people that needed to be pushed.

This.

This was outside of the order Nathaniel Cartwright knew.

This was in a realm of chaos, and he couldn't find his way out of it.

Art still stared at him anyway.

He didn't know if she was reading his mind.

He didn't know if she *could* read his mind.

He didn't know what she could do.

Alex stared straight ahead, the ever-present scowl deep on his face.

Nate found himself not giving two shits right at that moment.

So it was *surprising* when he was finally able to find his voice again. He hadn't been expecting it. He was still lost in the storm in his head. But then he opened his mouth and said, "Pull over."

Alex looked startled. "We don't have time—"

"Pull over."

"Nate, I can't—"

"Pull over!" he bellowed, slamming his hands against the dashboard, fingers grazing the imprints left by the girl sitting next to him. *"Pull over! Pull over! Pull—"*

"Do it," Art said, cocking her head at Nate. "Please."

Alex snarled at her but did as she asked. There was a pull-off up ahead on the right, a widening of the road meant for slower vehicles to stop and let others pass. Nate was out of the truck even before it had stopped moving, stumbling a little as his feet hit the pavement. His legs felt numb—hell, his entire *body* was numb—and he was sure he'd go down. Somehow he was able to remain upright. He sucked in great gasps of air, trying to fill his lungs as much as possible, chest expanding so much that it almost *hurt*.

"I think he's hyperventilating," he heard Art say from inside the truck, and he struggled to not start laughing hysterically. If he did, he'd probably never stop. "I saw someone do that once in front of me. It was before you."

He didn't hear Alex's response because he was walking around the back of the truck, squinting against the brightness of the tail-lights. Nate crossed the blacktop to the other side of the highway until he hit the opposite guardrail. He put his hands on it. The metal was cold against his skin. It was almost shocking, and it grounded him.

He breathed in through his nose and out through his mouth.

Below him, he could see the forest stretching out, the canopy blocking his view of the ground. The sun had mostly set, the sky orange and fading toward the darkest blue. Stars were beginning to appear overhead and—

So later, after we escape the bad men with the guns and the helicopters, we probably should tell you that I'm pretty much not from around here. And by around here, I mean this planet.

That set him off all over again.

He wasn't sure how long he'd been bent over, gagging even though nothing was coming up, when he felt a hand on his back. He flinched against the touch, but it was firm and warm, rubbing in a slow circle.

It wasn't the hand of a little girl.

He opened his eyes.

Alex stood next to him, a wary look on his face. One hand was on Nate, the other held a water bottle.

"That for me?" Nate asked hoarsely.

"Figured you needed it. Bad taste in your mouth."

Nate nodded. He took the water bottle but didn't open it. Not yet. "Art?"

"In the truck. She's . . . She didn't want to make it worse."

Nate appreciated that.

"Are you attached to the truck?"

Nate didn't know what that meant. "What?"

"The truck. You said . . . your parents. They left it to you. After they died."

"Yeah. Right. I don't—"

"We need to get rid of it."

"I don't understand." He was breathing evenly now, but the world was still blurred around the edges like he was caught in a dream.

"They know what to look for. The plates. The make and model. It'll be easy for them to track us. They'll put out a BOLO to the local cops."

That . . . wasn't helping Nate feel any better. "You're saying we have to ditch it."

"Yes."

"And then . . . what?"

"Find another car."

"You mean steal one."

"Yes."

Nate stepped away from him. Alex's hand fell back to his side. "But that's *illegal*."

Alex stared at him. "That's not a priority right now."

"Right," Nate said, feeling the panic starting to rise again. "My bad. I forgot. What's grand theft auto in the face of a little girl lifting three-thousand-pound vehicles and throwing them at helicopters."

"Exactly. I'm glad we're on the same page. You should drink the water."

For a split second, Nate thought about chucking the water bottle at Alex's head, just to be defiant. It was a close thing.

He opened the water bottle instead.

The water felt good going down.

His mouth still tasted bitter, but there wasn't much he could do about that now.

He had questions. Of course he did. Too many of them. He didn't know where to start. He needed answers. He was rational. He liked things in order. If there was a mystery, he could solve it, because *everything* could be solved if you went after it long enough. He was tenacious. Once he got that itch under his skin, he would pick at it until it bled just to see how far it went.

But for the life of him, he couldn't find the words now. "No. The truck. It's not—it doesn't mean anything."

"Good," Alex said.

"What if I'd said it had? Meant something, that is."

Alex shrugged. "I would have told you that you needed to get over it."

"You're an asshole."

"I know."

He had to ask *something*. "What is—"

Alex shook his head. "Not now. We have to keep moving. Later. Okay?"

No. That wasn't okay. Nothing about this was okay. But Nate nodded.

Alex went back to the truck. Nate could see Art watching him through the windshield.

He could run. Right now. While Alex was distracted, he could run. He wasn't in the greatest of shape, but he could be fast when he needed to. Head back toward where they'd come from. Back toward the soldiers. Because soldiers were good, right? They were good people who did brave things and Nate could trust them. They would take him in, and everything would make sense again.

He glanced back down the road.

He wondered what had happened to the helicopters. If they'd crashed.

Like that helicopter in California. During the training exercise that wasn't a training exercise.

Something big happened there, Ruth whispered in his ear. *Something that no one outside is supposed to know about.*

So many questions.

A mystery.

An itch under his skin.

He didn't run down the road.

He went to the truck.

Art was smiling at him as he opened the passenger door. "You made the right choice."

He didn't know what to say to that.

✦

There was a bar, a roadhouse in the middle of nowhere. Nate didn't know where they were. The sun was long gone.

A cluster of motorcycles was parked outside the bar. A few trucks. Old neon signs hung on splintered wood, buzzing brightly in the dark. Loud music came from inside, drums and guitars.

"How quaint," Art said. "Maybe we should go inside. We've been on the trail a long time. I sure could use a sarsaparilla."

"We're not going inside," Alex said.

She folded her arms and pouted. "You never let me do anything fun."

He ignored her. "That one," he said. "Near the back. The Chevy C/K."

"Why that one?" Nate asked, peering out into the dark. It looked old. It had a black paint job that had seen better days. The hood was rusted. The tires looked a little low. There was a Confederate flag in the back window. It was everything Nate thought you'd find in a backwoods bar in the middle of the mountains.

"Dust on the windshield."

"And?"

"It hasn't been moved in a few days."

"Maybe because it doesn't work."

"We'll find out."

"We don't even have *keys* for it."

"Have you never stolen a car before?" Art asked, squinting up at him.

"No," Nate said. "Never really came up."

"Oh. Well. We won't need the keys. I can hot-wire it. Alex taught me."

Nate didn't know what to do with that. So he did nothing.

Alex pulled the truck into the gravel parking lot, turning off the headlights. There was no one outside the bar. They drove toward the back and stopped when they were next to the C/K. Alex put the truck in park. "Art and I will take the Chevy. Nate, you take the truck. Follow us out of here, and we'll stop farther down the road and transfer everything."

"Don't drive away," Art said, eyes wide as she stared at Nate. "If you do, there is nowhere you can run where I couldn't find you."

Nate gaped at her.

"Knock it off," Alex said, cuffing the back of her head.

"I was just kidding!"

"Does he look like he knows that?"

"It's not *my* fault Nate's mind is being expanded in ways he never expected. The same thing happened to you when—"

"Let's go."

Art grumbled under her breath as she followed Alex out of the truck, scooching along the seat. Alex helped her down, and she took off toward the C/K. Before he closed the door, Alex looked back at Nate. "She's just joking."

Nate nodded dumbly.

"But don't drive away. Because I will find you."

Nate nodded again.

Alex closed the door.

Nate shifted across the bench seat. He put his hands on the steering wheel.

He almost drove away.

Instead, he watched Alex and Art through the windshield. They stood on the driver's side of the C/K. Alex lifted the handle. It was locked. He said something to Art, but Nate couldn't hear. He picked her up, lifting her to the door. Art put her hand on the handle. There was a beat where she didn't move, and then she pulled the handle.

The door opened.

She grinned up at Alex.

Nate almost drove away again.

Art climbed into the truck through the driver's door, all awkward limbs as she went from one seat to the other. Alex followed her, closing the C/K's door behind him. He almost looked too big to fit in the truck. Both Art and Alex bent over the front console, arms moving.

A moment later, the truck roared to life.

Art sat back up and gave Nate a thumbs-up through the window.

Nate didn't give a thumbs-up back. He didn't know how to act toward a girl who could stop bullets in midair.

And yet, when they pulled out of the gravel parking lot, Nate followed the taillights in front of him.

His skin was itching something awful.

+

"Should we say something?" Art asked.

She was standing next to Nate, who was staring at his father's truck. Alex was transferring everything to the C/K. The bar was miles behind them. They had stopped outside of a town called Mason's Corner. There was a bridge that went over a river. The embankments were steep.

Art tugged on his hand.

He looked down at her.

"Should we say something?" she asked again.

"About what?"

"Your truck."

"Why?"

She frowned. "Because we have to leave it behind. Like we left the cabin."

"I don't understand."

"These things were your things. That were given to you. And now they're being taken away from you."

He struggled to find the right words. He wondered if he should be speaking to her at all. "It's not . . . that isn't what—" He sighed. "It doesn't matter."

"Why?"

"They're just . . . things. I don't know if I would have kept them anyway."

"Those photographs on the wall. You don't miss them?"

He shook his head. "That was . . . an old life. One that's not mine, not anymore. It didn't—I don't know that it ever belonged to me. It wasn't real."

"Because it's just . . . things."

"Yes."

She nodded slowly. "I think I get that." She glanced at Alex. "He's not just a thing. He's not a photograph. He's real. He's mine. That's why I take him with me." She tugged on his hand again, her hand so small in his. "And that's why we took you with us. Can I tell you a secret?"

Nate didn't know if he could handle another secret. He was struggling with the last one. "Uh—"

"I took some of your books."

"Oh . . . kay?"

"I put them in my bag."

"That's . . . fine."

"I felt bad about it."

"You . . . can feel bad?"

She grinned up at him. "Oh sure. I can feel lots of things. I feel so bad right now. But I really wanted the books, and I knew if we had to leave fast, there wouldn't be time, so I kept putting books in the bag Alex got for me. Sorry. Wow. I feel better. Thank you."

"You're welcome?"

Alex finished transferring everything they had left to the C/K. He told them to get in the truck, but Art shook her head. "We have to say something."

"About what?" He was scowling again.

"About the truck. Nate is sad because we have to leave it behind, and he doesn't have anything left besides us."

Alex got a strange look on his face.

"I'm not *sad*," Nate said, pulling his hand from Art's.

"Kind of sad," Art said. "If you don't want to, I can. Dear Truck, thank you for helping us escape the bandits trying to take over our valley—"

"And that's enough," Alex said. "We need to move. Nate, put the truck in neutral."

"Why?" Nate asked. "Aren't we just going to leave it—"

"We're going to crash it," Art said gleefully.

And that's exactly what they did. Nate, against his better judg-ment, put the truck in neutral. He pushed against the open door. Alex was at the rear of the truck, hands flat against the tailgate. Art helped by pushing Alex's legs.

The truck rolled forward.

It was easier than Nate expected it to be. One moment the truck began to roll, and the next, it was gone over the edge. They watched as it bounced down the hill, knocking down young trees. Somehow, it didn't flip. It ended nose down in the river below.

"I thought there'd be an explosion," Art said mournfully. "I set my expectations far too high."

"Are you okay?" Alex asked him.

"I have no idea," Nate said, staring down at his father's truck.

They didn't stop until the sky was beginning to lighten the next morning. And even then, it was only because Art told Alex that if he fell asleep at the wheel and killed them all, it'd defeat the purpose of running away from the soldiers and the helicopters. Alex looked as if he was going to try and argue but ended up yawning instead.

"See?" Art said. "Nate doesn't want to die either. Right, Nate?"

"Right," Nate said.

"Fine," Alex muttered. "I'll find something."

There was an old motel that had seen far better days, but the VACANCY sign was lit up, and Nate's eyes felt as if they were filled with sand. He didn't think he'd sleep, but he needed to get out of the truck for a little while before he cracked in two.

Alex told them to wait in the truck.

"Do you even have money?" Nate blurted. "You can just take my card and—"

Alex snorted. "You can't use your cards. Ever. In fact, you need to get rid of them. Everything is cash only from this point on."

Nate blinked. "Why?"

"Because a credit card can be tracked," Alex said slowly, as if he thought Nate was an idiot. "And the whole point of this is to *not* be tracked. I have money. It'll last. For now."

He shut the door behind him, leaving Art and Nate in the semi-darkness.

What happened when this was all over? He could go back to . . . whatever his life had been before, right? Yeah, he'd been living a half life the past couple of months. But the whole goddamn point of coming to Oregon was to find his way again. When he couldn't sleep back in his last days in D.C., he imagined how things could be. He'd move to the cabin at Herschel Lake and find some way to grieve. For himself, his parents, the remains of a once-promising career. And when he'd finished, maybe he'd make his way back down to Roseland. He'd find a job in one of the shops. He'd become a townie. Or maybe he'd go a couple of towns over and work at the local newspaper, a weekly thing whose biggest stories were about Roseland getting a new traffic light or how a local 4-H club member raised a goat that won the blue ribbon at the Douglas County fair.

They were small dreams. They were the dreams of a man who couldn't fall asleep and thought about the best possible ending for himself after all that had happened.

"He's very good at this," Art told Nate after a few minutes of silence. "So you don't need to worry."

"I'm not worried."

"A little worried. You keep twitching."

"I'm not—it's fine."

"I like motels."

"Great. Wonderful."

"Do you think anyone has ever committed suicide here?"

Nate closed his eyes and wondered if there was any going back.

The room was . . . well. The nicest thing Nate could think to say was that it had four walls and a ceiling. There were two twin beds, one of which had a metal coin slot and a sign that promised MAGIC FINGERS for a quarter. There was a bland painting of a bowl of fruit on the wall, a TV with a layer of dust on the screen, and bright blue carpet with a large stain in the far corner that Nate decided he would ignore for the duration of their stay.

Art chose the bed with the Magic Fingers. She asked Alex for a quarter. Alex said he didn't have a quarter. Art put her hand flat against the coin slot. A moment later, the bed began to shake.

"Whooaaaa," she said. "That was unexpected."

Nate stood at the door, clutching his duffel bag against his chest as if it could protect him.

"You can take the other bed," Alex said gruffly. "You need to get some sleep."

"Yeah," Nate said. "You know what? Suddenly I'm not very tired.

In fact, I don't really know what I am right now, but it's definitely not tired."

"You can sit on the bed with me," Art said. "These fingers are magic. It might make you feel—oooh, a TV! I love TV."

"I know you have questions," Alex said, pushing Art toward the edge of the bed as he sat down heavily. She grabbed the remote off the nightstand between the beds and started pressing buttons. "But they'll have to wait. I need to get a few hours in before we have to get back on the road."

"Sure," Nate said, slightly hysterically. "That's fine. That's A-okay. In fact, I don't have any questions at all."

Alex snorted. "Sure." He toed off his boots before reaching behind him and pulling out his gun. He lifted the pillow and set it underneath. He scrubbed a hand over his face as he lay down. He was too big for the bed, his feet dangling off the edge. Art sat between his legs, attention focused on the TV. Alex closed his eyes and breathed through his nose.

He was asleep a moment later.

Nate stared at him in disbelief.

"He does that," Art said without looking at him. "Part of his training. He can sleep anywhere. Only takes a few seconds. It's a pretty neat trick, if you ask me."

Nate just nodded.

"He's right, though," she said, glancing at Nate. "You should sleep."

She was right. He needed to sleep. Instead he asked, "What are you?"

She smiled. "I'm your friend." She turned back to the TV. "What's this show? I've never seen it before. Why is that woman sucking on that mechanic's penis? That's not how you pay for car repairs, is it? That's certainly a strange transaction. Why doesn't she just give him money? Isn't that what currency is for?"

Sure enough, a large-breasted woman was choking on a dick belonging to a man in oil-stained overalls. That broke Nate's determination to stay right where he was. He took three steps forward, dropping his bag before snatching the remote out of Art's hands. She squawked angrily, but he ignored her, frantically trying to find the

166 · TJ KLUNE

right button. The mechanic opened his mouth to spill more fresh horror, but then the screen went dark.

Nate breathed a sigh of relief.

Art glared at him. "I was *watching* that."

"It's not for little—girls. Or whatever you are. You have to— wait. Until you're older."

She rolled her eyes. "I'm older than you," she muttered under her breath.

Nate thought his eyes were going to pop out of his head. "What did you just say?"

She smiled sweetly at him. "Nothing. Gosh, I'm tired now. I'm going to sleep too. Good night!"

He watched as she curled up between Alex's legs, her head resting against his thigh. She closed her eyes, and a moment later, she too was asleep.

"What in the actual fuck," Nate whispered.

✦

He didn't plan on sleeping. His thoughts were moving too quickly for him to even *consider* sleeping.

Which is why he was surprised when he was pulled from a deep slumber by a hand on his shoulder. He shot up, gasping, jerking away from the hand. He fell off the bed and landed face-first on the blue carpet.

It smelled medicinal.

Nate groaned as he rolled over on his back.

Alex stared down at him. His hair was wet, and he wore the same jeans he had on before, this time with a tight black tank top.

Nate wasn't prepared for such a view so early in the morning.

He closed his eyes. "What."

"You fell off the bed."

"I noticed. What time is it?"

"Two."

"In the afternoon?"

Alex sounded amused when he said, "Yes. In the afternoon. We need to get moving. You should shower before we go. I don't know the next time you'll get one."

THE BONES BENEATH MY SKIN • 167

"Great," Nate muttered. "Fantastic. Artemis was watching porn earlier."

"She told me. She asked me why the mechanic didn't just take money instead."

"I made her turn it off."

"She told me that too. She wasn't happy about it."

"She's *ten*."

Alex didn't reply.

Nate opened his eyes. Alex was still looking down at him, but there was a wary expression on his face.

Nate sighed. "She's not ten."

Alex didn't answer.

"Is there any chance I dreamed all of this? Like the helicopters and the guns and the explosions."

"It wasn't a dream."

"Dammit."

"We need to talk."

"The last time you said that to me, you told me that you were on the run trying to get a little girl back to her parents."

Alex shifted awkwardly. "That wasn't . . . entirely false."

"Oh great. Just as long as it wasn't *entirely* false."

"You wouldn't have believed me—us—at the time."

"I'm not going to like this, am I."

"I don't know. It's . . . a lot to take in. At first."

"Where is she?"

"Finishing up in the bathroom."

Nate nodded. He thought about staying right where he was, but somehow he managed to push himself up. He was surprised when Alex reached down to help him up. He stared at Alex's hand for a moment before grasping it. Alex's skin was warm. His grip was firm. He pulled Nate up swiftly. Nate overshot and lost his balance. He fell against Alex. An arm went around his back. Nate's hands were on Alex's chest. Nate swallowed thickly as he looked up at Alex and—

"Are you guys hugging?" Art asked. "That's so nice. I like hugging too. I don't know if you're doing it right, though."

Alex scowled and stepped away.

Art stood in the doorway, her braids damp, her skin a little red. Her overlarge red shirt had white lettering on it. It said LIFE WOULD BE TRAGIC IF IT WEREN'T FUNNY.

"I think we should have pancakes," Art said. "That's the food you get when you're on the run. I read that once."

Nate grabbed his bag and pushed past her without a word. The shower should have been his safe space. It was where he did all his thinking. It was where he figured shit out.

Except it looked as if there were the beginnings of mold in one tiled corner, and the water was lukewarm at best, and the *only* fucking thought that went through his head was made up of words that he never expected to hear in his lifetime.

And by around here, I mean this planet.

It was, without a doubt, one of the most frustrating showers in his life.

✦

"Wow," Art said, staring up at the waitress. She sat in the booth near the window. Alex was next to her. Nate was across from them. "You're a waitress, right?"

The woman smiled down at her. She was young and pretty, reaching up to curl a lock of yellow hair behind her ear. Her name tag said PEGGY, and she had a smile that lit up the room. "I am," she said, standing a little too close to Alex for Nate's liking. Not that it mattered, of course. Because that wasn't important in the face of so many other things. Like the fact that there was a little girl sitting across from him who apparently had superpowers.

Art leaned forward. "Are you the quintessential small-town girl waiting tables but who has dreams to make it to the big city and get signed to a record label or dance for money?"

Peggy's smile faltered.

Nate choked.

Alex smiled tightly. "She watches too much TV. Art, what did we talk about when it comes to waitresses?"

"Not to ask questions," Art said, sighing as she fiddled with a paper napkin. "Because it's none of my business if they want to dance for money."

Nate struggled to breathe.

Peggy's smile returned in full force. A hand lingered on Alex's shoulder. "That's all right. Curious thing, isn't she?"

Art frowned. "I'm not a *thing*. I'm a *person*."

"Of course," Peggy said. "Coffee for you?"

"Two coffees," Nate said. "And an orange juice."

They stared at him.

He realized it'd come out very demanding. He added, "Please."

Peggy nodded. "Will be right back with that. You let me know if you need anything. Anything at all." She sashayed away, hips swinging side to side.

"What's wrong with her?" Art asked, looking after Peggy, brow furrowed.

"She's like the woman with the mechanic," Nate said. Then, "Uh, I mean, what?"

Alex glared at him. "There's nothing wrong with her. She's just being nice."

"Huh," Art said. "The other waitress was nice, but it wasn't *that* nice. I thought all waitresses were supposed to have dreams to move to the big city. Does she want to suck on your—"

"What about waitresses already in big cities?" Nate asked, trying to change the direction of the conversation.

Art squinted at him. "I don't know. I've never been to a big city. I didn't know they had waitresses there too. I'm going to have to re-think everything I've ever learned. Nate, you may have just doomed your planet."

Nate felt himself pale almost immediately.

"She's joking," Alex grumbled.

"What's that look on your face?" Art asked. "Is that what sheer terror looks like? I mean, yesterday you looked scared because of the guns and the helicopters, but this certainly isn't *that*. I don't know if I've ever seen someone look so white before."

"Answers," Nate said. "Now. Right now. Every answer. Immediately."

"And here we are," Peggy said, appearing out of thin air. In one hand, she carried a small glass of juice. In the other, she had a pot of coffee. Nate wanted to ask her if she was aware her timing was terrible, but he managed to keep his mouth shut. She set down the juice in front of Art, who proceeded to watch it suspiciously. She poured Alex's coffee first, leaning down just a little over the table.

Alex didn't take the bait. He was looking directly at Nate.

Peggy didn't seem deterred.

She poured Nate's coffee with less cleavage involved. "Have y'all decided what you wanted to order?"

"Pancakes," Art said, poking her finger into her juice. "And bacon. In fact, please just cover my pancakes in bacon. I don't even want to be able to see pancakes because of all the bacon."

"Eggs," Alex grunted. "Scrambled. Toast. Sausage. Hash browns."

Peggy's hand had found his shoulder again. Nate was thankful Alex had worn another plaid shirt over the tank top. He probably would have reached over and broken her fingers if they'd been on skin.

She turned to him and arched an eyebrow. "Just the coffee," he said as politely as possible.

"He'll have the same as me," Alex told her.

Nate glared. "I'm not hungry."

"You need to eat," Alex said, jaw clenched.

"Just the coffee," Nate repeated.

"Same as me," Alex said again.

Nate's hand tightened around his coffee.

Peggy looked back and forth between them. "All right. I will . . . get that order in. Let me know if you need anything else."

No one watched her this time as she walked away.

"Do you think this juice is okay?" Art asked, watching it drip from her finger. "I don't know if I can trust waitresses now."

"It's fine," Alex said, reaching over for the little ceramic bowl that held individual packets of cream and sugar. "Drink it."

"Sir, yes, sir," Art muttered, but she just watched another drop fall from her finger back into the juice.

Nate flinched when Alex jerked the coffee mug from his hands. He took two packets of sugar and poured them into the coffee. He picked up a spoon and swirled the liquid around before shoving it back over to Nate. "You're going to eat."

Nate didn't know what to do with any of this. "You don't get to tell me what to do."

"He's a staff sergeant," Art told him. "He outranks us both. We have to do what he says, or we'll be thrown in the brig." She frowned. "Or we'll be killed. I'm not quite sure which one is worse."

"What the hell is going on?" Nate demanded in a harsh whisper. He leaned forward. He probably looked a little manic, but he was allowed after everything he'd been through. "What is this? Jesus fucking *Christ*, do you know how fucking nuts all of this is?"

"I know," Alex said slowly. "But it's not—"

"All I wanted to do was go to my goddamn *cabin*, and now I've been *kidnapped*. By squatters. Why did you kidnap me?"

Alex's eyes narrowed. "I didn't kidnap you. You could have stayed if you'd really wanted to."

"Yeah. And then been arrested by the water guy!"

"He wasn't a water guy," Art said. "He was lying. Didn't you realize that?" She looked at Alex. "Why does Nate still think he was the water guy?"

"I gave you a choice," Alex said quietly. "I didn't—you let us stay. You said we could stay."

"Oh sure," Nate said, skin crawling. "Victim blaming. Sure. That's just wonderful. Out of all the cabins in the goddamn *world*, you just happened to choose mine. Of course that's how my life works."

"He doesn't believe in destiny," Art told Alex. "I don't think he believes in very much at all."

Alex looked as if he didn't know if he could be angry or not. "I'm—it's not like—I'm *sorry*, okay? It's not like you—"

"You're *sorry*? How is that supposed to make *any* of this better—"

"I am what your kind calls an extraterrestrial," Art said. She'd found a straw somewhere, but instead of bouncing it on the table to get it out of the wrapper, she was peeling it slowly down the side. "As in not from this Earth. And I was held prisoner in the Mountain for thirty years until Alex broke me out a week before we met you." She finished with jazz hands.

Nate heard the words. Individually, he knew what each of them meant. He understood the sentences. He knew where they began and where they ended. But for the life of him, he couldn't *process* them, couldn't fit them together in the shape of something he could comprehend.

His mouth opened once, twice, but no sound came out.

"What did we talk about?" Alex asked her.

"We've talked about many things, Alex."

"Art."

She sighed. "You told me I can't just say things like that because I might break Nate."

"And what did you just do?"

"Broke Nate. But! To be *fair*, you just told me that. I never agreed to it."

"Art."

"It's for *science*, Alex. Just look at what we're learning. If, say, the test was to see how much Nate could take, we would have our answer. And the answer is not very much at all. How disappointing."

Nate took a long drink of coffee. It was hot. It burned his tongue. He winced.

"Just . . . not now," Alex said. "Not yet. Wait until we're back on the road."

"You really think having us all in an enclosed space like the truck and having this conversation is going to be a good thing?" Art asked him. She cocked her head. "Though I suppose he's already thrown up out a window once before. He'd be used to it by now if he had to do it again."

Nate tried to speak again. He failed miserably.

Art finally finished peeling the straw. She put it in the juice, stared at it for a moment, and then leaned forward slowly. She wrapped her lips around the straw, hollowed her cheeks, and drank. She sat back as she swallowed. "Okay. Nothing hurts. It wasn't poisoned."

Peggy chose that exact moment to reappear. She looked as if she'd freshened her makeup in her absence. Nate didn't know how to tell her that his entire worldview had shifted in the short minutes she'd been gone. She set down Art's plate first, before Nate's. Alex was last, of course. "There," she said. "Doesn't that just look fine, if I do say so myself."

"Bacon," Art breathed. "So much bacon."

"Thank you," Alex said, voice gruff. "We'll let you know if we need anything else."

"You do that, sugar," Peggy said, winking at him. "I'm at your beck and call."

"You really like lipstick, huh?" Art asked her.

"Pardon?"

Art shrugged. "Lipstick. You must like it. I mean, you're wearing a lot of it. Did you try and eat it too? Because it's all over your teeth. I've never worn lipstick before, but I don't think you're supposed to eat it."

Peggy blanched. "I—didn't. Enjoy your meal." She hurried away.

"That was rude," Alex told her, but even Nate could see the way his lips were twitching.

"I was merely pointing out that she had lipstick on her teeth," Art said. "It was the polite thing to do. Just because you don't know how to be polite doesn't mean I don't. Do I like sausage?" She was eyeing his plate.

"You have bacon," Alex reminded her. "Eat that."

"But I think I would like sausage."

"Give me a piece of your bacon. We can trade."

"Are you out of your *mind*? That's not—partner, you're lucky we're stuck together. Otherwise, I'd have half a mind to call you out for pistols at dawn."

Nate tried to speak. He couldn't form words.

Alex eyed him warily. "Eat your food. You're gonna need it."

Art grinned at him through a mouthful of bacon.

Somehow, Nate ate his food.

Of course, he didn't taste a single bite.

CHAPTER ELEVEN

They stayed on back roads when they could as they continued north. Alex said he didn't want to take a chance on main highways, though it might have been quicker. Before they'd left the diner, he'd switched out the license plate on the C/K with one on another truck in the parking lot. Art kept watch, whistling a jaunty tune. Nate sat in the truck, trying to keep his breakfast from making a reappearance.

He needed to ask more questions. Where they were going. What the plan was. Why they needed to go east. What planet Artemis Darth Vader had come from, and how she'd been captured thirty years before yet still managed to look as she did now. The easy questions.

He wondered if the cabin still stood or if it'd been razed to the ground by the water guy who wasn't a water guy.

He didn't know what it meant that he could think such a sentence.

Alex had switched on the radio an hour after they'd left the diner. He'd turned the dial until he found a station playing news. They talked about baseball. About the weather. About Markham-Tripp, the comet that was getting closer and closer, and man, those folks in the mountains were going to have *such* a sight, away from the light pollution of the big cities. Another three weeks and it'll be the brightest it'll *ever* be, how about that? And now, a song that's already *five years old*, can you believe *that*, it's Garth Brooks with that thunder rolls and lightning strikes.

There was nothing about soldiers outside of Roseland. About the downing of Black Hawk helicopters. About two men and a little girl on the run. Not a single word.

It was like none of it had happened at all.

Like they didn't even exist.

Nate looked out the window, watching the trees go by.

Art sometimes sang along with the radio while she read a book Alex had gotten from her bag. *Silver Canyon* this time. A gunslinger named Matt Brennan falls in love with a rancher's daughter. It wasn't Nate's favorite. Art wore her sunglasses, pushing them back up on her face every few pages. One of the lenses looked scratched. It'd probably happened during their escape.

It was early evening by the time they crossed into the Willamette National Forest. There were more clouds in the sky. If they kept going, they'd hit rain sooner rather than later.

Nate was brought out of his stupor when he felt the truck starting to slow. He blinked, looking over at Alex. He was scowling, which wasn't anything unusual. But it was deeper than Nate had seen before.

"What's wrong?" he asked, the first time he'd spoken since they'd left the diner.

Alex shook his head.

Art hummed as she folded the corner of the page and closed the book. "He's mentally preparing himself."

Nate didn't like the sound of that. "For?"

She looked up at him. He could barely make out her eyes behind the dark lenses. "The conversation we're about to have. He's worried you're not going to believe us. Or that you're going to do something to hurt me. Or leave us."

"Art," Alex warned through gritted teeth.

"What? You are."

"Maybe we should just keep driving," Nate said, fidgeting in his seat. "We don't need to talk about anything. We can just pretend that nothing happened."

Alex grunted. Nate didn't think that was any answer at all.

There was a pull-off up ahead on the right. Three wooden picnic tables sat in the grass next to a black metal trash can. Pine trees swayed in the breeze. The grass was a brighter green than Nate had ever seen before. There was no one else there.

Alex stopped the truck next to the tables. An empty paper cup sat on one of them. Red and white, the word COKE on the side. "Get out."

Nate shook his head furiously. "No. I'm fine right here, thank you."

"Nate. Get out of the truck. Now."

"Or *what?* You gonna shoot me and—oh dear god, please don't shoot me."

Alex rolled his eyes. "I'm not going to shoot you."

"He won't shoot you," Art said, patting Nate on the knee. "We like you too much to make you bleed. And besides, that would just slow us down if you were shot."

"And I could have shot you many times already," Alex said. "I don't need to start now."

"That isn't as reassuring as you think it is," Nate muttered. "Okay. *If* I get out of the truck, do you promise not to leave me here?"

"Only if you want to be left here," Alex said. He didn't sound happy.

"Okay. Um. That's . . . fine. I'll just get out now." He opened the door. The air felt heavy. He sucked in a deep breath.

"Wow," Art said. "Could you possibly move any slower?"

Jesus Christ.

He stepped out of the truck. The ground was solid beneath his feet. He could see squirrels running up tree trunks. Birds were singing. He could almost convince himself that everything was normal. That everything was fine.

Art took his hand.

He looked down at her.

"It'll be okay," she told him. "You'll see. You just need to listen, and I promise it'll be okay. I won't hurt you. I don't *want* to hurt you. And I know you don't want to hurt me. You're different. You're like Alex. He's special."

Nate didn't know what to do with that.

He allowed Art to pull him over to one of the picnic tables. She made him sit down before she went to the other side of the table. She crawled up on top of it and sat in front of Nate, legs crossed, elbows on her knees, chin in her hands. "Hi," she said as she stared at him.

"Hi," Nate managed to say in return. He tried to look away, but it was damn near impossible.

"So. Pretty crazy, right? The past couple of weeks."

"That's one way to put it."

Art smiled at him. "I know. I'm just trying to make light conversation to make you feel better."

"It's not working."

"Yeah, I'm not very good at it. There are . . . nuances I haven't yet mastered. You're very complex."

Nate chuckled weakly. "I'm really not."

"Oh, I wasn't talking about you specifically. I meant humans in general."

Nate felt like he'd been punched in the stomach. "That's . . . I . . ."

She lifted her sunglasses and set them on top of her head. "But you are too, Nate. More than you give yourself credit for." Her eyes were like the grass, so brightly green.

"Can you read my mind?" Nate blurted.

"No," Alex said gruffly, coming to stand at the edge of the table while still scanning the tree line. "She can't."

"But I am telekinetic," Art said cheerfully.

Nate wheezed.

Alex sighed. "She's . . ."

"Seventh Sea," Art said. "Do you remember saying that at the cabin?"

Nate could do nothing but nod.

"Do you know what that means?"

"No."

"It's code," Alex said. "Sea. S-E-A. Also means the letter C. As in *contact*. There was a man in the seventies. His name was Hynek. He published a book where he described a scale of contact between us and . . . others. Initially, he posited three kinds of contact." His shoulders were stiff. He looked as if he'd rather be doing anything else other than talking. It was a familiar sight, but it didn't make Nate feel any better. "The first is a visual sighting of an unidentified object less than five hundred feet away, enough to make out detail."

"This is fun," Art said. "I'm having fun."

Alex ignored her. "The second is where physical effects are felt. Animals reacting. Cars malfunctioning. Radios going on the fritz. Evidence left behind. Scorch marks. Traces of chemicals." He glanced at Nate. "Sometimes in the second level, it affects people. Paralysis. Discomfort."

Art wiggled her fingers at Nate. "Are you feeling any discomfort right now?"

"Yes," Nate said.

Art frowned at her fingers. "Huh. I didn't know I could do that. Should we see if I could paralyze you?"

Alex wasn't having any of it. "Contact of the third kind is when there are . . . beings present. Those that seem to be piloting the objects seen in the first kind. It's also called first contact."

Art sighed. "Contact of the first kind is objects seen, but contact of the third kind is seeing something *alive*, and that's also first contact. So unnecessary."

"Jesus," Nate said, voice breaking. "You're serious."

"Yes," Alex said bluntly. "I am. Extensions came after Hynek. Clarifications. Pushing it further. The fourth kind is abduction. The fifth kind is communication. The sixth kind is death of a human or animal in relation to contact."

Nate closed his eyes. "And the seventh?" Because what could be worse than abduction and death?

"The seventh is me," Art said quietly. "Though it doesn't quite fit."

"Contact of the seventh kind is a hybrid," Alex said. "Either produced sexually or by artificial methods. It's . . . *she's* not a hybrid. It's not like that with her. It's more . . . symbiotic."

"Nate," Art said.

He opened his eyes. In front of him sat a little girl. A man stood near her. They spoke of things that should be impossible. Things that shouldn't exist. Nate . . . he'd never really given much thought to such things. Oh, he knew of Roswell and the stories behind it. He knew of lights in the sky. He'd even seen a couple of episodes of that new show *X-Files*. For fuck's sake, he'd spent *years* in D.C., and he *knew* about secrets. But this wasn't something he thought about. How could it be? Because it was *bullshit*. If pressed, Nate would have said that humans were alone. That *if* such things existed, *if* there were life beyond Earth, they would be single-celled organisms on planets far, far away, in acidic oceans or buried in igneous rock. Nothing intelligent. And *if*, on the extreme off chance, there *was* intelligent life somewhere out there, he didn't think they'd come *here*. What would be the point?

He didn't believe in shadow sects of the government. In men in black. In Area 51. The world was dark enough already without those things. And there was no proof. There had never been any solid proof. Just stories. That's all they were. Stories. Yes, some mysteries needed to be solved, questions that needed to be asked, but they were earthbound with logical explanations.

Until now.

If they were to be believed.

Art cocked her head. "You're thinking too hard."

"You can't read my mind."

"No. But it's not that hard to tell. Your forehead is wrinkled. You do that when you're thinking."

"It's not—you really expect me to accept this. To take this at your word. To just . . . *believe* you. *In* you. In this."

"Do you know Cisco Grove?" Art asked, and Alex bowed his head.

"No," Nate said.

"It's in Northern California."

"I don't—"

"It's a campground. There was a man."

"Oren Schraeder," Alex said.

"Yes," Art said. "Oren Schraeder. What a lovely name. It just . . . rolls right off the tongue, doesn't it? Oren *Schraeder*. Anyway. He was a hunter. On a camping trip. He came upon something he didn't expect to see." She pointed at her chest. "Me."

"You," Nate said stupidly. "Like . . . this. Like how you are. Now."

She laughed. "No. Of course not. That would just be ridiculous. How could I look like I do now if I'd never been here before? Honestly, Nate. That's just crazy."

Nate didn't know how to answer that, so he said nothing.

"He was scared, of course. It was dark, and he'd wandered away from his campsite. He'd thought he'd do a little night hunting. He had a bow and arrow and a light attached to his head, and then he found me. I wasn't going to hurt him. I wasn't even going to try and communicate with him. But I was curious. I'd never seen one up close before." She was barely blinking. "A human."

"Oh my god," Nate said, fingernails digging into the wood of the table. "Oh my god."

She laughed. "He said the same thing. We . . . aren't shaped like you. Like anything, really. We're . . . fluid. The closest description you can understand is gaseous. Almost like liquid smoke."

"She didn't mean it," Alex said quietly. "It was recon only. Nothing more. There were others, but she'd found herself alone."

"They left me," Art said simply. "It's my fault, but I can't blame them. I was lost. I wasn't supposed to be where I was. I am young, younger than you might think. I shouldn't have been out there alone. But I—I needed to see for myself. Who you were. What you were made of. What you could be."

"This isn't real." Nate rubbed a hand over his face. "None of this is real."

"He tried to run," Art said as if he hadn't spoken at all. "And even though I knew it was wrong, I chased after him. He was very fast. But I was faster. It was . . . instinct, I think. Or a word close to it that doesn't exist in your language. I felt the need to chase."

"It's a symbiotic relationship," Alex said from the other side of the table. "Like a parasite. She . . ." He glanced at Art.

"It's okay," she said, reaching over and touching the back of his hand. "I know how it sounds. Some scary stuff."

He nodded slowly. "She infected him. Took him over. Have you ever heard of cordyceps?"

"No." Nate felt like he was floating.

"It's a fungus in nature. There's a type called *Ophiocordyceps unilateralis*. It's an entomopathogen. It infects insects, altering their behavior."

"Makes bugs go a little nutso," Art agreed, twirling a finger at the side of her head and crossing her eyes. It was so strangely endearing that Nate felt like screaming.

"It's similar to what Art is. Was. Except she doesn't have damaging effects on the host like the fungus does. She's not here to harm. She's not here to hurt."

"I don't like hurting things," she said. "It doesn't make me feel good. I was curious, that's all. Like you are."

"Oh," Nate said, eyes wide. "That's . . . that's great. That's just . . . great."

"Lights had been seen that night," Alex continued. "Above Cisco Grove. It's only a couple of hours away from the Mountain."

Art grimaced. "Talk about picking the worst spot to come to."

"The Mountain was already in play before her. It'd been set up in the late forties after the end of World War II. The original intent was to study and perfect biological warfare. There'd been a plan in place by the Japanese to use the plague as a biological weapon against civilians in San Diego in September of 1945. But the Japanese surrendered before that, and it was never enacted. The powers that be wanted to be at the forefront of such a movement so they could never be caught unaware. There was hope that by perfecting such weapons, they could also create cures. There was a front put in place, a base in Maryland started in 1943 called the United States Army Biological Warfare Laboratories." Alex looked down at his hands. "The Mountain was secret. It was meant to do all the things the base in Maryland could, but without the oversight. They weaponized anthrax. Tularemia. Brucellosis. Q fever. But that changed on September 5, 1964."

"Because of Art," Nate said, head spinning.

"Weird, right?" Art said, picking at the splintering wood of the table. "All it took was me coming here and everything changed. It's almost flattering. I mean, if you think about it that way."

"Oren Schraeder was assigned to the Mountain," Alex said flatly. "Of all the people for her to infect, she chose the one person she shouldn't."

Art rolled her eyes. "How the heck was I supposed to know? It wasn't like he was in uniform or anything. He was wearing a hat with floppy *ears*. That didn't necessarily scream *please don't possess me*."

Nate gaped at her.

She winked at him.

"The Mountain sent a convoy," Alex said. "They found Oren. He wasn't acting . . . normal."

"I didn't know how to make his legs work," Art said with a wince. "Or his arms. Or mouth. Or anything, if I'm being honest. Well. Except his bowels, which was *extremely* uncomfortable. I didn't even know how to get out. Not then. When they found us, we were lying on the ground. Oren was drooling and making weird noises, and I couldn't figure out how to make him stop. They thought he'd been attacked somehow. Or infected back at the base. They quarantined him. And brought us both back to the Mountain."

"It wasn't until they used a positron imaging scan that they saw her," Alex said. "She looked like a ghost trapped within him. Embedded into his brain. Tendrils in the gray matter. They didn't know what to make of it. Of him. Of what they were seeing. They said it was cancer. Or an infection. But nothing on the Mountain could cause what they were seeing."

"It took two years for me to be able to figure out how to make him work," Art said. "And then I started talking and—"

"They *believed* you?" Nate asked incredulously.

"What? No. Of course not. That would just be ridiculous. They thought something had happened to his brain. It wasn't until I fried their machines in the next room that they started taking me seriously." She laughed. "You should have seen the looks on their faces. It was pretty funny, looking back on it. Especially when I started to talk."

"What did you say?" Nate whispered.

She turned her face toward the sky. "I told them I'd come from a faraway place. That they weren't alone. That the universe was far bigger than any of them could have possibly imagined." She sighed. "And that I was ready to go home. If they'd just see fit to let me out, I'd be on my way and that would be that."

"They didn't," Alex said, hands in fists at his sides. "They believed her. After a time. But they didn't let her go."

"Questions," Art said. "So many questions. How and why and where and what does it all *mean*? They asked how many of us were there. Where had I come from. What our plans were. If we were hostile. If we were going to take over your planet and enslave the human race." She puffed out her cheeks. "*Take me to your leader.*"

Nate thought the sound he made was a laugh, but it felt like a sob.

"And the *tests*." Art threw up her hands. "All the tests. They poked and prodded and *inserted*. They showed me images of water and fire and earth. Of people helping others. Of women in pretty dresses and men in top hats, walking arm in arm down the street, smiles on their faces. Of atoms splitting, causing death and destruction. Of guns and sickness and men marching, arms raised. Of people dancing. That . . . I think that was my favorite. I liked it when I saw people dancing. It made me feel happy." She looked away. "I don't think I'd ever felt what it means to be happy before that."

"They don't have . . . emotions," Alex said. "Not like we do. Not that she could define in any way that they could understand. It was because of Oren that she began to feel it. He was a host, and she was the parasite, but instead of turning him into her, she began to turn into him."

"What happened to him?" Nate asked, dazed. "The man. Oren. Was he . . . in there? With you?"

She winced. "I wasn't . . . very good. It took me a long time to learn. For a while, I could hear him. But he wasn't hurting. He wasn't even really awake. It was more like . . . Do you dream, Nate?"

He nodded slowly. "Everyone does."

"Dreams are tied to how you form memories," she said. "They're . . . the things you learn. Stuff that's happened to you. The people you've met. Experiences you've had. They get lodged in your head, and you dream about them. Sometimes you dream of the fantastic. Sometimes you have nightmares. But then you wake up and you *breathe*, and everything is okay again. It was like that for Oren. He was . . . dreaming. I could feel them sometimes. He dreamed of fishing. He dreamed of a beautiful woman whispering in his ear. He dreamed of a monster chasing him through the woods." She cleared her throat. "That one was my fault. But . . . we talked. He was aware. He knew, after a while, what was happening. It was strange, really. He . . . *accepted* it. He began to become curious. About me."

"What happened to him?" Nate asked again, a cold chill running down his spine.

"He stayed as he was for years," Alex said. "He didn't . . . age. He stayed twenty-four years old for twenty years."

It was as if all the synapses in Nate's head fired at once. His mind felt whited out. Blank. He couldn't form a single coherent thought.

"It was another test," she said, and for the first time, he thought she sounded *angry*. Of all the things that had been said, of all the things he'd seen and heard, the *anger* in her voice scared him the most. It was laced with bitterness, her words more clipped and hard. "I didn't know that. I thought I could trust them. I shouldn't have, but I thought I could. Time passed differently in the Mountain. Time passes differently *everywhere* here. We don't . . . mark the passage of time. Not like you do. Not with anniversaries or parties or balloons or cake. It has a different meaning. It's . . . fluid. It can bend. It's not the straight, rigid line you think it is. Time and space never are. I—" She shook her head and looked away.

Nate watched as Alex reached up and put a hand on the back of her head. She leaned into it and closed her eyes. He was comforting her. Like he'd done it before. Like he knew what she needed.

Nate's eyes burned.

The air smelled of rain.

"It was before me," Alex said. "A year before. She . . . They called it a transfer. There was a girl. Her name was Emily. When she was nine years old, she developed encephalitis. There was nothing that could be done. She was in a coma and had been for three months. Her parents, they . . . were told she wouldn't wake up. But they persisted. They always persisted. They kept going. They kept *her* going. Until one day, they were killed when their car was T-boned by a truck at an intersection four blocks away from the hospital."

"They died instantly," Art said in a dull voice. "They felt no pain."

Alex nodded. "There was no one else. Emily had no other family. No one to worry about her. To care about what she—" Alex coughed. "They found her. I think they were looking for someone like her. Someone who wouldn't be missed. It was . . . very official, I'm told. They took Emily from the hospital in Pasadena and brought her to the Mountain."

"They told me that they wanted to see if I could help her," Art whispered. A drop of rain splashed on the left lens of her sunglasses. "Because I could . . . heal. Sometimes I could trick the body into thinking it was healing faster than it was." She shrugged. "It's the time thing again. It moves differently."

He was shot. By a jerk who wouldn't get out of the way.

"Jesus Christ," Nate said hoarsely. He looked at Alex. "You *did* get shot. You fucking bastard. Rubber bullet my goddamn *ass*."

Alex scowled at him. "I didn't know you. Would you have really believed that a little girl had healed me if I'd told you at the time?"

"I don't know if I believe you *now*."

"You do," Art said, watching him. "It's hard overcoming what you know to be true, I know. You're hardwired that way. Some more than others. But you do, Nate. You know everything we've said is the truth."

Nate shook his head furiously. "No. No, I *don't*—"

"I tried to heal her," Art said, voice flat. "I tried to do what they asked of me, but they *lied* to me. They didn't care about the girl. About Emily. They didn't give a *damn* about her. They didn't care that she had no one. That they had *stolen* her. They just wanted to see what they could do. If they could make me . . . if I could . . ." Her chest heaved.

"Electrical impulses," Alex said. "In the neurons. Across the synapses. They found if they overloaded them, if they essentially fried the brain, it would force her out. And so they did. It was a test. An experiment. A way to fight back in case the others returned for her. If others became . . . possessed."

"That's all they thought about," Art said, brow furrowed. "About *fighting back*. Like we are something to be feared. They didn't know it was already too late for me here. Too many things had changed."

"She latched on to Emily," Alex said, and Nate thought that if he could have gotten his legs to work, he'd be running away as fast as he could. "It was the only place for her to go. She wouldn't have survived for long. Too much of her had been twisted up in our genetic makeup. She wasn't . . . who she'd been before. So she did the only thing she could."

"It wasn't like Oren," Art said quietly. "Emily wasn't dreaming. It was cold and dark and empty for a long time. I almost couldn't find a way to . . . do it. But there were enough electrical impulses left, just a hint of a spark, to let me take her. Oren dreamed. Emily was already gone. It took me almost a year to open my eyes on my own. But I did it. I did it. They didn't think I could. They didn't think I *would*. But I did. I proved them all wrong. And I *scared* them because of it, even more than I already had. And I *liked* it. I *liked* that more than I should have, and it made me happy. I wanted to see it more. I wanted them to *all* be scared of me. And then he came."

"Alex," Nate said. "Alex came."

She nodded. "And things were . . . different. After that. It was a test, of course. It was always a test, but I knew that. And when you know, you have power over it. You can change the outcome. Make it how you want it. But Alex, he was . . . different than everyone else."

"You didn't like me at first," Alex said, and Nate swore he was almost smiling.

"You didn't like *me*," Art retorted. "You were mad and mean, and you said that you wanted nothing to do with me. But you still came back."

"I did."

"Why?" Nate asked.

Alex blinked. "Why what?"

"Why did you keep coming back?"

Alex shook his head, and even before he spoke again, Nate could see the walls shoring back up. "It doesn't matter," he said gruffly. "It's not about me. It's about her. It's about getting her home."

"How?" Nate asked, suddenly feeling the smallest he'd ever felt. If this were real, if this were all true, nothing would ever be the same. He wanted to think they were crazy. That they were liars. But he'd already seen things he couldn't explain when it came to Artemis Darth Vader. And no matter how he tried to force it away, it still washed over him, pulling him under.

"Don't quite know yet," Art admitted. "But they're coming back for me. I can feel it." Her voice took on a dreamy note. "It's like . . . a song in my head. I can hear them singing, and I know they'll return. I just have to wait."

And then she fell silent. Nate felt drops of rain on his head and shoulders. The storm would be on them soon. They were waiting on him. He just didn't know what to say.

Finally he said the only thing he could. "Why?"

She arched an eyebrow at him. "That's vague. Why what?"

He felt hollowed out and empty. "Why here? Why us? Why did you come here?" He brushed away a tear that spilled down his cheek.

And when she leaned forward, when she put her small hands on his face, he didn't flinch. "You think yourself alone. You think yourself lost. We wanted to show you that there was so much more than this place. We didn't come to hurt you. We didn't come to save you. Only you can do that. We came to be your friend. To make you understand that, in the end, you are never alone."

After that, Nate drifted.

✦

Another nameless motel in the middle of nowhere. They had crossed into Washington late in the evening. Nate didn't think they knew exactly where they were going, but he didn't ask. He didn't know how.

They left him alone in the motel room while they went to get food. Nate sat on the edge of one of the beds, staring down at his hands. Underneath the pale flesh of his palms, he could see the twisted shape of veins. He turned his hands over and saw the bones beneath his skin as he moved his fingers up and down.

They were giving him time. Giving him space to see what he would do. If he would even be here when they returned. It'd be easy, wouldn't it? To get up and grab his bag. To walk to the motel office and ask to use the phone. He could call the police. They wouldn't believe him at first. Who would? Maybe he wouldn't even have to tell them. Not everything. He could say they'd taken him from his home. Surely people were looking for them. Maybe they'd have Alex as a kidnapper. A man who had stolen a child from her home, and won't someone *please* help them find this little girl? He could do that. He could do that so easily. And then, if he was lucky and if it still stood, he could return to the cabin, close the door behind him, and never think about Artemis Darth Vader or Alex Weir ever again.

There was a moment when he felt his legs tense, like he was preparing to stand.

He didn't.

They brought back fried chicken. Mashed potatoes. Corn. Biscuits. Colonel Sanders smiled sagely from the side of the red-and-white bucket. Art looked relieved when Nate was in the spot they'd left him. Alex looked . . . like Alex, though his eyes did widen briefly. Art told him that she brought him food because she was *providing* for him. She had gone out and shot it her*self*, partner, and she cleaned and gutted and cooked it over an open fire under a cascade of stars in the night sky. She'd heard a lonesome coyote howl as she played her harmonica, hoss, and she hoped he was mighty hungry.

He blinked slowly at her.

She groaned loudly when she ate her first bite of fried chicken, eyes rolling back in her head. She raved that it was on par with bacon. By the time she finished, she had mashed potatoes on her cheek, and her lips were shiny with grease. Her eyes were drooping, and she leaned back on the bed, patting her stomach happily. "That's the ticket," she said. "Whatever else you guys got going on here, you did well with all the food."

Nate didn't eat much. He picked at it, but he had a hard time swallowing it down.

Alex ate perfunctorily and quickly. He kept glancing at Nate, but he didn't say a word.

Nate thought about curling up on the bed away from them and trying to sleep. He didn't know how successful he'd be.

It was Art who slept first. She'd brushed her teeth and made Alex undo her braids. Her hair was crimped and kinked as she shook it out. She'd changed into her pajamas, the same ones she'd worn every night since Nate had met her for the first time. She was asleep even as her head hit the pillow.

Nate had never felt more awake in his life.

Alex moved quietly around the room, picking up the remains of their dinner.

Nate had nothing to say to him. He didn't think he wanted to hear either of them speak again for the rest of the night.

Which is why he was surprised when he spoke. "You took her."

Alex tensed, hands freezing over the empty Styrofoam container that had held mashed potatoes before Artemis descended upon it. His fingers twitched.

"You took her from the Mountain."

"Yes."

"Why?"

Alex glanced over at him, looking as if he were gearing up for a fight. He was defiant when he said, "I would do it again."

"I'm not—"

"If I had to do it all over, I would do it again."

And Nate believed him.

"They were hurting her," Alex said, shoving empty containers into paper bags. "They weren't—it wasn't—they didn't *care* about her. Not who she was."

"But you did," Nate said quietly.

Alex didn't answer. Instead, he dropped the bags into the plastic trash bin in the corner. The room smelled like stale fried food and harsh cleaning products. Nate was getting a headache.

"I get it, okay? I—"

"No," Alex said coolly. "You don't. You don't understand the first thing about her. About me."

"I'm trying."

"Why are you still here?" Alex asked, turning around and glaring at him. "You could have left while we were gone. You could have put us behind you and *left*."

"But I didn't."

"I *know* that," Alex snapped at him, glancing at Art. She was snoring quietly. When he spoke again, his voice was lower but still charged. "I know you didn't. I don't get *why*."

"Why did you tell me about her?" Nate countered.

Alex looked frustrated. He reached up and ran a hand over his short hair. The mask he wore—the man, the soldier—was slipping again, farther than Nate had ever seen it. He wondered if Alex even knew it was happening. "Because, you—you just—you would have asked *questions*. And you wouldn't have stopped."

"So you could have made something else up," Nate said. "Like you did the first time."

Alex shook his head. "You wouldn't have believed me."

"And what makes you think I believe you now?"

"You do."

"How do you know that?"

"Because of that look on your face. That pale, wide-eyed look. I know that. I've seen it before. In the mirror after they showed me who she was for the first time. After they explained to me what I was seeing. I looked the same. You believe."

Nate swallowed thickly. "I don't know what to believe."

Alex sat on the edge of the bed, careful to keep it from shifting and disturbing Art. He reached down and began to unlace his boots.

"I thought about it."

Alex hesitated, but then lifted his foot and slid the right boot off. "I know you did."

"I thought about walking right out that door."

"I know."

"Finding a phone and calling the cops."

Alex pulled off the left boot.

"But I didn't," Nate said. "Because I couldn't make myself move. No matter how hard I tried."

"We," Alex said.

Nate turned slowly to look at him. The room was dark. Through the window, the red neon from the VACANCY sign filtered in, outlining Alex. "What?"

"Back at the cabin," Alex said, head sagging. "When he showed up the first time. The Enforcer."

"The water guy."

Alex snorted. "Yeah. Him. I should have seen that one coming. I—" He scrubbed a hand over his face. "When I saw his truck. You asked me a question. You said, what should we do?"

Nate waited.

"You didn't say *you*. You didn't say what should *I* do. You said *we*. Us. You didn't know who we were. We'd broken into your cabin. I had a gun. For all you knew, I could have been some . . . some kind of *creep*. Taking a little girl to the middle of nowhere."

"The thought did cross my mind." Nate winced. "Uh. I mean—"

Alex sighed. "I know. I don't blame you. Not for that. I—it doesn't matter. But you said *we*."

"I don't remember."

"I know. It's—you stayed."

"I did."

"Even after everything. Even with how crazy it sounds."

"Yeah."

"Why?"

"I don't know."

Alex didn't seem too happy with that answer. "How did you know? When you came back to the cabin, you said Seventh Sea. How did you know about it?"

That startled Nate. "Ruth."

Alex looked sharply at him. "Who?"

"Ruth. She's—an old friend." Nate felt his face growing hot. "I might have asked her to look you up."

Alex just stared at him.

"To be *fair*, your story about being a bodyguard sounded like bullshit, so."

"That was Art's idea," Alex muttered. "Her second one. She first wanted to tell you that she'd been kidnapped by bandits and that I'd ridden in on a white horse and rescued her."

Nate choked out a laugh. "She's . . ."

"Yeah," Alex said tiredly. "She is. What did Ruth tell you?"

"Something about Seventh Sea. About . . . you. That you'd disappeared ten years ago. Become a ghost. There were men there. They claimed to be NSA."

"They weren't NSA."

"I know. She knew that too. She covered her tracks. She'll be okay. She's faced far worse than government drones."

"They already knew about us. About you."

"That's what the water guy said. He was watching us, wasn't he? The whole time."

"I think so."

"Why?"

"Another test," Alex growled. "That's all it ever was. To see what she would do. To you. Out in the real world."

"You took her," Nate said again. "From that place. From the Mountain."

"I had to."

"You gave up everything. Your life. Your job. To get her out."

"Yes."

"Why?"

"It doesn't matter. We need to sleep."

That didn't sit well with Nate. "That's not fair."

"I don't care," Alex said, pushing himself up the bed.

"You don't get to keep shit from me. Not anymore."

"I get to do whatever the fuck I want."

"Obviously," Nate said bitterly.

"What the hell is that supposed to mean?"

"What happens after?"

"After what?"

"After *this*. After you get her to wherever she needs to go. What happens then? I just . . . go back to my life the way it was before? Go back to—" Nothing, really. Nate had absolutely nothing. The cabin had been the last thing. The truck, but that was in the bottom of a ravine. "And what about my brother?"

"What about him?"

"He has a family. If they know who I am, then they know who he is."

Alex didn't respond.

"You think about her," Nate said, voice low. "I get that. I do. I really do. But do you ever stop to think what you've done to me?"

Nothing.

"You don't, do you? Because you do whatever the fuck you want. It doesn't matter who gets in your way. You brought me into this. You made me a part of this. Everything that happens from this point on is because of you. And maybe the same thing happened to you. Maybe you didn't ask for any of this. For her. But you need to remember—"

And there it was, wasn't it? That little thing he'd forgotten in the face of everything. Randy. The water guy who wasn't a water guy. He'd known more about Alex. What had he said? His file. Alex's file. It'd been detailed and—

Did you ever wonder why they picked you? Out of everyone? Why they chose you. They picked you because you were broken.

They picked you because they wanted to see if it would latch on to you. Like a host. Symbiotic.

They wanted to see what it was capable of in the face of human grief. I think even they were surprised just how far it went. You thought you were a glorified babysitter. You didn't know that you were part of the test.

"Who was it?" Nate whispered. "Who was it that you were grieving over—"

"Don't." It was one word. A single syllable. But Nate heard everything Alex didn't say. It was a warning. A threat. Nate could push, he really could, but it wouldn't end well. For any of them.

He lay back in the bed and stared at the ceiling, feet hanging off the edge to the floor.

Shadows stretched along the walls.

He knew Alex wasn't asleep, even as the minutes ticked by.

Nate was exhausted, but he couldn't close his eyes.

Then: "I did what I had to." It was said quietly. Barely above a whisper.

Nate said nothing.

"She . . . No one deserves to be in a cage. No one."

Alex was sleeping a moment later.

Nate stayed awake long into the night.

✦

Toward dawn, he slipped from the room, leaving Art and Alex asleep in the bed.

The mountain air was cold. He could see his breath rising around his face. He pulled the collar of his jacket up and rubbed his arms.

A logging truck went by without slowing.

The motel office was dark.

There were no other cars in the parking lot. Their truck sat quietly in front of the room. Out in front of the office near the street was a large wooden electric pole.

And next to the pole was a phone booth.

Nate looked back at the motel room door he'd shut behind him. He thought about going back inside. About taking off his coat and climbing into bed, pulling the thin, scratchy comforter over his head. Of waiting until Alex rose and muttered they needed to get back on the road.

I get to do whatever the fuck I want.

Nate went to the phone booth.

The metal door screeched on its hinges as he slid it open.

He fished in the pocket of his jeans for the couple of quarters he'd found at the bottom of his duffel bag.

He dropped them into the coin slot.

He picked up the phone.

He pressed the receiver against his forehead and took a breath.

And then he dialed the number from memory.

He wasn't even sure what day it was as the call connected and began to ring over a crackling line.

In his head, he could see it. The house that he was calling. He'd been there just once. It'd been . . . before. Before his parents had found him in the cabin. Before everything had gone to shit.

It rang seven times before there was an answer, a single word thick with sleep. "Hello."

Nate couldn't find his voice.

"Hello," the voice said, sounding a little more awake. A little angrier. "Who is this? Do you know what time—"

"Ricky."

A beat of silence. Then, "Nate? Is this—what the hell?"

"Yeah."

"Why are you calling so early?" *Why are you calling at all?*

He let it go. He said, "I need you to listen. Don't talk. Just listen."

"Why are you—"

"Rick."

"What?"

"People are going to ask you questions. About me. I'm sorry for that. I know—I know you don't . . . just. Whatever they tell you is a lie. I need you to remember that. Whatever they say . . . Do you remember when you showed me how to skip rocks at the lake?"

"Nate?" He sounded alarmed now. "What's going on? Where are you?"

"It doesn't matter. Just—I don't know when we're going to talk again. Okay? And I want you to know that—I'm not mad. About everything. I want you to know that. I'm not mad. There are things, Ricky. Things that are bigger than you and me. Things that I never thought I'd see. Things you wouldn't believe."

"Have you been drinking? Nate, what the fuck are you—"

"I love you."

Rick didn't respond. For a moment Nate thought he'd hung up. Then, "Nate. Are you okay?"

Nate laughed hoarsely. "I don't know. I don't know anymore. But something big is happening. Something I can't explain. And I just needed to—to hear your voice again. Skipping rocks. Remember?"

"I remember." Rick sighed. "You weren't very good at it."

"Yeah. I learned, though. You taught me how. There's—do you believe there are things greater than us?"

"I don't—Nate, what are you *talking* about?"

"Nothing. Nothing. I've gotta go. Just—thank you. For showing me how to skip rocks."

"Nate, wait—"

He hung up the phone.

His hands shook.

Eventually, he left the phone booth and went back to the motel room.

Alex and Art hadn't moved.

She was snoring against his shoulder.

Alex's chest rose and fell.

Nate climbed back into bed and waited for the sun to rise.

CHAPTER TWELVE

They headed east.

Nate asked where they were going.

Art grinned up at him. "I have no idea. Isn't that awesome?"

Nate let it go.

✦

They kept to back roads. Alex said main highways were off-limits if at all possible. They couldn't take the chance.

They hadn't made the news. There was nothing about them on any radio station Nate could find. Nothing in any papers he got when they stopped for gas.

Alex said that didn't mean civilians weren't looking for them.

✦

There were beasts in Montana.

Art demanded they pull over, jumping up in the seat, stretching over Nate and plastering her face against the window. "Alex!" she cried. "Alex, *look* at them! Alex, pull over, pull over, pull *over*."

He thought Alex would keep going. Would tell her they didn't have time to stop.

Art had said time was fluid. That it could bend.

Alex stopped.

In a flat field with a snowcapped mountainous backdrop was a herd of bison. There had to be dozens of them.

Art was scrambling over Nate and out the door even before Alex had turned off the truck. The air was cool. Nate stared after her for a moment before turning to tell Alex that it'd been good of him to stop.

But Alex wasn't there.

His door was open, and he was crossing around the front of the truck.

Art stood at the top of an embankment, gazing down at the bison below. She was waving her arms wildly, face alight as she glanced over her shoulder at Alex as he approached. He didn't speak, but it didn't matter. Art did enough talking for the both of them.

Nate thought he should stay right where he was.

This didn't concern him.

This wasn't about him.

Alex looked back at the truck and arched an eyebrow, jerking his head toward the field.

Nate was out of the truck before he realized he was even moving.

". . . and they're so much *bigger* than I thought," Art was exclaiming, nose a little red. "I mean, you see *pictures* of them, but that doesn't show *anything*. Look at them! They're *huge*. Oh my heck, there are *babies*. Alex! Nate! Look at the *babies*."

Nate came to stand next to Alex. Their shoulders brushed together by accident. Alex was warm. Nate didn't move away.

But then the breath was knocked from his chest because Art was right. They *were* big, far bigger than he ever expected them to be. And they were close. He could hear them snorting and snuffling, heads bent low as they grazed. "Wow," he breathed. "That's . . . wow."

Art laughed. "Right? That's what *I* said."

"You ever seen these before?" Alex asked him.

"No. There aren't too many bison in D.C."

Alex rolled his eyes. "Imagine that."

"You?"

Alex looked back out at the animals. "Once. A long time ago. It was . . . yeah."

Nate didn't push. He'd already gotten more than he expected.

But then Alex said, "I was just a kid. Road trip. Went through Glacier. Yosemite. It—haven't seen them since."

Art tilted her head back, looking up at them. "Were they this big back then?"

Alex shrugged. "Bigger, even."

Her eyes widened. Then, "Do they taste like bacon? Can we get one and see?"

Nate coughed explosively.

✦

He asked questions. Of course he did. It was in his nature. It was who he was.

The *problem* with asking questions was that sometimes he didn't want to know the answers. Not exactly.

"Greys," he said suddenly as they drove down a bumpy road.

Art hummed but didn't look up from her book.

"Aliens." He breathed heavily through his nose. "Big heads. Big black eyes."

"What about them?" she asked.

"Are they . . . are they real?"

She looked up at him. "You really want to know?"

He nodded slowly.

"Yes. They're real."

"Oh," Nate said, unsure what to do with the information now that he had it.

"Yeah, but honestly? Those guys are jerks. Seriously. If you ever meet one, just punch it in the face."

Nate didn't know what to do with that either.

Alex snorted but said nothing.

Art's face scrunched up. "They have a weird obsession with probing. Like, okay, we get it, you want to see what the insides look like, but my word, there are *scans* that can do that. You don't need to stick something up an anus to find out. I think they just have a rectum fetish. Do you know what fetishes are? I do. It's when you—"

"Art," Alex said.

Art sighed and went back to her book.

Nate rolled down the window, trying to gulp in as much fresh air as possible.

He didn't ask any more questions for the rest of the day.

✦

They had a routine when they stopped.

They didn't want to be seen all at once. Two men traveling with a girl could be memorable. Motels were fine. They'd park far away from the office, and either Alex or Nate would go in, leaving the other two in the truck.

Same with food. Only one of them would go inside.

Gas stations were trickier. Some had cameras. Art would slide from the seat, lying down by Nate's legs. Alex would go inside and pay. He'd come back out and fill the tank. It was quick and easy. No one ever paid them any mind.

Until Havre, Montana.

It was a little town near the Canadian border. They'd swung south before heading north again. They were spinning their wheels, waiting for *something* to happen, for Art to tell them the way. She'd said it wasn't time yet, that she'd know when and where she needed to go. She'd tried to explain it to Nate, telling him it was a tug in her head, because she didn't *need* to speak where she'd come from. The first time she'd ever even *had* a mouth was with Oren.

That had sent Nate spiraling for hours.

She'd laughed at him.

Alex had scolded her.

She'd apologized.

Nate wasn't sure she'd actually meant it.

"We need to stop," Alex said, approximately a week after Art had sat on a picnic table and told him she was an alien from another planet. "Need to fill up." It was late afternoon, and they'd probably need to start looking for a place to spend the night soon. There were heavy-duty sleeping bags packed in the bed of the truck that they'd managed to grab before fleeing the cabin. Art had wanted to use them immediately. Nate had said he'd rather have a bed if at all possible.

He'd never seen such a look of betrayal on a space princess's face before.

He'd almost felt guilty.

Art nodded but didn't look up from her book. "Tell me when I have to get on the floor, partner. I'm with a cowboy about to partake in a shootout to save the woman of my dreams from the clutches of her evil oil-baron uncle."

Alex glanced over at Nate. "I blame you for those books."

Nate rolled his eyes. "Just because you don't know how to read."

"He knows how to read," Art said. "He just doesn't like to. It's because he doesn't have an imagination."

"And you do?" Nate asked before he could stop himself.

She looked up from her book. "Of course I do. Don't most people?"

There were times like this, times when Art seemed so damn human that he could almost forget what she'd told him while she sat on a picnic table in the middle of nowhere. That she was essentially a ghost possessing the body of a little girl who'd been in a coma that she'd never wake from. And when he *did* remember, when she said something like having an *imagination,* it threatened to send him into another state of panic. He'd never thought about it much before this. Never thought about the implications of what it could mean to find out humans weren't alone in the universe. It was science fiction. It was aliens coming down in their spaceships and blowing up buildings and trying to enslave the human race. It was little green men with lasers or robots with spindly fingers. They were monsters from deep space, and that's *all* they were to Nate. He'd never had any reason to believe otherwise.

But here she was, in the body of a ten-year-old girl. She liked reading. And bacon. And her sunglasses were on her head, and she was staring at him with such an inquisitive look on her face, like she couldn't wait to hear his answer. It was so fucking outside of the realm of what Nate considered possible that he couldn't even begin to fathom what it meant.

So he said, "Yeah. I guess. Most people do."

She nodded before turning back to her book. "Except Alex."

"Except Alex."

"I don't have time for an imagination," Alex muttered, but he kept glancing at Nate like he knew *exactly* what he'd been thinking.

Art had been . . . vague about where she'd come from. She said it was much farther than humans had ever been before, which—okay. That was probably true. Because the universe was terribly vast, and from Nate's rudimentary knowledge of astronomy and space travel, he didn't think they'd gotten very far outside of their own solar system, much less the galaxy. He remembered, loosely, a quote he'd read from Carl Sagan, who said there were more stars in the heavens than grains of sand on all the Earth. It hadn't meant much to Nate then. He hadn't really given it more than a passing thought.

But now?

The thought was wondrously horrible.

He thought about asking Art if there were others out there. Other . . . aliens. Besides the asshole Greys.

He couldn't find it in himself to force the words out. He didn't think he wanted to know the answer.

Sometimes he could almost make himself believe he was on a road trip with a man and his daughter.

Who'd broken into his cabin.

And then forced him on said road trip when soldiers and helicopters came.

He was pretty close to spiraling when he saw the sign.

Havre, Montana.

"We'll stop here," Alex said. "In and out. We'll be quick. Find somewhere down the road to stop for the night."

Nate didn't say a thing.

✦

It was cooler here than it'd been at Herschel Lake. There were still patches of snow on the ground, dirty and gray. Havre itself wasn't anything spectacular. It looked like any other small town they'd driven through over the past week. The sun was weak overhead, and the clouds were thin and wispy.

They stopped at the first gas station they came to. Art was on the floor of the truck, her head lying against Nate's knee, her focus still on her book. Nate brushed a hand through her hair. She hummed a little and leaned into it.

The station had four pumps. Unleaded was a buck twenty, something Alex grumbled about. It'd gotten more expensive the farther north they'd gone. Nate had asked about money, asked how their impromptu trip was being funded a few days before. Alex had stared at him for a long moment before showing him the contents of a secret pocket in his duffel. Inside were rolled bundles of cash, held together by thick rubber bands. It'd been quick, just a now-you-see-it, now-you-don't, but it'd been enough.

"You planned this," Nate had told him, trying to keep his voice even. "Her. You planned it."

Alex had shaken his head. "Not intentionally. Not at first. But once I started, I had to be careful. They'd have gotten suspicious. Ended up taking a year."

Nate hadn't said much after that, still stuck on *they'd have gotten suspicious.* The ever-omnipotent *they.* Those in the Mountain. The ones who'd held Art. *They* were the ones chasing after them, most likely in the form of the water guy. They wanted her back.

Nate understood why.

They pulled up to the pump, the gas tank on the passenger side. Alex turned off the truck. "I'll be quick."

Nate smiled tightly at him. These stops always soured his stomach. Rattled his nerves a bit. Nothing ever happened, but he was paranoid. He'd earned the right after everything.

Alex opened the door and slid out of the truck. He paused for a moment, raising his arms over his head as he stretched. Nate absolutely did not look at the thin sliver of the skin on his back as his flannel shirt rose above his jeans.

Alex closed the door behind him.

Nate watched as he glanced around, taking in the gas station. There was a car parked in front of the small convenience store. Their truck was the only one at the pumps.

Quick and easy.

Alex rounded the front of the truck and headed toward the store. The truck's engine ticked as it cooled.

The air in the cab felt stuffy. Nate cracked the window and took in a deep breath of cool air.

Art turned another page. Then she said, "Alex likes you."

"So you've said," Nate told her, hand still in her hair.

"I know. Just wanted to remind you in case you forgot."

"I didn't."

"Okay. It's just he can act like he doesn't sometimes."

"I know."

"He doesn't know how to show emotions."

Nate snorted. "That might be an understatement."

She squinted up at him. "Just don't give up on him."

"I wasn't—what do you mean?"

"He's going to need someone . . . after."

Nate didn't like the sound of that. "After what?"

She bit her bottom lip. "After I go home. He's . . . he thinks he can be alone. But it's not good for him. He's . . . he needs someone. Like you."

Nate hadn't really thought that far ahead, aside from that night in the motel. He wondered if it was because he still didn't necessarily believe it. Oh sure, he knew *something* was going on. After all, he'd seen Humvees being thrown into helicopters. But the idea of there being an *after* was nebulous at best. They had been almost aimless as they'd driven on, Alex asking Art every now and then if she was *getting anything*. She'd shake her head and say something about how it wasn't time yet, that she'd know when it was and *where* it was. What that meant . . . well. Nate didn't know if he was prepared to find out yet.

So, no. He hadn't thought about *after*. He was barely thinking about tomorrow. It'd have been like he was in a fugue state if everything weren't so startlingly sharp around him, as if he were seeing colors for the first time.

"I don't think he'll need anything," Nate said slowly.

She shook her head. "You're wrong. He's not like he was before. Things have changed. He'll need someone like you. No. You know what? Not someone like you. Just . . . you."

Nate looked out the window toward the store. He could see inside. Alex was at the drink coolers, probably getting Art her juice and Nate his Gatorade. Nate had asked for one once the first time they'd stopped, and every time after, Alex had made sure to buy one. It wasn't—it wasn't *anything*. It was probably just to shut Nate up so Alex wouldn't have to listen to him bitch and moan about being thirsty. It was fine. Everything was fine.

"I don't know if that's true," Nate finally said. "He's going to be fine on his own."

Art wasn't happy with that. "Why won't you believe me?"

"It's not that I don't believe you. It's that—oh *shit*."

"What?"

He ignored her, focus on the brown car that had just pulled up in front of the store.

Three words were emblazoned on the side.

HILL COUNTY SHERIFF

"Stay down," Nate hissed at her. "Don't move."

"Is it him? The water guy?"

The fact that she'd picked up on what Nate had called the Enforcer would have been hysterical if Nate hadn't suddenly felt like a bucket of ice water had been dumped on his head. "No. Cop."

"Alex?"

"Still inside." And he hadn't seen the new arrival. He was moving toward the front counter, plastic bottles in his hand. Nate screamed in his head, trying to force him to look over, to just turn his fucking head so he could—

And Alex did just that. One moment his attention was focused on the store clerk. The next, his head jerked toward the window, eyes narrowed in time to see the deputy pull himself from the sedan.

The deputy was a squat man with thinning blond hair. His cheeks were flushed a little, mirror shades covering his eyes. He wasn't looking into the store. No, his attention was focused on the truck. He stared at it for a moment, head cocked. He nodded at Nate when he saw him inside, and it looked like he was going to walk over.

Instead, he turned back toward the store, closing the door to the sedan behind him.

Nate felt a hand tightening on his knee.

He looked down.

Art's forehead was resting against his thigh, her fingers digging into his jeans. She was breathing shallowly, these quick little breaths like she was on the verge of a panic attack.

"Art," he whispered. "*Art.*"

She didn't answer him.

"Shit," he muttered, glancing back up at the store. The deputy was inside. Alex was at the counter. The store clerk was ringing him up. The deputy was moving toward the coolers, but then he stopped. His shoulders stiffened slightly. He glanced back over his shoulder at Alex. Then he looked out the window at the truck.

"Come on," Nate said. "Come on, hurry up, hurry *up*."

Art continued to breathe quickly.

Nate pressed his hand against her head.

His thoughts were racing. They were *get out* and *what's taking so long* and *it's fine, it's fine, everything is fine.* And then came a voice that *wasn't* his, and it felt intrusive and clawing and bright, and it said, *Alex, Alex, Alex, please don't leave me, please be safe.*

Nate knew that voice.

He turned slowly to look down at the little girl sitting on the floor of the truck.

Her eyes were closed. Her chest rose and fell.

And then he heard a *third* voice, rough and deep in his head, and it said, *Be ready, be ready in case we need to move. If you have to, you leave with him. He'll keep you safe. Nate is—*

There was a complicated flurry of images in his head. The cabin. The lake. A field of flowers. A woman with black hair. A little boy with bright blue eyes. And Nate, Nate, Nate. Nate in the kitchen in the morning looking sleepy as he sipped a cup of coffee. Nate standing by the lake. Nate sleeping against the window of the truck. Nate angry, Nate scared, Nate *laughing,* and he'd never *seen* himself this way. He looked wild and fierce and *vital.* It was too much too soon, and Nate was drowning under the onslaught. The images were accompanied by shifting emotions, from anger and grief to tentative trust and heartache like Nate had never felt before. He was overwhelmed by the intense *loneliness* of it all, like he was alone and had been for a very long time.

He blinked, a lump lodged firmly in his throat. "What's happening?" he managed to croak.

Then: a clear, unambiguous thought.

Nate?

He said, *Yes.*

The door to the convenience store opened.

Alex, whose voice he'd heard in his head, was walking toward them, a hardened look on his face.

Nate's skin was crawling.

Art sighed against Nate's leg.

She said, "You felt it, didn't you?"

Before Nate could answer, another voice called out, "Hey, you there. Hold up a minute."

The deputy had followed Alex out the door. Alex was only halfway across the parking lot. He stopped, the plastic bag in his hand bouncing on his thigh. He squared his shoulders and turned around toward the deputy. "Yes?"

The deputy wasn't smiling, but his hand wasn't on his gun, either. "That your truck?"

"Yes."

"Nice rig."

"Thanks."

"Thinking about getting myself a truck like that."

"That right."

"Sure is. Got a Ford right now, but my daddy had a Chevy when I was a kid. I loved that truck."

Alex shrugged. "Don't have any complaints."

"Washington, huh?"

Alex didn't respond.

The deputy stood a few feet away from him. "License plate. Washington."

"Yeah."

"On a trip?"

"Me and a buddy."

"Where ya headed?"

"South Dakota."

The deputy nodded. "Strange route to take from Washington. All the way up here."

"We went through Glacier."

"Pretty, right?"

"Sure," Alex said, and Nate decided right then and there that if they got out of this, if they managed to escape without seeing the inside of a prison cell, he was going to make Alex work on his small talk.

"What's in South Dakota?"

"What the heck," Art muttered. "Is every human this nosy?"

Nate felt like screaming.

"Badlands," Alex said.

"Oh yeah!" the deputy said. "Great park, if you've never been."

"First time."

"Camping?"

Alex nodded.

"Sounds like a good time." The cop glanced over Alex's shoulder at the truck. Nate almost waved at him but decided against it at the last moment. "You and a buddy. That's it?"

"That's it." Alex sounded as if he were done with the conversation. Nate should know. He'd heard that tone of voice many times in the past couple of weeks.

"Well, y'all have a safe trip, all right?"

"Thank you."

The deputy turned back toward the store.

Alex turned toward the truck.

Nate's stomach flipped.

Then, "One more thing."

Alex's jaw clenched before he glanced back at the deputy.

"You serve?" the deputy asked.

Nate wondered if the deputy had a death wish. The gun was sitting in the glove compartment. All he had to do was grab it. Sure, he didn't know the first fucking thing about guns, but it couldn't be that hard, right? Safety off, finger on the trigger. Point and shoot. He didn't need to kill anyone. Just a warning. That's all it'd have to be.

"It's just you carry yourself like a soldier," the deputy said. "My daddy was in Korea. Had almost the same haircut and everything."

And Nate could *feel* how much that rankled Alex. Somehow, he *knew* that Alex wanted to correct him, telling him that he wasn't a soldier, he was a *Marine*, and there was a goddamn *difference*.

Instead, he said, "Long time ago. Old habits are hard to break."

The deputy nodded. "Thank you for your service. Never did

myself, but I know what kind of man it takes to enlist. My daddy taught me that."

"Appreciate it."

"Sure. All right, then. Best let you get on your way. Have a good day, sir." The deputy gave a jaunty salute and turned back toward his car.

Alex was moving even as the deputy did. He went to the pump and started filling the truck.

The deputy's car didn't move.

It took perhaps two minutes for the truck's tank to fill.

It felt like it went on for hours.

Eventually, Nate heard the telltale click on the pump's handle.

Alex screwed the gas cap back on as he put the nozzle back.

He was around the front of the truck and opening the door. He tossed the bag inside before he sat down. He wasn't looking at either of them.

He reached down and grabbed the exposed wires, rubbing them together.

Nothing.

The truck didn't start.

He pressed the wires together again.

No spark.

Alex grunted and tried a third time.

Nothing.

"Fuck," Nate breathed.

"Art," Alex snapped. "Let go."

Art looked up. Her eyes were wide.

"Let go," Alex said again, and Nate *knew* the moment she did, even though he didn't know *what* she was doing. One moment his head was stuffed full of voices that didn't belong there, and the next, there was only his own thoughts. It felt like he'd breached the surface after being under for far too long. He gasped in a deep breath as Alex pressed the wires together again. They sparked. The truck roared to life.

He put it in drive and pulled away from the pump, heading toward the road.

"What the fuck was that?" Nate demanded. "What the hell—"

"Why?" Alex growled, and it took Nate a moment to realize the question wasn't directed toward him, but at Art. "Why did you—"

"Because he fits," Art said. "Like you. It's not quite the same, but you know it as well as I do."

"He didn't want this. He doesn't want any of this."

"Have you asked him?"

"I don't *have* to. He's told us both enough that he—shit."

"What?" Nate asked, not sure if he wanted to know the answer. "He's following us."

Nate looked out the rear window.

The deputy was behind them.

"He's in this," Art said, still seated at Nate's feet. "You know he is. He's here. With us. He hasn't left. He won't leave us. He won't leave *you*."

"Don't," Alex said, the warning clear in his voice. "I don't know what you think you're doing, but you need to stop. You hear me?"

"Just because *you* can't see it yet, doesn't mean—"

The light bar on the deputy's car flared to life, flashing red and blue.

"Fuck," Alex snarled, banging a hand against the steering wheel. "Art, get back up on the seat. And don't you say a goddamn word, you hear me? Nate, get the gun. Keep it hidden."

Art moved.

Nate did not.

"*Now*, Nate."

Nate moved. He popped open the glove compartment. Alex's gun was sitting on a pile of paperwork. "If he runs the plate, we're—"

"I know."

"You can't just kill him."

Alex wouldn't look at him. He pulled the truck to the side of the road. He broke apart the exposed wires and shoved them back into the dash as the truck fell silent. He put the panel back in place, banging on it with his fist.

Nate took the gun and set it in his lap. Art handed him her coat, and he laid it over the gun. "We'll be okay," she told him. "You'll see."

He tried not to flinch. "I thought you said you couldn't read minds."

"I can't."

"I heard—"

"That wasn't mind reading, Nate. Jeez. Give me *some* credit. Even if I could, I wouldn't do that to you without your consent. That was just me forming a connection with you so you could hear what Alex and I were talking about in our heads. I wanted to keep you in the loop so you would—why are you staring at me like that?"

"Do you not *hear* yourself when you talk?" Nate demanded. "What the hell do you mean *connection*?"

She frowned. "I don't know how I can be any clearer. I simplified it as much as I could so your smaller—but nonetheless fascinating—human brain could have a basic understanding of—"

"Both of you shut the hell up," Alex snapped. "Not a word, you hear me? He's coming."

Alex rolled down his window.

Sure enough, the deputy walked up to the side of the truck.

"Hey," he said, a smile on his face. "I hope I didn't startle you. I just—well, well, well, who do we have here?" His smile widened at the sight of Art. "Hello. I didn't see you at the gas station."

"I was lying down," Art told him, voice sticky-sweet. "I was so tired. I was still wearing my seat belt, though, because that's the law."

"Aren't you just precious," the deputy said. "Good girl. Always wear your seat belt."

"I want to be a police officer when I grow up, so I know the law very well," Art said. "My daddy said you have to be very brave to do that, so you must be very brave too."

"Well," the deputy said, blushing slightly. "I don't know about *that*. That's very nice of you to say. This big guy your daddy?"

She nodded. "He's so awesome."

"Well, you need to tell your daddy he's got a taillight out."

She gasped. "Daddy! That's against the *law*." Her eyes filled with tears. "Are you going to take him to jail?"

The deputy looked taken aback. "No, no," he said quickly. "Of course not. Your daddy is a hero as far as I'm concerned. Just going to let him off with a warning. No one's going to jail. No one's even getting a *ticket*."

A single tear tracked down Art's cheek. "Oh, thank you, sir. We're going on a road trip, and I know that would make my daddy feel so bad if you took him away from me."

"No need to feel bad," the deputy assured her, and Nate could do nothing but stare in *awe* at the way she was playing him. They'd been lucky that he hadn't run their plates. They wouldn't have even matched up with the truck they'd stolen. "Just wanted to make y'all aware so you can get the bulb changed out before you get too much farther. Don't want to get pulled over again now, do you?"

"No, sir," Art said with a sniff. "I'll make sure he gets it taken care of right away. Daddy's special friend here will make sure too."

The deputy's smile faltered a little. "Right. That's . . . that's just swell. Y'all have a good afternoon, okay?"

Art's tears were gone as quickly as they'd come. "Thank you, Officer!" she chirped.

The deputy nodded and turned back toward his car behind them. He pulled out and made a U-turn, heading back toward the gas station.

"Wow," Art said, slumping in the seat. "That was close. It's a good thing I learned how to work tear ducts pretty early on, right?"

Nate didn't know what to say to that. Maybe it was better that way.

+

They didn't stay in Havre. In fact, Alex made it a point to get them as far away from Havre as he possibly could. They'd stopped in the next town over at some local body shop and bought a bulb, cheap. Alex replaced it without a word, and they'd been off again.

They were still on the road long after the sun had set. Nate didn't ask where they were going because he didn't think even Alex knew.

Art had fallen asleep between them, head resting on Nate's shoulder, snoring softly near his ear. He was pretty sure she was drooling, but he didn't have the heart to shove her off, even if she'd somehow gotten inside his head.

Alex had turned reticent again, the look on his face making it clear that he wasn't in the mood for any kind of conversation.

Nate let him brood. For a couple of hours.

But then he couldn't take it anymore.

He didn't know how he'd lasted as long as he had. He was almost disappointed in himself.

"I heard you," he said, flinching at how loud his voice sounded inside the cab of the truck after the lengthy silence. "In my head. I heard her too."

Alex grunted.

"That's not a good enough answer. Not after this. You don't get to be stoic. Not after everything. I *heard* you, Alex."

Alex's hands tightened on the steering wheel. "I know."

"I *saw* things. Just—*pictures*. I don't—"

"It's—the closest word she can use to describe it is bonding. It's . . . familial."

"Familial."

"It's how she—they don't have the structure we do. They aren't *born* like we are. But they have . . . families. Or at least a semblance of one. She's—there was just me. And now there's you. She's bonded with you. Like she has with me."

"And now she can read my mind," Nate said, sounding rather hysterical. "And you can too." Nate tried to block out all the thoughts he'd had of seeing Alex naked, because *that* wasn't something he was willing to share. But the more he tried *not* to think about it, the more he *did* think about Alex with sweat on his bare skin, chest heaving as he leaned down to—"Oh my god. No. Absolutely not. You *stay out of my*—"

"I can't read your mind," Alex said with a sigh. "She can't either. It's a connection. Like a radio or a phone. Just . . . without the radio and the phone. I can't see or hear anything you don't want to show me. The same for you. For her. And it's not on all the time. She facilitates it. I can't do it now. And neither can you."

That . . . didn't make Nate feel any better. "Did you ever talk about me before today with your voodoo mind spell?"

Alex snorted. Nate thought maybe it was his version of a laugh. "Really. *That's* the question that comes to your mind."

"It is. And you need to answer it."

"Yes."

"Aha! I knew it. When? And what did you say about me?"

Alex glanced over at Nate. "That first night you showed up. Art was curious about you. And I wanted to shoot you in the head and bury you in the woods."

"Wow," Nate said. "I'm shocked. Really. That's so surprising, coming from you."

"I didn't do it."

"Thanks. Thank you for not putting a bullet in my head. I mean that."

"You're welcome."

"I was being *sarcastic*."

"I know."

Nate couldn't reach over and slap him upside the head because he had an alien in the body of a little girl sleeping on his shoulder. "You're infuriating."

"You're annoying."

"Don't be rude."

"Like a gnat in my ear."

"You're still not funny."

And wonder of all wonders, Alex chuckled. Nate shouldn't have liked the sound as much as he did. It wasn't safe. Nothing about this was safe.

"I heard her," he said slowly. "And you."

"We covered that. You're repeating yourself again."

"And you said that it's a bond. Family."

"Right."

"So she thinks of me as . . . what?"

"I don't really know," Alex admitted. "There's—it's complicated. No one understood it at the Mountain. Not really. There wasn't . . . they thought it was metaphysical. There was no actual quantifiable evidence of it. It hadn't happened before—before I was assigned to her. It was just another thing they didn't understand. Nothing changed, at least not physically. She bonded herself to me, and they thought they would see evidence in my brain scans. That there would be physiological changes. But there was nothing there."

"That's hardly surprising that you don't have anything between your ears."

"Har-har."

Nate thought hard. "But now she sees me as part of . . . this?"

Alex didn't look very happy at the thought. "It seems so."

He didn't know what to do with that. "This is stupid. Like, this is the stupidest thing that's ever happened to me. I can't even begin to express how stupid this all is. You have to realize that, right? How ridiculous this sounds?"

"You'll get past it," Alex said. "I was where you are at one point. I thought the exact same things you're thinking right now. Even more, probably."

"Yeah, okay. But you've had ten *years*. I've had two *weeks*."

"Fair," Alex said, though it sounded begrudging. "She's . . . complicated."

"You are too."

"Not really."

Nate considered letting it go right there. Letting Alex off the hook, at least for now. Instead, he said, "And you?"

"What about me?"

"It wasn't just Art."

Alex's body language was all but *screaming* for Nate to back the fuck up. "I don't know what you're talking about."

And since Nate apparently had no sense of self-preservation, he said, "You're lying. I heard you. I saw . . . what you see." *About me* was left unsaid.

Alex was scowling again. Nate wondered when that had become comforting. "It didn't—"

"Does that mean you like me?" Nate wondered aloud, as if Alex wasn't capable of reaching over and strangling him with one hand. "Because I think that means you like me. At least a little bit."

"Absolutely not," Alex retorted. "I don't like *anything* about you."

"Well *that's* certainly not true. You seemed to like how I look in the morning when I drink coffee. Saw that image a couple of times."

"Shut up," Alex said through gritted teeth. "That's not . . . I didn't know you'd see that. And it doesn't mean anything. All I was doing was telling Art that she'd be safe with you in case something happened to me."

"Wow," Nate said. "You must *really* like me if you think that."

"I hate you," Alex said.

Nate grinned in the dark. "I don't know that you do, buddy. What is it about sleepy me that gets you so—"

"I will kick you out of this truck and leave you here without a second thought."

"Yeah, yeah, yeah. I get it. You've had enough feelings for one day. Relax. You look like you're about to break the steering wheel. We don't have to talk about how much you think about me laughing or any other various images of me you apparently have stored up in your head—oh my god, I was *joking*. Don't you *dare* pull over, Alex."

Alex pulled the truck back onto the road from where he'd slowed on the shoulder. "You done?"

"I'm done." He wasn't, but he figured the rest could wait. There was still the woman he'd seen. The boy. They'd been mixed up with everything else. But he'd pushed Alex enough for one day. He had an idea of what that had been, but he wasn't ready to force it upon Alex. "It's just . . . a lot. You know?"

"I know." Alex still sounded wary. "I had time to process. To understand. You haven't. You'll get there. But everything can't happen all at once. I forgot that, I think."

"Did that hurt?"

"What?"

"Admitting you were wrong."

"I didn't admit *anything*."

Nate laughed quietly. "Sure, Alex. Okay." He glanced down at Art. Yes, she was definitely drooling on him. "You love her, don't you."

Nate thought he wasn't going to get a response. Art had told him that Alex had a hard time showing any emotion, but Nate didn't think that was quite right. Alex did show emotion, but most people just couldn't see it. And that was okay. Because he remembered Alex's hands deftly braiding her hair. That was enough for him.

But Alex surprised him.

He said, "She's all I've got left."

That hurt to hear more than Nate expected it to. He'd felt Alex's loneliness. Felt the way it wrapped around him like a shield. The way Art had been intertwined with him, like she was a part of him. Nate understood that more than he cared to admit. But wasn't there more to it than—

Things have changed. He'll need someone like you. No. You know what? Not someone like you. Just . . . you.

Nate had seen hearts break up close.

It was the look on his mother's face as she stood silently while his father screamed that he wouldn't have a faggot for a son.

It was the look on his own face in the mirror after he'd come home from being fired for doing something he'd never thought he was capable of.

He didn't want that for Alex. Not again. The dark-haired woman. The boy. Maybe he had more than a good idea of who they were. What they'd been to Alex. What the water guy had meant when he'd said the test had been to see what Art would do in the face of Alex's grief.

But it would happen regardless. If Artemis Darth Vader left, if she . . . returned to wherever she'd come from, it would happen again.

Nate would witness it up close, no matter how much Alex tried to keep it locked up. If they stuck with each other.

If they stayed alive.

He understood now why Art had asked him.

And he thought Alex knew that too. That he was already preparing to say goodbye.

"You've got me too," Nate said before he could stop himself. "I'm . . . okay? You just—you have me too."

Alex didn't respond.

But then Nate didn't expect him to. He stared out into the night sky and the stars above. They twinkled brightly out here in the middle of nowhere.

One seemed brighter than the others.

And it looked to have a trail behind it.

"Huh," he said. "Would you look at that. That's . . . What was it called? Markham something. The comet. I think that's the comet."

Alex grunted, but that was okay with Nate. It was comforting somehow.

He watched the comet for the longest time.

Eventually he closed his eyes and slept.

CHAPTER THIRTEEN

They had another close call in Wahpeton, North Dakota, two days later. A cop had followed them for a couple of miles just outside of town on a straight stretch of road. Just when they thought they were about to get pulled over again, the cop turned off in another direction.

Nate had breathed out a sigh of relief, unclenching his hands, his fingernails leaving marks on his palms.

Alex hadn't spoken much for the rest of the day.

They headed south, and Nate knew they were floundering. From what he'd gathered in the bits and pieces he'd managed to get from Alex, the plan had only extended so far as to get Art away from the Mountain as quickly as possible. They'd initially meant to go farther than they had, but Alex had been gutshot and they couldn't even be sure he'd survive, much less that Art could heal him enough for him to move. They'd found the cabin by a sheer stroke of luck. Nate thought the car they'd been in was at the bottom of Herschel Lake, though he didn't ask.

They'd just crossed into South Dakota when Art said, "What are the Badlands?"

Alex glanced at her before looking back at the winding road ahead. Nate had offered to drive, but Alex didn't seem to trust him to get them out of danger if they were discovered. He tried not to be too insulted about that. "What?"

"Back at the gas station with the deputy. You said we were going to the Badlands."

"It's a national park," Nate told her because Alex was brooding again and Nate couldn't be sure he'd actually answer. "They found a lot of dinosaur bones there. I think."

"We should go there," Art said.

That got Alex's attention. "Is it . . ."

She shook her head. "No. Not like that. I just want to see dinosaurs."

"Right," Nate said. "You know that dinosaurs are all extinct."

She looked at him strangely. "Everyone knows that, Nate."

"So you know we won't actually see dinosaurs, then."

She rolled her eyes. "Sometimes you seem very smart."

"And other times?"

She smiled at him. "Other times it's a good thing you're pretty. Isn't that right, Alex?"

Nate gaped at her.

Alex frowned harder.

"We should go to the Badlands," she decided. "And please don't say no. I don't want to force you to do my bidding with the power of my mind, but I will if I have to."

Nate choked.

"She's messing with you." Alex sounded extraordinarily grumpy. "She can't do that."

"Hey! *He* didn't know that. Why do you have to ruin everything?"

Alex reached over and ruffled her hair. "You've already freaked him out enough as it is."

"I'm not *freaked*," Nate said.

Art squinted at him. "Sort of freaked. And no, before you ask, I'm not reading your mind. You're just . . . twitchy again."

"I can't wait for you to go back to your planet," Nate muttered.

Art laughed.

✦

They stopped at a small country store outside of Onaka to get a map. Art had demanded to be let out of the truck to go inside, claiming that she'd been a prisoner for three decades and she'd be *damned* if Alex was going to make her stay behind. Alex looked like he was going to argue, but Nate had headed him off, saying he'd take Art inside while Alex stayed behind.

"Fine," Alex said, though he didn't sound like he meant it. He pulled out his wallet and handed Nate a couple of bills. "In and out. Don't get sidetracked."

Art grinned up at him, climbing to her knees on the bench seat and leaning over to plant a loud kiss against Alex's cheek. That soft look Alex seemed to get only with her made a brief appearance before it disappeared behind his mask again. She turned toward Nate. "What are you waiting for? Out. Out!"

He did as the space princess asked, opening the door and getting out of the truck. She followed quickly behind him before taking his hand and pulling him toward the store. She was forceful when she needed to be. Nate managed to glance back at Alex. He was watching them through the windshield. Nate winked at him.

Alex didn't look away.

The store was small. It had basic foodstuffs and toiletries. Coolers with soft drinks and cases of cheap beer. There was an older man behind the counter, his face wrinkled and kind. He greeted them as they came in, a bell dinging overhead as the door opened. An ancient radio crackled on a shelf behind him next to rows of cigarettes.

"Hello," the old man said, giving them a little wave. "Help you find anything?"

"We need a map," Art announced, pulling Nate toward the counter.

"I can probably help you with that," he said, smiling down at her. "Anything in particular?"

"We're going to the Badlands."

"Ah," he said. "Good choice. I've probably got something here that can help a traveler on their way." He looked up at Nate. "On a trip, are we?"

Nate nodded. "Sure." Better to say as little as possible.

"Let me see what I can find," the man said, starting to dig through a drawer.

On the radio, a voice was speaking, sounding almost frantic. ". . . and they don't *want* you to know. They want to keep it a *secret*. They don't think you're *ready*. But we know that's not the case. We know what we're capable of, what we *want*. And what we want is the *truth*. You really think Markham-Tripp is *just* a comet? Of course not! You heard what Johnny Brown said on this very show yesterday. He's an *astronomer*. He knows what he's talking about.

And if he says there's something in the tail of the comet, you bet your sorry butt I'm gonna believe him. The size of *Saturn*, he said. Why do they think we won't find out the truth? Why does the United States government really believe we won't see what they see? I'll tell you why, friends. They think we're *sheep*. They give you the fluoride in your water, telling you it's to keep you *healthy* when it actually makes you docile. The men in Washington smile their politician smiles and say *Trust us. We've got your best interests in mind.* And then they drop their pesticides and say it's for the *crops*. You expect us to believe that? Man has been farming for *thousands* of years without the aid of poison. It's only within the last century that they've started talking about insects that are *damaging* our way of life. You *really* think that's the case? No. No. *No*. We're being *experimented* on. We're being *tested*. We are in the world's biggest laboratory, and no one even knows it! Except you, my friends. Which is why it's my duty to tell you that there is *something in that comet*. We've been visited before, you can take that to the bank and *cash it*. And we're about to be visited again. Johnny Brown took *photos*. He can *see* it. They are coming, people. The question is what are we going to do about it?"

Nate stared at the radio. He was startled when the old man dropped a couple of maps on the counter. "You'll have to forgive me," he said, reaching over and switching off the radio, cutting off the announcer mid-squawk. "Sometimes I like listening to him. Steven Cooper. He's a crackpot and he talks trash, but it's *good* trash, you know? Conspiracies and such. I don't believe a single word he says, but he's entertaining."

"Yeah," Nate managed to say. "I . . . I've never heard of him."

The old man chuckled. "I'm not surprised. He's got his own radio show talking spooks and how the Russkies killed JFK and he's got *proof*, but he never seems to share it. Now that that comet's on its way, he's all up in a tizzy about it. Thinks it's a sign. Had this guy who claimed to be an astronomer a couple of days ago. Says a goddamn UFO is flying in the tail of it." He glanced down at Art. "Pardon my language, miss. Don't you be repeating that word now, you hear?"

Art nodded. "Oh, I would *never*. UFO, you say? How fascinating. You don't believe in them?"

The old man shook his head. "I've seen some things, sure. But little green men? Why, I think it's all flights of fancy. I mean, if such things existed, why would they come here of all places?"

"To help," Art said seriously. "Maybe this place is like the bright beacon in a vast, dark space. Maybe they see the potential of us, but also how easily we could be lost. It's a fine balance, don't you think? The line between love and fire is very thin."

The old man's brow furrowed. "I suppose. Aren't you a little young to be thinking about such things, though? Little girl like you should be playing with dolls, not thinking about flying saucers."

"I have unique and varied tastes," Art told him, picking up one of the maps off the counter. "I can like dolls and study UFOs at the same time. Just because I'm a girl doesn't mean I'm not capable of deciding what my interests should be."

"Right," the old man said slowly. "Meant no offense, of course. Your daddy here can decide that better than I ever could."

"He's not my daddy," Art said, opening the map with her little hands. "My daddy's in the truck. This is my daddy's special—"

"How much for the map?" Nate asked quickly, hoping it'd be enough to distract them both.

"Tell you what," the old man said. "Consider it a gift from me to you. Little girl is smart. Smarter than I could ever possibly be. Seems wrong to charge you for something so little as a map when it's going to lead you on an adventure."

"Thank you," Nate said, stepping behind Art and reaching over her, trying to gather up the map.

"Nate," she scolded him, tilting her head back to look up at him. "I can do it."

"Fine," Nate said with a sigh. "We gotta get on the road, though, okay? Your dad is going to get worried if we don't get back."

"Protective, is he?" the old man asked.

"You have no idea," Art told him. "One time, a man tried to take me from him, and my daddy took his gun and—"

"That's probably enough," Nate said, putting his hands on Art's shoulders, steering her away from the counter, the map jumbled in her hands. "Don't need to share everything with strangers. We've talked about that."

"But *everyone* is a stranger unless you talk to them! How do you expect to get *anywhere* if you don't—"

"She reads a lot," Nate said hastily over his shoulder. The old man was staring after them. "All those books. Gets ideas in her head that she should *probably keep to herself.*"

"Nate, you're tearing the map! Be careful, it was a gift from that nice man who doesn't believe in aliens but still listens to crazy people talk about them!"

The bell rang overhead as they went out the door.

Alex sat up in his seat, watching them through the windshield.

"Well," Art said, folding the map expertly. "That certainly was an adventure, don't you think?"

✦

Somehow she managed to find Steven Cooper on the radio in the truck.

Nate gave serious consideration to opening the door and leaping out onto the highway. He'd seen enough movies to know that as long as he tucked and rolled, he'd probably only end up with a few broken bones.

". . . and this, friends, *this* is what they don't want you to know. That they already have extraterrestrial technology incorporated into our warships and our aircrafts. Think about it. In the last century, we made more leaps and bounds in technology than we have in the history of humanity, and we're just supposed to believe it was *natural*? That it came from the human *mind*? Poppycock. We were *shown* how to fly. We were *shown* how to split atoms. Why, even *now*, there are military installations that have *laser beams* that can shoot *thousands* of miles. Do you really think that we did this all on our own? That's *bull.* And that, of course, leads to the question of *why.* Friends, I'll tell you *why.* It was to prepare us. Because one day, the truth is going to come out, and it will be brought into the light kicking and screaming. There will be nothing to stop it. We are going to know the truth of all things. The truth, of course, being that we were being *prepared.* There are messages hidden in lines of code. To make us subservient. To make us *zombies.*"

"I love him so much," Art breathed.

"Jesus Christ," Alex muttered.

"I mean, he's obviously wrong about everything," Art said to no one in particular, gaze fixed avidly on the radio. "No one showed humans how to do anything. You all figured that out all on your own. Which, by the way, good job. Well. Mostly. You guys seem to care more about blowing stuff up than curing diseases. That's kind of backward, but then who am I to judge. And there's no ship in the comet's tail. Do you *know* what they're made up of? I mean, the very idea is ludicrous. And even if it wasn't, it wouldn't *help* space travel. If anything, it would *hinder* it. Can you believe this guy? He's amazing, but honestly."

Nate didn't know what to say to that.

". . . and let's talk more about Markham-Tripp. You see it, friends. It's visible now to the naked eye. It's called the event of the century. That we won't see something like this again in our lifetime. But why was this just discovered *last year*? Shouldn't NASA have been able to spot this a long time ago? They have enough satellites in the sky. Well, the satellites that haven't yet been sold off to the shadow government and used to *spy* on its people. You know all about that in the sixteen-part series we did last fall. But Hubble should have been able to see this coming *years* ago. Why is it that a man named Markham and a man named Tripp were the only two able to find this? Of course, that's what we're being told, right? Tell me, friends. Just *who are* Markham and Tripp? Why have they never been photographed? Why have they never been seen on TV? They've been interviewed in a few papers, but gosh, friends, do you know how *easy* it would be to fake that? All it'd take is a couple of yes-men under orders to act like they were amateurs with their little telescopes in their backyards surrounded by white picket fences and two-point-five children and they were able to find something that even the biggest observatories *in the world* weren't able to see. You know what I say to something like that, friends. If it sounds like a pig taking a bath, it's *hogwash*."

Art laughed gleefully, clapping her hands.

"They're coming, friends," Steven Cooper said. "They're coming, and there is nothing we can do to stop it."

✦

There were several campgrounds listed on the map for the Bad-lands. They decided on Sage Creek, as it seemed the most remote. It took them only a few hours to reach the entrance, where they paid the fee to a bored-looking kid with acne scars sitting in a ram-shackle wooden booth. He'd welcomed them to Sage Creek with barely restrained disdain, telling them there was no running wa-ter and the bathrooms were pit toilets clearly marked and to enjoy their stay. Art looked pleased. Even Alex seemed okay with it.

Nate was stuck on *pit toilet*.

The campground itself was flat and barely marked. In the dis-tance, they could see rocky hills rising against the horizon. Alex pulled the truck as far into the campground as he could, picking a spot away from the handful of other campers already set up with small tents and portable grills.

Art practically climbed over Nate to get out of the truck, de-manding that Alex show her what a pit toilet was because she needed to pee. She corrected herself then, saying she didn't *really* need to pee, but she was trying to force herself to go so she could see the pit toilet.

They left Nate sitting in the truck, reeling.

He watched them through the windshield as they headed toward a lean-to made of rope and wood that looked as if it would fall over with the slightest of breezes. Art's nose wrinkled as they got closer, and he choked out a laugh at the look of horror on her face. Alex said something to her, and she grabbed his hand, trying to tug him back toward the truck.

They were being chased by men in helicopters with guns.

The little girl was from another planet.

They didn't know where they were going.

He didn't know what would happen when all was said and done.

If he would even have a life to go back to.

And yet somehow, Nate felt more at peace than he had in a long time. He watched as Art dug her feet into the earth, trying to stop Alex from pulling her toward the pit toilet. And Alex was *laughing*.

He had a small smile on his face and crinkles around his eyes. His teeth were flashing, and he was *laughing*. Nate's breath was knocked from his chest at the sight.

Yes, they were on the run.

Yes, they didn't know what tomorrow would bring.

But here, now, in this moment, Nate was almost . . . happy.

He got out of the truck.

"Alex! *Alex*. I changed my mind! I don't want to see the pit toilet. *Alex*, let me go!"

"Oh no," Alex said, and Nate could *hear* the laughter in his voice. "You wanted to see it, I'm going to show it to you. Trust me when I say it's not the worst thing in the world. It could be a hundred degrees in the desert and it's your job to dig the shit hole for everyone else."

"Great! Good for you! I don't want to hear your *war* stories, what the heck! Nate. *Nate*. Help me! Save me!"

"Yeah," Nate said, leaning against the front of the truck. "I think I'm going to stay right here, thank you very much."

"I've been *betrayed*," Art gasped, suddenly boneless as she flopped toward the ground. Alex's grip on her arm was good enough that she didn't fall. Instead, her feet dragged through the grass.

"Oh, we'll get him over here," Alex promised her, glancing back at Nate, eyes bright. "Trust me on that. He's going to have to poop at some point."

Nate made a face. "I really wish you hadn't said that out loud."

Alex's smile widened.

He didn't pull her all the way over. She was gagging dramatically, clinging to his leg and demanding that he carry her because her body no longer worked thanks to the stench. Nate had to swallow past the lump in his throat when Alex did exactly as she asked. He bent over, wrapped his big arms around her legs, and hoisted her up. She climbed him like a monkey, sneakers against his arms and chest until she managed to make her way around to his shoulders, her legs draped over his front. She put her hands in his short hair, tugging gently. "We need to go find dinosaurs." She looked at Nate. "And *yes*, Nate, I know they aren't real. Not anymore."

"You coming?" Alex asked him, jerking his head toward a marked trail on the other side of the campground.

If this was happiness he felt, it was dangerous.

But Nate found himself not caring.

✦

They had a fire built as the sun began to set. Alex managed to scrounge up a flat pan and opened three cans of soup, pouring them in before he held the pan over the fire. They were out of earshot of the nearest campers, a young couple who had waved from a distance but otherwise left them alone.

Art was in the back of the truck, spreading out their sleeping bags, already excited by the idea of camping under the stars. She babbled about the rocks she'd seen, the hills she'd climbed. She lamented over the lack of dinosaur bones, asking if she could use the power of her mind to bring some up from the earth. She'd had a wicked smile on her face when she said that last bit, glancing at Nate out of the corner of her eye. Nate knew she was trying to get a reaction out of him, but he kept his face blank.

She looked slightly disappointed but moved on, talking about how warm the sleeping bags would be and how she thought it was going to be more comfortable than the motel bed they'd had *last* night, which was the absolute *worst.*

Alex grunted in all the right spots, the good mood from earlier in the day faded slightly. He wasn't back to his default scowling, which Nate was thankful for. Nate was almost . . . relaxed. His muscles were tired from their hike, but it was a *good* tired, almost down to his bones. His muscles felt stretched, his skin still warm from the sun. He'd probably be slightly pink tomorrow, but he'd worry about it then. The air was already cooling off considerably, and he'd found a coat in the truck. He thought it was Alex's. He'd put it on anyway. Alex hadn't said a word, but maybe his gaze had lingered just a little bit longer before going back to their dinner.

They sat huddled together on the tailgate of the truck when the soup was ready. Alex was in the middle, holding the pan on his lap. They each had a plastic spoon and took turns digging in. Alex was a line of warmth down Nate's side, their shoulders and arms brushing together.

They watched the sunset as they ate.

When they finished, they barely moved away after Alex put the pan down behind them.

"Would you look at that," Art said dreamily as the last of the daylight fell away.

Nate looked up.

It wasn't like in Oregon. Or Washington. Or even Montana. It certainly hadn't ever been like this in D.C. For the first time, Nate thought his eyes were open and he was actually seeing what was above him.

They were beneath a universe of stars, brighter than he'd ever seen before. They seemed to stretch on forever, more so than he could possibly comprehend. He'd never felt so small in his entire life.

"Wow," he breathed. "That's . . . wow."

"Yeah," Art said. "Isn't it?"

Nate felt Alex's hand brush against his own, but he didn't look away from the sky above. It could have been an accident. Nothing more.

"They didn't let me see . . . anything," Art said suddenly. Nate felt Alex stiffen next to him, but they both kept quiet. "While I was in the Mountain. Not like this. I begged them. I pleaded with them. I promised to show them what they wanted. All I wanted to do was go outside and look toward the sky. But they said no. They thought . . . I don't know what they thought. That maybe if I saw the stars, I could use them to communicate or something ridiculous like that. They didn't understand that all I wanted was to look up and see what I could see. How different it would be to be staring at the stars from this side of the universe."

Nate's heart was thundering in his chest.

"Alex came, and I asked him to describe the sky for me. He . . . wasn't very good at it at first. What did you say, Alex? When I asked you?"

Alex snorted. "I told you it all looked the same."

"That's *right*," Art said, and Alex's fingers touched Nate's. "It all looked the same. And I *laughed* at you until I realized you were serious. That you actually thought that. I think . . . I think that was the first time I ever felt sadness. Like, actual, true sadness. I'd been scared. I'd been angry. But I'd never been *sad*. Not until then. Not until you. Do you remember what I told you?"

"You said that I needed to go outside and not come back until I looked at the sky again. Really looked at it."

"And you did."

"I did."

"Why?"

"Because it felt like the right thing to do."

"And what did you see?"

Alex sighed. "That it was so much bigger than I ever thought it could be. That there was this . . . expanse to it. Something I'd never seen before."

"You felt tiny."

"Yes."

"Like you were nothing but a speck of sand on a beach."

"Yes."

"It's humbling to find that out," Art said. "Even in grief. Especially in grief, I think. You taught me that. I didn't understand it. Not before. And when you came back in, you described the night sky to me so well that I could *see* it. I could see it through your eyes, and it was like we were standing there side by side in the middle of nowhere, looking at the stars together. It was good. It was very good, Alex."

Alex didn't speak at all. Nate thought Art wasn't expecting him to.

"You set me free," she whispered. "And now I can see the stars for myself. Nate. Look. Can you see it?"

Nate followed her finger to where she was pointing.

"It's faint," she said. "The star. Do you know it?"

"No," he admitted. "I don't."

"You call it VL62 Cass. Which—honestly—you're all terrible at coming up with names for things. Where's the imagination? Your ancestors were so much better, even when they thought the stars were gods. I mean, who the heck looks up and says, oh look, it's my favorite, VL62. How pretty."

"Art," Alex said.

"Yeah, yeah. VL62 Cass is in Cassiopeia. It's also one of the far-thest stars that a human can see with the naked eye."

"What about it?" Nate asked.

"Beyond it is home. Far, far beyond it."

Nate hadn't thought he'd had it in him to be surprised at any-thing anymore. After all he'd heard. After everything he'd seen. He didn't think he was capable of shock.

He was wrong.

"I don't . . ." he managed to say. "That's . . ."

"I know," she said, and he believed her. "You're all capable of such great and terrible things. And in such a short amount of time. You are surrounded by millions of those like you, yet you can still feel alone. You're so angry and powerful and wonderful. And so fragile. You can break into pieces and feel so lost. I didn't get that. Not . . . before. I don't think any of us did. You're complex and yet so simple at the same time. It's a dichotomy that shouldn't be possi-ble. When you smile, it's like the sun is out. When you cry, it's like you're trapped in shadows and you can't find your way back to the light. You can hold a gun to your enemy's head and pull the trigger in the name of what you call God. You drop bombs and scorch the ground beneath your feet. You hurt each other. You love each other. You scream words that fall on deaf ears. You hate that others aren't like you. They scare you, even though they want nothing more than to *be* you. You make yourselves a home out of nothing. You carry each other until your knees give out and you stumble. It's almost impossible to understand. None of us could get that. Not until they felt a heart beating in a chest like I have. Not until I felt the bones beneath my skin. We're not alike. Not really. We're separated by time and space. And yet, somehow, we're all made of dust and stars. I think we'd forgotten that. And I don't know if you ever knew that to begin with. How can you be alone when we're all the same?"

Nate blinked away the burn in his eyes.

"Also," she added, "you have bacon, which to be honest, I might recommend a total planet takeover just to have. Like, complete hu-man annihilation."

Nate felt like he was choking. "Artemis Darth Vader."

"That's my name, don't wear it out."

"I don't think I've ever met anyone like you before."

"I should hope not. If you had, I would have to ask if you'd been anally probed before, and that would have been awkward. I probably would know the guy who did it."

Alex surprised them both by laughing.

They stared at him as he bent over, arms wrapped around his waist, and *laughed*. It sounded as if it came from deep within his chest, forcing its way out as if it'd been waiting for a moment to break free. It was rough and quiet, but it was there. Nate felt warmth blooming inside him at the sight of this man, this strange and delightfully scary man, laughing over something as childish as an *anal* probe.

Nate could do nothing but laugh too.

Art followed them both.

There, under an expanse of stars so very far away and a comet growing brighter by the hour, they laughed.

✦

She slept between them, out almost as soon as her head hit Alex's rolled-up jacket that Nate had given her to use as a pillow. Her eyes closed, and she started snoring immediately, the sound so much larger than it should have been from such a little girl. Nate would never not be impressed by it.

He brushed his teeth before drinking from a water bottle and swishing it around. He spat the water into the remains of their fire, hearing the embers hiss and sputter. He thought that maybe he should visit the pit toilet, but he couldn't bring himself to stumble over to the lean-to in the dark. He'd tough it out. If push came to shove, he'd wander off a little ways and piss out in the open, something he hadn't done since he was a kid.

Alex was already in the bed of the truck, sleeping bag pulled up to his chest, hands behind his head. Nate swallowed thickly at the sight of his biceps straining against the sleeves of his undershirt, and looked away. He climbed into the truck as carefully as he could, not wanting to wake Art.

The sleeping bag was warmer than he expected it to be. They'd been in the cabin. His parents must have bought them before they'd . . . well. Before. He wondered if they'd used them, if they'd taken them from the cabin and down to the lake and slept underneath the stars, the sound of waves against the beach lulling them under. The thought alone caused him to shiver.

He pulled the top of the sleeping bag up to his chin and laid his head down on his duffel bag. He closed his eyes and tried to sleep.

He couldn't.

He turned on his side toward the other two.

Alex had shifted into the same position, watching him over Art's head, eyes glittering in the dark.

"Hey," Nate whispered quietly.

"Hey," Alex whispered back.

He opened his mouth to ask what the plan was, what they were going to do tomorrow or the next day or the day after that. Instead, he said, "My father killed my mother."

Alex inhaled sharply but didn't speak.

Nate thought he should stop. That Alex didn't need to know any more. That this wasn't the time or place or *person* he should be telling this to. "He shot her. And then he shot himself. I hadn't seen them in years. I wasn't . . . what they expected me to be."

Alex nodded slowly.

"I didn't—I didn't even go to the funeral. I wasn't sure how I was supposed to feel. Sad because they were my parents? Angry that they let me go like I was nothing? I told myself I didn't owe them anything. I told myself I was a coward."

"Why?"

"Why what?"

"Why did they . . . What did they expect you to be?"

"Straight," Nate said, and it was *freeing*. It was *terrifying*. There was a chance—though Nate thought it was smaller than it once had been—that Alex would look at him with disgust, but it felt good to say it out loud. There'd been people who had known, but they weren't . . . important. Ruth, maybe. She'd known. But then wasn't like now. This was Alex.

"Oh" was all he said.

"Yeah." Nate chuckled weakly, hoping he hadn't just made a mistake. "I think I surprised them. Well, I *know* I surprised them. They walked in on me and my boyfriend."

Alex coughed. "That's what you meant. Back at the cabin."

"Yeah."

"Shit."

"Yeah."

"That's . . . rough."

"Always know the right thing to say, don't you."

"I'm trying."

Nate winced. "I know. I didn't—mean it. Not like that."

"I don't care."

And yeah, that hurt. More than he expected it to. "I'm sorry. I didn't—"

"No," Alex said quickly. "I didn't—I meant I don't care that you're . . . not straight." He sounded flustered.

"Oh," Nate said. "That's . . . good? Yeah. That's good. Thanks. And I don't know why I'm thanking you. That's weird. I just . . . Thanks. I guess. And I thanked you again, what the hell—"

"Nate."

Nate snapped his mouth shut.

"It's fine. I don't—it's not a big deal."

"Good. That's good."

Alex looked like he was steeling himself for something. He looked away, then back at Nate, then away again. He opened his mouth once, twice. Then, "I'm . . . a little like that. Um. Both. I like . . . both."

Nate blinked. "Bisexual. That's . . . cool. Cool. Yeah. Cool, cool, cool."

"Did I break you?"

"Shut up."

Alex's eyes crinkled again, like he was amused. "I think I broke you."

"You didn't break me. I'm just . . . surprised."

"Why?"

Nate shrugged. "I dunno. You're . . . you know. All . . . you."

"Because that cleared things up."

"I don't know what else to say!"

234 • TJ KLUNE

"Shh. You're going to wake her up."

"I doubt she can hear anything above her snoring."

Alex chuckled quietly. "She's always been like that. Like a chain-saw."

"It'd be endearing if it wasn't so obnoxious."

"You get used to it."

Alex would know, right? He'd had years to figure that out. "She's . . . happy."

Alex's smile faded slightly. "Yeah?"

"Yeah. Was she ever happy? In the Mountain?"

Alex's gaze hardened slightly, but Nate didn't think it was directed toward him. "Sometimes. When I was with her. They . . . There were times when they kept us apart. They wanted to test and see how far and how strong the bond was between us. The longest time they kept us separated was almost seven months. She . . . Neither of us did very well toward the end."

Nate wanted to ask what was going to happen when she went home, if that bond would break. He couldn't bring himself to do it. Instead, he said, "They didn't care about her, did they? The people in the Mountain."

Alex shook his head. "Not really. Not like I did. There were a few. They . . . treated her all right. But even they thought she was nothing more than a parasite in a little girl. An animal in a cage. They didn't see her for what she actually was. Not like—not like I did."

"What did you think when they first told you? I wouldn't even know how to begin to explain her to anyone."

Art snuffled in her sleep, turning her face toward Alex. Her hands twitched. Nate wondered if she dreamed. And if she did, what those dreams were made of.

"I—they brought me in. To the Mountain. Told me that I was being granted access to a special project. That I was going to be part of something extraordinary. That if I agreed to what they were asking me, sight unseen, without explanation, I could never go back. I had nothing left. So I said yes."

And as Alex spoke and Art slept between them, Nate's eyes glazed over and the stars above melted around them, streaking brightly toward the Earth as if they were falling. He could see the images in his head, flashes growing sharper through the haze and he—

✦

He thinks, sure, yeah, whatever. Classified. He's heard it before. He knows how it works. They know *he* knows how to keep his mouth shut. He's a lifer. Career. Enlisted when he was eighteen years old and never looked back. His mom was a drunk, and his dad was in prison serving twenty-five to life for armed robbery where a gun had been fired. *That* was what had nailed dear old Dad, the discharge of a firearm in the commission of a felony.

And Alex Weir, scrawny little Alex Weir, knew even then that if he didn't get out, if he didn't break the cycle, he'd end up just like them.

So when he marched into the recruiter's office, ink barely dry on his high school diploma, he knew he was making the right choice.

Eleven years later, they tell him that he's going to be part of something unlike anything he's ever witnessed before. He's numb, his heart lying in pieces in the pit of his stomach, but he's listening. He's never been the curious sort. He's need-to-know, a good Marine doing what he's told. He knows how to follow orders, which is why he almost *hesitates* when they ask him questions instead of telling him what to do.

A man is sitting across a desk from him, and Alex has no idea who he is. He's not in uniform. He's wearing wrinkled khakis and a polo shirt, and he says his name is Greer. He has a thick file folder on his desk that he's barely glanced through that Alex briefly saw his own picture in. Alex wants to ask what this is about, wants to know what his file says. He thinks momentarily that he's getting discharged, and that *terrifies* him, until Greer says, "This is . . . big, bucko. Bigger than anything you've ever seen in your life. You gotta be sure about this because there's no going back."

He's never been curious.

But god, is he curious now. Even through the pain that's soaked into his bones, he wants to know what this is all about.

He has nothing left, so he says yes.

Greer's smile doesn't quite reach his eyes.

They test him. They poke and prod him. He undergoes an EKG. EEG. MRI. He's x-rayed. They hook him up to wires from head to toe and say it's called 3D mapping. They take his blood. His plasma. His semen. They do a spinal tap. They test his vision. His reflexes. He runs on a treadmill, mile after mile after mile until he thinks he's going to drop.

It goes on for six months.

Greer comes back, after.

He says, "It's time."

Alex is flown from Phoenix and taken to the Mountain for the first time in the spring of 1985. He's thirty years old, and he has lost everything.

He thinks it's going to be experimental weapons. Or armor. Maybe even robots. His imagination had never been something grand (his mother always said he was far too dour and serious as a child), but he's seen movies. He knows that sometimes science fiction really isn't fiction at all. There's always going to be a new type of warfare, and he's good at what he does. He's decorated. People follow him. He's street-smart and quick on his feet. His body has been honed. He's ready.

Which is why he falters when they take him deep inside the Mountain to a room with floor-to-ceiling glass walls.

Inside the walls—the *cage*—is a little girl.

She's wearing pink sweats and a blue tank top. She's sitting cross-legged in the middle of the floor, head cocked to the side as she watches him with bright eyes. There's a bed. A bookshelf filled with books. A partition with a toilet and a shower behind it. A green, leafy plant that looks as if it is growing wildly out of control.

And her, of course.

He thinks, oh, you bastards, you bastards, you knew what you were doing, you knew why you asked me to do this, how—

He says, "What is this?"

This, Greer tells him, is the Seventh Sea.

The little girl rolls her eyes.

"I don't understand."

"I know," Greer says. "But you will."

They take him from the room. From her cage. Before he's through the door, he glances back at her over his shoulder.

She waves at him.

He doesn't wave back.

And when they *tell* him what she is, where she's come from, how long she's been there, *everything,* he says, "Bullshit."

Greer laughs. "I said the same thing, bucko. But I can assure you, it's true. All of it is true."

(Nate felt it here. This moment. This terribly singular moment when everything Alex had ever known about how the world worked shattered with the greatest of ease. In the bed of the truck, he trembled.)

They give him a few days to . . . process. He meets with people who talk to him about things like *biology* and *genetic makeup.* They say things like *no verifiable DNA* and *Ophiocordyceps unilateralis.* He doesn't get it. He can't comprehend. He's a grunt. Give him a gun and tell him where to shoot, and he'll pull the trigger. Give him a map and point to where the enemy is, and he'll figure out a way to flank them. But tell him that the little girl in the room is an extraterrestrial, and he doesn't know what to *do* with that. He doesn't know how to *reconcile* it with everything he knows.

They take him back into the room.

The girl says, "Hello again," and Alex's knees buckle beneath him.

No one moves to help him up.

The girl says, "People do that a lot around me. It's weird, right?"

They don't give her a name. Not a real name anyway. They call her *Seventh Sea* or *it* or *that thing that came from outer space.*

It takes four months for Alex to work up the nerve to actually talk to it without being angry. To the thing that came from outer space.

To her.

The leaves are changing color on the trees in the forest on the Mountain when he says, "Hey."

She blinks, just once, and says, "Hi, Alex."

He lets her in. God help him, he lets her in.

She's . . . not what he expected. She likes to read. She laughs when he tells her about a dog he had when he was a kid, a stupid mutt that always seemed to trip over its own feet. She asks him questions about anything and everything. What is his favorite color. Has he ever been to the ocean. Has he ever ridden a horse. Has he ever petted a penguin. (Blue. Yes. No. What the hell?)

(Nate laughed. Or at least he thought he did. He couldn't be sure.)

At first, there's always someone in the room with them. Multiple someones. They stay in the background, typing on their computers, writing on their notepads, poring over the readouts that never seem to stop printing. They whisper behind him, always speaking in low voices, never interrupting Alex and the Seventh Sea until it's time for him to go.

He's in awe of her.

He resents her.

He doesn't know what to do, because this is *tearing* at him. The first year is the worst because he's still in mourning. He's still *grieving* over everything he's lost. And here she is, this thing that came from outer space, and she smiles at him now, every time he comes into the room. She tells him she doesn't like it when he goes away. She asks if they can watch a movie. There's a TV set up, a big black VCR underneath. They bring in tapes. Comedies. Cartoons. Westerns. She loves those the most. She'll sit on the ground against the wall that separates them, elbows on her knees, chin in her hand, and she'll be *enraptured* by the sight of cowboys and Indians, of bandits robbing a train.

He'll sit too during movie time. He's offered a chair. He takes it. He uses it. At first. But eventually, he's sitting on the ground too, six inches of bulletproof glass separating them.

Sometimes, the power flickers and goes out. It never lasts long.

"Wiring," Greer tells him. "It's terrible here. I don't think we were meant to go so far inside the Mountain."

In the second year, he goes inside her cage.

They tell him to wear a hazmat suit.

He tells them to fuck off.

She's fidgeting. Hopping from one foot to the other.

There are many men in the room with them, standing back and watching. Waiting.

Two doors lead into the cage. He stands in front of the first, and the electronic lock shifts from red to green. The door slides open slowly. He walks in. It closes behind him. Above, fans whir to life and a faint mist sprays over him, tasting faintly medicinal. The fans slow and eventually stop. The second door opens.

He walks into the cage.

She's hugging him even before he realizes she's moved.

Her little arms are wrapped around his waist, her head resting against his stomach, and he *hates* her, hates everything she represents.

But he puts a hand on the top of her head and says, "Hello."

It's during the fifth year that she bonds with him.

It happens with the greatest of ease.

One moment she's reading aloud to him from the book he's brought for her (*Mrs. Frisby and the Rats of NIMH*), and the next, he's hearing it in his head. He doesn't understand what's happening at first, doesn't understand why her lips are no longer moving but he can still *hear* her. Except it's not just words, is it? He can *see* Mrs. Frisby and Nicodemus and Justin and Jeremy and Dragon. But not as if they're real. No. It's how *she* sees them, this little girl they call Seventh Sea, and she's *telling* him the story inside his head, and it's overwhelming. Too much so.

He faints.

They don't let him see her for a week.

They ask him what happened.

They want to *understand.*

He thinks about lying. About keeping this just between himself and the girl.

But he has a duty.

He tells them.

When they let him back into the room, the relief on her face is palpable. "I'm sorry," she tells him, stricken. "I never meant—"

"It's okay," he says gruffly.

She looks down at her hands. "I was . . . sad. When you were gone."

(Nate felt his heart break. He wanted to reach out and press his fingers against Art's sleeping face, but he couldn't move. He wasn't even sure he was awake anymore.)

And oh, doesn't *that* set them off. In the years they've had her, when she was Oren and when she was as she is now, she *never* said anything about sadness. She's never said anything about emotion at all. Oh, they've seen expressions on her face. She smiles. She frowns. She gets angry, rare though it is. But she's never emoted *aloud*.

She has now. She was sad when Alex was taken from her.

For the first time, there in the fifth year, Alex thinks she doesn't belong here.

It's a dangerous thought.

So goddamn dangerous.

So much so, in fact, that he doesn't let himself think of it again for the longest time.

Not until the ninth year, at least.

During the ninth year, they bring in a woman who calls herself only Laura, and she changes everything. Alex is told they're not getting the results they need, that they've plateaued and the higher-ups are demanding answers. Greer, whom Alex has only seen a handful of times since being brought to the Mountain, grins ruefully at him. "She's a hard-ass," he says. "Hope you're ready, bucko."

Laura's no-nonsense. She's older, maybe in her early fifties. She wears the same drab blouses, the same lab coat, the same pair of horn-rimmed glasses day in and day out. She doesn't smile the first time she meets the Seventh Sea. She doesn't even look shocked. Alex wonders what she's thinking as she walks slowly around the cage, gaze calculating. For her part, the girl (*Artemis*, she'd shown him in his head in the sixth year, *you can call me Artemis*) doesn't seem affected. She stands in one spot, spinning in a slow circle, watching Laura.

Once Laura has circumnavigated the cage, she looks at Alex for the first time. "You're the one she's bonded with."

"Yes, ma'am," Alex says.

"Good." She glances over his shoulder at the guards near the door. "Get him out of here. I don't want to see him in here again until I say."

"What?" the girl (Artemis, Art) says, sounding alarmed. "No, wait, what are you—"

Alex thinks about fighting. Thinks about grabbing one of the rifles and telling this woman, this Laura, that she won't take Art away from him. That she won't separate them.

He doesn't.

And Laura does exactly that.

For *seven months*.

It's . . . agonizing. There are moments, brief though they are, when he can still *feel* her, little short bursts of images in his head. Alex doesn't know if it's the distance that's weakening the bond, or if it's something grimmer, but it's *barely there*. And when it *is* there, it's bright flashes of *pain*. Like they're *hurting* her.

Alex doesn't eat. There are days when he doesn't get out of bed. It goes on like this for two months. He's sick. Feverish. He knows he's being monitored, that he's part of this just like Art is, but there's nothing he can do to stop it.

In the fourth month, he demands a meeting with Laura.

It takes three weeks.

He's led to her office, which used to be Greer's. "He's . . . retired," Laura tells him when he asks. "Fishing. Golfing. Whatever one does when one is no longer needed."

Alex doesn't believe her.

"Do you understand why?" she asks him. "Why we have to break her?"

He keeps the mask firmly in place. He won't allow it to slip. Not to this woman. She expects it. He won't let her have it.

"No," he says.

She nods slowly. "I thought not. Tell me, Mr. Weir. What do you think will happen if they come back for her? If she's something important? What if they decide that what we've done here is equivalent to firing the first shot?"

Alex doesn't respond.

Laura sighs, sitting back in the leather chair behind the desk. "We have to be prepared for an invasion. They aren't like anything we've ever seen. How can we hope to stop them if we don't understand them? This isn't . . . this isn't like Roswell, Mr. Weir. These aren't beings of flesh and whatever fluid they call blood. They have the potential to be nothing less than a biological weapon. They won't attack from above. They will attack from *within*. We run the risk of being nothing but hosts to an advanced race that has evolved far beyond anything we have ever seen before. Do you really think we can sit idly by and let that happen? Or should we be prepared for every eventuality?"

She's . . . not wrong. Alex knows this. But in his secret heart, in that place that's only begun to put itself back together, he doesn't believe it. At all. "Why?"

Laura arches an eyebrow. "Why what, Mr. Weir?"

"Why would they do that? Why would they come all this way just to attack us? To take us over. If they are as advanced as you seem to think they are, won't they have evolved past such desires?"

"Pragmatism has no place when dealing with the unknown. If someone comes uninvited through the back door, you don't welcome them into your home. You get your gun and show them who lives there."

"Shoot first, ask questions later," he says bitterly. "Art would never—"

"Art?" she asks, deceptively soft.

He closes his eyes.

"Ah," Laura says. "I see."

She keeps him away for three more months.

(Nate had never hated anyone he'd never met before. He hated Laura.)

He never figures out exactly *why* he's allowed back into the room with the cage. He doesn't know if it's because Art demands it, if she says she'll tell them what they need to know. He's not sure, but he doesn't care, because the *relief* he feels when he sees her again is all-encompassing, though he doesn't allow the stony expression on his face to change. It doesn't matter, because she knows. The bond between them flares to life, and he's *assaulted* with images from her, pictures in his head that are like seeing a sunrise for the first time. She's *happy*. Oh yes, she's many other things too (hurt and angry and scared), but she's *happy*.

(Nate felt like he was barely breathing.)

Hello, Artemis says in his head.

Hello, he pushes back.

And she *smiles.*

Deep in his mind, away from where even Artemis can see, Alex begins to think that things shouldn't be the way they are.

Things return to . . . well, not *normal,* because nothing about this is normal. Laura seems to take a step back, though Alex is sure she's never too far away. They still run their tests, but it's not as extensive as it was in the months they were separated. Art tells him little about what she went through no matter how much Alex asks. He doesn't know if he's grateful or not.

At one point, she asks him how long she's been in the cage.

He tells her it's been almost thirty years.

He flinches when she speaks aloud and says, "Huh. That's not very long at all."

Time has . . . no meaning. At least not to her. She tries to explain it to him, but it's too abstract for him to understand. Thirty years to a human could be considered a lifetime. In thirty years, a person could be born, learn to speak and walk and think. They grow during that time until they reach adulthood. Their minds solidify. They become who they are.

It's different for Artemis. Time is fluid. Thirty years is nothing.

He asks her once how old she is.

He gets back a complicated series of images that makes him believe *centuries,* but that she's still considered a child where she comes from. A word that almost seems like *youngling.*

Toward the end of the ninth year, she sends him an image and a collection of words.

He sees stars.

And he hears *I think they're coming back for me.*

Every morning after that, he wakes up before the sunrise. He leaves the Mountain for the base below. He walks along the edges of the fences. He memorizes the perimeter. He counts the soldiers. He counts the number of steps it takes from the Mountain to the back gate. To the front gate. He tells himself his duty is to his country. That he needs to stop this now.

He can't. He can't. He can't.

(*Oh my god*, Nate tried to say out loud. *Oh my god*.)

His mind is sharp. It always has been. He can retain so much in very little time. He learns all the escape routes out of the Mountain. How often the guards rotate their shifts. How many are where. He finds their weak points. There are three rotations. Four in the morning till noon. Noon till eight at night. Eight until four in the morning.

The 4:00 A.M. switch is the weakest. The men leaving are tired. The men coming on are barely awake. The sky is dark.

And the wiring inside the room where she's held has never gotten better. The power still comes and goes, especially during storms. They have backups, sure. Generators. But they take a good few minutes to kick in. There are contingencies in place. Art's cage never opens when the power is out. He thinks she can open it if she wants to, but she hasn't yet, and he hasn't worked up the nerve to ask her why. The cameras in the room fall silent. The only light comes from the row of emergency lights along the floor showing the way to the exits.

Alex doesn't know if he can do this.

He doesn't know if it's the right thing.

The decision is made for him when he overhears Laura one afternoon, almost ten years to the day since the first time he was brought to the Mountain. He hasn't heard from Laura in months, so he's surprised to find her in the room with Art. Laura doesn't see him, her back to him as she faces Artemis.

She says, "Soon. I think it'll be soon."

And then she turns and leaves, brushing by Alex without so much as a nod in his direction.

He doesn't know what *soon* means.

But he knows he doesn't like the sound of it.

He hears whispers in the few days that follow. He's such a recognizable face in the Mountain that people tend to think he's there doing what's asked of him. Maybe they don't realize he can hear them. The scientists in the room speak of plans to do what they'd only done once before. With Oren Schraeder. To forcibly remove her from the body that she inhabits.

Except this time, they aren't going to provide her with another host.

If it's gaseous, they whisper, it can be broken down to the smallest of molecules. Instead of learning what they can from the host, why not go directly to the source? Surely there are secrets embedded in . . . whatever it is. They're not finding out anything new. They don't want to be replaced like Greer was. Some of them have been there for *decades*. There needs to be an endgame.

And it's coming.

She stares at him curiously. "What is it?"

"Do you trust me?" he asks her.

And the image that she sends back to him is so full of love and light that it knocks the breath from his chest. She does. She trusts him very much.

Okay, he thinks in response. *Okay*.

It's stupid, really. It won't work. It *shouldn't* work. Alex has never been lucky that way. He knows far too well that even something planned to the last detail can still go to shit at a moment's notice. His entire life has been a prime example of just that.

But he's still got to try.

And maybe he's been planning it for longer than he's aware. After all, there was a *reason* he'd been pulling money out weekly and stuffing it under his mattress, right? Why else would he have done such a thing unless he was always going to do this?

He's conscious of the choice he's making for weeks.

But he thinks it maybe goes back almost a year.

And then everything aligns.

He waits until he knows Laura is off the Mountain. She leaves every month or so for a week before returning. He doesn't know where she goes. He wonders sometimes if she has a family waiting for her. And if she does, what they think she's doing when she leaves for work. He thinks they'd be surprised to know their loved one has ordered the decimation of the thing inside the little girl.

Coincidentally, it's during one of her absences that the threat of a strong spring storm comes in.

Now, he thinks. *Now. Now. Now.*

He doesn't sleep that night.

He knows he should.

But he can't.

Instead, he watches the digital clock as the numbers click by.

It's three thirty when he's moving.

Thunder peals overhead, faintly echoing inside the Mountain.

He takes nothing with him, not that much remains. He's already loaded a jeep in the motor pool at the back of the base days before. No one even looked in his direction when he took clothes from Art's cage. He's done her laundry before.

There are a few people out and about, but it's late (or early, depending on how you look at it), and they're all dead-eyed. They nod at him but say nothing more. He heads to the security room next to where Art resides. Inside is a sleepy-eyed man that Alex barely knows. He's surrounded by monitors. Rock music plays from a small stereo.

"Hey," Alex says just as the monitors flicker with another rumble of thunder.

"Hey," the man says, glancing over his shoulder. "You're up early."

Alex shrugged. "Couldn't sleep. How's our girl?"

"Hasn't moved in hours," the man says, nodding toward one of the monitors. A thin stripe of static rolls up the screen. There's the faint outline of the bed. She's on her side, comforter pulled up to her neck.

The man yawns, jaw cracking.

"I can take it from here," Alex offers. "You've only got another fifteen minutes before shift change, anyway."

The man glances at him hopefully. Alex has done it a handful of times in the last year preparing for this exact moment. "Yeah? Dude, that would be *awesome*. I got a date with one of the townies tomorrow." He frowned. "Later today, I guess it is now. Waitress. Dude, she is hot. Got this set of tits like you wouldn't believe."

Alex waves him away. "Get outta here. Get some sleep. Don't want to fall asleep on your dream girl."

"Or do I?" the man asks, waggling his eyebrows. He stands, hands above his head as he stretches his back. Before he leaves the small room, he pats Alex on the shoulder. "Thanks, man. This is really cool of you."

"No problem. Hey, is it Reyes and Jones on guard duty?" He already knows the answer, but it's good to get confirmation.

"Yep. Got their table set up outside its room. Cheating at cards again."

Alex forces a chuckle. "Assholes."

"Don't I know it. Thanks again, Weir. I'll see you tomorrow."

He's out the door without looking back.

Alex listens for his footsteps to fade.

The monitors flicker as the storm grows overhead.

He looks back to the screen for the camera near Art's bed.

She's not sleeping.

Instead, she's wide awake, standing underneath the camera, staring straight into the lens.

He makes quick work of the recording equipment. He rips wires. Old coffee is poured on electronics.

One by one, the screens turn to snow.

He's moving now, out the door and down the hallway. He stops at a T-intersection, the metal grating beneath his feet groaning slightly. He takes a deep breath. He's doing the right thing. He's doing this for her.

He turns down the hall to the right. Reyes and Jones are sitting near the entrance to Art's room, small folding table set up between them, rifles set off to the side, leaning back in their rickety chairs. Jones has a lit cigarette in his mouth, smoke curling up around his head. There's an ashtray stuffed with discarded butts near his right hand. Cards are spread out between them.

They look up when they hear him approaching. "Weir," Reyes says. "What are you doing up?"

"Couldn't sleep."

Jones laughs. "Getting old, buddy?"

"Must be," he says, already having decided upon how to dispatch them with minimal noise. "I need to get inside."

Jones's smile fades a little. "Can't do that, big guy. You know the rules. No one inside until six. Protection, you know? We don't want it to hurt anyone."

Alex snorts. "You really think she's going to hurt me?"

Jones and Reyes share an uneasy look. Oh, and he *knows* what that means. They, like most everyone else below his pay grade (and maybe even a few above), don't know what to make of him, don't know if he's entirely human anymore. He's heard their whispers, saying that he's been brainwashed, that it's gotten inside his head too, that it's *infected* him, making him do its bidding. They're wary of him, yes, but they're also *scared* of him. They're afraid of what they don't understand.

Which is good. Because they should be.

"No," Reyes says slowly. "We don't think *she's* going to hurt you, but orders are orders. You know?"

"I outrank you."

Neither of them have reached for their rifles yet. Foolish, really. "True," Jones says. "But this is *above* you. You know that."

"I do," Alex says, smiling. "I'm just playing around, guys. Yanking your chain a little."

They both relax.

He goes after Jones first, as he's the quicker of the two. Alex has got two *decades* of experience under his belt. Even though he's been assigned to this project for ten years now, he hasn't let himself get out of shape. He's as strong as he's ever been and still able to move quicker than a man half his age.

He has his hands over Jones's face, slamming his head back against the rock wall behind him. Jones grunts, slumping down in his chair.

Reyes moves faster than Alex expects. He's already raising his rifle as Alex spins toward him. Alex grabs it by the barrel, sight digging into the flesh of his palm. He snaps it to the side, breaking Reyes's trigger finger. The rifle does not go off. Reyes opens his mouth to cry out in pain, but all that comes out is a harsh croak as he gets the heel of Alex's palm slammed against his throat. His eyes bulge as Alex grabs him by the back of the head, slamming him face-first into the table. It collapses at the force of the impact, and Reyes goes down with a low grunt. His eyes are fluttering as he rolls to his side, nose bleeding in rivulets down his cheeks. He stares blearily up at Alex and opens his mouth, but Alex's boot meets his face, and he's out.

Less than a minute has passed since they greeted him.

He drags an unconscious Reyes to the panel next to the door leading to Art's room. He holds his hand up to a black pad. For a moment, nothing happens. Then a thin blue light scans down the length of his hand. The door slides open.

He drops Reyes to the floor.

Art watches as he enters her room. The low lights flicker overhead. He moves quickly, needing to get to the computer before the power—

The lights go out.

There's a beat of silence, and then the emergency lights pulse white along the floor.

"No," he whispers, because her fucking cage is *locked*, it's—

She's standing against the glass wall nearest him.

She puts her hand flat against it.

He feels it in his head. The whispers. The images. She thinks of impossible stars.

Spiderweb cracks burst underneath her palm.

Alex takes a step back.

The wall of glass shatters.

But the pieces don't fall.

She lowers her hand and walks through the glass slowly, pushing sharp shards out of her way.

She stops in front of him, a small smile on her face. "Are we going on an adventure?"

He says, "Time to saddle up and hit the trail."

(Nate was gone, gone, gone.)

He takes her by the hand. His grip engulfs hers.

They flee the room.

She doesn't comment on the two men they have to step over.

He's moving down the hallway, the way out already mapped in his head. He glances down at his watch. The shift change is coming up in ten minutes. The hallways are dark, the generators not yet having kicked back on.

They bypass the main thoroughfares. It's easier to stick to the smaller paths. Fewer people. But there will come a point where they won't have a choice. Each exit to the Mountain will have at least two guards posted with two more on the way.

But that's what he's counting on.

They reach the closest exit in less than five minutes.

He peers around the corner.

Two men stand in front.

He has to be quick.

He lets go of Art's hand and thinks, *Stay.*

He walks around the corner.

The man on the right sees him first. He looks to raise his rifle but stops when he recognizes Alex. "Sir," he says.

"What are you still doing standing here?" Alex growls. "The generators haven't come up yet. There are *protocols* in place. Why haven't you checked in yet?"

Right glances at Left. "Shift change hasn't come through. We thought we'd wait until—"

"You thought wrong," Alex snaps. "Move your asses and—"

Then, from behind him, "Holy shit, what the hell is it doing *out*—"

He turns. Shift change was early. Two men stand, guns pointing toward Art, who has moved into the hallway.

Fuck.

Left and Right moan behind him.

"Hello," Artemis Darth Vader says. "It's nice to see you."

She jerks her head to the right.

All four men slam against the walls, rifles falling from their grasps and landing on the ground.

"Huh," Art says. "They weren't as heavy as I thought they'd be. I may have overdone it. Poor guys. That's gonna hurt when they wake up."

Alex grabs a key card off one of the men near the door. He waits. Nothing. The power is still off.

He's starting to panic. "Come on. Come *on*—"

The lights kick on overhead. He doesn't know if it's the power coming back or the generators, but it doesn't matter.

He slides the key card through the black slot on the wall.

It beeps.

The door slides open.

"Let's go," he says. "We have to hurry."

They run down a long hallway. They're close. So close.

They reach the last door. This one isn't locked electronically. He shoves it open.

Rain slams against his face. He takes in a deep breath of cold air. His skin is instantly soaked. Art gasps at the wave of *wet* that washes over her, and later Alex will realize it's the first time she's been out of the Mountain in over three decades. It'll hit him and hit him hard.

Lightning flashes overhead.

Thunder rolls.

He grabs Artemis by the hand again and pulls her out into the storm. The gravel on the path crunches beneath their feet. Alex blinks away the rain. Ahead of them, he can see the spotlights at the entrance to the base moving slowly back and forth, the guards pacing in their towers.

They head away from the front gate. Alex leads them off the main path, keeping to the trees and the shadows. They freeze briefly as two soldiers run by. They wait until the soldiers disappear around a corner before they move again.

The motor pool is empty this early in the morning. The mechanics don't come on shift for a few more hours. The warehouse housing vehicles belonging to the government of the United States of America is large, but Alex knows exactly where they need to go.

They enter through a side door and close it behind them. Rain drums on the ceiling overhead. Art is shivering, but there's nothing he can do about that now. He remembers the first time he found out she *could* be cold, and it had shocked him more than he expected it to. And then he'd learned she could be hungry and happy and experience *pain*, and he still wonders if this is worth it to her. From the bits and pieces she's given him, it's not like this for her when she's . . . how she normally is. She doesn't *experience* emotions or sensations, not to the extent humans do. At least she didn't before.

There are days he wishes for that. Days he wishes he could push it all away.

He doesn't know if she wants the same thing.

He doesn't know how to ask.

They move down rows of Humvees and jeeps and armored vehicles with mounted machine guns across the top. He's briefly considered taking one of those, but it wouldn't be very subtle, now would it? He can't imagine driving down a road and *not* getting pulled over because of the large weapon attached to the top of their vehicle.

The jeep is gray. It's a newer model (most of the vehicles in the warehouse are—taxpayer dollars at work in this secret government facility experimenting on an alien life force) and fully gassed. He's stocked it as best he could while remaining inconspicuous. His duffel bag is already inside, filled with clothes and cash. He's grabbed a similar bag for her. There's some food and water, but it isn't much. He couldn't take more without drawing suspicion.

And now that they're here, now that he's opening the door for her and she's climbing inside, he realizes how crazy this is. How spectacularly bad of an idea this is. Oh sure, he's *thought* it was nuts before, but it was abstract. He's had other things to focus on besides the fact that the chances of this working—of them actually escaping—are slim.

He has to try.

He puts her seat belt on.

She touches his hand. "We're going to be okay."

He nods tightly.

He steps back and shuts her door. He's around the front of the jeep when a voice says, "I told myself you wouldn't be this stupid. I hate it when I'm proven wrong."

Laura's standing a few rows down, flanked by two men. He doesn't recognize them, but he can figure out who they are. Or rather, what group they belong to.

Enforcers.

An elite group of men in the Mountain whose primary job is this *exact* moment.

They are trackers. Hunters.

If there is a breach, they are the ones sent to find and contain.

He's seen a few of them around the Mountain before. There were whispers about who *exactly* they worked for. From what Alex has gathered, they are privately contracted by the United States. It gives deniability in case it is needed.

They're armed, but then so is Laura. She has a pistol in her hand, a blank look on her face.

"You have to know this won't end well," she tells him, not unkindly.

Alex says nothing. He's already planning in his head.

Laura nods, as if she's expected his silence. "I don't know what it's capable of, Mr. Weir. I don't think even you know. It has infected you."

The massive doors at the front of the warehouse are still closed. The jeep is reinforced, so they'll still have a chance. This doesn't have to be the end.

Except Laura raises her gun and *shoots* him.

(Nate thought he was screaming, but no sound came out.)

It's so quick that he doesn't have time to react. He's been shot before, once, in the Al-Asimah province in Kuwait back in 1982. It'd been in a port city, a through-and-through on his right arm. It'd hurt, but he'd been able to grit his teeth and fight through it.

This isn't that.

At first, he's unsure of what's even happened. One moment he's standing in front of the jeep, hands in fists at his sides, and the next he's staggering against it, his abdomen on fire. He can hear Art yelling behind him, and he takes in a ragged breath. It hurts, holy fuck does it hurt. His vision is starting to tunnel, but he's trying to fight it.

One of the Enforcers hands Laura a thick circular band of metal. He knows what that is.

The thing in the little girl behind him had once inhabited the body of a young soldier named Oren Schraeder. After a time, it was decided to see if they could hurt it. Her. Him. They tried many things. Chemicals. Gas. Injections. But it wasn't until they electrocuted the *hell* out of Oren that they realized how they could at the very least *contain* it.

The Enforcer has handed Laura a collar capable of shocking the wearer with *thousands* of volts.

Art has never had to wear it before.

But the threat has always been there.

Alex doesn't think it's just a threat now.

And apparently neither does she.

Because Alex feels it building. It's like a storm in his brain.

Artemis is *pissed*.

Get in the truck, he hears in his head. *Now*. He's never heard her sound so cold.

The vehicles around him begin to rattle.

The Enforcers take a step back.

Laura's eyes narrow.

She raises her gun again and—

The ground cracks beneath his feet as he lurches toward the driver's side of the jeep. He hears one of the Enforcers shout in warning, and there's the crack of gunfire, and he swears he *hears* the bullet cutting the air as it hurtles by him. He's got one hand wrapped around his middle, and he knows he's bleeding. It's *bad*, but Art has told him to move, so he's moving.

He's at the door and jerks it open. He grits his teeth through the pain as he climbs inside. He fumbles for the keys he's hidden in the visor and closes the door behind him.

Art isn't looking at him.

She's staring straight ahead, eyes wide and vacant.

Alex follows her gaze out the window.

"Fuck," he breathes.

Dozens of vehicles have risen into the air. They hang suspended at least ten feet off the ground. The Enforcers have their weapons raised toward them as if bullets will stop what is about to happen.

Laura, though. She's staring straight at them, gun raised, collar in her other hand at her side.

"Drive," Art tells him in a low voice.

He starts the jeep.

He sees the exact moment Laura decides to pull the trigger again. Her shoulders tighten, and she lets out a deep breath.

Alex shifts the jeep into drive.

He slams his foot on the gas pedal.

The vehicles begin to rain down. There are loud shrieks of metal as they crash into the ground, glass shattering, hoods popping off and flipping into the air. Farther into the warehouse and off to the right, a Humvee explodes, the fire bright in the dark, shrapnel embedding itself into the walls.

The Enforcers are running, trying to dodge what's coming from above. One almost makes it to a side door when another jeep lands on top of him. Alex doesn't see what happens to the other one.

Laura doesn't run. She walks slowly toward the oncoming vehicle, firing her weapon with sharp precision. The bullets hit the reinforced windshield and deflect away. Her aim is true; the windshield chips right in front of Alex's face.

He doesn't slow.

She doesn't jump out of the way like he expects. When the jeep strikes her at nearly thirty miles an hour, destruction still falling from above, she's on the hood and against the windshield, a bright splash of blood spraying against the glass. And then she's up and over the jeep.

"Doors," Alex says. "Art, *doors*."

Artemis hums a little under her breath. The sliding doors shudder in their frames, and there's a moment when Alex thinks they'll slam into them head-on. It'll be over before they ever exit the warehouse.

But then the doors are *torn* off their hinges, the entire front *wall* of the warehouse breaking away as if a massive tornado is spinning outside. They're in the warehouse, and then they're out in the dark and lightning, rain slashing against the windshield. He's driving one-handed, his other hand holding the wound in his side.

From there, it's like a dream.

He hears alarms blaring, knows they're being fired upon, but no bullets seem to hit them. He's floating, maybe just a little, hearing whispers in his head that tell him everything is going to be all right. Everything is going to be just fine. They'll be okay.

He believes the whispers.

At one point, there's a spotlight shining down on them, and he hears the *thumpthumpthump* of rotor blades, but then there's a jarring crash and an explosion somewhere in the distance.

They burst through the back gate and onto an old logging road. The road is muddy and slick, water rolling down the hills around them. His focus is on keeping his eyes open. He has precious cargo. Nothing can happen to her.

Art will tell him later the next crash he hears is an avalanche behind him, one of the rocky hills giving way and falling onto the road, washing it out. "We got lucky," she'll say. "The storm must have loosened it."

He won't believe her, but he won't say a word about it.

She's telling him to move his hand, Alex, move your hand, and he groans as he does. Then *her* hand is on him, and it feels *hot*, like she's *scalding* him. He somehow manages not to scream.

Three days later, they find a sign pointing them toward Herschel Lake.

Art says, "There. We should go there."

Alex says, "We have to keep going. We have to get as far away as we can."

Artemis Darth Vader shakes her head. "No, Alex. We have to go to the lake. I know it. You have to trust me."

He does. She's the only thing he has left.

So he turns up the road toward the lake and—

✦

Nate blinked slowly, feeling as if he'd just awoken from the most vivid of dreams.

Artemis was snoring, head on Alex's shoulder.

Alex was watching him.

Neither of them spoke for what felt like hours.

Then, "She . . . How did you . . ."

Alex said, "I don't know. It's . . . what she does. The connection. The bond. With me. With you."

"We have to get her home," Nate said, and he wasn't sure if he'd ever believed in anything more in his life. "We have to find a way to get her home."

He didn't expect Alex to raise an arm. He didn't expect the hand coming toward his face. The fingers trailing along his cheek. His jawline. The thumb brushing over his lips.

He leaned into it because it was the only thing he *could* do.

He turned his head slightly and pressed a dry kiss into Alex's palm.

Alex's eyes widened, but he didn't pull away.

Nate reached up and took Alex's hand in his own. He slid a little bit closer until he could tuck Alex's hand against his chest. It was warm.

Alex sighed as if in relief and closed his eyes. Nate watched as he fell asleep a moment later, arm resting over Art.

Nate fell asleep soon after under the sea of stars and a comet that burned brightly.

The next morning, over powdered eggs that tasted like shit, Art said, "You know where we have to go."

Alex rubbed a hand over his face. "Are you sure?"

She nodded slowly. "It's . . . I think it's the right thing to do. Before."

Nate glanced between the two of them. "I'm not going to like this, am I?"

"Saddle up, partner," Art told him. "There's rough days ahead."

CHAPTER FOURTEEN

Five days later, Nate stared out the window as they passed a black carriage being pulled by a single horse. Inside the carriage sat two men dressed in dark clothes with wide-brimmed hats. Both had thick beards. They waved as the truck passed them by. Art waved back cheerily.

"You've got to be kidding me," Nate said as they passed a sign welcoming them to Bird-in-Hand, Pennsylvania.

Alex snorted. "Afraid not."

"He's *Amish* now?"

"No. But there's a good-sized Amish population out here. Mennonites too. It seemed to fit him . . . after. There's a tendency to eschew technology of any kind. It makes sense if you think about it."

"Nothing about this makes sense. Literally nothing."

"Try not to worry too much about it."

Nate turned slowly to gape at him.

"Yeah, yeah, yeah," Alex said, a small smile on his face. Ever since that night in the Badlands, it'd been making more of an appearance. Nate wasn't complaining. He was rather fond of the crinkles around Alex's eyes when he smiled.

"Do you think I'll get to ride a horse?" Art asked for what had to be the hundredth time. "If he has horses, that is. But, I mean, he lives on a *farm*, right? He *has* to have horses. It's like, the law."

"I don't think that's quite true," Nate told her.

She rolled her eyes. "You don't know that. And—" She gasped. "Oh my heck, what if he has *pigs*? What if there's *bacon*?"

"You just had bacon yesterday, remember? You told the waitress at the restaurant to just, and I quote, *keep it coming, sweetheart.*"

"She stared at me weird after that."

"Probably because you called her sweetheart."

"I saw it in a movie once. Wanted to try it out and see how it went. Upon retrospection, I don't have the chops to pull it off." She sighed dreamily. "Pork chops."

"You're so weird," Nate said, and he didn't know if he'd ever meant anything more. She acted like such a human sometimes.

"Please, if you'd had to subsist on nothing but the energy around you for centuries until you finally got to have taste buds for the first time, you'd say the same thing."

And then there were those other times when she said shit like *that*.

"Christ," Nate muttered.

"Still working on him," Art said with a frown. "Why do humans say his name in vain while others use the idea of him to make themselves think they're better than everyone else?"

"I don't even want to get into that conversation with you," Nate said. "It's futile."

"But, *Nate*."

"No. Absolutely not."

"Later," Alex said. "We're almost there."

Nate glanced at him. "Are you sure about this? I mean, he doesn't even know we're coming. You said he doesn't have a phone."

"He doesn't. But . . ."

"He knows," Art said. "He knows I'd come find him."

"How?" Nate asked, unsure if he actually wanted the answer.

Art winked at him.

"That's not an answer."

"I know. I'm practicing being mysterious. Is it working?"

"You're an alien from another planet. You don't *need* to be any more mysterious."

"Oh. Wow. I never thought about it that way. Huh. I need to rethink a few things. Hold on."

Nate sighed and looked back out the window.

✦

Bird-in-Hand wasn't big enough to even be called a town. It was more of a village, and it took only a couple of minutes to pass through and leave it behind. Alex had a map open in front of him on the steering wheel, glancing down at it every now and then with a frown on his face. Art sat between them, hands folded in her lap as she hummed quietly to herself.

Ten minutes outside of the village, Alex said, "I don't know where it is. Maybe we already passed it. We should turn around and—"

"We didn't," Art said. "It's up ahead on the right."

Alex sighed and crumpled up the map and tossed it to the side. "Maybe you could have told me that before I opened the map."

"You looked like you had it under control. It isn't my fault you're not very good with directions. You're a man, after all."

He glared at her. "Do I even want to know where you heard that one?"

"Probably not. Look. It's there."

Nate followed where she was pointing. Up ahead on the right was an old mailbox in the shape of a barn. Next to it was a dirt road surrounded by empty fields. In the distance, Nate could see a large copse of trees. Above them rose a thin black smudge. Smoke.

Alex slowed to a stop just before the road. They hadn't seen another car since they'd passed through Bird-in-Hand. "Are you sure about this?" he asked her, leaning forward against the steering wheel to study the road. He winced slightly, and Nate knew his back was probably bothering him from the almost nonstop driving they'd done since the Badlands.

"I think so," Art said, face scrunched up. "It feels like the right thing to do."

"And nothing else, huh?"

She shook her head slowly.

Nothing else being the enigmatic way of asking if her . . . people . . . were here. Or on their way. Or signaling somehow.

"Not yet," she said. "I think there are things I have to do first. And he's one of those things."

She sounded unsure. Nate didn't like that.

"All right," Alex said. "But you stay with me at all times, you hear me? I don't want you out of my sight." He glanced at Nate. "Either of you."

Art laughed. "What's the worst that could happen?"

Alex and Nate both groaned.

"What? Why did you guys do that? What did I say?"

Alex turned onto the dirt road.

✦

In the trees sat a rambling farmhouse, well-kept with a sloping roof covered in what appeared to be solar panels. There was a chimney rising up on either end. It was white with blue shutters on each of the windows.

Next to it sat a large barn. The mailbox they'd seen looked to be almost an exact replica, albeit smaller. It was a rusty red with white trim, the big sliding doors open.

It looked almost like an oasis after all they'd been through. It was late April now, and unseasonably warm. But, shaded by the trees, the house looked inviting. The grass was green, and the fields around the house looked as if they'd been recently tilled. Nate wondered what would grow there. Given the bare knowledge he had of the area, he thought it would be corn.

Next to the farmhouse was a garden of flowers and tomato plants and other things he wasn't sure of. He was a city boy mostly, or at least he had been for the past few years. He'd never had a garden of his own. He'd had a plant once, given to him for his apartment, but it'd died within a month. He hadn't been too surprised. He'd watered it maybe twice.

There were a few trucks next to the barn. Two older sedans.

And *people*.

He could see a few in the fields.

A handful in the garden.

Some carrying hay out of the barn.

Two sitting on the porch in old rocking chairs.

They were dressed in jeans and work boots. The men wore white shirts. One of the women had a tank top. Some had hats.

They all looked up at the same time, watching the truck approach.

An icy chill ran down Nate's spine.

One of the women on the porch got up and went inside the farmhouse, the screen door slapping shut behind her.

"Who are these people?" Nate asked. "I thought you said it would be just him."

Alex was frowning. "I thought it would be."

"They're here because of him," Art said, and they both looked down at her as Alex stopped the truck a short distance away from the house. "I think they know. And they believe him."

Nate wanted to tell Alex to turn around. To drive away. To get them the hell out of there. He didn't have a good feeling about this, and if there was anything he'd learned to trust over the years, it was that twist in his gut. Maybe sometimes it'd led him astray (or at the very least, he'd ignored it, instead choosing to sink down on his knees and suck the thick cock of the junior senator, hands tugging in his hair as he choked), but usually he was spot-on.

They should leave.

He had opened his mouth to say exactly that when the woman who'd gone inside came back out.

And she was followed by another man.

Instantly, Nate knew this was who they were here to see.

He wasn't what Nate expected. He'd been only twenty-four years old when he'd stumbled around in the dark in Cisco Grove, California, in 1964. And after that, he'd been held in the Mountain for twenty years.

If everything Alex and Art had told him was true, Oren Schraeder would have been born in 1940.

Which would have made him fifty-five years old now.

He looked younger than Alex.

Oren's skin was tan, as if he spent his days out in the sun. His hair looked almost white and was pulled into a ponytail that rested in front of his left shoulder. He was lean and fit, jeans dusty and streaks of dirt across a white shirt that looked like what the other men wore.

He had a smile on his face, wide and toothy. He raised a hand and wiggled his fingers at them.

He stayed as he was, Alex had said. *For years. He didn't . . . age.* He had stayed twenty-four years old for almost twenty years.

Like he'd been stuck in time.

In stasis.

And only resumed aging after Art had been electrocuted out of him.

The woman who'd gone inside to fetch him leaned over and whispered in his ear. He waved her away. Watching. Waiting.

Nate turned to tell the others that this didn't feel right, but Alex was already out of the truck, Art scooting across the seat after him. He tried to help her down, but she told him she could do it herself. He stepped back to let her jump out of the truck.

Nate didn't want to follow them.

He did anyway.

Alex kept Art behind him as they slowly approached the farmhouse. The people stood stock-still in the garden and in the fields and in front of the barn as if they were all *waiting* for something.

Nate hurried to catch up with Art and Alex. Art took his hand, squeezing it tightly.

They stopped a short distance away from the farmhouse.

Nate saw the telltale bulge of the gun tucked in the waistline of Alex's jeans in the back. Where once the sight had frightened him, it now made him feel a little bit better. Funny how that worked out.

Nate didn't know who'd speak first. If there was . . . protocol for this sort of thing.

He was in over his head, though he'd be lying if he said some small part of him wasn't still thinking about how big a story this could be. How when this was all over, the narrative he could craft would probably get him hired anywhere he wanted. Or better yet, a book deal. Sure, he'd probably get pushback, but couldn't he provide proof? The things he'd seen. The people who'd come after him. The Mountain. They couldn't cover it up. Not all of it. He could expose them all. Maybe if they all got out of this alive and Artemis found her way . . . home, he could consider it. He could do *something.* People deserved to know, didn't they? They deserved to know what else was out there. That if it was anything like Art, it was benevolent and kind and not to be afraid of.

It was a small part.

But it was there nonetheless, having become clearer the more all of this had sunk in.

"Oren," Alex said. "Oren Schraeder."

The man on the porch nodded. "That's not a name I've heard in a very long time." His voice was higher-pitched than Nate expected, and softer. But he had a *presence* around him that made it hard to look away. There was something about him that drew attention. He radiated strength and something that closely resembled *peace*. It was the only thing Nate could find in his extensive vocabulary to explain it. He felt *soothed* by this man. "And it's one we don't speak out loud here."

He didn't like it.

"My name is Alex Weir."

"I know who you are," Oren said. "I've been expecting you."

Alex stiffened slightly. If Nate hadn't known what to look for, he'd have missed it. But he'd been side by side with Alex for weeks. He'd studied him closely, far more closely than he probably cared to admit. He knew what to look for. "That's good," Alex said.

Oren briefly glanced at Nate before looking back at Alex. "I see that you've brought a guest."

"This is Nate," Alex said. "He . . . found us."

Nate snorted. That was one way to put it.

"Did he now," Oren said. "What a thing to find. Tell me. Does he know what it is you have huddling behind you?"

"He—"

"I can speak for myself," Nate said. "You don't need to talk like I'm not here."

Alex didn't look too pleased at that when he glanced back.

Oren, however, was amused. "Indeed. My apologies." He bowed his head slightly. "I meant no offense."

"None taken," Nate said, dropping Art's hand and moving to stand shoulder to shoulder with Alex. "And yes. I do know."

"Interesting," Oren said, gaze boring into Nate. He felt like flinching, looking away. Somehow, he didn't. "How curious the people we find when we need them most. It's as if there is a higher power pulling the strings. Placing those in our paths that we can lean upon in our darkest hours."

The people around them murmured quietly under their breath as if in prayer. It was over almost as quickly as it'd begun.

"Tell me, Alex," Oren said. "Were you followed?"

Alex shook his head. "No."

"And you can be sure about that."

"Yes."

"Not even that pesky Enforcer?"

"The water guy," Nate muttered quietly.

"How did you know about that?" Alex asked, voice hard.

Oren's smile grew even wider. "I have my ways. When one has been through a life-changing experience as I have, one tends to keep one's ears to the ground. They didn't have them when I was in the Mountain. Not like this . . . Randy. He's tenacious. Or so I'm told."

"And what's going to stop him from coming directly here?" Nate blurted. He hadn't meant to speak, and he winced when Oren's gaze snapped back to him. It made his skin crawl. "If you are who they say you are, if you've . . . been a part of this, why won't they know to come here?" It was a question he'd asked Alex almost immediately when Oren's name was mentioned back in the Badlands. He'd received a vague response, followed by Alex asking him to trust him on this.

That hadn't been fair. But he'd gone with it, swallowing down further questions. Because he *did* trust Alex. And he trusted Art. If she thought they needed to come here, then they would.

But if he trusted them, then they needed to trust him. They wanted him safe. He wanted the same for them.

Oren laughed. A few of his people smiled at the sound, gazing up at him with what Nate thought was adoration. "Oren Schraeder committed suicide in 1991. Ate a shotgun shell in a motel room outside of Olympia, Washington. A terrible tragedy. Head was blown clean off. They identified him by the license he carried on him."

Nate felt numb. "Not the fingerprints?"

The man who had once been Oren Schraeder stepped off the porch and walked toward them. They didn't move. He stopped a few feet away, holding up his hands toward them.

Nate could see how unnatural they looked. Oh, he had the right number of fingers, thin and spindly though they were. But it was the *details* that weren't quite right. There were no lines on his palms. No creases. He could see the veins underneath his skin. A streak of dirt. Multiple calluses.

He had no fingerprints.

His fingertips were completely smooth.

"Do you know how hard it was to find someone who suffered from adermatoglyphia with my same blood type?" he asked. "I almost thought it was impossible. But I was provided with such a person who found their life no longer worth living. They were sad and alone. And in the end, they gave themselves to a higher power." His gaze flickered down before coming back to Nate. "They gave themselves to me so that I could escape the shackles that had tied me to those who would keep me chained for the rest of my life. He was a gift." He smiled again. "Oren Schraeder died. My name is Peter Williams, and this is my home. You are safe here, Nate. We live off the land, much like the people that have been in this area for centuries. We have the solar panels on the house and use propane in the kitchen. You are off the grid now. Nothing can find you here."

He stepped back.

Nate wished he could say that made him feel better.

It didn't.

Oren—Peter—leaned his head to the side like he was trying to peer around the great wall of Alex. "Hello there," he said, voice quiet.

Nate thought Alex wouldn't let her go. That he'd keep her right where she was, and that'd be a damn good thing.

Except she pulled away from his grasp and stepped around him. She stopped when she stood in front of them. Nate had to keep himself from putting his hand on her shoulder.

She stared up at Peter. Nate wondered what was going through her head. Eventually she said, "Hello."

Peter bowed his head again. "It's nice to see you as you are now. It was . . . brief. The last time."

She took another step toward him. "It was. Did you understand what was happening to you? When they separated us?"

"Not at the time," Peter said, voice barely a whisper. "I remember thinking how much it hurt and how quiet it was after. How alone I felt. And then I saw you. Her. As you are now, and I felt you *pulling* me. But I couldn't go. No matter how hard I tried, I could not follow."

Nate was startled when he looked around the farmyard to see

that Peter's people had their heads bowed. Their eyes closed, lips moving silently.

"I didn't know what they were doing," Artemis said. "What would happen. Do you believe me?"

"Yes," Peter said. "I believe you." He held up his hands, wiggling his smooth fingertips. "Maybe not at first. When you were torn from me, you took part of me with you. I was . . . bare. Wiped clean. I was Oren, but at the same time I wasn't. I had his memories. I could *remember* things that had happened . . . before. But taking you from me took everything from myself, and I had to figure out who I was. In that respect, I was reborn. I could become something more than I'd been before. Something greater. It was necessary, I think. In the end."

She cocked her head at him. "Are you happy?"

A flicker of *something* stuttered across his face, but it was gone before Nate could figure out what it was. What was left was a trembling smile and wet eyes. "I believe I am." He took in a deep breath and let it out through his nose. "I've been waiting for this day."

"I know," Art said. "It was time for me to see you again."

He sank to his knees in front of her.

She reached up and took his face in her small hands. His eyes fluttered shut as he leaned into it, moaning quietly.

"I never meant to take you from your life," she said, voice low. "I was scared. I wasn't supposed to be where I was. I froze you in time. You lost years because of me."

He shook his head as she held him. "And you gave me something more. This is who I'm supposed to be. This is what I was made for. Here. Now. This moment. And it's because of you I can say that. These are auspicious days. And now that you're here, I believe it can only get better."

She leaned forward and pressed a kiss to his forehead.

He sighed.

Art dropped her hands and stepped back until she bumped into Alex. He put a hand on her shoulder, squeezing gently.

Peter Williams stood slowly. His eyes were dry. The smile had returned.

His people followed suit.

It was creepy as all hell.

"What do you call yourself now?" he asked.

Art grinned. "Artemis Darth Vader."

There was laughter from the people of the farm.

Even Peter chuckled. "You are safe here," he said again. "They will not find you. You may rest your tired bodies without worry. Come. See what I have made in the wake of the earthquake you brought out in me."

✦

The woman who'd fetched Peter was named Dolores. She was in her sixties, with a kindly smile and dark eyes. She was short and trim with graying black hair. Nate noticed that her fingernails seemed to be bitten to the quick. She led them toward the kitchen, fretting over them all, but especially Artemis. The others had resumed their work, gazes lingering as they followed Peter and Dolores inside the house. Nate brought up the rear, and he glanced back through the screen door before it shut in time to see them all look away.

The house itself was wide and spacious, old wooden floors creaking with every step they took. There was a great room off to the left of the door with two large sofas piled high with decorative pillows. There were floor-to-ceiling bookcases filled with books completely covering a far wall. Artemis let out a squeal of joy at the sight of them and was ready to rush over, but Alex stopped her. She glared up at him, and Nate almost choked at how much she looked like Alex in that exact moment. He tried not to think about the future.

There were stairs directly ahead that led to the second floor, and a hallway next to them. To the right of the main doorway was a dining room with a long table that looked as if it would fit everyone on the farm that had been there to greet them. The table was old and looked like heavy oak.

Dolores made sure they followed her to the kitchen. Peter had disappeared somewhere farther into the house, telling them they were in good hands and that he had matters to attend to. Nate hadn't seen where he'd gone.

In the kitchen, a battery-powered radio played quietly with a voice that Nate recognized.

". . . and it's getting *closer*, friends," Steven Cooper was saying. "Can't you see that? Can't you *feel* it down to your very bones? It's getting closer, and there will be *contact*. We will finally behold the wonders of the universe, our minds expanding in ways that you couldn't even begin to comprehend. They are *coming* for us, friends. You mark my words. Soon, all will be revealed. All will be shown. And the picture that has been long kept hidden from us will be startlingly clear. We will see things that we have only imagined. They may try to hide it from us, they may try and tell us that it isn't *real*. But we have the *photographic evidence*. We have the *proof*. And don't even get me *started* on what our government is capable of. They work with the *Russians*. With the *Saudis*. They release AIDS upon the population to try and cull the herd. They want to control us by telling us we *need* vaccinations. That we *need* to drink the water. But we *know*. In two days, that comet will be as close as it will *ever* be, and we *know*. Caller, you're on the air. What are your thoughts on—"

Dolores turned the radio off. "I could listen to him all day," she said, almost sounding apologetic. "I know he's . . . a little out there, but . . ." She glanced down at Art before looking back at Alex. "How far off can he be?"

Nate didn't know what to say to that. He wouldn't have pinned Dolores as the type to listen to such bullshit. Granted, he didn't know the first thing about her, but still. She looked like someone's grandmother.

"I don't know," Nate said, for lack of anything else.

She barely gave him a glance. Her focus was on Artemis, who was looking wide-eyed around the sunlit kitchen. A window above the sink was open, with pots of flowers on the sill. Nate could hear people out in the yard, talking and laughing. "I bet you're hungry," she said. "You must have come a very long way."

"Yes, ma'am," Art said. "I could eat an entire pig right about now."

Dolores chuckled. "I'm afraid we don't have any pigs here. Or any meat at all, really. Peter believes consuming flesh makes the mind weaker. We have all converted to veganism. Nothing that comes from an animal is allowed in the house."

"Huh," Art said, cocking her head. "That sounds terrible."

"Artemis," Alex warned.

She winced. "Sorry. I didn't mean that the way it sounded. I merely meant to say that while we are staying with you, we will honor the traditions of your home. And then, after we leave, I will find a waitress to give me all the bacon I require."

Alex sighed.

Dolores didn't look fazed in the slightest. "I'm sure. We'll all sit for dinner at seven. There will be winter squash and lentil stew. But for now, I do have some freshly made chickpea fritters that I'm sure you'll love."

Art looked dubious. "Oh yes. That sounds . . . delicious."

Nate adored her.

Dolores smiled. "They are. I should know. I made them myself. Please, sit." She looked up at Alex and Nate, smile fading slightly. "You as well, gentlemen. Peter will return shortly to show you where you will be staying."

There was a small circular table in a breakfast nook in the kitchen. There were four chairs set around it. Art pulled out one of the chairs, climbed up and sat on her knees, hands on the table. A vase of wildflowers sat in the middle. She reached out and traced a finger along the velvety petals. "I like flowers," she said. "They're so colorful. We don't have ones like these where I come from."

Dolores dropped a plate on the counter. It didn't break, but it clattered loudly. "I'm sorry," she said quickly, face slightly red. "Clumsy of me. Just slipped right out of my hand." She turned toward the oven, switching on the light and leaning over to peer inside.

Nate stared at her back.

"It's fine," Alex said in a low voice.

Nate wasn't sure that it was.

And maybe Alex wasn't either, because he pulled his chair close to Art. He grabbed a third and set it next to his before sitting down. He nodded toward the chair. Nate sat. They were far too close. Their elbows bumped. Their legs brushed together. There was enough room for them to spread out, but this was . . . better somehow. More comfortable.

Dolores was still a little flushed when she came back, a tray filled high with fritters in her hands. She set it down carefully on the table, nudging the vase off to the side. The fritters were brown and crisp, oblong and flat, but Nate couldn't even be sure what a chickpea was. There was a dish with a white paste sitting in the middle of the fritters.

The presentation was immaculate.

"It's a garlic dill sauce," Dolores said. "Made from scratch."

"It looks wonderful," Nate said, trying to put her at ease. She looked more nervous than she had when they first arrived. He wondered if she was still stuck on Art's comment about the flowers. Nate didn't know if that was a good thing or not.

But Dolores acted as if she barely heard him. Her focus was again on Art. "Yeah," Art said. "It looks good. I can't wait to try it. Might I have something to drink? Do you have juice?"

"Oh, yes," Dolores said. "I have apple." She hurried back toward the fridge.

Art leaned closer to Alex. "What's garlic dill sauce, and why does it sound gross? Also, those hash brown cake things smell weird."

Nate snorted but covered it up with a cough when Dolores looked back at them over her shoulder.

Alex took one of the fritters and broke it in half. He dipped it into the sauce and took a bite. Art watched his every move. Alex chewed slowly. Nate could see the exact moment when Alex decided he hated everything going on in his mouth but was going to put on a brave face for Art. "It's good," he grunted.

"I don't believe you," Art said.

"Neither do I," Nate said.

Alex scowled. "Just eat it. We don't want to offend her."

Art squinted at him. "Why would she be offended? Don't you think it would be more polite to tell her that what she made is inedible so she doesn't make it for anyone else?"

Alex looked to Nate for help.

It wasn't fair.

Nate took the discarded half of the fritter Alex had left behind. He gave serious thought to skipping out on the sauce but decided to go for the full in-the-middle-of-nowhere-Pennsylvania-with-an-alien experience.

It was . . . terrible, frankly. Nate wasn't a vegan for a reason. The garlic was overwhelming, and he was pretty sure chickpeas were something he never wanted to eat again.

"Mmm," he said as he chewed. "So good."

Art stared at him suspiciously. "You're a better liar than Alex. I can't tell if you mean it or not."

But she took one of the fritters anyway. She brought it up to her nose and sniffed it. She grimaced but covered it up quickly when Dolores returned with a single glass of juice. Nate wished she were a more courteous host and had brought something for the rest of them, but he managed to keep his mouth shut.

"The sauce is good," Dolores told her as Art was about to take a sauceless bite.

Her shoulders slumped a little. "Yeah, that's what Alex and Nate said."

Dolores waited.

Art sighed and dipped the fritter into the sauce. She narrowed her eyes before taking a small bite. She chewed. She swallowed. She set the fritter on the plate. She picked up the juice and drank the entire glass in one go. She set the glass back down. "Wow," she said. "So good. And now I'm full."

Dolores frowned. "But—"

"We had a big breakfast," Nate said. "You know how it is."

"And we have to save room for winter squash and lentil stew," Art said morosely.

"Thank you, though," Alex said. "It was very kind."

"Of course," Dolores said, picking up the plate of fritters. "My apologies. I should have asked. Peter is always saying I try and feed everyone too much. When I had my grandchildren, I—" She paled and took a step back. Her smile was tremulous. "Well. I just like to cook."

Nate didn't like the look on her face. "It's okay. Maybe you could save those for later. I'm sure we'll be hungry again soon enough. And you have grandkids? Do they—"

"Dolores."

Peter stood in the entrance to the kitchen.

Dolores's eyes widened.

"Thank you, Dolores," Peter said. "You always make our guests feel welcome. I appreciate that more than I could ever say. That will be all for now."

Dolores nodded and scurried back into the kitchen. A moment later, the radio came back on and Steven Cooper began to rant and rave. She didn't look back at them.

"You'll have to forgive her," Peter said quietly. "She's . . . had a hard life."

"Why?" Art asked, staring after her.

Peter shook his head. "Things aren't always like they are on the Mountain. Yes, we were in a box. Yes, they poked and prodded. But we were fed and clothed. We were warm and safe. But it was . . . illusory. Like being in a snow globe. The outside world can be harsh and unforgiving. People can lose sight of their paths so easily. Sometimes they just need to see the light in the dark to lead them home."

"You've changed," Art said.

Peter smiled. "You're life-changing. Come. Let me show you where you will be staying."

✦

He tried it. He really did. Nate had to give Peter credit for that. To have the balls to try and separate them given how much bigger Alex was in comparison was something Nate didn't expect.

Peter led them back outside. People were working in the garden and yard. Out in the fields. From what Nate could tell, none of them seemed even remotely alike. A few looked younger than him. A couple were as old as Dolores. Everyone else was somewhere in between. They were white and Black. One appeared Middle Eastern. There was a beautiful Asian woman who waved at them from the rows of tomatoes.

They followed Peter toward the barn. They were greeted by a large man with a sloping gut and a bald head. "The area is ready," he told Peter.

"Thank you, Adam," Peter said, putting a hand on his shoulder. "You have done well today."

Adam seemed to glow under the praise. He glanced curiously at

Artemis, ignoring Alex and Nate, before he nodded and walked out toward the fields.

The barn was larger than it appeared. It was two levels. The first housed a small combine harvester off to one side. On the other side was a long workbench with hooks embedded into the wall above it. Farm tools hung from some of these hooks. There were many empty spaces. Nate figured it was because they were in the hands of the people working around the farm. Bales of hay were stacked around the interior of the barn.

There was a steep wooden staircase near the back of the barn that led to the second floor. The wood creaked beneath their feet as they followed Peter up the stairs. The handrail wobbled slightly. Alex was behind Peter, and Nate brought up the rear. Art was between them. Nate thought Alex had planned it that way. Nate was relieved he was being cautious. There was something just . . . off about this whole place. Maybe it was just his overactive imagination colliding with everything he'd gone through in the last month. Maybe Peter was weird because he'd spent over two decades with an alien having taken over his body. That probably changed a person.

The second floor of the barn had more hay, both loose and baled. Off to the right, the hay had been cleared. On the wooden floor sat a couple of air mattresses next to a stack of clean wool blankets and a battery-powered lantern. There was a window just above them, the swinging slats opening outward toward a long stretch of lonely fields.

"It isn't much," Peter said. "But the rooms in the house are filled. Regardless, you will be comfortable out here. I myself have spent many a night in the barn, looking out the window up at the stars. It will be cool, but the blankets should keep you warm. Obviously, Artemis will have her own room in the house to—"

So, yeah. Nate had to give it to Peter for at least *trying* that in the face of Alex Weir.

"Art will be staying with us," Alex growled.

Peter didn't seem to realize the dangerous ground upon which he was treading. "Surely not. There is a bed for her inside. *She* of all people doesn't need to be staying in a barn."

"I thought you said it was comfortable," Nate replied mildly. "You've stayed out here."

Peter smiled. It was so serene that Nate wanted to punch it down his throat. "Of course. But I am not *her*. She is different."

"Not that different," Art said, sounding nervous.

"Not happening," Alex said. "She's with us. There won't be a moment when she's out of my sight."

"Unless I have to go the bathroom," Art said. "Or I'm showering."

"Not helping," Nate told her.

"What? I'm not letting him in the bathroom when I have to *poop*, Nate. That's just gross!"

"What do you think could possibly happen to her?" Peter asked Alex. "Here, of all places? We are *safe*. My people know who she is. *What* she is. They know how special this moment is. For all of us. This is a monumental occasion for everyone, and I get the distinct impression that you don't trust me."

It was odd, really. Nate almost felt *bad*. Peter was earnest and charismatic, and Nate felt the edges of *guilt* crawling along his skin. He managed to shake it off, but Peter was *good*. Either he was being sincere, or he was a goddamn sociopath. Regardless of what else Nate had learned in his short life, it was always best to expect the worst. That way, you could be surprised when it turned out okay.

"I don't know you," Alex said. "I don't know your people. But I know Art. And Nate. We stay together, or we don't stay at all."

Nate thought Peter would argue. That he'd push.

He was surprised yet again.

"Of course," Peter said, bowing his head slightly. "You are our guests. I merely wanted to extend a courtesy to the Seventh—to *Artemis*. After all, I have known her for far longer than you have. She was *part* of me."

"If anyone cares about what *I* want, I'd be happy to tell you."

They all looked down at Art.

"Yes," Peter said. "I apologize. I should not be speaking as if you aren't capable of thinking for yourself. I . . . sometimes forget we're separate. It doesn't happen as often as it once did, but having you near again has . . . well. I am just happy to see you healthy and whole."

She reached out and touched his hand. She didn't linger. "I understand. But Alex gets twitchy when I'm not around. And even though we're safe here, he sometimes gets in trouble and needs me to rescue him. I need to keep an eye on him. It makes me feel better."

"She has a point," Nate said as Alex scowled down at her.

"She does *not*."

"Curious," Peter said, staring at the three of them.

"What is?" Art asked.

"The people we choose to surround ourselves with. Me, here. And you. Maybe I don't see it the way you do. Maybe I will be surprised."

Nate thought they were being insulted, but he couldn't quite figure out how.

"No matter," Peter said, taking a step back. "If you wish to remain with . . . these men, then I will defer to your decision. Feel free to make use of the facilities inside the main house. You are free to come and go as you please. Dinner will be served in front of the house at seven. Please join us then." He glanced down the stairs toward the front of the barn. "Ah, and it looks as if your bags have been brought in."

Sure enough, their duffel bags were stacked next to the combine. Nate hadn't even heard them being placed there.

"It is an honor," Peter told Art. "As always. I may not understand who you have chosen to bond with, but I trust that you will help make sense of it all. You opened my eyes once before. I believe that you can do it again."

He turned and made his way down the stairs.

They watched as he walked out of the barn.

"I still taste chickpeas in my mouth," Art grumbled. "Being vegan is the absolute worst."

CHAPTER FIFTEEN

The sky was pink and orange, and the blue was fading toward black as they left the barn a little before seven. The stars were beginning to flicker, and Markham-Tripp was blazing brightly in the north. Steven Cooper said two more days and the comet would be as close as it'd ever be.

Art walked between them, holding Alex's hand as they stopped outside the barn. She gasped at the sight in front of them.

The front yard had been transformed. Two long wooden picnic tables had been pushed together. White tablecloths covered them. There was a line of baskets on the tables filled with flowers of almost every color imaginable.

Tiki torches had been staked into the ground, the wicks lit and burning brightly. Chinese lanterns were hung from the trees, the thin paper red and green and flickering brightly. Strings of white lights had been wrapped around the trunks of trees.

It was wonderful.

It felt off somehow.

People were milling around the tables, whispering among themselves. Some held glasses of lemonade. Others were setting the table—plates, silverware, and cloth napkins. The man they'd seen at the barn was grunting as he hauled an old record player down the porch steps before setting it on the ground near the table. It appeared to be hand-cranked, something Nate had never seen before in person. Dolores patted his arm before she bent over and unlatched the bottom of the player. Inside were numerous record sleeves. She flipped through them before deciding on one and pulling it out. She slid the record out and placed it on the player. She gripped the crank and turned it slowly.

A moment later, the sounds of Billie Holiday began to spill out over the yard, the sound crackly and haunted.

It was one of the most surreal moments of Nathaniel Cartwright's life.

"This is so pretty," Art said, eyes alight. She tugged at Alex's hand. "Isn't this pretty?"

"It's pretty," Alex said begrudgingly. Nate reminded himself to give him shit for that later.

Art tugged him forward.

The conversation stopped almost immediately as everyone turned to look at them.

At *her*.

"Hello," she said. "This is very nice. You guys did a good job. I'm super impressed."

They all sighed almost at the same time.

"Thank you," Peter said, appearing on the porch. "We wanted to show you just how much we appreciate you. For everything that you are. Please, sit. We will begin momentarily."

Dolores and the man from the barn walked past Peter and into the farmhouse. An older Black man stepped toward them. His fingers twitched. He walked stiffly. His gaze darted from Art to Alex and back again.

He stopped in front of them. He cleared his throat. "I would be honored if I could show you to your seat."

"You're like a waitress," Art told him, smiling wildly. "I like waitresses."

Nate didn't bother correcting her.

The man didn't either. In fact, he seemed to relax upon hearing her words. He looked as if he wanted to reach out and touch her, but one look from Alex seemed to change his mind. He turned, and they followed him toward the end of the table. A chair had been set up, a thick cushion on old wood. He pulled the chair out for her. Art laughed as she climbed onto it, holding on to the armrests as he lifted it slightly to set her closer to the table. Alex sat on the bench to her left. He nodded for Nate to take the spot opposite him.

The man said, "Actually, sir, those seats are for—"

Alex glared at him.

He backed away slowly.

Art leaned toward Nate. "Do you think they stopped being vegans in the last couple of hours so we can have bacon?" she whispered to him.

"I don't think that's quite how being vegan works," Nate whispered back.

She looked disappointed with that.

He patted her hand.

Alex's foot pressed against his under the table.

He looked down at the tabletop, feeling his face grow warm. They hadn't—that is to say, nothing had *happened* between them, not really. There was intent, oh *fuck* was there intent, but when you were running for your life with an alien at your side, it wasn't easy to act on said intent. Ever since the night in the truck when he'd seen (dreamed?) the escape from the Mountain, then pressed a kiss to Alex's callused hand, he'd been careful, not wanting to push Alex further. It was frustrating, especially with moments like this, Alex's leg warm against his own, but he—there were things he didn't know. Many things. The woman he'd seen the first time the bond had flared to life because of Art. The little boy. He—he *knew*. How could he not? But he also knew how grief worked, how it could be all-encompassing. He didn't want to push Alex for something he wasn't ready for. He wasn't even sure if he *himself* was ready for it. It didn't help that now probably was not the best time to even be thinking about it. Art needed to be his focus. Not this . . . whatever it was happening between them.

But Jesus Christ did he want.

Maybe after, they could—Nate didn't know.

He didn't know what would come *after*.

If Alex would even be coherent. He'd lost before. Someday soon, he was going to lose again. Artemis was going to leave, and Nate was going to have to pick up the pieces.

He'd do it, though. Of course he would. He'd see this through to the end.

Peter had followed Dolores and the other man into the house. They all reappeared, one after another, each carrying a large Crock-Pot filled with what Nate thought would be the winter squash and lentil soup. The Asian woman from the garden came out of the house after them, carrying two large baskets filled high with thick slices of bread.

Dolores set her Crock-Pot between Alex and Nate, in front of Art, smiling shyly as she did so. The man from the barn set his in the middle where the two tables met. Peter put his at the other end of the table, where another chair had been set up.

Billie Holiday sang that she didn't want her man to explain.

The people of Peter's farm came to the table and sat. A young man with acne scars sat next to Nate, glancing at him out of the corner of his eye. A woman sat next to Alex, a quiet smile on her face as she used his shoulder as a prop to seat herself. Her fingers trailed along his biceps. Nate decided he wasn't a fan.

Alex pressed his foot into Nate's ankle.

Nate understood.

Peter tapped the side of his glass with a spoon. Everyone quieted down as they looked toward him. He smiled at them, taking a moment to look at each of them in turn. His gaze stayed on Art the longest.

"I have spoken," he said, "many times about my . . . experiences in the place known as the Mountain. The things I saw. The things I learned. When one—when an intelligent being chooses you like I was chosen, it can do nothing but change you. When you come out on the other side, you are scraped raw, hollowed out because *everything* you thought was real before suddenly seems so trivial. The things that mattered, the tiny little things that we think day to day, are *nothing* compared to the cosmic force that works around us."

Billie Holiday sang that she was a fool to want you, that right or wrong she can't get enough without you.

Peter said, "It . . . was life-changing. I was broken down and rebuilt from my very foundation. And when I was once again alone, I knew, I just *knew* that I needed to make the world a better place. Or at least a little corner of it." He smiled, gaze sweeping around the farmyard. "I like to think I succeeded."

The people around him murmured in agreement, heads bobbing up and down.

"We've all had to make sacrifices," Peter said. "Every single one of us. To be here, now, in this moment, means we've given up something else." He looked at Nate. Nate tried not to flinch. "And maybe we don't quite understand our purpose yet. But now that she is here, now that she has come, I know we'll soon see things quite clearly." He raised his glass from the table. "To Artemis. For showing me the way."

His people raised their glasses toward her. "To Artemis."

Nate and Alex didn't move.

Artemis cocked her head.

They all drank as one.

Peter set down his glass. "Now," he said cheerfully. "Let us eat this fine meal Dolores has so lovingly prepared for all of us. This is a celebration. Which means it's time to start celebrating."

He sat down in his chair as Dolores smiled at him.

The food was served, the stew being ladled out, the bread being passed around. Something that resembled butter was served in small dishes for the bread, but since it was supposedly vegan, Nate passed. He didn't want to know what it'd been made from.

Art appeared uncertain as she stared down at the stew in front of her. She picked up her spoon and poked at it briefly. She waited until Alex took a bite before she followed suit. "Wow," she said, overbright. "This is really good. Like. I am so happy I am having this right now."

Nate wouldn't look at her for fear of bursting out laughing.

He managed a few bites before he just decided to pick at the bread.

He thought maybe he'd sneak out to the truck later and see if they had any of their soup left. The image of them huddled in the barn under cover of night sneaking soup from a can caused him to snort.

He felt Alex's boot press against his ankle.

He looked up.

Alex's eyebrows were raised in question.

He shook his head.

It was fine.

Everything was fine.

Yeah, maybe these people were a little weird. Maybe he didn't understand them, but hell, he'd never been through what Peter had been through. He didn't know him. Or them. What had led them to be here. On this farm. How they had so quickly accepted these strangers. This girl. They hadn't seemed surprised about anything having to do with her. Instead, they were almost . . . reverent. Like they were in awe of her.

Nate understood that more than he cared to admit.

It was probably nothing. They just . . . needed someone like Peter. Nate could see why. He was—there was just something about him that Nate couldn't quite put his finger on. He barely seemed to blink. He was almost always smiling. And calm. Eerily calm.

It was fine.

Everything was fine.

✦

The meal was over, and the people of the farm pushed away from the table, clearing their dishes and setting them into a large plastic tub filled with soapy water that had been set near the porch. No one commented on how little the three guests seemed to eat, their bowls still mostly full, bread in small shredded pieces on the plates. Nate tried to help but was quietly told it wasn't necessary. That he was their guest, that he'd come with *her* and wouldn't need to lift a finger.

Billie Holiday cooed that she was all about you, body and soul, spending her days in longing, always for you.

Nate stared in shock as Peter offered a hand toward Dolores and bowed low. Dolores giggled like a girl far younger, blushing, bosom heaving. She took Peter's hand, and as he chuckled, he led her to an open patch of grass near the record player. He pulled her close, and they began to dance, swaying slowly back and forth.

Others joined them a moment later. A man and a woman. Two women. A group of three, all standing in a lazy circle, hands holding hands, shuffling feet as they spun slowly.

"What is that?" Art breathed. "Alex, what are they doing? Is that . . . is that *dancing*?"

"Yeah," Alex said quietly. "It's dancing."

"Like that movie," she said, sighing dreamily, eyes reflecting the lights around her. "The one with the pretty woman in the dresses. What was it called?"

"*Hello, Dolly!*"

"Yeah, that one." She glanced at Alex before looking down at her hands. She looked . . . nervous, something Nate hadn't really seen on her before. She looked at Alex again before smiling and fidgeting with the tablecloth.

Nate understood.

Alex did too. Even before Nate could speak, Alex said, "Do you want to dance?"

Art shrugged.

"Art."

"Maybe a little," she muttered.

"Do you want to dance with me?"

She shrugged again.

Oh yeah. Nate had seen heartbreak up close before. And he felt it then, too, in his chest. Right down the middle. He understood, briefly, what Peter had meant by scraped raw. There was this girl, this perfect little girl, who wasn't a girl at all. And she wanted to dance.

Alex pushed himself up from the table.

He held a hand out to her.

She blushed.

Nate wondered when exactly he'd started to love them both. When he had allowed himself to feel something he didn't think he was capable of.

But he was, apparently.

He had.

He knew it then.

Somehow, he had.

Art hesitated, but only for a moment, before she took Alex's hand. Billie began singing about the wishing well, and that she'll be seeing you, that she'll always think of you that way, like a summer's day.

Alex led Art to the middle of the grass. The others moved out of the way. Dolores danced with her cheek pressed against Peter's chest. Her eyes were closed, and she looked as if she didn't plan on moving from that spot for a long time.

Peter was watching Alex and Art.

Nate's heart was in his throat as Alex told Art to stand on his feet. She smiled up at him, a dazzling thing that caused Nate's hands to shake. She did as he said, gingerly stepping onto the tops of Alex's boots, as if she feared she'd hurt him somehow. He helped her, her hands in his. Once she had her footing, he began shuffling his feet through the grass. It was awkward, and Alex was stiff, but as Billie told them she'd find you in the morning sun, Art looked as if she'd never been happier than she was right then. She smiled up at Alex, and Nate thought Billie was right. It was the morning sun.

I didn't get that. Not before, Art had told him. *I don't think any of us did. Not until they felt a heart beating in a chest like I have. Not until I felt the bones beneath my skin. We're not alike. Not really. We're separated by time and space. And yet, somehow, we're all made of dust and stars.*

He hadn't understood what she'd said. Not really. Not before. Not until this moment.

And perhaps for the first time, he truly understood the depth of how much Alex Weir loved Artemis Darth Vader.

He wondered if there would be anything left of him after she was gone.

They danced.

And as the song came to a close, Artemis stepped off his feet, lifting a single finger and beckoning him down. He bent over, and she kissed his cheek before she whispered in his ear, glancing at Nate, a coy smile on her face.

Alex tensed.

This couldn't possibly be good.

Art took a step back.

Alex stood upright.

Billie, of course, chose that moment to begin singing how sure she was crazy, crazy in love, she'd say.

Alex turned toward him as Billie said she'd walk through fire.

He held a hand out for Nate, palm up toward the stars and an ever-bright comet, fingers slightly curled.

Nate stared at him for a moment, unmoving.

The determined look on Alex's face faltered slightly.

"Nate," Art hissed. "He's asking you to *dance*. You have to say *yes*."

That got Nate moving. He stood quickly and immediately stumbled forward, tripping over the chair. He nearly fell, but at the last moment, felt strong arms around him, holding him tightly. His face was pressed against a throat rough with stubble. He inhaled involuntarily, and there was a scent of clean skin and sweat and something he couldn't quite make out.

"Fuck," he muttered.

He felt more than heard Alex when he chuckled. "That was . . . I don't know what that was."

"Shut up."

"No, seriously. I don't know if I've ever seen you move that fast before."

"You're still not funny."

The arms tightened a little around him.

Nate had to remind himself to breathe.

And then they began to move.

Nate's hands were trapped between them, curled into Alex's flannel shirt, holding on for dear life. It wasn't—they were off, just a little. Their knees knocked together more often than not, and Alex stepped on Nate's feet more than once. If Nate wanted to do this properly, he'd probably step back just a little, put some space between them. But he was good with where he was, and Alex didn't seem inclined to let him go anytime soon. It wasn't the best dance in the world, but it was theirs, and it was enough.

Billie sang.

They danced.

Yeah. He understood heartbreak, all right.

It was all dust and stars.

✦

He awoke, blinking in the dark, unsure of his surroundings. He was almost instantly calmed by the sound of a little alien snoring loudly at his side. He turned his head slowly. The air mattresses had been pushed together earlier that night, Art sleeping between them as in the truck. There hadn't been a question of sleeping any other way.

He'd dropped off pretty quickly, the events of the day heavy on his shoulders. He didn't know what to make of Peter's farm, and his thoughts were dizzy with *Alex, Alex, Alex.*

Speaking of.

Alex was gone.

Nate blinked again, trying to clear the last remnants of sleep.

He pushed himself up.

He scrubbed a hand over his face, the air mattress shifting underneath him. Art grumbled quietly in her sleep, turning over to face away from him.

Nate looked around the barn. The window above him was still open, and the night air was cool. He stood, rubbing his hands together. Alex had given him one of his flannel shirts to sleep in. It was a little big, but Nate hadn't complained.

From what he could see, Alex wasn't on the second floor of the barn, unless he was hiding behind bales of hay.

He'd probably gone out to take a leak. Right? That was plausible. That had to be it.

It wasn't like Peter came and did anything to him. That—that was just stupid.

And of course now he was thinking about Peter and what he was capable of more than anything else.

He looked down. Art slept on, snoring loudly again. He made his way to the stairs, holding on to the hand railing tightly as he took each step down. The wood creaked ominously under his feet, but soon he felt solid ground and breathed a sigh of relief.

The doors to the barn were closed. Unless he'd gone out the front and then closed them again, Alex hadn't left that way. He—

"What are you doing?"

Nate, standing in the dark on a farm in Pennsylvania, far away from everything he'd ever known, let out a slightly strangled scream before slapping a hand over his own mouth.

He heard a choking sound and turned to see Alex standing near another barn window, struggling not to laugh.

"You *asshole*," Nate hissed at him. "What the fuck is *wrong* with you?"

"I don't know if I've ever heard you make a sound like that," Alex managed to say. "Holy hell."

"Yeah, well, see if you ever get to hear any *other* sounds I make, you fucking prick." He blanched almost immediately. "I didn't mean . . . just—Jesus Christ."

Alex recovered first. "I'll keep that in mind," and it was a dark promise that Nate didn't know what to do with.

So he deflected. "What are you doing?"

"I could ask you that same question."

"I woke up. And you weren't there."

"I didn't go far. I wouldn't do that to either of you. Not here."

Nate believed him. He hesitated, but then forced himself to move until he stood next to Alex. The air through the opened window was almost cold. He shivered slightly, elbow bumping against Alex's.

"You're shaking," Alex said quietly.

"I'm fine."

Alex sighed. "Just . . . Come here."

Nate didn't know what he was asking for. He didn't know what he could give. But Alex raised an arm, settling it across Nate's shoulders, tugging gently until Nate was pressed against him. It was warm and nice, and Nate was instantly on edge.

"Relax," Alex said near his ear.

"Easy for you to say," Nate muttered.

"Maybe."

A beat of silence. Then, "Why are you down here?"

"Couldn't sleep."

Nate snorted. "You? I thought you could fall asleep wherever you wanted."

"Most times. It's . . . There's a lot to think about."

Nate waited. He didn't know if Alex was going to offer more, but he didn't think it was his place to ask.

He didn't have to wait long. "This place. It's . . . off somehow."

Nate was a little relieved at that. "Right? I mean, they're nice people and all, but it's a little too utopic. It reminds me of those old tent revivals they used to have. Peter's like a traveling salesman disguised as a fire-and-brimstone preacher. He's selling them on what they want to hear."

"And what do they want to hear?"

"I don't know. But it's—maybe all they wanted was a little bit of hope. It's easy to get lost. It's even easier to try and latch on to someone you think can show you the way."

Alex grunted. "Maybe. I can't quite put my finger on it."

"Art doesn't seem to think anything is wrong."

"I know. And that's what worries me."

Nate gingerly laid his head on Alex's shoulder. Alex tensed, but it was brief. His fingers dug into Nate's skin, a silent welcome. "There's still something there."

"What do you mean?"

"Between her and Peter. Or Oren. She was in him for . . . what. Twenty years? And the way she's bonded to you and—and to me, it's just . . . She was torn from him. They both said as much. What if something was left? How did she know how to find this place?"

Alex shook his head. "I don't know. Even after all this time, I don't understand some of the things she can do."

"Do you think she's keeping things from you?"

"No. At least not intentionally. She . . . wouldn't do that."

Nate didn't know if he believed that but kept the thought to himself. "How long are we going to stay here?"

"I don't know. However long she thinks we need to. Or however long it takes for me to put us in the truck and drive. Whichever comes first."

Nate looked out the window at the night sky. He found Cassiopeia almost immediately. His gaze shifted toward Markham-Tripp, brighter than it'd ever been. It looked as if it were streaking across the sky, its tail seemingly longer than it'd been the night before. And then he asked the most ridiculous question of his life. "What are the chances of there actually being a UFO in that thing?"

Alex laughed quietly. "I don't think that's very realistic."

"There's a little girl upstairs who's an alien and can move things with her mind."

"Right. No. I don't think there's a UFO in the tail of the comet. That's for the crackpot conspiracy theorists."

"The same ones that have said we've been visited before when we actually have?"

"Not like . . . not like they think."

Nate stepped away, suddenly frustrated. Alex's arm dropped back down to his side. "That we know of. How many other Mountains are there?"

"I don't . . . What are you saying?"

"Alex," Nate said, exasperated. "You can't possibly think this is isolated. What if there are others? What if—"

"I don't care about others," Alex said, that familiar scowl returning. "This isn't about them. It's about her."

"I know that. But—what if? What if there are more? What if there are other little girls that—"

"Don't."

Nate shook his head. "I'm not trying to manipulate you. I'm just saying—"

"I know what you're trying to say. This isn't a story, Nate. This isn't a fucking lead that you can chase down so that you can get back whatever it is you think you lost before. You can't use this— her—to get your life back."

"That's not fair."

"You've thought it."

"I—" But he had, hadn't he? Of course he had. "Maybe. But not for a while. And you can't blame me for that. This—what's left, Alex? After this? What's going to happen to us? What are we going to do? You can't think everything will just go back to—"

"I hated her."

Nate stopped talking.

Alex wouldn't look at him. He ran a hand over his head and down the back of his neck. "At first. I hated her. When they took me to her. I . . . knew. What they were doing. Or at least I had an idea. Yes, I was in awe of her. I was shocked that something like her could exist. That I wasn't—that *we* weren't alone. It was a secret. The biggest one the world had ever known, and it was being told to me."

He turned toward the window, resting his elbows on the sill, staring off into the night. The farmhouse was dark, the only light coming from a flickering bulb on the porch. Nate went to stand next to him, making sure to keep a careful distance between them. Alex was radiating *do not touch,* and Nate needed to hear what he had to say.

"And she was curious about me. She talked. A lot. She asked me questions. If I liked horses. If I'd ever jumped from the top of a waterfall. If I had ever gone sledding. She told me about stories she'd read. Books about cowboys and bandits and dragons stealing princesses and the knights who came to their rescue. She wanted me to play board games with her. She wanted me to sing with her. She asked me why I didn't smile. Why I looked angry all the time. Why I was mean to her. What it meant to be sad. Why are you sad, Alex? What happened to make you the way you are?" He chuckled bitterly. "And I hated her. Because she didn't dance around my feelings. She didn't—I don't think she's capable of that. There's . . . nuances that she doesn't understand. Verbal and physical cues she doesn't get. She says whatever's on her mind. Even when I yelled at her. Told her to shut the fuck up. To leave me alone. She wouldn't."

Nate hadn't seen any of that when Alex had shown him before. But he had seen the woman. The boy. Which meant . . . he didn't know what that'd meant. "Grief," he said slowly. "The water guy said that you were part of it. Part of their experiment. To see how she would react in the face of grief."

"Yeah," Alex said hoarsely. "That's what he said, isn't it? And maybe I didn't understand the complexities behind their thinking, but I knew . . . something. I don't think it was supposed to go as far as it did. I don't think they thought I would let it. That I would let *her.* In my head. In my . . . heart. I didn't ask for it. It just happened."

"But you didn't fight it."

"No. I didn't. Because I learned that she wasn't just this . . . thing. That she wasn't just an experiment. A creature to be studied. A prisoner. She's living and breathing and has thoughts of her own, these stupidly wonderful thoughts that make her more human than anyone else I know."

He had to ask. He had to. "Who were they?"

Alex stiffened, and Nate was sure he'd crossed a line. But then,

"We married young. She got pregnant before I deployed for the second time, and when I came back, her parents insisted we get married, and I—I said yes. Because it was the right thing to do. We'd been together since we were seventeen years old. It was—good. We loved each other. A lot. Maybe not as much as someone should when they get married, but . . . it was good. Mostly." He wiped his eyes. "And the kid was born, and I didn't know it was possible to love something so completely at first sight. He was early, and we were scared. They let me take emergency leave because it was touch and go for a while. He was so *tiny*, and he had to stay in the hospital for weeks. They told us that we needed to prepare, just in case. But I would sit next to his incubator and whisper in his ear that he needed to *fight*. He needed to prove them all wrong and *fight*. And he did. Somehow, he did. Two months after he was born, we took him home.

"I loved her. And him. While I was gone, she'd send me letters and pictures of him, and I'd show them to everyone, whether they wanted to see them or not. I told myself it was enough. That I could make this work. That I had more than most, and it was . . . good. It was going to be good. And it was. For seven years, it was."

Nate closed his eyes.

"Stupid, you know? I've been pinned down by gunfire in the dead of night in a desert thousands of miles away from home, sure I was never going to see them again. I've seen friends blown up when an IED under their Humvee exploded. I've held wives and mothers when their loved ones were being lowered into the ground. I broke an extraterrestrial out of a government base while being gutshot and chased by helicopters. But I couldn't stop her from leaving."

Alex sighed. "It wasn't fair to her. That . . . half life she was living. I was gone more often than not, and she . . . she wasn't getting from me what she needed. That wasn't fair. I didn't see it at the time. All I could focus on was *me*, what she was taking from *me*. She left. She took our son with her. For a while, it was bad. We'd yell at each other, accuse each other of making our lives miserable. But there came a day when I didn't have anything left to say. And so I listened to her. To what she was saying. And I heard her, I *really* heard her for the first time in years. We became friends. I think . . . I think I loved her more then than I did at any other point.

"He was nine years old. And it was something so simple. Car accident. Slick roads from the rain. A corner too fast. Her little car rolled into a tree. They told me it was instant, but I—I didn't believe that. I thought of them trapped with me half a world away, calling for me, begging me to come save them like I saved people whose names I never even bothered to learn. But I wasn't there. I wasn't there for them. And they died."

Nate opened his eyes. Alex was staring up at the sky. Nate reached over and took his hand. Alex squeezed it tight. "How long after did they bring you in to the Mountain?"

"Six months. They knew what they were doing. Because that kind of grief . . . it never really goes away. It doesn't heal. It festers. And they knew that, I think."

"And so you hated her."

"Yeah," Alex said. "I did. They were nothing alike. Her and him. He was . . . quiet. Always watching. She never stopped talking. He had this little laugh where he'd breathe out quickly through his nose. She was loud when she was happy. She wasn't him. He wasn't her."

"What changed?" Nate asked.

Alex shrugged. "I don't know. Not really. It . . . One day, I just stopped. Stopped being angry. Stopped blaming her. Myself. The open wound became a scar, and it didn't hurt as it once had. She knew it too. She told me once, a long time later, that when she made me laugh for the first time, it was the greatest thing she's ever done."

Nate bumped his shoulder against Alex's. "Can't say I disagree. I might have felt the same way when I heard it for the first time."

Alex cracked the barest of smiles. "You both need to set the bar a little higher."

"Har-har. You're still not funny."

"A little."

"Maybe." Then, "Thank you."

Alex arched an eyebrow. "For?"

"Telling me."

"You knew."

"I guessed. I saw . . . them, when we were at the gas station. With the bond."

"I know."

"You wanted me to see them."

"I don't—maybe. Subconsciously? To be honest, I'm still not quite sure how it works. I don't think anyone knows."

"Why?"

"Why what?"

"Why did you want me to see them?"

Alex sighed. "Really, Nate? You know, for a reporter, you're a little clueless sometimes."

"Journalist," Nate corrected automatically, barely hearing himself above his rabbit-quick heart. "Maybe I don't want to make any assumptions. You know what they say when you assume. It makes an ass out of you and—"

Alex kissed him.

It wasn't earth-shattering. It wasn't fireworks bursting. It was firm and dry, Alex's stubble scraping against Nate's chin. For a moment, he wasn't even sure what was happening. But then he opened his mouth just a little and felt the press of a tongue against his, a quick swipe that caused him to whimper slightly in the back of his throat. Alex was breathing through his nose, and their hands were still clasped, the angle of all of it so damn *awkward*, but it was more than Nate had ever felt before in his meager life.

He blinked slowly as Alex broke the kiss, pulling away with a wary look on his face. Waiting for Nate tell him off, to demand to know what the hell *that* had been. Nate couldn't bear to see that look on his face, so he leaned forward and kissed him again. Alex made a grunt of surprise. It was short and sweet. They were both panting by the time their foreheads pressed together, breathing each other in.

"I've kind of wanted you to do that for a while," Nate admitted quietly.

"Yeah?" Alex asked, and the smile was there again. "I kind of figured."

"Asshole."

"I've kind of wanted to do that to you for a while," Alex said.

"Yeah? I kind of figured."

Alex laughed and kissed his forehead before he pulled Nate close again. Nate wrapped an arm around his waist, turning his head until his nose pressed against Alex's neck. They stood there, in a barn under an approaching comet called Markham-Tripp, wrapped up in each other. Nate thought about pushing for more, asking what this meant, where it could lead, what would happen to them . . . after. But for the life of him, he couldn't make himself speak the words aloud. Instead, he pressed himself farther against Alex and just breathed.

It was enough.

CHAPTER SIXTEEN

Nate made his way into the farmhouse the next morning. Alex and Art were out in the fields with some of Peter's people, Art having demanded she see horses immediately once she'd found out about them. It was a good distraction, because she'd woken up between them the next morning and immediately stared at them suspiciously.

"Why is your chin all red?" she had asked Nate, narrowing her eyes at him.

Stubble burn, but he hadn't known if he'd wanted to explain that to a nosy alien. "Must have slept on it funny." He glared at Alex, who was doing a terrible job of covering his laughter.

"You slept on your chin wrong," Art said dubiously.

Nate only shrugged. "Must have."

"Hmm," Art said.

So yes, he was thankful when Peter mentioned horses over breakfast, knowing that it was only a temporary distraction. Art would figure it out sooner or later. She couldn't read their minds, not really, but they were . . . bonded, somehow. And she was perceptive. He had an idea of what her reaction would be, and he didn't know if he was ready for it.

Alex hadn't looked very pleased at the idea of Nate staying behind, but Nate had waved him away. "It's fine. I'm going to see if they'll let me do laundry. We need it. We're all running out of clothes."

Alex nodded slowly. Checking over his shoulder to make sure they weren't being overheard, he dropped his voice. "Gun's under my bedroll."

Nate rolled his eyes. "I'm not going to shoot Dolores."

"Nate."

"Alex."

"Don't be difficult."

"I—"

Alex had pulled him inside the barn, just out of sight, and kissed him furiously. Nate was still a little shell-shocked that this was a thing they could *do* now, and barely had time to reciprocate before Alex stepped back. "It's just in case."

"Yeah," Nate said, slightly dazed. "Just in case."

When they'd stepped back out of the barn, Art had looked up from where she'd been watching the people in the garden. "Huh," she'd said. "You must have slept on your chin again in the last three minutes. Funny how that happens."

Thank god for those damn horses. They made for a perfect distraction.

He'd gone back up to the hayloft where their duffel bags sat and dug through them, finding everything that needed to be washed. He'd transferred it to one bag and slung it over his shoulder, making his way out of the barn and toward the house.

There were people in the garden, pulling weeds and aerating the soil. They stopped as he passed them by, each of them greeting him warmly with a broad smile on their face. It seemed as if they were . . . happier than they'd been the day before. Maybe it was the fact that Art was here. Maybe it was something else. But they were all smiles and kind words. It made Nate uneasy, but he responded cheerfully.

Dolores was in the kitchen, cleaning up the remnants of the breakfast she'd put out. There'd been large bowls of oatmeal with fruit and sugar. Art had not been a fan of the lack of meat.

And of course, the radio played in the background.

Their old friend Steven Cooper was on again. Nate wondered if he ever went *off* the air. "Tomorrow, friends," Steven was saying. "Tomorrow is the day. Why, even now, even during *daylight,* you can see Markham-Tripp. And *oh,* you know we've got them scared. Did you see that statement they released? *Nothing to worry about,* they said. *It's all a bunch of baloney,* they said. *It should be a fun event for the whole family,* they said. As if they don't know. As if they haven't been preparing for this *exact* moment for *years.* You're telling me, you're *really* going to sit there and tell me that this comet was only discovered *last year*? One of the biggest and brightest astrological events *of our lifetimes* was only spotted a *year ago. Hogwash,* friends. Pure and utter *hogwash.* They've known about this. For *years.* Why, sources even tell me that they've known for a *decade* about this thing. The comet is just a front. Don't let anyone tell you otherwise. It is *just a front.* You'll see. By this time tomorrow, we will all bear witness to the greatest event in human history or I'll eat my hat. Caller, you're on the air. What are your thoughts on what tomorrow will bring?"

The caller was a shrill man speaking in biblical verses, and Nate cleared his throat even as Dolores was nodding along with the radio.

She startled a little, turning around, bringing the wet cloth to her bosom.

"Sorry," Nate said, wincing slightly. "Didn't mean to frighten you."

Dolores laughed, an oddly braying sound. "Oh, Nate. That's . . . okay. It's . . . I wasn't expecting anyone there."

"Yeah." He nodded toward the radio. "Must not have heard me coming."

She nodded furiously as she reached over and turned down Steven Cooper. "It's just . . . these are big days, you know? I wanted to hear what Mr. Cooper had to say."

"Big days?"

She flushed. "The comet and all. It's . . . a once-in-a-lifetime event."

"So it sounds like. Cooper seems to think so."

She wrung the dishcloth nervously. "I know you think he's all poppycock and tomfoolery. That I'm probably foolish for listening to him like I do."

Nate shrugged. "I don't judge you for that at all. I mean, with everything I've seen lately, who am I to say that it's not something?"

Her eyes widened. "Right?" She sounded breathless. "I can only imagine what . . ." Her gaze darted over Nate's shoulder before she took a step toward him. "Can I . . . can I ask you a question?"

"Sure," he said slowly. "Though I reserve the right not to answer if I can't."

"Yes. That's . . . I understand. I . . . didn't believe. Not like I should have. Not like he wanted me to. Not for a long time."

"Not like who wanted you to? Peter?"

She nodded. "It was—you have to understand. The things he claimed. How fantastic they sounded. I mean, to hear it on the radio is one thing. But to hear it from someone in *person*. Someone who had *experienced* it . . . well. That was something else entirely."

A warning bell went off in Nate's head. "Is that how you met Peter?"

She brought her right thumb up to her mouth and started gnawing on the fingernail. "Yes. He said *things*. And I wanted to believe them, believe *him*. But it was hard. My daughter, she—she thought it was all a bunch of bull. She said I was acting crazy." She laughed a little wildly. "I told her that we all had things we believed in."

"You said something about grandkids yesterday. How you liked to cook for them."

Her smile trembled. "Yes. Oh, yes. I did. And I was very good at it too. I made them pies. Apple and cherry. And meat loaf. The kind with ketchup in the middle. They liked that most of all. They always ate it up so fast."

"You haven't always been vegan, then, huh?"

"Oh goodness, no. That was only after we came here. To the farm. Peter says it's better this way. That it makes the body healthier. Cleaner. We needed to be free from all the constraints of the lives we used to live." She blanched. "Oh, listen to me prattle on. I must apologize. You don't want to hear any of this. Peter always says I go on and on, and if no one is there to stop me, I might just talk myself to death."

"It's fine," Nate said. "I'm probably the same way."

She studied him rather frantically. "You are, aren't you. The same. Peter says you are. That you *believe*."

"Well, I mean. I've . . . seen things that wouldn't let me *not* believe, if that's what you're asking."

"Miracles," she whispered fervently. "You've seen the miracle that they are."

Nate frowned. "I don't know if I'd call them *miracles*, per se. But it's—it's been a very strange last few weeks."

Her eyes were wet and wide. "Is she everything you thought she'd be?"

"I don't—I never *thought* about her before I met her. I didn't even know she *existed* until I saw her for the first time." He huffed out a breath. "They told me at first that she'd been kidnapped and he was trying to take her back."

Dolores nodded. "Yes. Yes. Back. Away. To let her return." Her eyes darted to the bag slung over his shoulder. "Are you . . . Is everything all right?"

"What? It's—oh, this? No, everything is fine. I just was hoping to use your laundry facilities. We're running out of clean clothes, and I don't know when we'll get a chance to wash them again after we leave here."

"I don't understand," she said. "After you leave?"

"When Art needs to move on," Nate said. "We'll need to take her where she needs to go."

"Right," Dolores said. "Of course. I guess I wasn't . . . thinking." She took another step toward him. "I can do the laundry for you. It's one of my jobs here at the farm. I keep a tidy house."

Nate forced a smile on his face. "No, that's all right. You've done so much for us already. I can handle it. If you could just point me in the right direction, I'd appreciate it. Besides, it's mostly Alex's dirty clothes, and he really sweats through his boxers."

"Oh my," Dolores said. "He is awfully big. I can see that."

"Yes, ma'am. So, the laundry?"

"Down the hall. Last door on the right. Detergent is on the shelf."

He gave her one last tight smile and made his way out of the kitchen. He heard Steven Cooper as she turned the radio back up, telling everyone who was listening that it was going to be a bright and *glorious* future, my friends.

He paused for a moment at the stairs, looking up and wondering just how many rooms were up there. The house was big, but it wasn't big enough that each person on the farm could have their own room. He wondered if they doubled up. Or if Peter had his own room.

Ahead, past the stairs, were four doors.

The first was a door on the left. It was open. Inside was a half bathroom with an open window. He could hear birds in the trees. The tile inside was a clinical white. There was a bar of soap sitting on a dish on the edge of the sink. It was immaculately clean.

Three more doors.

Another on the left, toward the end of the hall.

One on the right.

And a door at the very end.

It was this door that caught Nate's eye. It wasn't like the others.

The doors in the house, from what he'd seen, were wooden.

The door at the end of the hall was metal.

And there was a padlock on the front.

He heard a voice coming from the last door on the left. He couldn't quite make out the words, but there were low, dulcet tones. It could have been a TV. Or a radio.

He walked down the hall.

On either side of him, hanging on the walls, were framed photographs.

He didn't understand what they were at first.

They were mostly black-and-white. Fuzzy and slightly out of focus. Some had numbers etched into the photo paper across the bottom, numbers too long to be dates. Almost like coordinates.

In each of them, buried in the blurry gray, were discolorations.

He could see clouds.

They were photographs of the sky.

And the objects that were in them.

Objects in the sky.

Lights. Shapes.

He'd seen things like them before. Of course he had. Everyone had. They were photographs published as proof of unidentified flying objects.

And there were at least a dozen of them on the walls.

That was . . . par for the course, now that he thought about it.

He wondered if Peter—Oren, that was—had wanted to be separated from Art when he had been. Or how aware he'd been during the two decades in the first place. Artemis had implied it had been a dreamlike state.

But Nate knew just how real dreams could feel.

The floorboards creaked under his feet.

The voice became clearer.

It was Peter.

Peter was speaking.

". . . and there is the potential for it to be reborn. It happens. Time is a circle. We've been at this point before. Maybe not exactly as we are now. There could have been an entirely different civilization than we know to exist right now. It is a *cleansing*. And we find ourselves at the threshold."

Nate took another step. The door was almost closed. He could barely see through a crack in the doorjamb. There were shelves of books. A telescope. The edges of a desk with a blue screen behind it. He thought he could make out the edges of an arm, as if Peter was sitting at the desk in front of the screen.

"Many may not believe my words," Peter said. "I can't force that belief. You and I are different people. I have . . . seen things. Things that seem to defy imagination. It's not fair for me to think you could understand when you haven't been enlightened as I have. There are times when even I seem to lose my patience, where I wish I could take you by the shoulders and shake you until you open your eyes to see what is right in front of you. It's not . . . We are more than what the world has made us out to be. There is *more* beyond the stars. More than you could ever imagine. And when I speak of this wondrous change, I do so only because there are those that can save us from ourselves. Those that show us that there is more. That is the purpose of the Light of Eve and—"

Peter fell silent.

Nate took a step back.

He heard what sounded like a chair moving from a desk, as if someone was standing.

He whirled around, glancing one last time at the metal door before he reached for the doorknob leading toward the laundry room. He was inside the laundry room and fumbling with the switch when the door to the office swung open behind him.

"Nate?"

He glanced over his shoulder, feigning surprise. "Hey, Peter. How are you?"

Peter eyed him curiously. "I'm fine. What are you doing?"

He nodded toward the duffel bag. "Laundry, if that's okay. I asked Dolores, and she pointed me in the right direction."

Peter crossed his arms over his chest. "That's . . . fine, of course. While you stay with us, anything I have is yours."

"That's very generous of you. We really appreciate it. I know Art does."

"Yes," Peter said, voice filled with disdain. "*Art.* Shortened, because a nickname is always necessary in this day and age."

"It's what she likes to be called."

"So I gather. She's . . . adapted. More than I expected her to. In ten years, she's become more human than she ever was with me."

"That—it was different, though, wasn't it?"

Peter cocked his head. "How so?"

"She was . . ." Nate fumbled for the right word. "Sharing. With you."

"Sharing," Peter repeated slowly.

"You were there. With her."

"I was."

"She's alone now."

"I don't know if that's true," Peter said. "She has the Marine." His gaze crawled down Nate before it went back up again. "She has you."

"I meant inside. She's . . . The girl was already gone. Before."

"Her consciousness had left."

"Yes."

Peter nodded. "The body is not the be-all, end-all, Nate. Do you know that?"

"It seems pretty important to me."

"It would, I'm sure. But it's merely a husk. The *soul* is what makes us human. Your flesh doesn't do that."

"I don't know if I believe in souls," Nate said honestly, unsure where this conversation was headed. He didn't like the way Peter was looking at him.

"What do you believe in?"

He shrugged. "I don't . . . know?"

"A higher power? A belief in something more?"

"Seems like if there was, we get the shit end of that deal."

Peter's brow furrowed. "How so?"

"We suffer. We suffer all the time."

"Through pain we're taught the lessons the soul must learn to achieve the highest state of consciousness."

"I'm just worried about surviving, if I'm being honest."

"Surviving what?"

Nate snorted. "I've been shot at more in the last few weeks than I ever have before in my life. I mean, the guy that turned on my *water* turned out to be an agent with a part of the government I'm not supposed to know about."

"Enforcers."

"Yeah. That's the one. He was nosy, but I mean, I thought that was just small-town living. How the hell was I supposed to know he was already watching us?"

Peter was barely blinking. It was unnerving. "You're very odd."

"Says the guy who got body-jacked by an alien for twenty years and yet barely looks older than me." Nate winced. "Shit. Sorry. That probably didn't come out like I wanted it to."

"I think it came out exactly like you wanted," Peter said evenly. "But I take no offense. I understand your point. You're very . . . direct."

"Good," Nate said, ignoring the trickle of sweat that ran down the back of his neck. "I don't want to make things difficult. You've been very kind to us since we arrived."

"Can I ask you a question, Nate?"

"Ye-es?"

"Who have you lost?"

Nate blinked. "Excuse me?"

"You're very . . . cynical for someone your age. It would suggest that you've experienced loss so young."

"I don't . . . What does that have to do with anything?"

Peter leaned against the doorjamb that led to his office. Nate could see a video camera set up on a tripod in the middle of the room over his shoulder. It was pointed at the desk where he'd been sitting before. The camera seemed out of place for a farm that was supposedly off the grid. "I'm merely trying to figure out who Artemis has aligned herself with."

"Aligned," Nate said, looking back at him. "What does that mean?"

"She's fond of you."

"I'm pretty fond of her too."

"And the Marine. That . . . Alex."

Nate bristled a little at the derision in Peter's tone. "He helped her when no one else would. He saved her life."

"Did he? And how did he do that?"

"She's here, isn't she? She's not still in the Mountain. She's *safe*."

"She is. More so here than probably anywhere else in the world. I'm glad you see it that way."

That wasn't what he'd meant at all. "And that's because of Alex."

"Is it?"

"Yes," Nate growled. "He rescued her. He risked his life for her. Hell, he almost fucking *died* for her. She means the world to him."

"Of course she does," Peter said soothingly. "It's almost like she's some kind of replacement for him, isn't it?"

Nate opened his mouth, then closed it again. Because *wasn't* that not too far from the truth? Wasn't that almost *exactly* what had happened? It was—oh hell. What was the psychobabble called? Transference. That sounded right. Transferring the feelings for one to another. It was . . . not unexpected. The people running the Mountain had been smart in choosing Alex, and more than a little cruel.

"Ah," Peter said. "I see it on your face. That's what it is, isn't it? She's a replacement." He sighed. "How unfortunate. I mean, the depths they would go to. I wonder if she knows. That's . . . that might just end up breaking her heart. That is, if she's capable of having her heart broken at all. They're not . . . They don't have emotions like we do. Not to the same extent."

That was a glaring untruth. Nate had seen it with his own eyes. Either Peter was lying to him, or he was clueless as to who Art really was. "That's not what this is," Nate snapped. "You don't know anything about them."

"Don't I? Out of all of us, Nate, who do you think would understand what they have—what they *are*—more? You? Or me? Because *I* know what it's like to be *engulfed* by all that she is—by all that *it* is. You see a little girl. You see her big eyes and her crooked smile and the way she dances on Alex's feet. And for all you know, that's exactly what she *wants* you to see. Have you ever thought of it that way? Clearly, you are intelligent. Has it never crossed your mind that she's showing you exactly what she thinks you want to see in her?"

Well . . . no. He hadn't thought that at all. She was—she was Artemis Darth Vader. She was inquisitive and kind and stared at Alex adoringly. She liked reading and waitresses and movies about space princesses. Of *course* that's who she was. Right? Yes, maybe if she were capable of deception, this would be the way to go about it, to play upon their emotions, to act the part of a bright-eyed, smiling little girl until she turned on them and—

No. He'd seen her. He knew her. She wasn't like that.

"No," Nate said. "Never."

Peter smiled, as if this was the answer he expected. "Do you want to know what I see?"

"I don't—"

"I see a god. I see a being who can impart knowledge far beyond what the human mind is capable of. I see, in part, our salvation."

Nate narrowed his eyes. "She's not yours."

Peter held up his hands in placation. "I know. She doesn't belong to any of us. If anything, she belongs in the stars. That's where she's from. And it is to there she must return."

He felt . . . better? Hearing that. That Peter thought she needed to go back to where she'd come from. It—well, it actually wasn't comforting, not really. Nothing about this place was. But as long as Peter understood what the endgame was here, nothing else mattered. Maybe they'd only be here for another day or two. Artemis would get what she needed from the farm. From Peter. From *Oren*. And then they would leave. It was funny when he thought about it. He'd been initially relieved that they'd found a place to stop for a few days. Now all he wanted to do was get back out on the road again, put the farm in their rearview mirror. "I agree," Nate said. "Just . . . you don't know what Alex has been through. What Art has. Hell, even though it doesn't compare, you don't know what I've been through."

"I don't," Peter agreed. "But you know loss, just as much as they do. Just as much as everyone here does. Tell me, Nate. Do you know what everyone in this place has in common? Why they came here as they have?"

Nate shook his head. He couldn't even begin to guess.

Peter *tsked* as if disappointed. "It boils down to this: *l'appel du vide*. It's a French phrase. It means, quite literally, the call of the void." He uncrossed his arms and stood up straight. "It's an urge for . . . destruction. Have you ever been driving down the road and thought to yourself, what would happen if I swerved into oncoming traffic? Or have you ever been on the edge of a cliff staring down into nothing and thought, what would happen if I just took *one more step*? It's not suicidal. It's an impulse. A need somehow embedded into our genetic code. Most don't act upon it because we are capable of rational thought. But there, buried in our lizard brain, is always the *what-if*. Your hands on the steering wheel and there's an oncoming semi. The tips of your shoes hanging into nothing. It's exhilarating. It's debilitating."

"I don't understand," Nate said, feeling slightly dizzy.

"I know," Peter said. "And that's okay. Maybe you have yet to experience it. You are so young, after all. But the people at the farm, they know of what I speak. They've all gone through *l'appel du vide* at one point or another. They all have a desire for something . . . more. Something further."

"And you . . . ? What. Think you can give it to them?"

Peter laughed. "You sound so dismissive."

"You sound like Jim Jones."

Peter didn't laugh at that. "Do I?"

"Have you ever heard him speak?" Nate glanced pointedly over Peter's shoulder at the video camera. "Or seen his tapes? Because I have."

"This isn't Jonestown," Peter said. "I'm not a demagogue."

"Aren't you?" Nate asked, suddenly curious. "Because Christ, you give a good speech, Oren. Sorry, I mean *Peter*. Hell, there are moments even *I* almost believe you."

"Belief," Peter said. "It's a funny thing when you think about it. It can be so fickle until it's solidified. And even then, there are moments so extreme that can cause it to shatter into the tiniest pieces. I had a belief, tenuous though it was. I thought I understood the order of the universe. But that was before my body was taken over by a being from the stars. That changes you, Nate. If you've never been through it, you can never understand it. It's . . . it showed me things. Expanded my mind in ways I never thought possible. And when it was taken from me, when they *tore* the Seventh Sea from my body, I was bereft. It felt as if I'd been forsaken. I felt *loss*, Nate. Like you. Like Alex. You may think of me as you do, but I am like you. I understand pain. And grief. I have felt alone while my heart broke just a little more with every beat. While our paths have been different, we have all been led here. To this moment. These people, those who have felt the call of the void, are here by choice, because they no longer wanted to *feel* alone. Can you not say the same?"

He wanted to. He really did. He wanted to tell Peter he was fucking crazy. That he was done with this conversation. If everyone else wanted to believe it, fine. That was their choice, but Nate wasn't going to be a part of it.

The *problem* with that was that he *could* say the same. It wasn't until he'd found Alex and Art that he realized just how lonely he'd been. After all, what did he have left? He had no job. His friends had abandoned him when news of his little scandal had broken. His parents were dead. His brother wasn't speaking to him. All he'd had left was a cabin in the middle of the woods in the mountains of Oregon (and God only knew if *that* still stood).

And if he *really* thought about it, if he allowed Peter's words to sink in, hadn't he felt the call of the void before? *L'appel du vide.* He had, hadn't he? There'd been that moment, months before. After his brother had called him to tell him their parents were dead, but before the call about the cabin and the truck. He'd been . . . dazed. He'd left his little apartment, his mind almost uniformly blank. He couldn't even remember how he'd gotten to Chinatown. One moment he'd been sitting on his couch, staring at the walls, and the next he'd been standing under the ornate arch, people milling around him. He'd blinked slowly, like he was just waking from a deep sleep, the remnants of a dream still clinging to him with sticky fingers.

It'd been late in the day and he should have been at work, but hell, *that* wasn't an option anymore, was it? He was numb. Everything felt numb.

He'd turned and headed for home.

And it was while he was standing on the Metro platform, waiting for the train, that he'd thought *what if?* It had been nothing more than a whisper in the back of his mind as he watched the light from the approaching train in the tunnel get bigger and brighter.

What if.

What if?

What *if* he took a step off the platform in front of the train? It would be quick, wouldn't it? A breath, a step, and then it would all be over, and holy fuck, it had *called* to him, the whisper becoming a goddamn *scream* in his head, brief and earsplitting, and he'd lifted his foot. He'd lifted his foot, his other leg tensing as he started to step forward and—

The train had *whooshed* by in front of him.

He'd taken a step back, eyes feeling like they were bulging from his head, heart thundering in his chest.

He'd gasped for air as he bumped into a woman behind him. He'd apologized, voice a croak, and the woman looked concerned, asking him if he was okay. He'd nodded, yeah, yeah, I'm fine, just—I'm okay. The train startled me. Daydreaming, wouldn't you know.

She'd smiled cautiously.

He'd sat on a bench, head in his hands, for close to an hour.

Eventually, he'd made his way home.

A couple weeks later, his brother had called. The cabin at Herschel Lake. Dad's old truck. That's it, Nate. That's all they left you, so don't ask for anything else. That's all you're going to get.

Yeah, Ricky. Okay.

"Nate?"

He jerked his head up.

Peter looked worried. "Are you all right?"

"Yeah," he said. "Yeah. I'm . . . fine. Look, Peter. I appreciate everything you've done for us. For Art. And . . . yeah. You're right. I don't understand what it is you went through with her. When she was . . . you. But she's different now. She's changed. Because of Alex."

"And you, I would suspect."

Nate shook his head. "No. It's not like that. She's—"

"You don't see it, do you?"

"What?"

"The way she looks at you. The way they both do. The three of you, you're . . . I suspect you're all connected. In one way or another."

Nate flushed. He couldn't help himself. "We've been through a lot together," he muttered.

Peter smiled. "I know. I think everyone here can say the same. And while you may not agree with our way of life, I hope you can respect it. We're all travelers, after all. Just trying to find our way."

Nate could get that. He really could. "I know. And I'm sorry if I came off as—I don't know. Rude. Or something. You've been nothing but nice to us, and I'm here accusing you of being . . ."

"Jim Jones?"

Nate grimaced. "Yeah."

Peter waved him away. "I can see where you'd come to that conclusion, far-fetched though it may be."

"Who were you recording the video for, then?"

Peter laughed. "A bit of self-indulgence, if you can believe it. Ever since I was freed from the shackles of the Mountain, I've created a video journal of sorts. To document my experiences so that one day, if all of this were to come to light, people would see the truth. How many people in this world could say they have been in my position?"

"Not many," Nate said. "At least, I would hope not."

"Precisely. I think it's important for the entire world to know what has happened here. To me. To us. You know as well as I do that the Mountain will do everything it can to cover this up. To keep the truth hidden in shadow."

Nate believed that completely. "We won't let them."

"No," Peter said, smile growing as wide as Nate had ever seen it. "No, I don't expect we will." He took a step back. "I'll leave you to your laundry. Thank you, Nate. This conversation has been most . . . enlightening. You are truly an extraordinary individual."

Nate didn't know what to say to that.

Then, "Peter?"

Peter Williams stopped in the doorway to his office. He looked back over his shoulder at Nate. "Yes?"

Nate nodded toward the padlocked metal door. "What's in there?"

Peter laughed. "Basement. We store chemicals and fertilizer down there for the fields and the gardens. We had kept such things in the barn, but they were stolen from us repeatedly. It can be used to manufacture methamphetamines, in case you didn't know. I will not be involved in the destruction of the human body, especially not for monetary gain. It was easier to keep it all locked away. Will there be anything else?"

Nate shook his head.

Peter closed the door behind him.

Moments later, Peter began speaking again, though the words were muffled now.

Nate turned back toward the laundry and went about what he'd set out to do.

✦

He waited until after lunch to pull Art and Alex into the barn. Art was babbling about the horses she'd seen, there had been *three* of them, and one of them had eaten an apple slice out of her *hand*, could Nate believe that? Could he really believe that?

It turned out he could.

Alex had looked a little worried when Nate had glanced around before nodding toward the barn. Peter had already gone back inside the house, and the others were moving rather lethargically toward their afternoon chores. No one seemed to be in any real hurry.

The comet was a white light against a bright blue sky.

"Is everything okay?" Alex asked him after they'd climbed up to the loft. "You were . . . quiet at lunch."

Nate shook his head. "I don't know. Honestly, it's probably nothing. I mean . . ." He struggled to find the words. "I had a talk with Peter."

"About what?" Art asked, sitting on a bale of hay, feet dangling above the floor.

"How well do you know him?"

"How well do we know anyone?"

"Art," Alex warned.

She rolled her eyes. "I don't know. For him, it's been a long time since I've seen him."

"But not for you," Nate said slowly.

"No. I told you. Time moves differently for me. It's . . . hard to explain."

"That can't be your answer for everything. That's dirty pool."

She snorted. "Your tiny human brain isn't quite capable of understanding the complexities of everything I am. Trust me on that."

"Be nice," Alex told her.

"I didn't say that to be *mean*. I was being honest. Literally, your brain could potentially explode if I showed you everything."

"Oh . . . kay," Nate said. "But you still haven't answered my question."

She shrugged. "He's changed."

"For the better?"

"Maybe? He was . . . angry. At first at me. Then at the people in the Mountain. He was disillusioned, I think, that his own people could keep him locked away. After a while, the anger faded. We talked. A lot. It was like a dream."

"Did you bond with him? Like you have with Alex?"

"And you," she reminded him. "You're part of this too. And no. It wasn't the same. We were sharing the same space. With you, I shared everything else."

That was . . . vague as usual. "Why are we here?"

She looked frustrated. "I don't know yet. I just know we have to be here."

"How?" Alex asked. "How do you know?"

"It wasn't—we're not still connected. Not really. That was broken when they forced me out of him. But I think a piece of me remained in him, or a piece of him was in me. Maybe he imprinted on me, or I on him. I don't know. We were only ever supposed to observe." Her shoulders slumped. "I messed up. It's no wonder they left me behind."

Nate sighed. "I'm not trying to make you feel bad, Art. I'm just trying to figure out why we're here. What the point of this is. This place." He gave them a quick rundown of the conversation he'd had with Peter outside his office. He didn't talk about the call of the void. He didn't tell them about standing on the edge of a Metro platform, the grand *what-if* of it all. He couldn't bring himself to share that. But even *without* that, he realized just how crazy he sounded. It was there, that gut instinct, but what proof did he have to back anything up? So what if Peter was weird? He'd been possessed by a fucking *alien* for twenty years. Of *course* he'd be weird.

Alex looked thoughtful when Nate finished talking. "So . . . what? You think Peter's in charge of some kind of cult?"

Nate shook his head. "I don't—no. I don't think he's a cult leader. I just . . . Maybe I'm overthinking everything." He glared at Art and Alex. "If I sound crazy, the fault rests on both of you."

"What?" Art said, sounding outraged. "Why?"

"Because all *I* wanted to do was go sit and brood in my cabin in peace! But no, you two just *had* to choose to break into that one and then point a gun at me, like, twelve times."

"Drama queen," Alex muttered.

"Alex wouldn't have really shot you," Art told him. "Even back then he thought you were cute."

Alex gaped at her.

She winked at him.

"That is *beside* the point," Nate said, though he was going to kiss the hell out of Alex later when no prying eyes watched their every move. "I'm just—this place gives me the creeps, okay? And maybe it's nothing. Maybe everything is fine. But it wouldn't hurt to keep an eye open while we're still here."

Alex nodded slowly. "It's . . . That's a good idea. I'm sure it's fine. But if it's not, it's better to be prepared. I'll start carrying the gun again. Just to be safe. We trust you, Nate."

Nate absolutely did not preen at that.

"Why are you blushing?" Art asked him. "I don't think I've ever seen your face turn that red before."

"Shut up."

"Uh-huh." She glanced between the two of them, a calculating look on her face.

✦

Dinner that night was held once again in the front yard. The same lights were strung up in the trees. The same torches were lit. There were the same plates, the same tablecloths. It was again another stew, though the ingredients were different.

Hell, even Billie Holiday was caressing their ears again.

But still. It felt . . . different.

The air was charged somehow. Like an electrical storm was approaching.

The sky above was clear as the stars began to shine.

The comet looked huge, almost as bright as the moon.

The people of the farm were quiet. Peter had spoken a few words at the beginning of the meal, but it didn't have the same gravitas as it'd had the night before. He looked distracted. His eyes were wide, and Nate swore he was barely blinking.

Nate didn't eat.

When the meal was finished, everyone got up to dance again.

They didn't speak. They clung to each other as they shuffled their feet in the grass.

Peter stayed for a single dance before he disappeared into the house.

"His mind is heavy tonight," Dolores told Nate as she watched the screen door swing shut.

"Why?"

She looked up at the sky. "Because sometimes, our choices are laid out in front of us, waiting for a decision to be made."

He'd barely dozed off when he felt a hand shaking his shoulder.

He opened his eyes.

Art was snoring next to him.

Alex was standing above him, staring down.

He sat up quickly. "What—"

Alex brought a finger to his lips.

Nate fell silent.

Alex jerked his head toward the stairs.

Nate nodded and stood slowly, careful not to jostle the mattress. Art smacked her lips and continued snoring.

He followed Alex down the stairs. He watched the play of muscles on Alex's back under his shirt in the low light. His skin felt hot. His eyes were heavy.

Alex didn't lead him to the window from the night before.

Instead, when they reached the barn floor, he took Nate by the hand, pulling him toward the rear of the barn. The moved around bales of hay until they were in a dark corner, out of sight from anyone who could enter. They were steeped in shadows. Nate could barely make out Alex in front of him as he turned, eyes glittering dully in the dark.

"What is it?" Nate asked.

Alex pushed him gently against the barn wall. The wood creaked under his back. A thick thigh was pressed between his legs, a foot kicking them farther apart. He gasped quietly as Alex applied pressure to his groin, heat pooling low in his stomach.

He tilted his head back against the side of the barn.

Lips and teeth trailed along his neck. Alex hadn't shaved in a few days, and Art was going to figure things out sooner rather than later as his skin felt as if it were being scraped raw.

"You're going to need to be quiet," Alex whispered in his ear. "Do you think you can do that?"

"Why?" Nate asked. "What do you think you're going to do?"

He felt Alex's smile against his cheek. "What do you think?"

"Art—"

"Is sleeping. And will stay that way if you keep quiet."

"Pretty goddamn sure of yourself," Nate whispered, biting back a groan as the thigh on his cock and balls pressed even harder. "Fucking grunt, huh? Think you're so goddamn good?"

Alex kissed him then, and it was more than it'd been the night before. At the window, under the stars, it'd been tentative. Unsure. Almost shy. It wasn't like that now.

Now there was teeth and tongue and a big hand wrapped gently around his throat, holding his head in place as Alex worked his mouth over. Nate felt small and breakable, knowing Alex could most likely snap him in two if he wished. He didn't resist when he felt pressure on his jaw from a thumb, Alex breaking the kiss as he turned Nate's head, teeth finding the cords in Nate's neck, biting down gently.

He couldn't believe they were doing this now. Here, of all places. Surrounded by the weirdest people he'd ever met in his life. He didn't know what had gotten into Alex.

But he sure as shit wasn't complaining, especially when the pressure eased between them slightly, enough for Alex to reach his free hand down between them. He palmed Nate's dick through his jeans, the ache of it almost too much to bear. Nate groaned again, Alex hissing in his ear that he needed to be *quiet*. Nate was about to snark something back, to tell him to fuck off and get on with it, but there were two fingers in his mouth then and a voice telling him to *suck*.

He did. Alex's skin tasted slightly salty as Nate rolled his tongue against the fingers. Alex had the digits pressed almost to the back of his throat, and Nate's eyes rolled slightly. Alex snapped open his jeans, and there was a hot hand down the front, groping him roughly. He tried to speak around Alex's fingers, wanting to tell him it was okay, that he could take it, that he could go harder, but all he managed to do was drool on his chin.

Alex shoved Nate's jeans down his thighs, effectively trapping his legs. He pressed up against Nate again, still fully clothed, his fingers in Nate's mouth pressing down against his tongue. He rolled his hips against Nate. The slide of skin against denim made Nate feel like he was burning up.

Nate bit down gently, teeth sinking into Alex's skin.

Alex grunted near his ear. "Don't have anything," he muttered. "Nothing that could work and not hurt you. But we're gonna do something. You trust me?"

Nate nodded, babbling incoherently around Alex's fingers.

"Good," he said. "I'm going to take my fingers out of your mouth. I want you to get my hand as wet as you can. You do that for me, and I promise I'll make it worth your while. You like the sound of that?"

Yes, Nate said with his eyes, wide and wet. *Yes. Yes. Yes.*

Alex pulled his fingers out of his mouth with a wet *pop*. He held the hand in front of Nate's face. "Do it, then."

Nate gathered spit in his mouth and spit on Alex's hand before licking his palm, spreading his saliva around as best he could. Alex groaned quietly, reaching up to twist Nate's nipple through his shirt. Nate's hips jerked at the bright flare of *pleasurepain* that bowled through him. "You like that, huh?" Alex whispered. He did it again. Nate moaned against Alex's hand. "Yeah. You really do, don't you?"

Nate did.

"I'm not wet enough. More."

It only took another minute before Alex pulled his hand away and took a step back. Nate's heated skin felt sharply cold. He watched as Alex unbuttoned his own jeans and pushed them down around his hips. He used his dry hand to pull his own dick out. Nate could barely make it out in the dark, but he could see the head through Alex's fist. He watched as Alex hooked a finger under his shirt and rucked it up under his armpits, exposing his hairy torso. Alex spit down. It landed on his dick. He used the hand that Nate had gotten wet to spread their saliva around, coating the length.

"Turn around," he grunted.

Nate did. He turned his head, cheek pressing against the rough wall of the barn.

"Press your ass out."

Nate felt a bright flash of *shame*, or something close to it. He felt exposed, more so than he'd ever been before. He did as Alex told him to do. He felt fingers trace along the crack of his ass, brushing along his hole. He pushed his ass back into the touch. The fingers continued down between his legs until they came to his balls. Alex tugged on them, first one and then the other. It went on for a long minute, Alex *pulling*, stretching his nuts. Nate was sweating, and harder than he'd ever been in his life.

"Pull your balls forward," Alex told him.

He did. His thumb pressed against the base of his dick, and he grabbed his balls, pulling them forward.

"Squeeze your thighs together. Hold them tight."

He got it now. He was on board with this, yes, sir. He pressed his thighs together, letting his balls drop on the front of his legs. His dick bobbed in front of him, the tip hitting the wall. He pushed his hips back a little more. He didn't need a fucking splinter.

He felt the press of Alex's dick against the back of his thighs. There was a brief moment of resistance, but then the length of his cock was between his legs, trapped between Nate's thighs. His cockhead bumped the back of Nate's balls.

They both groaned at the sensation. Alex gave an experimental thrust, and then another one, and the hairs on Nate's legs were pulled, little needle pricks that caused his eyes to roll back in his head. He felt Alex pull out almost completely and heard him spit again. It hit the crack of his ass, dripping down. A finger rubbed against it until it pressed between his thighs above Alex's dick, making it wetter.

"There it is," Alex breathed as he pressed back in until his hips met Nate's ass. "Right there." He pulled back and pushed in again, dick rubbing along the length of Nate's taint.

He squeezed his thighs tighter, hearing Alex grunt behind him. Nate's hands were pressed flat against the wall of the barn, and it was all he could do to just hold on. Alex gripped his hips, the sound of bare skin slapping along with sharp exhalations.

Alex reached around and pressed a hand against his stomach before he was pulled against Alex's chest. To keep the angle just right, Nate was standing on his tiptoes. He rested his head on Alex's shoulder as Alex sucked on his neck. He closed his eyes when Alex's hand wrapped around his dick and began jacking him off in time with each thrust.

Nate reached up behind him and wrapped an arm around the back of Alex's neck, letting him take the weight.

Alex bit down the moment he came, a warm splash against the back of his balls.

His hips stilled as he panted against Nate's neck, his orgasm causing him to tremble.

"Please," Nate managed to say. "Please."

Alex chuckled darkly before swiping his thumb over Nate's cockhead. He squeezed Nate's dick and started jacking him again, his grip tight. Nate fucked Alex's fist until his thighs were trembling. He grunted as he came, streaks hitting the barn wall in front of him.

They stood there, Nate held tightly against Alex. Nate turned his head until his lips found Alex's jaw. The angle was awkward, but Alex met him partway.

"Fuck," Nate muttered as he broke the kiss. "Jesus Christ. Where the hell did you learn to do that?"

"You make do when you need to," Alex said, smiling against the side of Nate's head. "And I needed to."

"Yeah. You did." Nate kissed him again.

✦

They cleaned up as best they could. There was a rain barrel outside in front of the barn. They splashed water on themselves, getting rid of the evidence. It wasn't ideal, but it'd have to do for now until Nate could shower later. The farmhouse had surprisingly good water pressure, though Nate hadn't spent long in it that morning, not wanting to waste the hot water when there were so many people living on the farm.

Before he could go back into the barn, Alex stopped him.

He looked back.

Alex said, "I . . . Thank you."

Nate arched an eyebrow. "I feel like I should be thanking *you*."

Alex shook his head. "Not . . . for that. But yes, that too, I guess. I mean for . . . everything. I don't know what we would have done without you."

Nate smiled. He reached up and cupped the back of Alex's neck. "You would have been just fine."

Alex leaned down, pressing his forehead against Nate's. "Maybe. But this—it's better. This way. With you."

"Yeah?"

"Yeah."

"Good. Because I'm pretty sure you're stuck with me."

Something complicated crossed Alex's face as he pulled back, but Nate was getting better at reading him. It was disbelief warring with hope. "This is going to get difficult."

Nate knew what he meant. They were approaching the end. Or at least *an* ending. Whatever came after was still in the great beyond. It was nebulous, this future, though there would be a point when it would need to be made clear. "We'll figure it out."

Alex nodded, his brow furrowed. "There are people who could take us in. After. While we figure out what to do next."

"People?"

He looked away. "Friends. Contacts. And I think the story needs to be told. Of Art. Of the Mountain. So everyone knows. And I think you need to be the one to tell it."

Nate was shocked. "Are you sure?"

"Yeah. It might be our only chance. Know someone who'll listen?"

He thought of Ruth, a cigarette dangling from her lips. "I might."

"Good. We'll worry about that then. It'll take time before we can speak. Maybe a long time. And it might make us a bigger target, but there are ways to disappear when you need to." He sighed and turned his face skyward. Then, "Would you look at that."

Nate looked up.

Above him, the comet was blazing, brighter than anything else in the sky.

"Wow," Nate whispered in awe. "That's—that crazy guy. Steven Cooper. He said tomorrow is going to be the brightest the comet will ever be before it starts its sling away."

"He's not wrong."

"Makes you wonder if he knows other things we don't."

Alex snorted. "Maybe. We should get some sleep. Tomorrow we need to figure out where to go next."

"Okay."

He let Alex lead him back inside by the hand and back up the stairs. Art hadn't moved, hair spread out around her on Alex's rolled-up jacket. Alex squatted beside her, running a hand across her forehead. She leaned into it but continued snoring.

It was there, plain as day.

How much he loved her.

Nate didn't know why Peter couldn't see it.

Maybe it had started as transference. But it was beyond that now.

Heartbreak up close. Yeah. No matter what, it was going to happen.

Nate settled down on the mattress. Alex did the same on the other side. Art sighed in her sleep, turning toward Nate. Alex and Nate watched each other over her head.

"Good night," Nate whispered.

Alex smiled.

And then they slept.

✦

He awoke when a hand pressed tightly over his mouth.

His eyes flashed open.

It was dark.

People were standing above him.

He tried to shout, but it came out muffled.

Something flared to life in his head, a string connecting him to the two people lying next to him. Images flew, coated in anger and fear. He heard the snarl of electricity, and Art was *screaming* between them and—

A pinprick in his right arm.

Instantly, the world began to melt around him.

He couldn't move his arms.

His legs.

"Shh," Oren Schraeder/Peter Williams whispered above him. "It's time, Nate. It's time. It's time for us to leave this world and take our place amongst the stars."

Nate struggled to keep his eyes open even as Alex shouted weakly somewhere off to his left.

But it was no use.

Everything bled together until he was gone

gone

gone

CHAPTER SEVENTEEN

Nate.

He was standing on a street in a nice suburb. The lawns were mown, and the hedges were freshly trimmed. Flowers bloomed, and people walked on sidewalks. They waved at each other as their dogs tugged on their leashes, as children shouted around them from their bikes.

One house in particular caught his eye.

It was made of brick. It had a large porch with two rocking chairs. The mailbox was green with ladybugs painted on it.

He knew this house.

He'd grown up here.

This was his home before—

Nate.

He looked up.

There, next to the sun, was a comet.

He looked back at the house.

Gone was the summer's day. The sky was cloudy and gray above him. The hedges were thin and dead. The flowers were gone. The air was cold. There were little patches of dirty snow along the sidewalks. The grass was brown. The streets were empty.

"Wait," he said, taking a step toward the house.

A low rumble came from his right.

He turned his head.

An old truck was coming down the road. Its headlights were on, but dim. He recognized that truck, didn't he? Yes. The last time he'd seen it, it'd been at the bottom of a ravine, right? After—

It pulled up to the curb in front of his old house.

His father sat inside.

He looked . . . older. Far older than he'd been when Nate had seen him last, screaming at him in the cabin in the woods that he'd *never* have a faggot for a son, that he needed to get the fuck out and never come back. Time hadn't been kind to him. His face was craggy and heavy. The bags under his eyes were purpled, like bruises. Nate watched as his father looked up at the house, fingers tightening around the steering wheel.

And then he got out of the truck.

Nate knew then what this was. He tried to move forward, but it was like he was underwater. His limbs were heavy. It hurt to breathe.

"No," he said. "No, no, don't do this, Dad, don't *do this*—"

"He can't hear you."

A little girl stood at his side, staring up at him sadly.

Artemis Darth Vader.

"He can't hear you," she said again. "Because this isn't real."

"No," Nate said. "We're here. He's *right there*."

And he was. His father had closed the door to the truck before he made his way up the short driveway to the house. There was a light on inside that Nate had missed before. His father pulled the collar of his jacket up around his neck as he reached the porch.

He took each step slowly.

Nate screamed at him to stop.

He didn't.

He tried the handle to the front door.

It was locked.

He knocked. And waited.

The door opened.

He couldn't see past his father, but he knew his mother had answered the door.

His father began waving his hands wildly.

He was shouting, but Nate couldn't make out his words.

His mother tried to shut the door.

His father pressed a hand against it.

"We need to go," Artemis said, tugging on his hand. "We have to find Alex. Nate, we have to find Alex before it's too late."

Nate shook loose from her. He managed another step forward, but the pavement beneath his feet started sucking him down like quicksand. He struggled against it but only made it worse.

At the house, his mother had managed to close the door.

His father was going back to the truck.

Nate knew what came next.

He shouted at his father. Begged him. Pleaded with him. Told him to stop, don't do this, please don't do this, it's not too late to stop this, Dad, please.

His father ignored him.

Nate sank farther into the road. It was up to his knees now.

Artemis said, "We have to hurry. Peter is going to—"

His father opened the truck.

Pulled out a shotgun.

And for a moment, for a brief, shining moment, he *hesitated*. Nate could *see* it. That look on his face. That look of comprehension. Of *horror*. As if he understood right then and there what he was about to do. What he was truly capable of. And Nate had hope. He had hope that things could change.

Nate, can you hear me?

He ignored the voice from the comet. It couldn't help him now.

"Yes!" he cried. "That's right. Dad, that's *right*. This can't happen. This *can't happen*."

The look slid from his father's face. His jaw grew slack, mouth opening slightly.

He turned back toward the house.

He left the door to the truck hanging open.

He carried the shotgun in one hand.

Up at the house, Nate saw the curtains open. He saw his mother in the window. She was crying. She had a phone pressed against her ear. She disappeared, and the curtain fell back against the window.

The door was locked again when Mitchell Cartwright stood on the front porch. His ex-wife, now Linda Cook, had locked it before getting on the phone with the police. His brother, Ricky, had told him this . . . after.

His father pulled shells from his pocket. He loaded the gun.

He aimed at the door.

There was a concussive blast. A lick of fire.

The door fell open.

His father went inside.

Nate was up to his waist in the road. Art stood next to him, staring up at the comet bursting through the cloud cover. She told him she couldn't help him. Not with this. Time didn't move backward, she said. Forward, yes. Even side to side. But never backward.

Inside the house, on the second floor, came another shotgun blast that echoed throughout the neighborhood, and Nate *knew* that was the moment his father murdered his mother.

He howled up at the gray sky above, the comet heading straight for them.

From the house, the shotgun fired again.

His father, blowing his own head off.

He did it, Ricky had told him, voice thick. Didn't leave a note. Didn't say *why*. He just killed her. And then he killed himself.

Nate, I need you to listen to the sound of my voice, the comet said.

"No," Art said, sounding urgent. "Nate, I need you here with me. Please. I need you to help me. To help Alex. He needs our help. He needs *you*. He loves you, can't you see that? He loves you, and I need you too—"

"Yes," Nate said. "Yes, yes, yes."

"Good," Artemis Darth Vader said, and there was a great white cloud of *something* floating around her. It pulsed brightly with a kaleidoscope of colors, some that Nate wasn't sure existed in his world. His mind wasn't capable of comprehending what was in front of him, and when Art reached for him, her hand wrapped in the beautiful sheen that was swallowing her whole, he understood that this was what she *really* looked like. This was who she *really* was, and it was more than he ever expected, more than he ever thought possible, and when their hands touched, it was like a miniature sun had gone supernova in his chest. He was *engulfed* by it and—

They stood on a rain-slicked road.

There was a snarl of metal in front of them, wrapped around a tree. It took a moment for Nate to understand that what he was looking at had once been a *car*. It was barely recognizable aside from a single tire that somehow had remained intact, spinning lazily.

Alex Weir was on his knees in front of them, pounding his fists against the road.

He was screaming.

Art tugged on Nate's hand.

He looked down at her.

"Do you remember what I told you?" she asked. "About how he'll need you after I'm gone?"

"Why do you have to leave at all?" Nate demanded. "Why can't you—"

The tree cracked and fell.

There was a dull *fwump* as fire began to spread along the car.

Alex tried to crawl toward them.

His hands sank into the road.

Nate took a step and—

"There you are," Peter said, a smile on his face. "Hello, Nate. I'm glad you—"

The rain beat down from above. Alex was snarling as he tried to get to the car.

The pavement beneath Nate's feet began sucking him down.

Nate. Nate. *Open your eyes. I need you to open your eyes.*

"Alex," Nate said.

Alex turned and looked over his shoulder. Nate's heart broke at the anguish etched on his face. "Nate?"

Nate nodded. "Listen to me. This isn't real. None of this is real. Okay? I know it hurts. I know you feel helpless. But we can't go back. We can't change what's already happened. You have to remember that. This isn't real, but I am. And Artemis is too."

Recognition flickered across Alex's eyes. "Artemis."

"Yes. *Yes.* Artemis. Art. She needs you. Okay? *I* need you. Something's wrong. Something's wrong and we have to—"

Nate's head snapped to the side as if he'd been slapped.

He opened his eyes.

Oren Schraeder stood in front of him. He wasn't smiling. "You will listen to me," he said, voice flat. "Wake up. Wake up. *Wake up.*" He raised his hand and slapped Nate across the face again and—

Alex was trying to get to Nate. The car burned behind them in the rain.

Nate looked over his shoulder, wanting to shout at Art to help them.

She was gone.

"Fuck," he whispered.

*Nate. Nate. NateNateNate*NATENATENATE—

Alex ripped his hands free from the ground with an angry growl. He stood up. The road was solid beneath his feet. He ran toward Nate.

Nate tilted his head back toward the falling rain. Water sluiced down his face.

"I'm here," he heard Alex say. "I'm here, and we're gonna get out of here. We're gonna—"

Everything exploded in white.

Nathaniel Cartwright opened his eyes.

His thoughts were fuzzy and loose. His head felt as if it were stuffed with cotton. He blinked blearily, trying to get his eyes to focus. It almost worked. He saw through a filmy haze, the edges around him blurred.

There was a metal table in front of him.

On the other side of the table was Alex.

"Alex," he said. Or at least he *tried* to say. In the end what came out was a garbled sound that didn't resemble *Alex* at all.

Alex was awake, though his eyes were vacant.

Nate tried to lift his arms.

He couldn't.

He looked down.

He was seated in a chair. His arms were sitting on the rests. He wasn't secured to the chair. There were no manacles around his wrists. His legs weren't bound. He was free. He was free to move.

He tried to stand.

He understood the concept. He told his body to move. The synapses fired. His arms twitched. His toes shifted in his boots.

But that was it.

"Are you here?" a voice asked.

He slowly looked back up.

Peter stood off to the right of the table. He was frowning. Nate didn't like that.

He said, "What the fuck did you do to me?"

What came out was just a low groan.

Spittle dribbled onto his chin.

"It's difficult," Peter said, nodding slowly. "Or so I've heard. Sco-polamine. It's also called Devil's Breath. It's derived from a flower that grows on a shrub. Strange little plant. Only found in Colom-bia. The natives used it in their rituals for centuries. Burundanga poisoning. Sometimes it's a powder that can be blown into your face. Other times it can be made into a liquid and injected."

Nate didn't understand what Peter was talking about. He tried to get up again. Tried to raise his arms so he could wrap his hands around Peter's neck and choke the fucking *life* out of him. But the very *idea* of attacking Peter seemed so irrelevant, so far away, that it was just easier to let it go.

"It causes hallucinations," Peter said. "And for that, I apologize. I know they can be . . . so lifelike. Seeing things that you don't want to see. I can only imagine what it was like for you. I never like to see suffering if I can avoid it. But this . . . I think this was unavoidable."

Peter was wearing what looked like a white dress or a sheet. Nate didn't know why it mattered. Why he focused on it. Maybe it was because he'd only ever seen Peter in jeans and a white shirt. Like everyone else at the farm. But now, the white fabric was sitting loose on his shoulders and billowed around his body.

It was . . . odd.

He tried to ask Peter why he was wearing something so ridicu-lous, but his mouth only twisted, and his tongue barely moved.

"It's almost time," Peter said. "I don't expect you to understand. How could you? You haven't seen the things I have. You haven't had it inside of you. I argued at first. I fought against it. It took me a long time to figure out I wasn't dreaming. And when I did, I *railed* against it. This . . . this *thing* inside of me. Oh, it said it came in peace. It said it wasn't going to hurt me. It had just gotten *separated* from the others and had gotten scared. It was almost . . . childlike. This spirit. This ghost. I was haunted. And I had no choice."

He smiled ruefully. "But . . . eventually I stopped and started to listen. And it was only then that I understood that I'd been chosen. Out of all the people in the world, out of all *six billion people*, it had chosen *me* to act as its vessel. It had chosen *me* to bring enlightenment to the world. I felt . . . powerful. I felt loved. I felt *joy*. And I promised myself that I would never forget the lessons I learned. That I would do what I could to spread the gospel of the Seventh Sea. And when it was torn from me, when they *took* it from me and then *discarded* me as if I were nothing, I knew what I needed to do. I knew what it was asking of me. Which is why I made this. This place. These people. The Light of Eve. It was my way of spreading the gospel of the Seventh Sea, of trying to make the masses understand that we are not alone. That we have been *lied* to, and that there are *gods* among us."

"Alex," Nate tried to say. "Alex. Alex. Alex."

Alex blinked slowly, mouth slack. He didn't appear to be tied down either.

"Nate," Peter said. "Turn your head to the left."

Nate said, "Fuck off."

But in reality, he said, "Mmph," and slowly turned his head to the left, just as Peter had asked. In fact, doing what Peter asked seemed like the best thing to do. It felt *good* to do what he asked. It felt *good* to have Peter telling him what to do.

And no matter how hard he tried, he couldn't fight it.

To his left, near the table, was a video camera set on a tripod. It looked to be the same one Nate had seen in Peter's office the day before. A red light on top blinked on and off, on and off.

It was recording Peter's sermon.

But the camera fell away when he saw where he was. And what lined the wall.

The floor was a large concrete slab. Exposed fluorescent lights flickered overhead. The walls were made of wood.

And lining those walls, all around them, were white metal bunk beds, stacked two high.

On each of the beds lay a person dressed similarly to Peter. All white. Their feet were bare.

There was a difference, though, between them and Peter.

The people lying on the beds had black velvet cloths covering their faces.

None of them moved.

"They have chosen," Peter said quietly, "to put their trust in me, to allow me the honor of releasing them from the shackles of their humanity. They will rise from this plane of existence, their souls like *gas*, and they will follow the Seventh Sea to where it will take them into the tail of Markham-Tripp. We will give ourselves to the gods that are coming for us. We will be rejoiced. We will be *revered*. You may look at me again. Nate, look at me."

Nate turned his head. It felt as if the muscles in his neck were seizing. "What . . . you . . . *done?*" Nate managed to ask.

"The void, Nate," Peter said. "The call of the void. *L'appel du vide*. They felt it. They were lost souls. They had *nothing*. They were drug users and whores and degenerates. They were being taken *advantage* of. They were the discarded. The forgotten. All of them had stood on the edge of that cliff, looked over, and thought about *jumping*. But for what? What purpose would it have served? What would it have done? Their life would have had no meaning." Peter walked around the table behind Alex. Nate tracked every step he took. Peter stopped next to a bed. The person upon it was smaller than the others, and plumper. It was a woman, and she was still breathing, though it was rapid and shallow. Peter smiled down at her lovingly. He fell to his knees next to the bed. The bottoms of his feet were dirty. "I took them in. I gave them a purpose. I showed them that there was . . . more to this world than they could ever understand on their own. I told them I would lead them to salvation, and the only thing I required from them was their trust. The only thing, Nate. I promised them I would never hurt them. I would never call them names. I would love them as if they were my own. Because in the Light of Eve, they *are* my own. My people. And soon, they will enjoy their reward." He reached under the bed.

And pulled out a gun.

A pistol. An old six-shooter. It looked like every clichéd gun Nate had ever seen in a Western. Art would love it. Down that old dusty trail, partner.

Dolores took in a deep breath. Her fingers shook. "Shhh," Peter said. "It's all right. You will reap your reward soon enough. Shhh." He pressed a hand against her forehead. "A cocktail. Ketamine with

330 • TJ KLUNE

fentanyl. They took it voluntarily. They slept and dreamed of stars, knowing I would give them peace. I need you to remember that. I didn't force them. In the end, they chose this."

Nate could do nothing as Peter raised the gun and pressed it against the side of Dolores's head. He pulled the trigger. There was a muffled crack as her head jerked to the side. She didn't take another breath. Nate could barely see any blood at all.

"There," Peter said quietly as he lowered the gun to his side. "There. Almost done. She . . . she was one of the first to join me. In her previous life, she was a retired teacher. A grandmother. She was being used, of course. Her children only came to her when they needed something. Her grandchildren only told her they loved her when she gave them presents. She was lonely, Nate. She was very lonely listening to the call of the void. I don't know how much longer she would have lasted if I hadn't found her. But I did, and I gave her a purpose again. I told her of the things I'd witnessed. Of the god that had been within me. That I was going to share it with her, and the only thing I required was that she come with me. That she give up her empty and meaningless life and come with me." He leaned over and kissed what seemed to be the tip of her nose under the black fabric. "Do you know what she said to me? She said thank you. I will never forget that."

Peter stood back up. He looked around the bunk beds. No one else was breathing. He must have killed everyone while Nate was caught in a dream. He felt a tear fall down his cheek. He couldn't raise his hands to wipe it away.

"It's almost time," Peter said. "Time for me to keep my promises made to my people. We will rise to the spacecraft in Markham-Tripp, and we will be free of this place. One last thing remains to ensure our success."

He walked back toward the table, opening the cylinder of the gun. Spun it around. It clacked and echoed in the room. The basement. They had to be in the basement. Behind that metal door with the padlock.

Peter showed Nate the contents of the cylinder. Five chambers were empty. One had a bullet inside. He did the same for Alex, though Alex's eyes were still unfocused. Peter spun the cylinder

again before snapping it closed. He set the gun on the table between Nate and Alex. "Don't touch that," he said.

And then he walked away toward a door in the wall to the right.

Get the gun.

Get the gun.

Get the gun.

Get the gun get the gun get the gun GET THE GUN GET THE—

He didn't move.

He stared at it.

He wanted it more than anything.

But he didn't move.

"Nate," Peter said. "Alex. Would you look at me, please?"

They both turned their heads.

In the open doorway, standing next to Peter, was Artemis Darth
Vader.

Her eyes were wide. Her face was wet. And she looked *furious*.

Good, Nate thought. *Good. Good. Good.*

But upon her head sat a halo of sorts. It was black and metal, and
wires were attached to it that ran down her arms, the ends of which
ran into filmy white electrodes stuck to her bare skin.

And she was *shaking*, her hands like claws, her fingers spasming
out into hooks.

She was being electrocuted.

He knew what it was.

He'd seen something like it before, though it'd been more sophis-
ticated.

"A trick," Peter said, his speech slightly slurred. "Something I
learned within the Mountain. It's crude but effective. It . . . con-
tains her. Her telekinesis. She is, in all senses of the word, trapped.
But she will be free. She will lead us home."

He forced her to take a step forward. Her mouth twisted, her
little legs shaking. Her eyes started to roll back in her head, and she
gave such a cry of *pain* and *fury* that Nate reached for the gun and
raised it and fired it and killed Peter right where he stood and—

The gun sat in the middle of the table untouched.

Peter brought her in until she stood next to the table. The camera was trained on all of them.

"I want to go home," Peter said quietly. "That's all I've ever wanted. I want to go home. Take us, Artemis. Take us away from here."

"I can't," Artemis said through gritted teeth. "I can't."

Peter sighed. "This can be easy. I promise you. Please don't make me do what you know I'm capable of."

"There's no ship," she spat at him.

"You *lie*," he snarled at her. "I've *seen* it. I've *seen* what's in your head because you put it in *mine*. Markham-Tripp is a *harbinger*. It is a *sign*. I know it's time. I know they're coming for you. Why else would you be here? Why else would you seek me out if it wasn't to take us home?"

The cords in Art's neck stood out as she tilted her head back, the wires attached to her pulling against the electrodes. "I came here," she said, hands jerking. "Because it was the right thing to do. Because I took so much from you. I came here. To say I'm sorry. To tell you that I care about you. That your world is harsh and unforgiving, but there is so much beauty in it if you only know where to look. I felt it. Your pain. Your uncertainty. Even long after you were gone. I didn't come here to take you home. I came here to show you that you already *were* home."

"No," Peter said, head snapping side to side furiously. "No. No. *No*. Not true. *Not true*. I know what this is. I know what all of this is. This is a test. This is another test to prove my faith. To show you what I am willing to do. I accept. I will prove to you how far I am willing to go." He looked at the camera. "I will show you all."

Then, "Alex. Look at me, please."

Alex did, eyes cloudy.

"There is a gun in front of you. Nod if you understand."

Alex nodded.

"There is one bullet inside. We are going to play a game. Alex, I want you to pick up the gun. I want you to point it at Nate's head. Do it now."

"Alex!" Art cried. "Don't. Please don't do this. *Please*."

Nate felt little jolts in his head, like something was trying to burst through the fog. He thought he heard Art screaming somewhere deep in the recesses of his mind, but it was so inconsequential to him.

Alex put his hand on the tabletop.

He slid it until his fingers bumped into the gun.

He picked it up.

He pointed it at Nate. Right at his head.

"Take us to your ship," Peter said to Art.

"There's no ship! There's no ship! There's no ship!"

Peter sighed. "Alex, pull the trigger."

Alex did.

There was a dry click.

Nate barely flinched.

"One down," Peter said. "Five to go. Alex. Give the gun to Nate. Nate, take the gun from Alex."

Alex's hand was trembling as he held the gun toward Nate. His mouth was in a tight line. His eyes were narrowed.

Nate took the gun from him.

"Nate, point the gun at Alex."

"No," Nate managed to say, but he couldn't stop his arm from rising. Couldn't stop his finger from wrapping around the trigger.

"Devil's Breath," Peter said. "It's really rather fascinating. Takes away your choices. Your free will. While it's in your system, you will do as you're told. Nate, shoot Alex."

Alex stared at him.

Nate's finger tightened on the trigger.

Art said his name, but it was lost under the electrical *snap* of electricity coursing through her.

Nate pulled the trigger.

The hammer fell.

click

"How fascinating," Peter said. "Nate, put the gun on the table."

Nate did.

"Do you see now?" Peter asked Art, a hand in her hair. "What I'm willing to do for you? What I am capable of? Please, take us home."

"There's nothing there," Art said, voice breaking. "Peter—Oren— I wouldn't lie to you. I would do it if I could. But there is *nothing there.*"

He backhanded her across the face.

Her head snapped back.

"You *lie*," he whispered hoarsely. "I've seen it. I saw it. The lights in the sky. The night you came for me. The night you *chose me*. I saw it. You said they would come back for you. You said it would come again. And I know it's almost here. I can *feel* it."

"There's no ship!" she shouted at him. "That's not how this works. That's not how *any* of this works. Those lights? They weren't a fucking *ship*."

"Alex," Peter said coldly. "Pick up the gun and shoot Nate."

Alex did as he asked. The gun was pointed at Nate's head almost quicker than he could blink. He pulled the trigger.

click

"Three left," Peter said. "One of them will *die* unless you do it and do it *now*. Is this what you want? Do you want to see one of them with a bullet in their head? How could you do this? How could you let this *happen*?"

"Alex," Art pleaded. "Fight. Please fight this and—"

Her head snapped back again as Peter pressed a button on the side of the halo. Her eyes rolled back into her head. A thin string of spit dripped down her chin.

"Gun on the table, Alex."

The gun went on the table.

"Nate, pick up the gun."

Nate picked up the gun.

Through the fog, there was an image of flowers blooming in a field. Of rocks skipping on a lake. Of sleeping in the back of a truck under a sea of stars.

Of Alex. His big hands. Standing behind Art, braiding her hair.

The fog was cracking.

"Shoot Alex," Peter said.

Nate's finger tightened on the trigger.

And he thought, *What if I don't want to?*

What am I doing?

Why am I—

Nate was seated at the table in the cabin. Art was next to him, plate piled high with bacon. Alex set down a cup of coffee in front of Nate, made just how he liked it. He felt Alex lean down and press a kiss to the side of his head.

"It's okay," Alex whispered in his ear. "I promise. It's okay. I forgive you."

He pulled the trigger.

click

Alex sat down across from him at the kitchen table.

Art said, "What should we do today?" through a mouthful of bacon.

Alex shrugged as he took a sip of coffee. "Whatever we want."

"Really?" Art asked, eyes wide. "What*ever* we want?"

"Sure. That all right with you, Nate?"

Nate nodded. He was crying, but it didn't matter. "That's all right with me."

Alex reached across the table and grabbed his hand. "In case—you have to know. I—I'm not very good. At this. With you. But you have to know. Nate, I—"

Peter said, "Alex, take the gun from Nate."

Alex did.

"Point it at Nate's head."

Alex did.

"Are we going on an adventure?" Art asked them at the kitchen table, eyeing their clasped hands gleefully.

"Yeah," Alex said, a soft smile on his face. "Yeah, I think we are."

"And we're going to go together, right?"

"Together," Nate said.

"Alex," Peter said. "Pull the—"

"*Wait.*"

Nate blinked slowly in the basement of the farmhouse.

"What is it?" Peter asked, looking down at Art.

"I'll do it," she said. "I'll take you. Just . . . please. Don't hurt them. Please don't hurt them."

The fog was burning away.

He saw how red his skin got when Alex's stubble rubbed against it.

He saw them sitting in a diner in the middle of nowhere, Art smiling widely at the waitress.

There were bison roaming fields, larger than any of them expected.

And they were *together*. All of them were together. It was Nate and Art and Alex, and they were singing along with the radio, they were on the dock at the lake, they were running for their fucking *lives*, but they were together, always together, the three of them.

"It's why I chose you," Art told them through all the shifting memories. "It's why I chose the both of you. You made me a home out of nothing. Out of a place where one should not exist. You carried each other until your knees gave out and you stumbled. I didn't get that at first. I don't think anyone can. Not until they know what it means to be human. We're not alike. Not really. We're separated by time and space. And yet, somehow, we're all made of dust and stars. I will never forget that. You will never be alone because I will always be with you."

"I will take you to the ship," Art told Peter in the basement. "I will take all of you to the ship in the tail of the comet."

"You will?" Peter asked, eyes bright. "I knew you would see it my way. I knew you would—"

"I know," she said, reaching over and taking his hand. "I know you did. And I'm sorry I let it get this far. Please, Peter. Take this thing off me, and I will lead you all home."

He nodded. He reached out and pulled the electrodes off her arms. They dangled down around her shoulders, hanging from the halo. He turned the screw that fastened the halo to her head. The metal creaked but loosened. He pulled it off and let it fall to the floor.

"All I ever wanted," he told her as he fell to his knees in front of her, "was to leave this place."

"And you will," she said, cupping his face with one hand. "I'm sorry that it took me so long. I didn't understand what I was capable of. I do now."

He leaned into her palm. "It's okay."

The fog parted with the rays of bright, bright sunlight.

Nate saw Alex's eyes clear across from him.

The barrel of the gun wavered.

And from above them came a sound that Nate couldn't quite place.

A hum, like an electric current.

The farmhouse around them began to shake.

"When we were connected," Art said quietly, "I could hear you. And you could hear me. Do you remember?"

Peter nodded.

"And I knew your thoughts. When I was taken from you, I couldn't hear them anymore. It was very quiet for a long time. But I learned you, Oren. Even now, I know what you're thinking."

He breathed a sigh of relief. "Tell me. Tell me what I'm thinking."

"Nothing," Alex growled as he pressed the barrel of the gun against the side of Peter's head.

He pulled the trigger.

The gun fired.

Peter jerked to the side, a small arc of blood trailing behind him. He fell to the floor, staring sightlessly toward the ceiling.

"I'm sorry that it had to come to this," Art told him quietly. "But I would never let you hurt them."

"Nate," Alex said sharply as he stood. He wobbled a little before catching himself. "Nate."

Nate looked up at him.

"Are you with us?"

"Yeah. Yes. It's . . . I'm okay."

"Good. We have to go. Now."

The walls were trembling.

"What's going on?" Nate asked, throat dry. "Is this—is this you?"

Art shook her head slowly. "No. That's not me."

And from above them came the sound of a small explosion.

"Fuck," Alex muttered. He crouched down next to Peter, grabbing his hand and putting the gun against it, curling his fingers around the grip. Alex stood and moved quickly toward the stairs that led to the metal door.

The frames on the bunk beds rattled. Dolores's hand slid from her chest and hung off the side.

"They found us," Art whispered.

"Who?" Nate asked.

She said, "The water guy. The Enforcer. The—"

Her head rocked back.

Her mouth opened and worked.

Her eyes went opaque.

She stood rigid, as if once again electrified.

"Art?" Nate whispered.

He reached out for her. He took her hand in his. He felt the little bones beneath her skin and—

CHAPTER EIGHTEEN

It was white.

Everything was white.

His eyes were (*weren't*) open.

He was (*wasn't*) human.

He didn't understand.

But there were *voices* in his head, whispering numbers and letters, lines and colors. They were *pulsing,* and there were so many of them, thousands, hundreds of thousands. It was too much. He felt like he was being torn apart from the inside out. He could see everything. He could feel *everything.* Nate opened his mouth to scream, but it came out as a shape, a spinning triangle that looked as if roots were growing out of it.

He couldn't qualify what he was seeing. Hearing. Feeling. Nothing made sense.

He heard another voice, somewhere inside. It said, "Nate" and "Nate" and "You have to let go, you have to let *go*" and he—

He snapped his eyes open.

He was pressed against Alex's chest, big arms wrapped around him, holding him close. Art stood next to them. The *thumpthumpthump* of the helicopter above was fainter, but it still shook the walls. Footsteps sounded on the floors above them, feet pounding against the wood. There had to be dozens of people in the house.

"What the hell was that?" he whispered.

"Home," Art said, expression pinched. "They're calling me home. It's almost time." She shook her head. "You could have been killed."

"I didn't mean—"

"I know. But it was . . . a lot. Even for me." She looked toward the ceiling again. "They're coming."

"What do we do?" Nate asked, closing his eyes and breathing Alex in. He was exhausted.

"The door is locked from the inside," Alex said. "It's made of reinforced steel. It'll take the Mountain time to get in."

"But it won't hold them forever," Art said. She sighed. "There's no other way out, is there? No other door?"

"It doesn't matter," Alex said, holding Nate even tighter. "As long as your people get you out of here, the rest doesn't matter."

Nate opened his eyes.

Art was staring up at Alex as if betrayed. "What?"

Alex squeezed Nate before letting him go. Nate stepped back, hands shaking.

Alex crouched down in front of Art. She glared at him fiercely. "Why did we do this?" he asked her.

There was a banging on the metal door.

"No," she growled at him. "No. Stop. You stop it right now. You hear me? You don't get—"

"Art."

She shook her head and took a step back, just out of reach.

"You need to listen to me," he said. "The whole reason we did this, the reason we came this far, was to find you a way home. That's the only thing that mattered."

She rubbed a hand over her eyes. "No. Stop. Alex, please stop."

"And I told you that if something happened to me, you would need to keep going. Do you remember? You promised me."

"Well, I didn't mean it," she snapped. "I'm not leaving you behind. I won't do that. I *won't.*"

"You need to go home," he said roughly. "Nate and me. We can handle ourselves. Okay? Just . . . go."

"Shut up, Alex. Shut *up.* Shut *up.*"

"Art—"

"No! And you just *lied* to me."

"I'm not lying about—"

"You *did.* You *lied.* You said the reason we did this was to get me home. That that was it. That that was the only thing that mattered. That's not true."

"I don't—"

"You saved me because you *love* me," she shouted at him, voice breaking. "You love me like I love you. Like I love Nate. Like *you* love Nate. You love me because we belong together. You are my *friend*. And friends don't leave each other behind. Not now. Not like this." Uncertainty flickered across her face. "You do love me. Right?"

"You stupid girl," Alex said, hanging his head. "You stupid, stupid girl. Of course I love you. Of course I do. The both of you. How could I not?"

Nate put a hand on his shoulder, fingers digging in. "She's right. About everything. We're in this together."

"Until the end," Art said firmly. Her eyes suddenly sparkled. "One final ride, ain't that right, hoss?"

For a moment, Nate thought Alex would fight against it. That he'd shout at her to leave. To get the fuck out of his sight and never come back to this goddamn planet.

Instead, he stood slowly. He looked at Nate, then back at Art. He scrubbed a hand over his face. He squared his shoulders.

"One final ride," he said.

She grinned wildly. "Then saddle up, partners. It's time to take back our valley."

✦

It went like this:

Nathaniel Cartwright was twenty-seven years old.

His parents were dead.

The only family he had left had forsaken him.

He'd gone to a cabin in the middle of the woods to mourn the loss of everything he'd known.

Instead, he'd had a gun pressed to the back of his head.

Instead, he'd found a man and a little girl who was the strangest person he'd ever met.

He'd been scared of them.

Of who they were.

And later, of *what* they were.

But fear can be a funny thing. You can fear what you don't understand, but in the end, you can still be brave. You can still stand up for what's right.

Nate hadn't understood that before. Not really.

He did now.

"Stay behind me," Artemis Darth Vader said, eyes alight. "No matter what, stay behind me. I promise you I'll show you the way."

They followed her up the stairs, Alex gripping Nate's hand so hard it felt like his bones were being ground to dust.

Sparks were coming around the door, and a line of molten red appeared across the top.

They were burning their way in.

Art stopped in front of the door, cocking her head at it.

A moment later, she reached out and knocked on the door.

The sparks stopped.

There was a beat of silence. Then from the other side of the door came a voice. "Hello?"

"Hello," Art said through the door. "Is this the water guy?"

"What? What water guy?"

"Randy."

A pause. Then, "No."

"Is he here?"

"Who is this?"

"Is. He. *Here.*"

"Not in the house" came the reply.

"Huh," Art said. "Thank you. If I asked you to leave, would you?"

"Kid, we've got orders. Open the door or we're going to break it down."

"You didn't answer my question."

"No. We're not leaving. Look, do you live here? We're looking for—"

She laughed. It sent chills down Nate's spine. "Oh, I know who you're looking for."

Muffled voices from the other side. "You do?"

"Yes. The Seventh Sea, right?"

"Yeah, we're—"

"You found her."

Silence. It stretched on for what felt like *hours.*

Then, "Holy shit, run, run, *run*—"

The air around the little girl in front of them seemed to *bend,* the walls and door warping. Nate felt a harsh pressure in his ears before the metal door was ripped off the wall with a heavy groan, jagged cracks splitting around them. It floated out in front of them, moving into the hallway of the farmhouse, scraping against the plaster of the walls.

He heard men shouting, the sound of feet pounding the floors trying to get away.

Art didn't hesitate. She took the last step out of the basement, and there was a *push* that Nate felt down to his bones. The metal door hurtled down the hallway, gouging the walls around it, knocking down everyone who hadn't made it toward the front of the house.

"It's time to go," she said over her shoulder, her hair billowing around her head.

She walked down the hall.

They followed.

A man in full tactical gear burst from a door on the right. Peter's office. He swung his rifle in their direction, eyes wide behind the mask covering his nose and mouth. Art barely twitched, and the man was knocked into the ceiling with a loud crash, plaster raining down around him as he fell to the ground, landing on his stomach. He didn't get back up.

Alex reached down and picked up his rifle, snapping it free from the harness.

Nate grabbed a dropped metal baton.

"You know how to use that?" Alex asked.

"It's a stick," Nate said. "You hit people with it."

Alex snorted but didn't say anything more. They followed Art down the hallway.

Soldiers lay sprawled on the ground where they'd been knocked down by the basement door, which had landed near the stairs. The front doorway to the farmhouse had been blown open, the wood around the frame charred. Two men ran down the stairs as they passed, but before Alex could swing the rifle in their direction, Nate stuck the baton between the posts, tripping the man in front. Both men tumbled the rest of the way down. They landed on the floor and immediately tried to get up. Art barely glanced in their direction before they were sent flying into the kitchen, slamming into the stove and oven. They didn't get back up.

"Do you want to trade?" Nate asked Alex, feeling oddly giddy. He was most likely about to die, but he couldn't remember feeling so alive.

"Bastard," Alex said, but his answering grin was crazed and beautiful. He reached down and picked up a walkie-talkie from one of the fallen soldiers.

They headed for the blown-out doorway.

The front yard was filled with dozens of soldiers, black rifles pointed at them as soon as they stepped out onto the porch. There were armored vehicles and a helicopter above them. It was so close Nate could see the pilot inside, mouth moving soundlessly.

The grass was flattened by the force of the spinning blades.

Art cocked her head at them.

He should be frightened. He knew he should be scared for his life. Chances were he was about to die there on the porch of a farmhouse belonging to a dead cult leader. He hadn't done half the things with his life he'd wanted to do. He'd never hiked Machu Picchu. He hadn't swum in the crystal-clear waters of the Maldives. He'd never been on a roller coaster. He'd always wanted to learn how to swing dance. He'd never tried calamari, though it was probably disgusting.

And strangely, somehow he was okay with it.

He was okay with all of it.

He'd been lonely. He'd been sad.

But he'd found a purpose.

He'd found a reason. Two, in fact.

If he died right here, right now, there was a very real possibility that he'd done something good. That his life had mattered. That he'd loved and been loved in return.

And sure, there was *fear* with all those guns pointed at him, his human brain wondering if it would hurt in the end. But it was *negligible*. It was *unimportant*.

He'd read about last stands before. Of a group of people, beaten and weary, rising against a much greater force. Outmanned. Outgunned.

He knew what it meant.

His hand tightened on the baton. It wouldn't do much.

A man pushed his way through the soldiers. He carried a bull-horn.

He didn't look like he had when he'd come to the house posing as an employee of public works. That man, the water guy, had been smiling a little too widely, full of *aw shucks* and *golly gee*. Even when they'd run into each other in the store (quite a coincidence, that, Nate thought dryly), he'd been oddly intimidating, but it still hadn't meant much.

It was different now.

The water guy, Randy, wore black trousers with a UTG tactical leg holster around his thigh. A black pistol with a silver handle was attached to it. He had a white shirt under a black leather jacket. On his face sat mirror shades, reflecting the bright early-morning sunlight.

Nate looked up toward the sky.

There, among the clouds and fading stars, was Markham-Tripp.

It burned against the deep, deep blue.

It was a good day to die.

Nate looked down at the yard again when Randy brought the bull-horn to his lips and said, "It's over. You have to see that." His voice echoed across the yard, audible even against the *thumpthumpthump* of the Black Hawk.

Art looked back at Alex. She held her hand out. For a moment, Nate thought she was asking for the rifle, but Alex handed her the walkie-talkie instead.

She frowned at it as she turned forward again, fiddling with the knobs at the top. Once she'd gotten it where she wanted, she held it out in front of her, wiggling it at the water guy. With her free hand, she held up two fingers.

The soldiers tracked her every movement.

For a moment, Randy didn't move.

Then he looked over his shoulder and barked out something Nate couldn't quite make out.

One of the soldiers came forward, handing him another walkie-talkie.

Randy twisted the dial across the top before nodding up at Art and holding it against his ear.

"Can you hear me?" Art said into the walkie-talkie.

"Yes," he said through the bullhorn.

"Good. There are people inside. They lived here. They're dead."

"Did you kill them?"

"No."

"Oren Schraeder?"

"Dead."

Randy turned his head away from the bullhorn and said something to the soldier next to him. The soldier didn't react. He came back to the bullhorn. "That's unfortunate. He was . . . There's never been anyone quite like him."

"He said you could never find him here."

Randy smiled almost ruefully. "Yeah. I bet he did. He was right, as much as it pains me to admit. We didn't . . . We had no idea where he'd gone after he left the Mountain. He was *supposed* to remain under surveillance, but he managed to give us the slip. Never really believed he took his own life, but I couldn't find a way to prove it. He was good. Better than he had any right to be. Makes me wonder if you had anything to do with that."

"I didn't."

"You expect me to believe that? I've seen what you're capable of. What you can do to a mind. We're lucky someone spotted your vehicle driving through the last town. Imagine our surprise when we found out who you'd come here to see."

"You're going to let us go."

Randy laughed soundlessly. "You know I can't do that. Look, this has been . . . fun. You've lasted a hell of a lot longer than anyone expected. We could have taken you back at the cabin at any time, but we *let* you stay. We *let* you live with Alex there. We understood that maybe a change was needed. To expand the parameters of the experiment. Change the variables, if you will. To see what we could see." He glanced at Nate. "And then the variables changed even further with the introduction of Mr. Cartwright here. That . . . wasn't expected. But we were curious to see what you would do. To see what you both would do. The end result was unexpected."

"He's mine."

"Do you understand, Mr. Cartwright, what it is?" Randy asked. "What it's capable of. It's infected your mind. It has taken you over. It is *controlling* you. It's how they do it. It's how they work. They infect you until you can do nothing but obey. We are trying to stop that. We are trying to protect the world from things like them. Because they will come for us again. And we need to be ready. Look what happened to Oren. We found a way to remove it from him, but it was *still* able to find him even after all this time. We can't let it do that to anyone else. It's not a girl. It's a *thing*. It belongs in a cage, locked away so we can find a way to stop it before it's too late."

"Wow," Nate said. "He's pretty out there, huh?"

"Enforcers usually are," Alex muttered.

Nate plucked the walkie-talkie from Art's hand. He found the button on the side. There was a squeal of static as he brought it close to his face. "I think I'm good right here, thanks."

"What about your brother?" Randy asked. "Nate, what about Rick? Don't you think he'd want you to come home? Don't you think he wants to see you again? You call him Ricky, right? Nate, I know he wants to see you. Hell, he told me as much. I've talked to him, Nate. Personally. He's a nice guy. He doesn't understand why you won't come home."

And that . . . that was *smooth*. Nate hadn't expected that. He should have. "Rick?"

Randy nodded. "Yes, Nate. Rick. He's waiting for you, okay? All you have to do is come to me. Fight it, Nate. Fight whatever's going on in your head. Whatever *it's* making you do. I know you can do it. It's . . . probably too late for Alex. But you? Nate, think of Rick. Think of your brother."

Art looked up at him, a sad smile on her face. "I understand," she said. "Maybe I wouldn't have before, when I first came here. But I do now. Family is important. It's everything, Nate."

She was right, of course. Family *was* everything. Which is why he said, "I have my family right here."

Alex's eyes were wide.

Nate handed the walkie-talkie back to Art. She kissed the tips of his fingers after taking it from him. In his head, he felt her. Felt her reach. There were images of flowers blooming in fields. She was happy.

"Nate sends his regards," she said into the walkie-talkie. "You can still leave. All of you can."

"You know I can't do that," Randy said, voice harder than it'd been before. "How do you see this ending? Surely you can't stop all of us. I know what you can do. But you can't be everywhere at once. I will kill Alex Weir right here, right now. I will take him from you unless you give yourself up. I will take both of them."

Even before he finished speaking, Nate flinched when a bright light flashed in his eyes. It was only a split second before it faded. He blinked against the afterimage. He looked down. Across his chest were red dots, wavering slightly.

He swallowed thickly as he looked over at Alex. Alex had the same dots on him.

He followed to where Alex was looking and saw a group of men lined up on the second floor of the barn, standing at the open windows, rifles pointed in their direction, laser sights grouped over their hearts.

"Why?" Art asked.

"Because I can," Randy said simply. "Because I will do anything I have to in order to protect this country. This planet. There is nothing I wouldn't do to keep my people safe."

"We mean no harm. We never have."

"I don't believe you. Complacency means death."

"Shoot first, ask questions later."

"Yes."

"You learn you're not alone," Art said. She almost sounded like she was pleading with him. The images in Nate's head were getting more vivid. "That there is more to this universe than just yourselves, and your first reaction isn't to welcome it with open arms but to trap it. To study it. To *hurt* it. And when it doesn't do what you tell it to, you threaten it with destruction. You threaten to take from it what it loves."

"You don't know *how* to love," Randy said coldly. He reached up and took his sunglasses off, fumbling with them before dropping them to the ground. "That is inherently human. Which you're not. You aren't capable of such a thing."

"Even after all this time, after everything you've done to me, after everything you've seen, you still know so little about me. About what I can do. You're right. I'm not human. I'm not like you. But I know what it means to be loved. To have friends. To have people I would do anything for. And I know how it makes me feel when those people are threatened." She looked up at the soldiers in the barn, then the helicopter, then back at Randy. "You really should let us go."

"I can't do that."

Art nodded. "So be it."

Nate could see the moment the words sank in for Randy. His eyes narrowed. His mouth was a thin line. He lowered the bullhorn. The men around him tensed.

And when Randy shouted, *"Don't hit the girl!"* Nate knew that he'd mattered.

In the end, he'd mattered.

He closed his eyes against the sound of gunfire cracking over the farmyard. In his head, flashes of images: his mother in the kitchen, sashaying back and forth as she baked a cake for his twelfth birthday. His father putting a hand on his shoulder the day he graduated and squeezing it gently. He and Ricky under a fort made of pillows and blankets, using flashlights to read comic books late into the night.

But there were other things too. Flashes that didn't belong to him.

He saw Alex walking hand in hand with a little boy with a quiet laugh.

Alex standing in front of a man in a suit, nervous as he stared at a woman in front of him, a devilish smile on her face.

Alex in front of a girl in a cage, seeing her for the very first time.

Alex, his side feeling like it was on fire, watching through the window as a young man pulled up in an old truck in front of the cabin.

Then they were *merging*, and there it was, right? That first kiss,

awkward and sweet and oh so fucking *devastating*. He felt Alex's
nervousness, his fierce *want*. He'd been irritated at first, even had
himself halfway convinced that Nate had come from the Mountain, had come to try and take Art away from him.

But he'd learned, slowly but surely, that there was so much more
to Nate. So much more to them both.

And then there was Art, and Nate was seeing things he couldn't
understand. There were *structures* under triple suns that burned *pink*,
structures that were so close to being familiar but off just enough
that he couldn't understand them, couldn't quite make them out.
And there were these *beings*, these beings made of iridescent white
light, and they were *swirling* around, speaking in a way that Nate
couldn't comprehend. It wasn't even *words*, but there was intent
there, and one of these lights, one of these bright gaseous things
was almost . . . familiar. It moved along a path made of some kind
of shiny metal, and it was *young*, and it was *sad*, though it didn't
understand what sadness was precisely. But there was such a per-
vasive sense of loneliness coming from it that Nate felt like he was
drowning in it.

It wasn't like the others.

It was like Nate. It was like Alex.

And it was *here*. It was in the woods, and there was a man standing in front of it, and it was thinking *can you help me? can you please
help me?* although it wasn't *quite* in those words. And Nate saw the
moment a younger Oren Schraeder understood what was happening to him, understood what it was he was seeing in front of him.

The gunfire around them ceased.

Nate felt no pain.

He opened his eyes.

Surrounding them were hundreds of bullets, floating in midair.

Art's eyes were wide and angry.

There was a moment, a brief, terrible moment when Nate *felt* that
anger, felt what she wanted to do. She wanted nothing more than to
send those bullets right back where they'd come from, send them into
the heads and hearts of the men who thought they could take from
her. Before this place, before she'd come here, she'd never understood

the concept of violence. Of revenge. Randy had been pretty close when he'd said she wasn't human, that she couldn't experience something such as *love*. But that had been before. Before Cisco Grove. Before the Mountain.

She knew love. She knew rage. She knew violence.

And she wanted revenge.

Alex said, "No. Art. No."

And so she let it go.

The bullets dropped, clattering against the wooden porch, bouncing down the stairs and into the grass in front of the farmhouse.

The only sound came from the *thumpthumpthump* of the Black Hawk above.

And then Artemis Darth Vader was moving.

She took her first step down the porch stairs.

The soldiers began to shout.

Some fired.

The bullets ricocheted away as if hitting a large barrier around her.

She looked up at the helicopter.

It wobbled.

She jerked her head toward the barn.

It hurtled toward the snipers.

They shouted as they scrambled backward.

The helicopter crashed into the barn, the blades spinning through wood, causing it to splinter and break apart. The front of the barn fell *inward* under the weight of the helicopter. Nate half expected it to explode, but somehow, it didn't. It fell through the second floor with a screech of twisting metal and landed on the ground, a great cloud of dust curling up around it as the broken rotor blades came to a halt.

The men in the yard looked dazed.

Randy didn't.

He reached down to the gun holstered on his thigh.

Nate was running even before he knew what he was doing.

He hit the grass just as Randy slid the gun from the holster.

He was almost to Art when Randy pointed the gun at her head.
He almost looked . . . regretful.

Nate reached Art and wrapped his body around her, shielding
her from Randy.

"Thank you," he whispered to her. "For everything."

A gun fired.

And it—

Nothing happened.

He opened his eyes.

Alex stood on the porch, rifle raised.

Nate turned in time to see Randy falling to his knees, a hole in
the center of his forehead. His eyes were sightless. A drop of blood
trickled down over his nose. He fell face-first into the grass.

There was silence in the farmyard.

Then the soldiers raised their guns again.

And Artemis Darth Vader said, "No."

✦

Later, when the police arrived, sirens wailing, radios squawking
with bewilderment, there would be confusion. They would find the
remains of a helicopter in a barn, bewildered soldiers slowly picking
themselves up from the ground where they'd been knocked off their
feet, vehicles overturned and lying upside down. The sun would be
high in the sky, and when the bodies were discovered inside the
half-burned farmhouse, black cloths over their faces, a man lying
on the ground with a bullet in his head, a pistol lying beside him,
the picture would slowly start to become clearer.

In the days that followed, there would be reports all over the
news, reporters breathlessly exclaiming how a cult had faced off
against the military before retreating back inside the farmhouse,
where they met their end at the hands of their leader. The pundits
would say it was David Koresh and Waco all over again. So-called
experts would weigh in, attempting to explain that people in *cults*
(the word uttered with disdain) were often gullible, easily swept
up in a grand design proselytized by a man with seemingly endless
amounts of charisma and a desire to prey upon those weaker than

him. He was most likely a sociopath, they would say. He would think himself a prophet.

And then there would be the tapes. The tapes where Peter Williams would sermonize his vision of the world, of a change that would come upon the Earth. He would speak of his time in a base called the Mountain (to which there was a resounding *of course it's not real* when those in the know were asked about such a place), and while there was the admission that he *had* been enlisted, it was clearly documented that Peter Williams had been honorably discharged years before due to mental health issues. That he claimed to be Oren Schraeder, a soldier who'd been born in 1940 and had died in combat, cemented the world's view on Peter Williams's lack of sanity. Add in that he'd claimed to be possessed by an *alien*, of all things, and . . . well.

He was just a crazy cult leader, they said.

Just another wacko.

✦

The stories that poured out of the farm tended to focus on those in the cult, and on the outrage at a military intervention that possibly forced the hands of those who died. Family members came forward, telling tales of woe about loved ones who had one day dropped everything and disappeared. A woman named Rachel cried in many interviews, her children at her side, speaking of her mother, Dolores, how they'd been very close, how her kids, who loved their grandmother very much, couldn't understand why she'd had to go away. "How am I supposed to explain this to them?" Rachel asked tearfully. "I mean, how could they ever understand?"

Others agreed with her, saying their loved ones weren't crazy, they weren't like this, this didn't *sound* like them, and why would they ever do such a thing?

It had to be his fault.

It had to be because of Peter Williams.

Some had their loved ones buried.

Others, like Dolores, were cremated.

Rachel said she'd spread her ashes but declined to answer where.

When asked what would become of Peter Williams, reporters were told his family had come and claimed the body, but had requested privacy, so no further details were provided.

✦

A statement was released regarding the downed helicopter. It'd been an ill-timed malfunction. It was similar to the incident that had occurred back in March when a Black Hawk had gone down outside the Marine Corps Mountain Warfare Training Center. The entire fleet would be checked to prevent such a thing from happening again.

✦

Aside from the deceased in the basement of the farmhouse, there was only one other casualty on the raid on the Williams Farm, as it would come to be known.

A soldier named Randy Forks.

He'd been shot by Peter Williams before Peter had fallen back into the house and taken his own life.

He was given a full military funeral.

A folded flag was handed to his brother.

Later when the brother was interviewed, he'd said he hadn't heard from Randy in almost a decade before he died. "Sad," he said. "Real sad. Randy and me, we never got along. But he's my family, you know? Sad that it had to end this way, killed by a crazy bastard who believed in aliens. What the hell is wrong with people?"

✦

A video camera was discovered in the basement where the bodies of the members of the Light of Eve lay.

But Peter Williams must have forgotten to put a tape inside, because the camera was empty.

✦

There was no spacecraft in Markham-Tripp, obviously. The comet began to fade as it hurtled away from Earth. Eventually, it disappeared from the sky. It wouldn't return again until the impossible year of 4380.

There was a queer sense of sadness. How could so many people be fooled into believing such a thing occurred and then take their lives because of it?

"It's a real tragedy," a man named Steven Cooper opined on his daily radio show broadcast coast to coast. "A real damn tragedy. It wasn't time. They came. I know they did. But it must not have been our time. They must not have found us ready yet. But they will, friends. Mark my words. One day they'll come back, and you'll see I'm right. Those poor souls of the Light of Eve were misguided. They went about this the wrong way. I don't know how or why they got it into their heads that they needed to off themselves to see what was plain as day for the rest of us. That Peter Williams must have messed with their heads. Come on, friends. Have you *seen* his rantings? He claimed to have been possessed by an extraterrestrial. *Possessed.* We all know that's not how this works. The Greys don't *possess* us. They aren't capable of such things. This is why UFOlogy is looked at with such disdain! When we have crackpots like *Peter Williams,* it takes away the validity of our *science.* Peter Williams was nothing but a hoax. A false prophet. I don't doubt our government is shady. I know that. *You* know that. What was the reason they were involved in the siege at the Williams Farm to begin with? Were they trying to avoid another Waco? Why wasn't this left up to state and local law enforcement? I have my theories. You know I do. You know I *always* do. Peter Williams suffered PTSD. One too many concussion blasts. It happens. He served, god love him. He did his duty. But he became *lost,* after. And he got it into his punch-drunk head that he was something more than he was. He deserves our pity, friends. They all do. I think that's why they came after him. Why the cops weren't involved. He was one of their own, and they hoped to bring him back into the fold. But make no mistake, friends: by taking their lives as they did, it may well have set those of us that believe back fifty years. They will come, friends. I guarantee it. Maybe not today. Maybe not tomorrow. But they will come. Caller, you're on the air. What do you think about all this madness—"

✦

Eventually, they left Rick Cartwright and his family alone.

The men in uniforms stopped coming to the door, though non-descript black cars followed him for months.

They wouldn't tell him much, only that his brother had been a traitor, that it'd cost him his job at the *Post*, and that he was involved in something Rick would never get the details of.

He was curious, sure, but he wasn't like Nate. He didn't feel the burning need to ask question after question.

He let it go.

There were days he wouldn't even think of his brother at all. He was a very busy man, and he had a family to support.

But every now and then, he'd stop and think about skipping rocks along the surface of a lake, his little brother's voice ringing in his ears. He'd think of how Nate had sounded on the phone that late night, and how he'd called him *Ricky*.

✦

A woman named Ruth who lived in Washington, D.C., watched the news coming out of Pennsylvania, a cigarette dangling from her lips. She was on an extended sabbatical, a decision she'd made after the men from the "NSA" had voiced their vaguely veiled threats toward her. She didn't know what had happened, didn't know where Nate was, but somehow she *knew* the Williams Farm had to do with him. With them. With the man and the girl.

"You keep running, kiddo," she muttered at the TV, smoke curling up around her head. "You keep right on running. Don't you ever stop."

She would die seven years later from a heart attack, having never heard from Nathaniel Cartwright again.

✦

There was no mention of two men and a little girl who'd found themselves on the farm. There'd been a BOLO issued on them, their photos circulated before the Williams Farm was swarmed by the military. A little girl taken against her will. Two men she was thought to be with. But in the spring of 1995, there was no such thing as Amber Alerts; in fact, the little girl for whom the Amber Alerts would be named wouldn't disappear until January of 1996.

The BOLO was eventually recalled. No connection between it and the Williams Farm was ever made.

It was as if they never were at all.

CHAPTER NINETEEN

But they *did* exist.

They *had* been at the farm.

"Wait here," Alex growled at them before making his way into the barn, climbing over a part of the crashed helicopter.

The porch of the farmhouse was on fire.

Nate wondered how long it would take to burn.

The farmyard around them was destroyed. Armored vehicles overturned. Men lay unconscious on the ground. Or at least, he thought most of them were. They'd all been knocked off their feet by Artemis Darth Vader, an invisible explosion that had caused the earth around the farmhouse to crack and shift. It'd been almost tornadic in nature, the aftermath, like a twister had touched down right there in front of the house and somehow managed to save them.

Art stared out at what her power had done.

Her hands were shaking.

Her skin was pale.

She said, "You almost died. If it hadn't been for Alex, you would have died. Why?"

Nate put a hand in her hair. "For you. Always for you."

She looked up at him. Her bottom lip was trembling, and her eyes were wet. A tear trickled down her cheek. "You love me."

"Yes."

"You love him."

"*Yes.*"

"I know now," she said. "What it means to be human."

He wiped away her tears. "What?"

"It means having your heart broken. There is nothing more human than a broken heart. How am I supposed to leave you both?"

He picked her up.

She cried against his shoulder.

Eventually Alex came out of the barn. He had their duffel bags over his shoulders. He caught sight of them and stopped, a look on his face that Nate couldn't place.

Nate shrugged helplessly.

"We have to go," he said gruffly. "While we still can."

✦

Miraculously, the truck they'd arrived in had somehow survived the onslaught in the farmyard. Alex threw the duffel bags in the bed of the truck as Nate climbed inside, Art still clinging to him.

Alex entered the truck, slamming the door behind him. He breathed a sigh of relief when the truck started immediately.

He put his arm over the bench seat, hand stretching over to Nate and Art as he reversed slowly out of the yard.

Nate felt Alex's fingers against his ear.

✦

They passed police cars and fire trucks with screaming sirens.

No one paid them any mind.

Nate looked in the side mirror. Behind them, he could see a plume of smoke rising from a copse of trees in the distance.

They drove on.

✦

That night, they stopped at a motel in the middle of nowhere after crossing from Pennsylvania into West Virginia.

Art was sleeping against Nate's chest.

Alex hadn't said a word as he'd gone inside.

He came back five minutes later, that same tight look on his face.

He was angry, Nate had slowly figured out. But Nate couldn't be sure at what.

He parked at the end of the motel, keeping the truck in the shadows as much as possible.

He climbed out again and shut the door behind him. Nate watched as he reached back in for their bags.

He walked toward the motel door at the end of the row, un-locked the door, and went inside.

"He's having feelings," Art said quietly, startling Nate.

"Oh?"

"Yeah. He's not very good at those most times."

"I think he's mad."

"Probably."

Nate sighed. "Are you hungry?"

She shook her head. "Just tired. Tomorrow we can get bacon. Tonight I just want to sleep."

"All the bacon," Nate agreed.

He carried her inside before setting her down.

Alex was sitting on one of the beds, face in his hands, shoulders slumped.

Art went to him, standing at his side, hand on his arm, whisper-ing in his ear. Nate didn't listen. It wasn't for him.

He went into the bathroom and closed the door.

It was dingy but serviceable.

He splashed water on his face before daring to look at himself in the mirror.

He didn't recognize the person who stared back at him. His hair was shaggier, and he had stubble on his face. His eyes seemed harder somehow. Wilder. He breathed in through his nose and out through his mouth, trying to stave off the panic clawing at his chest.

✦

Art was asleep when he came back out, only the top of her head visible under the comforter, snoring loudly.

Alex was awake, watching the old TV in front of him, the vol-ume low.

There were overhead shots of the farm. The chyron across the bottom of the screen screamed that MILITARY SHOWDOWN WITH DOOMSDAY CULT ENDS IN DEATH.

Alex stood from the edge of the bed and switched the TV off. He glanced at Nate, that same pinched look on his face.

He nodded toward the door.

Nate followed him outside after looking back at Art. She was still asleep.

Alex walked around the side of the motel, out of sight from the office and the road. It was dark. The stars were twinkling. The comet seemed duller than it'd been before.

Nate could barely make out Alex in the dark. Crickets chirped and frogs croaked in the woods behind the motel.

Nate said, "What's going—"

"Don't."

Nate stopped and waited.

It didn't take long. "What the hell were you thinking?"

"About?"

"Don't be an asshole," Alex growled. "You know what I'm talking about."

Yeah, so maybe he did. "I did what I thought was right."

"You could have *died*," Alex said, taking a step toward him. His hands were in fists at his sides, shoulders stiff. "If I hadn't—if Randy had—"

"I'm here," Nate said quietly. "Now. With you. We're safe."

"You don't understand," Alex said, voice hoarse. "You—Nate. What if you'd—" He broke off, chest heaving.

"Thank you." Nate moved toward Alex slowly, hands raised as if placating a cornered animal. "For saving me. I know it was—"

"You *don't* know," Alex snapped. "You *don't* know. If I hadn't seen him, or if he'd moved one second faster, you would be *dead*. Don't you get that? You fucking *asshole*. How dare you. How dare you try and—"

Nate kissed him.

Alex didn't respond, at least not at first. Nate reached up and wrapped his arms around Alex's neck and kissed him for all he was worth.

And then Alex essentially *collapsed* against him, as if his strings had just been cut. He grunted into Nate's mouth, arms coming up and circling Nate, holding him close as he kissed him back, more teeth than anything else.

"Stupid," he muttered as he broke the kiss. "You're so stupid. You can't do that. You can't do that to me. Please. Nate. Please don't do that to me. I can't do this. Not without you. Not—"

Nate hushed him, telling him that they were all right, that they were fine, that they had made it, they had made it, and soon, so soon, it would be over and they could move on to whatever came next.

Alex shuddered against him, and in the dark, they held each other for a long time.

When they made it back to the room, Artemis was sitting up in the bed.

"Hello." She smiled quietly at them. "It's almost time."

Nate and Alex exchanged a look before Alex said, "Are you sure?"

She nodded but wouldn't meet their eyes. "I'm going home."

They slept that night in the same bed. It was a tight fit, but they made it work. Art lay on top of Alex, curled against him, snoring under his chin.

When Nate dreamed, it was of numbers and code and flowers blooming in a field.

The next morning, they ate a lot of bacon.

They didn't speak much.

It came to an end two days later in Dingess, West Virginia.

It was a nothing place. Not really even a town. A bump in the road. They drove past a post office. A worn-down sign for a place called Jamie's Family Restaurants. The sign had bullet holes in it.

It was dusk. The sky was orange. Markham-Tripp was fading. The stars were just starting to come out.

The trees swayed in the wind.

They came to an old tunnel. A green-and-white sign stood next to it.

HISTORIC DINGESS TUNNEL
CONSTRUCTED 1892

The road narrowed to a single lane through the tunnel. It was apparently very long, the light at the other end faint. There was no other traffic on the road. The air coming in through the open windows of the truck felt heavy. Staticky. It was getting harder to breathe.

"Here," Art said. "Alex, I think it's here."

Alex slowed the truck to a stop.

Nate noticed that there were no birds singing in the trees.

His head was filled with flowers.

His skin felt like it was vibrating.

He felt them. Alex and Art. Both of them.

The truck idled, rattling until the wires came apart, stopping the engine.

"Are you sure?" he asked, staring out the window. His voice was flat. His face was blank. Nate knew what he was doing. Shoring himself up. Cutting himself off. He thought Art knew it too and was trying to cover her hurt.

"Yeah," she whispered. "I'm pretty sure."

Alex nodded tightly, but he didn't move. His knuckles were white where he gripped the steering wheel.

Oh yeah. This was heartbreak up close.

Nate wondered if there would be enough pieces remaining to make a recognizable shape of what they once had been.

He opened his door.

Alex jerked his head to glare at him.

"Are we going on an adventure?" Art asked him, eyes wide.

Nate nodded. "That we are, hoss. Time to saddle up and hit that old dusty trail."

She gave him a trembling smile.

He climbed out of the truck.

His knees popped. He closed his eyes and took a deep breath.

Yeah. It was here. This was the place. He could feel it. He didn't know how. He didn't know why. But he could. It was *different* here.

Art followed him out of the truck. She reached for his hand. He squeezed it tightly. They walked toward the front of the truck.

Alex hadn't moved.

"You need each other," Art said softly. "You see that now, don't you?"

There was a buzzing in Nate's ears. "He needs you more."

She looked stricken at that. "I can't—Nate, I want—you don't understand. What I am. Who I'm supposed to be."

He looked down at her. "Space princess wasn't too far off, was it?"

She shook her head. "No. It wasn't. And I—I love him."

"I know you do. And he knows that too."

"You'll take care of him for me?"

"If he'll let me."

The expression on her face hardened. "He'll try and push you away. He'll try and say he won't need you. He'll be mean. He'll be cold. You can't believe him. Nate, he loves you, okay? You can't let him—"

"I won't." Nate cut her off before she could work herself into a panic. "We'll . . . we'll figure it out, okay? I don't know—somehow. I know it."

"As long as you're together, right?"

"Right."

"Because when you're together, you can do anything."

"Yeah, Art. Anything."

She tugged on his hand, pulling him down. The headlights of the truck were bright as he leaned forward. She took his face in her small hands, studying him. He didn't close his eyes. He didn't look away. He took his fill, just as she took hers. Everything hurt.

She said, "I wondered what you would be like. Humans. What you would be capable of. How your minds would work. How your hearts would beat. You are animals. Fierce and wild. You are harsh and brutal and beautiful. There is no one like you in all the universe. You have the power for such destruction within you. And such joy. It's a dichotomy that shouldn't exist, and yet here it is.

Within you. Within all of you." She leaned forward and kissed his forehead. Each cheek. The tip of his nose. "I'm glad we found you. I'm glad he has you. Remember that when you look up at the stars."

A tear trickled down Nate's cheek. There was nothing he could do to stop it.

She let go of his face.

He stood upright.

Alex stayed in the truck, hands still on the steering wheel. Art nodded sadly at him. "It's okay. I understand. It's . . . I—"

They came then.

Through all the things that had happened to them, after everything Nate had seen, he hadn't really thought ahead to this moment. To what would happen. How the end would be. If pressed, he would have said a ship would descend from the sky, smooth and silver, lights flashing. There would be a beam of blue light that fell upon Artemis, and she would rise into the ship before it shot off into the stars.

He hadn't expected this.

Time passed differently in the Mountain. Time passes differently everywhere here. We don't . . . mark the passage of time. Not like you do. Not with anniversaries or parties or balloons or cake. It has a different meaning. It's . . . fluid. It can bend. It's not the straight, rigid line you think it is. Time and space never are.

At the tunnel's entrance, electricity was arcing against the smooth stone. Rocks and pebbles on either side of the road slowly began to rise into the air. The hairs on Nate's arms stood on end. The air smelled like strikes of lightning.

There was a low rumble, and the air in front of the tunnel began to sizzle. It took Nate a moment to comprehend what he was seeing. It was as if the world in front of him was *tearing*, shredding into pieces and being swallowed into a hole opening up out of nothing. When it opened, the hole grew until it was almost as large as the tunnel behind it. Nate could no longer see the other end of the tunnel. Instead, he was staring into a gaping maw of white. It felt like he was staring into the sun.

"We learned a long time ago how to travel without the need

for ships," Artemis said beside him. "It expends a great amount of energy, and it can be very dangerous. But we can reach across time and space, crossing distances never before possible. It's a gateway."

And he could *hear* them on the other side. They were whispering in his head, unintelligible, soothing noises that caused his chest to hitch. He knew what Art was. He believed her. But here, now, seeing this swirling light in front of him, it hit him, and it hit him *hard*. They weren't alone. There were others. And maybe they were far away, and maybe he would never see anything like this again, but they weren't alone.

"Never," Art said fiercely.

"I thought you said you couldn't read minds," he managed to choke out.

"I can't. Not really. But you're broadcasting and we're connected, you and me."

"I love you," he told her, finally tearing his gaze away from the wonder in front of him. She was smiling at him, eyes wet. "I love you."

"I know," she said, smile widening.

He laughed. Of course he did. He couldn't do anything else.

She took a step toward the light.

Nate looked back to the truck.

Alex Weir still sat behind the steering wheel. He was as white as a sheet.

Nate pushed.

Big, rough hands braiding hair.

Rocks skipping on the surface of a lake.

Mouths full of bacon.

Reckon we might as well get on, ain't that right, hoss?

And love. So much love that Nate felt like he was *drowning* in it.

He watched as Alex's face crumpled.

Heartbreak. Up close.

And then Alex was throwing the door to the truck open, shouting, "Wait! Art. *Wait.*"

He was running.

She met him halfway, jumping the last couple of feet.

He caught her deftly, pulling her close. She wrapped her legs around his waist, arms going around his neck. His hand went to the back of her head, and he held her as she cried, as she told him she didn't want to go, that she didn't want to leave him, that she was hurting. "Alex, everything hurts because I never thought it could be like this. I never thought I could feel like this. I never knew it could be you. But it is. It *is* you."

And Alex was saying, "Hush, hush, baby girl, you hush now, you hear me? It's okay. It's okay. I need you to listen to me. Can you do that? There. There you go. Listen."

He said, "No matter where you go. No matter how far away you'll be, I'm always going to be with you. I love you. I love you. I love you."

He rocked her back and forth.

She sobbed into his neck.

Alex looked helplessly at Nate, face wet.

And there was nothing Nate could do.

Eventually, she quieted down.

Eventually, he set her back on her feet.

He reached over and wiped her cheeks.

She sniffled as she looked up at him.

"Go on, now," he said roughly. "You gotta get going."

She nodded slowly. "Adventure, right?"

"Yeah, baby girl. An adventure."

She took a step back.

And another.

And another.

She looked at Nate. Then back at Alex.

She turned around.

Artemis Darth Vader took a deep breath.

She squared her shoulders.

She walked toward the gateway shining in front of her.

And she—

She stopped.

Cocked her head.

The whispers grew louder. Nate didn't understand what he was seeing in his head. What he was feeling. It felt like spindly fingers running along the surface of his mind, pulling at memories. They didn't seem to care about . . . before. They went back far enough to when Nate felt a gun pressed to the back of his head as he stood in front of the generator in the shed. When they found it, when they found that image, the whispers sharpened, the fingers wrapping around it and *pulling*. Nate felt as if he were electrified, his head rocking back, fingers spread wide on his hands, toes curling. It was like he was *seizing*, but there was no pain, and he could still *feel* everything, could still *hear* everything, and those fingers *pulled*. They caressed over the flowers blooming in a field. They pinched at a helicopter being knocked from the sky. They curled in anger at men standing with guns. And they were soft, so fucking soft when Artemis and Alex sat across from him, both of them laughing, Art's mouth full of bacon.

They poked.

They prodded.

And when they came to Alex standing behind him, teeth in his neck, flesh hot and body hard, Nate thought, *No, that's not yours, that's not for you to see,* and they *listened* to him. They left it alone and pulled away.

Above it all, he heard Art say, "Yes. Both of them. They're mine. And I'm theirs. Why?"

There was a response, but Nate couldn't understand it.

"They have faults. They make mistakes. But they love me. And I love them."

The whispers were louder. Harsher, like the buzzing of bees.

"That may be so, but I would do it again. And again. And again. You may not understand them. You may not see their purpose, but I have seen their hearts. I have seen their souls. They are stars. They are dust. And I will remember them. Always."

A single voice answered. It sounded like bells ringing.

Artemis said, "I—I can? But what about—"

The bells rang louder.

She looked back at them, a strange expression on her face. She turned back toward the light. "Then yes. Oh yes. More than anything in all the worlds."

The light exploded around them, and Nate was knocked off his feet. He was out cold even before he hit the ground.

✦

When they woke, it was dark.

The stars were blinking overhead.

The comet looked stuck in the sky.

The tunnel was just a tunnel.

They pushed themselves up slowly.

They were alone.

Alex took Nate by the hand, and they turned toward the truck.

Something moved behind them. They both whirled around and—

EPILOGUE

He sang along with the radio.

Something about taking a sad song and making it better.

After, he laughed until he could barely breathe.

Coincidence, right? It had to be a coincidence.

Funny thing was, he didn't believe in coincidences.

Not anymore.

He wondered if today would be the day.

✦

He was halfway home when his old friend Steven Cooper came on the radio. His voice was rougher, and maybe he meandered more than he did before, but not much else had changed.

He was saying, ". . . and why wouldn't they think we would just *believe* them? Folks, you were *around* when we broke the story on chem trails. You were *there* when the government tried to convince us that Y2K was going to bring about the end of civilization. And yes, my friends, we were all there when those towers fell in New York. And we all know what *that's* about, don't we? How those towers weren't knocked down by a damn plane, no. It was a *controlled* demolition, friends. It was done on *purpose*. And the reason was clear as the nose on my face. Blame it on the Arabs! On the Muslims! The Iraqis and Afghanis! *That* way, when we invaded Iraq and Afghanistan, we would have the might of the *people* behind the war, when in fact, all we actually wanted was to clear a way for oil pipelines! Friends, there have been *hundreds* of such instances, both big and small, all these little pieces of a puzzle that, once put together, show a grand picture of where our world is headed. You have Katrina. The Indonesian Tsunami. Virginia Tech. Hell, you have that little town in Oregon. Roseland. It was *destroyed* by a storm that *only* seemed to circulate above that *one specific* region? And you are expecting me to *believe* that? It was a *test*, friends. The government was performing *experiments*. Longtime listeners will know that I've proven time and time again that we are test subjects and have been since the fifties. Ever since we had *contact*. Truman made a deal. You know he did. How else can you explain the technological revolution that followed his presidency? In the last sixty years, we advanced more than we have in the entire existence of the human race. And you *really* expect us to believe that wasn't done *without* guidance? What do we owe them when the bill comes due, friends? In six months, this year will come to an end. And the *Mayans* knew. They *knew*. It's why their calendar *ends* this year. They knew that *nothing* came after. Friends, it's my belief that here, this year, in 2012, we will see everything I've told you come to fruition. For whatever reason, they chose not to come back in '95 with the damn comet. Or maybe they did and Peter Williams and his friends are now far, far away from here—"

Nolan switched off the satellite radio then.

Sometimes it was better to listen to nothing at all.

✦

It was the middle of June, and the snow was mostly gone as he left Nain, Newfoundland, behind. It'd been a good winter, but Nolan was happy to see the green of spring. When the thaw had started in April, he'd felt like he'd been awoken from hibernation. It was by no means the worst they'd had since they settled in the cabin ten years ago. The winter of 2007 had been killer, and he'd been sure they weren't going to make it.

They had, of course, and had given serious thought to packing up and leaving, trying to find someplace new. But then spring had come, and summer, and Aaron had been taken on by a fishing boat out of Nain, and they'd been *happy*. They'd stayed. People in Nain knew them now, and they were friendly. Nolan helped at the shops in the summers when the cruise ships came, bringing tourists by the hundreds who marveled at such a quaint little seaside town before they climbed back aboard and disappeared.

Somehow they'd made a home.

Nolan heard seagulls calling through his open window. There was still a chill in the air, but he was used to it by now. It'd taken some time, but he'd figured out the more layers he dressed in, the better. He'd even learned how to snowshoe better than Aaron ever could, much to his chagrin.

He smiled softly down at the gold ring on his finger, chipped and worn. Nolan and Aaron Callahan, going on eighteen years now and still as strong as ever.

He was whistling by the time he turned down the old dirt road that led to the cabin in the woods, happy to be home from the grocery run. Aaron had volunteered to accompany him, but Nolan had waved him off. Aaron had only been back a couple of days after being out on the fishing boat for close to a month. He deserved his rest.

The cabin wasn't much, not really. A single story. Three bedrooms. One and a half baths. There was a deck on the back where they could sit and smell the ocean, though they were almost ten miles inland. It had a solid roof and a good foundation. It was home and had been for a long time. Maybe it wouldn't be forever. He thought they were getting closer to an ending, on the precipice of a new beginning.

It didn't matter.

Home didn't always have to be a place.

Home could be a person too.

Sadie heard the truck first, tearing out of the house, barking as she nearly stumbled down the porch steps. She'd been a gift from Aaron a couple of Christmases ago, a black-and-white Alaskan malamute puppy with bright eyes and a cocky strut. She'd grown (and grown and grown) since then to the beast she was today.

Said beast jumped up on the truck, front paws hanging on the door, frantically whimpering as she tried to reach Nolan to lick his face.

"Hey," Nolan said, laughing. "I was only gone for a couple of hours. Calm down."

"She's been sitting at the door since you left," Nolan heard a deep voice say. "Whimpering and everything. Like she thought you weren't coming back."

Even now, even after all this time, his heart fluttered in his chest. Aaron Callahan stood on the porch, as large a presence as he'd ever been before. He was fifty-seven years old now to Nolan's forty-four, but Nolan could only hope he'd look half as good nearing sixty. Aaron had always been a big guy. He was leaner now than he'd been at forty, but he was still strong. His hair was white, as was the full beard on his face, something he'd started to grow years ago, much to Nolan's delight.

Nolan wasn't too shabby either, or so Aaron said. They were both older, maybe only a little wiser, but they hadn't had to run for their lives in a long time.

"We need to break her of that," Nolan said, climbing out of the truck. "Separation anxiety is a bitch of a thing. I should know. I sit at the door whimpering until you get home too."

Aaron laughed as he walked down the steps, a throaty chuckle that Nolan still marveled over. Sadie licked his hands before she barked and ran around him in circles.

It'd only been a couple of hours, but Aaron hugged him just as hard as he had when Nolan picked him up at the docks a couple of days before. Nolan felt his bones creak, not as young as he'd once been.

"Happy you're home," he murmured into Aaron's shoulder.

"Me too," Aaron said. Nolan leaned back, and Aaron kissed him. His beard was scratchy, and his lips were slightly chapped, but it was still the best feeling in all the world.

Nolan sighed and melted into the kiss.

"The groceries can wait, right?" he muttered against Aaron's lips. "What say we get back inside, lock the bedroom door, and see what we see?"

"How's your back?" Aaron asked, eyes glinting.

Nolan rolled his eyes. "It's *fine*."

"You sure? You were bitching about it quite a bit yesterday."

"I can't *bend* like that anymore," Nolan reminded him. "Not that you have any room to talk. Remember what happened when you tried to fuck me up against the wall the last time?"

Aaron's eyebrows dipped, as they often did when he scowled. "I was having an off day."

Nolan snorted. "Sure. Keep telling yourself that, buddy."

Aaron kissed him once more, swift and sweet. "Rain check, okay?"

Nolan heard it then. In his voice. Saw it in the way he carried himself. And maybe, if he *really* thought on it, he'd known this day was coming. For weeks. Maybe he couldn't have said it would be right this moment, but he wasn't surprised.

"It's time, isn't it?" he asked quietly.

Aaron nodded. "Think so."

He didn't know how to feel about that. They'd made this place for themselves. Made a home, hidden away from the rest of the world. This could change everything. Scratch that. It *would* change everything. Eventually. It was going to take time, but once the decision was made, there would be no going back.

Nolan nodded tightly. "Yeah. Okay."

Aaron looked worried. "Hey. Hey. What's going on in that head of yours?"

Nolan shrugged. "I don't—I'm just overthinking things, I guess. It's just . . . everything is going to change."

Aaron reached out and stroked his cheek. "It will."

"We might not ever get this again. This moment. This quiet. This . . . place."

"Maybe," Aaron said. "But you'll always have me. No matter what. No matter where we are, I'm going to be right by your side."

Nolan smiled. "You sap."

"Your sap."

"Yeah. I just . . . I'm scared."

"I'm not going to lie," Aaron said. "It might get rough. It—there's going to be many people who won't understand. People who won't believe. People who will know nothing but fear. But it's going to be our job to help them. To show them the way. To let them know that there is nothing to be afraid of. It's just the next step. For all of us."

"You're sure about this?"

Aaron hesitated. Then, "Do you trust me?"

"Of course."

"Do you—do you regret . . . this? Any of this?"

"No," Nolan said as honestly as he could. "Never. I never have."

And that was the truth. For a long time, Aaron had felt guilty over . . . everything. The life they'd left behind. Cutting off all ties. Pulling Nolan into all of this. It'd taken a while for Nolan to convince him, but every now and then, Aaron's uncertainty still made an appearance. "Not one second." He paused, considering. "Well. I take that back. I could have done without the farm."

Aaron shook his head, a look of fond exasperation on his face. "I think all of us could have done without the farm."

"And then there were your so-called *friends* after. I regretted that quite a bit."

Aaron winced. "Yeah, that was probably on me."

"Hippies, Aaron. Your friends were *hippies*. And we had to stay with them. For *months*."

"You ever going to let that go?"

Nolan sniffed haughtily. "Probably not."

They were laughing when they kissed again. Nolan liked those types of kisses very much.

"We'll lock the bedroom door later," Aaron promised him in a low voice, reaching around and squeezing Nolan's ass through his jeans.

"Gonna hold you to that, old man. Help me with the groceries?"

Aaron did.

✦

The hippies had told him it'd be tough, but he had to stop thinking of himself as Nathaniel Cartwright. "Even when you don't realize it," a woman with glassy eyes and dreads had told him, "you think of yourself as Nate. It's all you've ever known. It happens unconsciously. You can't do that anymore. You have to be aware. You have to think it. You have to *live* it. Nathaniel Cartwright is no more. You're Nolan Callahan now."

"And what about him?" Nate (*Nolan*) had asked, nodding to where Alex was sitting, a frown on his face as his *friend* had him sitting in front of a blue screen, getting ready to take his picture. "Who is he going to be?"

The woman had grinned. "Aaron."

"Oh, that's—"

376 • TJ KLUNE

"Aaron Callahan."

Nate had choked. "Like . . . brothers?"

"Oh, I don't think he meant like brothers when he suggested it. Not like brothers at all."

Alex had refused to meet his gaze for a while after that.

It had been difficult. He never knew just how much his identity was wrapped in the two words *Nathaniel Cartwright*. The woman had been right; even if he didn't *think* those words, he *was* Nate. He had been for damn near thirty years.

So it didn't happen overnight.

Hell, it didn't even happen in the first couple of years.

There'd been quite a few awkward moments, new people met when he'd stumble over his name, dragging out the *N* and the *A* until he corrected it to *Nolan*, making it come out sounding like *Nnnnaaaa-olan. Nolan. My name is Nolan.*

He'd gotten a few funny looks over the years.

But there came a day when he realized he wasn't Nate anymore.

Nathaniel Cartwright had been a good person, mostly. He'd made mistakes, sure, but he'd always tried to make things right. He'd been lonely and lost. Directionless. It wasn't until the very end of being Nate Cartwright that it really hit him.

It hadn't been easy remembering to be Nolan Callahan.

But it had been easy to agree to become him.

All he'd had to do was look at Alex Weir.

He followed Aaron into the cabin, arms laden with bags of groceries, Sadie following her favorite human close, lest he decide to leave her again.

They set the bags down in the kitchen, and Nolan cocked his head, listening. There were the usual sounds of the forest filtering in through open windows, and the cabin creaking, but nothing else.

They didn't move to unpack the groceries. Nolan knew Aaron was waiting for him to ask. They weren't telepathic. They couldn't read each other's minds. But there had always been the intuition there because of Artemis Darth Vader. Even after the Dingess Tunnel, they'd been connected in ways that others were not.

Nolan thought about what was most important. What needed to be asked. "Why now? Why after all this time?"

Aaron looked out the window. His face was lined. He still looked tired, not having yet caught up with his sleep after his time at sea. But he was still as handsome as the day they'd met. "We promised her that her story would be told. That the world would know what happened."

"I get that," Nolan said. "I do. But it's been over seventeen years. I thought—haven't there been so many moments where the truth should have come out? After everything that's happened in the world. The deaths. The destruction. The disease and famine. We are compassionate, but we destroy everything we touch. How can we deserve this? Why is it *now*?"

Aaron looked over at him, eyebrows bunched on his face. "I don't always know."

Nolan sighed. "I know. I'm just . . . scared, I think. For us."

"C'mere," Aaron said, raising an arm.

Nolan went. Of course he did.

He fit perfectly under Aaron's arm, just as he always had. He wasn't sappy and maudlin enough to think that they were made for each other. That they were meant to be. But he remembered when she'd looked at him, back at Herschel Lake. A grunt had been standing behind her, braiding her hair, and she'd asked a man named Nate Cartwright if he believed in fate. In destiny.

He hadn't then.

But sometimes he wondered about that. About it all.

He looked out the window.

A young woman sat in a small clearing outside the kitchen window next to the cabin. She was facing away from them. Her hair was pulled back into a loose ponytail. She wore black leggings and an oversized flannel shirt. It looked like one of Aaron's. She sat cross-legged, her feet bare, hands on her knees. A pair of bright purple sunglasses rested on top of her head. Her shoulders rose as she took a deep breath and fell as she let it out slowly.

Around her, between the blades of grass, flowers began to bloom.

Nolan Callahan felt it in his head, as much as he saw it with his own eyes, a bright burst of colors that he felt down to his very bones.

When the light had faded at Dingess Tunnel, Artemis had still been standing on the road, an uncertain look on her face.

Alex Weir had made a wounded noise, falling to his knees, spreading his arms wide.

She'd run to him.

She'd told them later she'd been given a choice.

And in the end, she'd chosen them—chosen humanity—without hesitation.

They hadn't understood what it would entail.

Not then.

Not until she'd lost her first tooth three days later.

It was . . . slower. The aging process. She looked like she could still be in high school. But she was tall, statuesque, and astonishingly intelligent.

Artemis Darth Vader.

Or Ellie Callahan, as she was referred to these days.

Days that were apparently coming to an end.

The flowers were in full bloom.

She stood slowly, pushing herself up off the ground.

She glanced over her shoulder, and the smile when she saw them was blinding.

✦

They ate dinner that night on the back deck. The evening air still had some bite to it. The stew was warm and the coffee hot. Aaron had made it just as Nolan liked it.

"You've been quiet," Nolan said to Ellie. She'd barely touched her food.

She shrugged. "Just thinking, I guess."

Even though he knew, he still asked, "About?"

"Tomorrow." She looked at the flowers in the clearing. Sadie lay among them, gnawing on a bone. "I'm nervous. I didn't expect to be."

Aaron reached out and took Nolan's hand in his. "Why are you nervous?"

"I don't know. Just am, I guess. About what it means. What will happen next."

Nolan sometimes thought that she was the most human of all of them. Their sweet, fierce girl. "We'll be right there with you."

She smiled quietly. "I know."

"And you're sure?"

She nodded. "It's time. I can . . . hear them."

Nolan and Aaron exchanged a startled look. "Them," Aaron said slowly. "As in . . ."

"As in *them*."

Nolan's heart was pounding. "When did it start?"

She hummed a little under her breath. "A few weeks ago."

That old familiar scowl adorned Aaron's face. "Why didn't you say anything?"

"I needed time . . . time to figure out what it meant. After . . . after the tunnel, I knew I'd be cut off. That was part of the deal. Hearing them again, it—time is moving slower for me now. I understand it better. It took me by surprise." She pushed her bowl away. "But they're coming. They have so much to teach this place. So much to show the world."

Gooseflesh prickled along the back of Nolan's neck. "People won't understand. Maybe a lot of them. And not for a long time."

She laughed. He loved that sound. "I know. But my story needs to be told. *Our* story. Before." She looked up toward the sky. Aaron and Nolan followed her gaze. The stars were just beginning to come out. "This world is on the verge, I think. Of something bigger. Something greater. But it's a thin line. The scales can be easily tipped. And it's our job to make sure that doesn't happen. To make sure they don't heed the call of the void." She closed her eyes. "It will start small. The message. But it'll spread soon enough. One day, and one day soon, they'll be ready. The people. And we'll be the ones to show them the way."

✛

She hugged them before she went to bed, as she always did. She had a book in her hands, a dog-eared Louis L'Amour. She'd never stopped loving them, even after all this time.

And later, after the dishes were done and Sadie let out for the final time, Aaron led his husband by the hand to their bedroom.

He undressed Nolan slowly, worshipping every inch of bare skin he could find. They panted into each other's mouths, skin slick with sweat, and at their release, those colors burst in their heads again and again and again.

✦

After, Aaron lay behind Nolan, huddled close, arm wrapped around his waist.

"Tomorrow," Nolan whispered in the dark.

"I love you."

"I know."

"I should have never shown her that movie," Aaron said with a sigh.

But they laughed.

And then they slept.

✦

It happened one foggy June morning, in a remote corner of the Canadian wilds.

A camera was trained on a desk with three chairs behind it. It was live, streaming online for all the world to see. Only a handful of people would witness the initial broadcast, most of them stumbling upon it by chance. But within ten months, it would have spread across the world, shared far and wide by millions of people.

Some would believe it.

Most wouldn't.

That changed. Eventually.

But that came later.

This was now:

Three people came into view. Two men. A young woman. She sat between them, and anyone watching would see how much they adored her. How much they loved one another. They moved in tandem. They sat close. The men appeared nervous. The woman was calm. Almost serene.

One of the men, the older and gruffer of them, cleared his throat and said, "Are you ready?"

The woman looked at him, cocking her head. "Are we going on an adventure?"

And how he *smiled.* "Yeah, baby girl. I guess we are."

The other man reached over and took their hands in his. He said, "We good?"

The woman nodded. "We're good." She looked directly into the camera. "You won't understand. At least not right away. And that's okay. You may even think I'm a liar, and that's okay too. All I ask is that you listen until the very end before passing judgment. I have a story to tell you. Of a place under a mountain. Of the minds of men. Of what it means to be human, to make a home out of a place where one should not exist. And of what the future holds. For you. For me. For all of us." The woman smiled, eyes sparkling. "I am loved. I love in return. My name is Artemis Darth Vader. And I come in peace."

AUTHOR'S NOTE

Back in the day (2017), I submitted *The Bones Beneath My Skin* to my former indie publisher. The relationship between myself and this publisher was a bit strained—they were late on some royalty payments, and I wasn't happy about it. Still, I sent in the book because I didn't know any better. After all, I'd only been published with this publisher, and had been for years. I figured they'd get their act together sooner rather than later. So I submitted the book and told myself to get started on whatever was coming next. A few weeks later, my editor at this publisher contacted me and said, "Got your book. The publisher said this one is *weird*."

And that rubbed me the wrong way. It wasn't the editor—she was and is a lovely person. But the emphasis on the word *weird* told me a lot, especially in just the one word. This book, the publisher had decided, wasn't like my others, and that wasn't good. They wanted the same type of story told a certain type of way. I even remember being questioned by that publisher as to whether this book could be classified as a "romance" because it *only had one sex scene*. I was flabbergasted. How is sex necessary for romance? What about asexual people? Demisexuals? People who actively dislike sex? When did we decide that writing sex is the *only* way to show people falling in love?

I . . . wasn't happy. So I did something sort of stupid: I pulled the book from the publisher with a grandiosity only found in those who actively believe they've been wronged, and decided to self-publish it. With hindsight, that was the right move, as the publisher hit a new low the following year, seeing as how they weren't paying a great many people what they were owed. But I didn't know that then. All I knew was that I was going to delve into the wide and fascinating world of self-publishing.

Holy crap, my dudes. That shit is *hard*. Formatting, editing, artwork, ARCs, marketing, all of it having to be done by a single person. It gave me a much higher appreciation for the work that self-pubbed authors do. It can be humbling to figure out you really have no idea what you're doing.

But I did it, somehow. I self-published the book in 2018, and it came out. People read it—perhaps not as many people as would have had I stayed with the publisher, but that was all right. I was—and am—proud of this book. Nate and Alex and Artemis Darth Vader: the three of them formed a home in my chest and I loved them to bits.

That being said, the former publisher was right: This book *is* different. It *is* weird. But then, I'm the guy who made a socially anxious vacuum cleaner named Rambo into a main character. *The Bones Beneath My Skin* is an action movie in book form, perhaps the most action I've written in a book that didn't involve werewolves. Things explode and helicopters fall from the sky as a little girl (who may not be a girl at all) fights to protect those she loves. Oh, and bacon. So much bacon.

Check out that snazzy new cover thanks to Chris Sickels with Red Nose Studio. I wondered how he'd pull this one off because I had a *very specific* image in mind. The Dingess Tunnel—a real place, by the way—at the climax of the book. He took my idea, ran with it, and made it better than it had any right to be. Chris is just that good. Thanks, Chris.

Tor picked up the novel to rerelease, and I'm so grateful for it. As I write this, it's spring 2024, and I'm gearing up to release the sequel to *The House in the Cerulean Sea*. I've been with Tor for five years. I've released—so far—six new novels, and four rereleases with them. They don't care that I'm weird. In fact, they actively advocate for my weirdness. Really, there is no better publisher. How grateful I am to everyone at Tor. They have made my wildest dreams come true, and I'm so, so humbled to be part of their company.

And to you, the reader, as always: thank you for following me here and there and everywhere my brain takes me. Sometimes, we get to go to islands to see gremlins and their dads. Other times, we die and find a tea shop in the woods. Or the world ends and it is up to us to save our robot dad. Or we're superheroes who write flowery fanfiction. Or we're fuckin' werewolves with daddy issues who fight for our families. Thank you for coming on these journeys with me. I can't wait to show you just how weird I can be.

TJ "Weirdo" Klune
April 29, 2024

Read on for a sneak peek of *Wolfsong,*
Book one of the Greek Creek series,
the beloved fantasy romance sensation by TJ Klune.

Available Now from Tor Books

MOTES OF DUST / COLD AND METAL

I was twelve when my daddy put a suitcase by the door. "What's that for?" I asked from the kitchen.

He sighed, low and rough. Took him a moment to turn around. "When did you get home?"

"A while ago." My skin itched. Didn't feel right.

He glanced at an old clock on the wall. The plastic covering its face was cracked. "Later than I thought. Look, Ox . . ." He shook his head. He seemed flustered. Confused. My dad was many things. A drunk. Quick to anger with words and fists. A sweet devil with a laugh that rumbled like that old Harley-Davidson WLA we'd rebuilt the summer before. But he was never flustered. He was never confused. Not like he was now.

I itched something awful.

"I know you're not the smartest boy," he said. He glanced back at his suitcase.

And it was true. I was not cursed with an overabundance of brains. My mom said I was just fine. My daddy thought I was slow. My mom said it wasn't a race. He was deep in his whiskey at that point and started yelling and breaking things. He didn't hit her. Not that night, anyway. Mom cried a lot, but he didn't hit her. I made sure of it. When he finally started snoring in his old chair, I snuck back to my room and hid under my covers.

"Yes, sir," I said to him.

He looked back at me, and I'll swear until the day I die that I saw some kind of love in his eyes. "Dumb as an ox," he said. It didn't sound mean coming from him. It just was.

I shrugged. Wasn't the first time he'd said that to me, even though Mom asked him to stop. It was okay. He was my dad. He knew better than anyone.

"You're gonna get shit," he said. "For most of your life."

"I'm bigger than most," I said like it meant something. And I was. People were scared of me, though I didn't want them to be. I was big. Like my daddy. He was a big man with a sloping gut, thanks to the booze.

"People won't understand you," he said.

"Oh."

"They won't get you."

"I don't need them to." I wanted them to very much, but I could see why they wouldn't.

"I have to go."

"Where?"

"Away. Look—"

"Does Mom know?"

He laughed, but it didn't sound like he found anything funny. "Sure. Maybe. She knew what was going to happen. Probably has for a while."

I stepped toward him. "When are you coming back?"

"Ox. People are going to be mean. You just ignore them. Keep your head down."

"People aren't mean. Not always." I didn't know that many people. Didn't really have any friends. But the people I did know weren't mean. Not always. They just didn't know what to do with me. Most of them. But that was okay. I didn't know what to do with me either.

And then he said, "You're not going to see me for a while. Maybe a long while."

"What about the shop?" I asked him. He worked down at Gordo's. He smelled like grease and oil and metal when he came home. Fingers blackened. He had shirts with his name embroidered on them. Curtis stitched in reds and whites and blues. I always thought that was the most amazing thing. A mark of a great man, to have your name etched onto your shirt. He let me go with him sometimes. He showed me how to change the oil when I was three. How to change a tire when I was four. How to rebuild an engine for a 1957 Chevy Bel Air Coupe when I was nine. Those days I would come home smelling of grease and oil and metal and I would dream late at night of having a shirt with my name embroidered on it. *Oxnard,* it would say. Or maybe just *Ox.*

"Gordo doesn't care" is what my dad said.

Which felt like a lie. Gordo cared a lot. He was gruff, but he told me once that when I was old enough, I could come talk to him about a job. "Guys like us have to stick together," he said. I didn't know what he meant by that, but the fact that he thought of me as anything was good enough for me.

"Oh" is all I could say to my dad.

"I don't regret you," he said. "But I regret everything else."

I didn't understand. "Is this about . . . ?" I didn't know what this was about.

"I regret being here," he said. "I can't take it."

"Well that's okay," I said. "We can fix that." We could just go somewhere else.

"There's no fixing, Ox."

"Did you charge your phone?" I asked him because he never remembered. "Don't forget to charge your phone so I can call you. I got new math that I don't understand. Mr. Howse said I could ask you for help." Even though I knew my dad wouldn't get the math problems any more than I would. Pre-algebra, it was called. That scared me, because it was already hard when it was a *pre*. What would happen when it was just algebra without the *pre* involved?

I knew that face he made then. It was his angry face. He was pissed off. "Don't you fucking get it?" he snapped.

I tried not to flinch. "No," I said. Because I didn't.

"Ox," my daddy said. "There's going to be no math. No phone calls. Don't make me regret you too."

"Oh," I said.

"You have to be a man now. That's why I'm trying to teach you this stuff. Shit's gonna get slung on you. You brush it off and keep going." His fists were clenched at his sides. I didn't know why.

"I can be a man," I assured him, because maybe that would make him feel better.

"I know," he said.

I smiled at him, but he looked away. "I have to go," he eventually said.

"When are you coming back?" I asked him.

He staggered a step toward the door. Took a breath that rattled around his chest. Picked up his suitcase. Walked out. I heard his old truck start up outside. It stuttered a bit when it picked up. Sounded like he needed a new timing belt. I'd have to remind him later.

✦

Mom got home late that night, after working a double in the diner. She found me in the kitchen, standing in the same spot I'd been in when my daddy had walked out the door. Things were different now.

"Ox?" she asked. "What's going on?" She looked very tired.

"Hey, Mom," I said.

"Why are you crying?"

"I'm not." And I wasn't, because I was a man now.

She touched my face. Her hands smelled like salt and french fries and coffee. Her thumbs brushed against my wet cheeks. "What happened?"

I looked down at her, because she'd always been small and at some point in the last year or so, I'd grown right past her. I wished I could remember the day it happened. It seemed monumental. "I'll take care of you," I promised her. "You don't ever need to worry."

Her eyes softened. I could see the lines around her eyes. The tired set of her jaw. "You always do. But that's—" She stopped. Took a breath. "He left?" she asked, and she sounded so *small*.

"I think so." I twirled her hair against my finger. Dark, like my own. Like my daddy's. We were all so dark.

"What did he say?" she asked.

"I'm a man now," I told her. That's all she needed to hear. She laughed until she cracked right down the middle.

✦

He didn't take the money when he left. Not all of it. Not that there was much there to begin with.

He didn't take any pictures either. Just some clothes. His razor. His truck. Some of his tools.

If I hadn't known any better, I would have thought he never was at all.

✛

I called his phone four days later. It was the middle of the night.

It rang a couple of times before a message picked up saying the phone was no longer in service.

I had to apologize to Mom the next morning. I'd held the handset so hard that it had cracked. She said it was okay, and we didn't talk about it ever again.

✛

I was six when my daddy bought me my own set of tools. Not kids' stuff. No bright colors and plastic. All cold and metal and real.

He said, "Keep them clean. And God help you if I find them laying outside. They'll rust and I'll tan your hide. That ain't what this shit is for. You got that?"

I touched them reverently because they were a gift. "Okay," I said, unable to find the words to say just how full my heart felt.

✛

I stood in their (her) room one morning a couple of weeks after he left. Mom was at the diner again, picking up another shift. Her ankles would be hurting by the time she got home.

Sunlight fell through a window on the far wall. Little bits of dust caught the light.

It smelled like him in the room. Like her. Like both of them. A thing together. It would be a long time before it stopped. But it would. Eventually.

I slid open the closet door. One side was mostly empty. Things were left, though. Little pieces of a life no longer lived.

Like his work shirt. Four of them, hanging in the back. *Gordo's* in cursive.

Curtis, they all said. *Curtis, Curtis, Curtis.*

I touched each one of them with the tips of my fingers.

I took the last one down from the hanger. Slid it over my shoulders. It was heavy and smelled like *man* and *sweat* and *work*. I said, "Okay, Ox. You can do this."

So I started to button up the work shirt. My fingers stumbled over them, too big and blunt. Clumsy and foolish, I was. All hands and arms and legs, graceless and dull. I was too big for myself.

The last button finally went through and I closed my eyes. I took a breath. I remembered how Mom had looked this morning. The purple lines under her eyes. The slump of her shoulders. She'd said, "Be good today, Ox. Try to stay out of trouble," as if trouble was the only thing I knew. As if I was in it constantly.

I opened my eyes. Looked in the mirror that hung on the closet door.

The shirt was too large. Or I was too small. I don't know which. I looked like a kid playing dress-up. Like I was pretending.

I scowled at my reflection. Lowered my voice and said, "I'm a man."

I didn't believe me.

"I'm a man."

I winced.

"I'm a man."

Eventually, I took off my father's work shirt and hung it back up in the closet. I shut the doors behind me, the dust motes still floating in the fading sun.

ABOUT THE AUTHOR

Natasha Michaels

TJ KLUNE is the *New York Times* and *USA Today* bestselling, Lambda Literary Award–winning author of *The House in the Cerulean Sea, Under the Whispering Door, In the Lives of Puppets,* the Greek Creek series for adults, the Extraordinaries series for teens, and more. Being queer himself, Klune believes it's important—now more than ever—to have accurate, positive queer representation in stories.

Visit Klune online:
tjklunebooks.com
Instagram: @tjklunebooks

THE GREEN CREEK SERIES

The Bennett family has a secret:
They're not just a family, they're a pack.

The beloved fantasy romance sensation about love, loyalty, betrayal, and family.

Wolfsong is Ox Matheson's story.

Ravensong is Gordo Livingstone's story.

Heartsong is Robbie Fontaine's story.

Brothersong is Carter Bennett's story.

NOW AVAILABLE FROM TOR BOOKS!
The Green Creek series is for adult readers.

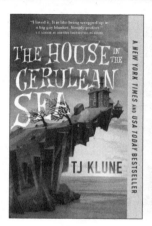

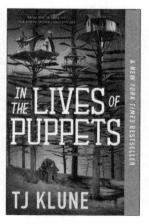